T0104051

Yukon Territory

THE CHALLENGE

STEWART N. JOHNSON

Order this book online at www.trafford.com
or email orders@trafford.com

Most Trafford titles are also available at major online book retailers.

Print information available on the last page.

ISBN: 978-1-4907-6497-9 (sc)
ISBN: 978-1-4907-6499-3 (hc)
ISBN: 978-1-4907-6498-6 (e)

Library of Congress Control Number: 2015914684

Because of the dynamic nature of the Internet, any web addresses or
links contained in this book may have changed since publication and may
no longer be valid. The views expressed in this work are solely those
of the author and do not necessarily reflect the views of the publisher,
and the publisher hereby disclaims any responsibility for them.

Trafford rev. 09/18/2015

 www.trafford.com
North America & international
toll-free: 1 888 232 4444 (USA & Canada)
fax: 812 355 4082

CONTENTS

ACKNOWLEDGEMENT

I want to first start off with my investor, Miss Breanna Gibson. Thank you, for without your efforts this book would have never went to print, and with many more books to follow. I am trying to find a solution on how to write a good tale, which I think this one was, as I finish this day September 1, 2015.

CH 1

A call to arms a new person is in charge

It was the winter of 2003, when another batch of hopefuls, surrendered, and left the Yukon Territory, their dreams of owning a piece of property dashed. The newly elected territorial Governor was elected, his name is Jim Hickson, a third generation politician, and native American Indian. He was from up in the valley of Old Crow nation, in the gold mining region of the upper Territory. It is typically covered in snow year around as it sits in the Arctic circle. He took office with zeal, and his first project was to end the challenge. But after he reviewed the newest hopefuls, he actually changed his mind. The field contained a sports personality to several hundred farmers. In the hallway, he sees his associate in charge of this game, to say, "Mister Governor, we need to talk" said Davy.

"Have a seat, what's this about?"

"You're no more than two weeks in office and your cancelling the challenge, why?"

"Well simply, were not getting the right people who want to live here, and make that area prosper, it's the only area with deep riches and according to the benefactor, it has to go to a worthy individual, not some company, ready to strip mine the property."

"That is true, but the challenge is our way of life, it supports tourism and"….

"And nothing, look it was all really once nice thought to get another few settlers, but now it's a joke after 10 years."

"Well instead of shutting this down, we take all the best candidates and narrow the field down to the best, find those that really want to be here, just yesterday, I read one, that said, "In the increase of this daunting task, I feel my vulnerability will succeed, now that is a statement of some sincerity."

"Well you may have a point, but what would be nice is if I could find me a conservationist, do you know any?"

"I put it out on the net, and still no responses" said Davy.

"Why do you think that?"

"Probably they don't want to live in below freezing weather, especially in Beaver Creek, where for six months there under snow."

"This wouldn't be half bad, but did you see some of the last years contestants, shelters, modest cabins, for themselves, all eight of them, and for working the land, nothing, not a single improvement, nor discovery, for them it was just around the cabins."

"They did do some trapping?" said Davy.

"Do some trapping, what catching artic rabbits, and shooting one deer, said Jim, the governor, to add, I want people who will first build something spectacular, and second improve the land, in addition I may allow Bear season out to November, instead of ending in October, No, what I really want to see, is vast improvement and the ability to share with one another, and make something out of that land, and make it profitably, too many reality shows create the falsehood of realism, I want the public to see a bunch of families who show, that they are here for others, and that conservation is the theme, and to succeed, and thrive, so let me see what you and the staff have chosen?"

"Well first off, our number one choice, is a current active duty Marine Corps Sergeant who is scheduled to get out May 10th, of this year. A combat veteran, whose job, is to scout, he is the number one tracker in all the services, so said those that know him, and his value to the services for the United States."

"How do you know that?" asked the Governor.

"Because they hold yearly challenges, and for the last four years, he won each year, he is the survivalist we are looking for, plus he thrives in the cold weather having spent the last six months in Alaska, as a guide to the excavations, of Mount McKinley, out to Fairbanks."

"That is impressive, all right he is in, next?"

"Well for our number two, we went way out there, it's the southernmost place, Missouri, a place called Liberal, where two vegetarians live raising vegetable, they say, we have a greenhouse we can live anywhere, and with a successful mushroom operation, they feel, they can grow mushrooms anywhere, but it's the "Vulnerability", to the elements which will stand us apart from everyone else" so says Brian Lewis.

"Alright, there in," said the Governor.

"Oh and with them they wanted to bring, a third, A brother to Lily", he shows him a picture of her and him."

"She is quite a looker, I say more the merrier, and if the three of them get along, I'm fine with that, but that person is excluded from the challenge, only eight."

"Yes sir, as for our next selection, it was really hard, but I guess the word "vulnerability" came up in his profile as well, he and his newly married wife, is John and Kimberly Locke, a third generational ranchers, plans to bring, 13 head of black angus cattle, with four of them pregnant."

"That should start a good herd, what of other stock and supplies."

"Well, were still requiring everyone to bring what they need."

"No, this year, let's give them a stipend, say, five thousand dollars each couple, and then when they get here, we match what they have left."

"That seems fair" said Davy.

"What do they have for resupply?"

"Beaver creek, has three stores, and an empty ghost town of lumber, windows and immediate supplies."

"Fine give them that, but only if they ask for it?" said the governor.

"Yes sir."

"So who is manning those stores?"

"I believe a couple, who we send out to other places, a Jake and Rita Wilson."

"Ah I know of them, they play fair, good, whose last?"

"Well that one was a two way tie, but that same vulnerability came up, so we chose, Billy and Laurie Holmes, a couple with varying degrees of talents, she is a veterinarian certified, with a thriving practice, and a pretty good one, so much so, we thought of hiring here."

"So do it" said the governor, maybe take over for old man Pilson".

"Well it defeats the purpose of the challenge, now does it?"

"Yes, I guess you're right, and what of him?"

"He is Billy and he is into animal husbandry."

"Good, good, place all the requirements down, and send them off via e-mail. As for the wager wire, place the favorite being the scout at 3-1, the gardeners 5-1, the ranchers, 7-1 and the farmers 9-1, for who will drop out the first," said Jim.

Meanwhile on maneuvers in Alaska, Matt, laid out on a side of a cliff, to get a spot, to zoom in for the sniper, and its new target, a mine shaft explosion, as he said, "On my count, 3, 2, 1, fire", off went the shot a mile away, and then it hit, and an explosion occurred, to hear, "Perfect shot, now come down." Matt crept back, then up, as his camouflage kept him hidden, from the others, as he stood, to feel his phone vibrate, he checked his message, he smiled as he was confirmed, to be part of the challenge.

Elsewhere, it was a few hours later, when Brian, found out, and Lily and him rejoiced. Thinking finally able to get out of the heat. As for the ranchers, it was instant they knew, and both were excited, as for the farmers, Billy knew first, and then his hard working wife, knew later, she knew he was only doing it to keep her close. He read what it said, "Your officially accepted, all we need is a physician to sign off on your health, that you are able to withstand these harsh conditions, in a later text I will send the suggest required clothing, you will live on 1280 acres divided into fourth's, and on that land, your free to trap, hunt, and kill year around, except grizzly bear, which opens, Sept. 1st and closes Nov 1st, good luck and good bye."

Billy was first to start preparing, by isolating his stocks, and a call to his sister Rose, who in the event that they were accepted, agreed to run the family farm, so she said, "I'll be there around may 15th."

A couple of weeks went by, before Matt called Anna, whom was happy to receive his call, as he said, "Hi Honey, I'm done with winter training, and I will be getting out, on May 10th, do you wanna pick me up?"

"Yes, where?"

"I'm at the airport now, well, I'll be flying into Lowry Air Force base in Aurora Colorado."

"Yes, I know where it's at, I'll see you soon", she slid her phone shut, to see her other sister Erica, to say, "My man is in town wanna come with me?"

"To the military base, sure."

Anna drove as her bigger sister rode along, to the base, where they had to show ID's, and they were let on, she drove to the terminal, and the two got out, as military men were everywhere, they were let in, and down to waiting, as the plane landed, he had his duffle bag in hand, as he came through the doors, she got up and jumped into his arms, and wrapped her legs around him, to kiss him, to say, "Your back, what of May 10th?"

"That is my discharge date."

"You're getting out, but what of Hawaii, and on to Scofield barracks, your next assignment?"

"Well, I just knew I couldn't be away from you any longer, besides I got a better offer?"

"Which is?"

"Hush, not in front of your sister."

"Oh right, okay, as he let her down, to see Erica, she embraced him, to say, "So when are you gonna make an honest woman of my sister, and whom do you have to fix me up with?"

"I have a few friends, but they like action."

"Ha, funny", as they laughed, as Anna yelled, "Enough you too, you think you two were a couple." Erica smiles at Matt, who turned to have his eyes on only his Anna.

Meanwhile, the days were ticking down, when finally the Locke family's clan blew up, and senior said, "How long before you were going to tell us?"

"Well soon?" said John his son.

"Soon, isn't long enough, I want you out, you should go back to Florida, and be with your mom, because you aren't the son who is supposed to be my kid."

"All I am here is a slave, I work, the steers, and for what pay, none?"

"You have room and board, and the great meals, your step mother makes for you."

"She is four years older than I, besides, Kim is a better cook than she is."

"Yes, about that, maybe I can convince her to divorce you, and she be my next wife.", with that John attacked, his father, and the two were at blows, as John junior pummeled his suppose father, as it escalated, when junior was thrown back, into the fireplace, knocking over all the wood, junior was angry, and clinched his fists, and just then Grand Pa, entered with a shotgun, to say, "Hold on there, Senior, I've had about enough, with you two, you don't go around beating on your son, and Junior, walk away, go back to your home, I'll deal with your father, as he left, and closed the door, and just then Grand Pa, took a swing, and connected his barrel with his son's face, and he went down in a heap, to hear, "If I ever witness you hitting my grandson again, I'll kill you myself."

Meanwhile, in Liberal Missouri, Brian had received notice that Charley could be part of this, but not in the challenge, so he could go as he liked", Brian nodded, to confirm, as they were assembling all of their plugs, in a peat moss lined box, set into a deeper larger box on a long double axel trailer, as the assembly for the trip was underway. A large glass greenhouse frame was set on it, as the glass was put in the back of the Jeep grand Cherokee, in between Styrofoam. It was a slow process, as Charley was still filling mail order orders, and had agreed to continue this operation. Lily was off to the local hardware store, to buy new seed to go with her already large collection, as her staple diet was eggplant, potatoes, and artichokes. She was looking forward to all the rich black topsoil.

Meanwhile, back in Denver, it was onto Anna's house, on the outskirts and into the foothills, to a place called Morrison, right next to Red Rocks park, she drove into her parents place, a sprawling five acres, nestled near a river, called turkey creek. Matt got out, to smell the fresh air, and so did the other two girls, when the door opened, and a flood gate of children was upon him, he looked at the modest two story house, as he went in, and up, in the middle was a courtyard, with a pool, it was nice, as another of the 12 children, said, "Matt, come outside, and catch praying mantis's" said Brad, the youngest to Anna, pulling on his arm, as Matt gets up, for him to see Mamma, who frowned at him, as he went outside, for her to say, "So how long, will he be here this time?" she said to her husband. "Mamma you have to admit, he is the longest, your daughter has ever dated, I think he is the one" said her father, liking him.

"They should, if it wasn't for him, we would have never come from Sicily to here, once, she met him, it was over."

"So you're in agreement with me Mamma?" said her husband.

"Yes, just when will he put a ring on her finger?"

"In due time, it's been a four year commitment, besides he is loyal to her."

"In time we will see."

Outside, Matt showed young Brad, a way of catching the mantis, as using bait, while the two sisters, sat on the upper patio, for Erica to say, "Aren't you worried someone else will come along?"

"No, why should I, I fell in love with him in Sicily, and if you don't forget, he got Papa, a work visa, to the space base in Littleton."

"It's true, he didn't have to do that, but look at how good he is with children, why can't I find a man like that?"

"Because you're trying too hard, you gotta let it flow."

"Trying too hard, you were topless when you met Matt."

"That is true, in Sicily, it's alright to go topless, here not so much, but I allow him to see everything now."

"Hush, you'll get in trouble with that talk."

"Who cares, he is my man, and for that I love and trust him, now run along, I have some knitting to do."

Later that night after dinner, Anna and Matt say their goodbyes, as Anna drives, back to their house, a modest three bedroom two bath, as she clicks the garage door, it opens, and she drives in, for Matt to see his red jeep, he gets out to admire, it, for Anna to say, "Don't worry I start it every week, it still runs good." They went inside, for Matt to say, "I want to talk with you?"

"Alright, as she takes a chair, he gets down on one knee as her excitement fills with anticipation, for him to say, "It's been four years apart, off and on, so I'd like to know, if you'll accompany me to be part of the challenge."

She looks at him weirdly, expecting something else entirely different, for him to say, "The challenge, remember I told you a while ago I applied", she looked at him to say, "What is this challenge?" she crossed her arms, with a stern look on her face, to say, "What of after you got to your next duty station, Hawaii, I would come, and we would be married?, is that still on the table?"

"Yes, but I didn't want to lead with that, and then you would have to go."

"Go where, we are happy here, and you will be my husband."

"I'm fine with that, but, let's do the challenge first."

"What is this challenge you talk of?"

"It's a place we need to go together for one year, if completed, we will have the land, some money and a place to call home." She sat thinking about it, and weighing the options, to say, as he looked up at her, "Where is this place to be exactly?"

"Yukon Territory?"

"Where is that, in Canada, or somewhere?"

"A bit higher, near Alaska?"

"Alaska, way too far away, what of my family?"

"After it's over, they could come up?"

"I don't know, and you say, after this we will get married?"

"Yes, but I didn't want to start with, asking you to marry, and then ask you to accompany me to this challenge."

"Listen, all I want to be is your wife, I'm celibate, for only one reason, a ring on my finger, after you put that on I'm all yours."

"Yes, but it's much more than that, it's the challenge."

"Alright, I will agree to go, under one condition?"

"What is that?" asked Matt.

"I have my satellite TV and recorder."

Matt looked at her, to think, "What do I have to do, to get electricity", to say, "Well I will try to get you some electricity."

"Why do you have to try, isn't there electricity already out there?"

"Well no and yes, I'll bring a generator, and you'll have your satellite."

"Then it settles it I'm going with you", she left the room, to go to her computer, to see, as she typed it in, to see a vast winter snow packs, and read, Klondike gold rush, still going on, it was a skiers paradise, as she thought, "I like to ski, and snowboard, and the fishing is incredible, not to mention lots of wildlife, and a way to get back to nature, then she saw, an icon, about the challenge and it came up, the challenge, pits four friends and family of two, against the harshest weather imaginable. From October to May you are snowed in, be prepared for twenty foot snow drifts, you must bring your own food, and or take it from the land, you start on June 1st, to June 1st., a complete 365 days, survive, and win the land, and the prize of a million dollars. Note if all make it, then those that really show a profit, and create something special wins the prize, plus land, you're on and a host of other things, this year's contestants have been chosen, as she clicked on that icon, to see the three others, curious, she clicked on hers first, at 3-1 odds to succeed, she was impressed, as she saw, a picture of her, that said Anna, L, from Palermo Sicily, now living with her boyfriend, in Denver, she has a degree from the university of Denver, in Metallurgy (Geologist) studying to receive her masters. Then clicked on his, Matt M, seasoned Marine Scout, a sergeant in the Marine Corps, stationed in Camp Lejeune North Carolina. Due to get out May 10th. He thrives in the winter snow and ice, watch out he is the favorite. She thinks "He is my man", as she clicked on Brian Lewis, a horticulturalist, who lives in liberal Missouri, with girlfriend, free spirit Lily White, a herbalists, they own a huge mushroom factory, all kinds by mail-order. Next she clicked on was John and Kim Locke, a third generation black angus cattle ranchers, and she raises prized chevron goats. A picture of both. Last was Billy, and his famous wife Laurie a world class veterinarian. She sold her stake in her practice, but with an option to buy back in, when she is done. They raise all forms of animals. Now she went back up to the top to see, all must report by May 28th, to Whitehorse, government building, for special instructions, and revisions. She then clicked on, destinations and routes to Whitehorse Yukon, as the data came back, 3295 approx. divide 60 miles per hour is about 55 hours or about 7 days travel. So she thought about when Matt was getting out, and knew it was time to get it all together.

Matt's leave was up and went back to Camp Lejeune, as for Anna, it was full speed ahead, her big brother Erick came over, help out now that the only ones loyal to her, knew about the challenge, to say, "What can I do for you Sis?"

"I need you to take the jeep down to get a service done."

"If you need a truck, I'll lend you the 1 ton."

"Thanks, but I know Matt would want to take the jeep, besides he has a dual winch on his, do you have that?"

"No."

"Precisely." As they went to the garage, she hands him the key, he pumps it a few times, all it did was click the battery over, for Erick to say, "I think the battery is dead, let me take it over to the dealership, I will have the mechanics go over it with a fine tooth comb."

"If you think it will help", she watched as Erick got out, and lifted the garage door, and undid the brake, using the wheel, pushed it back, got in, and hit the clutch, and it started, he rolled out to the street and off it went.

Meanwhile in Liberal Missouri, at the mushroom factory, a call came in for Brian, who said, "What is your order today?"

"None actually, I want to buy your operation?"

"It's not really for sale."

"Why not, your leaving for a year, and surely not taking it with you."

"Well were still shipping for another six months, till were up and running in Alaska."

"Listen this is what I'll do, later in the week, I'll send a representative, out there, to asset what you have and then make you an offer, the terms is all cash, how does that sound?"

"Sure, I'm welcome to all offers."

"Fine, you'll be hearing from me."

Meanwhile in Minneapolis, Minnesota, the most famous Vet, was working hard, at her job, while at home on their farm, Billy was sectioning off, those he was going to sell off for this 3400 mile trip, and knew what he was using his brand new 1 ton dually extra cab, long bed. He knew he was going to slide on his camper, for a place to live, till he gets the cabin built. Then it was out to see, each animal personally.

In Madison Wisconsin, it was a family gathering, to support John, and missing was his father, who took to a cabin to get away from the clan. John Junior had support from all of his uncles and aunts, and well-wishers, Grand pa, John said, "Take as many stock as you need, son."

"Thirteen if you please, and four of them pregnant."

"Well do, any hogs?"

"Yes, two sows pregnant."

"I don't know if that is wise, John, they may have a miscarriage, due to the vibration, said Uncle Tom.

"True, but I plan on doing it just before I go on the fifteenth."

"Oh then you should be alright?"

February, turned into March, and then April, as it was the wettest in years, flooding was happening in all of Nebraska, and other northern parts, all three families took a slow approach, to loading as much as they could get in their trucks, and repack. After April 15th a representative from the Yukon, made his way to Billy's farm first, he drove out there from the airport. Billy greeted him, he got out to say, "Hello, you must be Billy, my name is John Hughes, I represent the authority putting on the challenge." The two shook hands, for him to say, "It's sure hot out here, can we go inside?"

"Sure, right this way, as he gives him the tour of his log cabin, he built, for John, to say, "Is this what you will be building up there?"

"Yes, but a single level, I built this with a family in mind, now all my wife thinks about is work" said Billy dejected.

"Well there is plenty of that to do up north.," said John in an off handed way. John hands him a booklet, for Billy to look it over, and then two credit cards, to say, "The red one is the gas card, unlimited but just as long as it's just before or on the trip, in Whitehorse will take them back, the green card, is 5000 line of credit, buy what you need for the trip, also one last thing, your only allotted one vehicle and one trailer, but if you have a visitor, its unlimited what they bring up. Any questions?"

"No." said Billy, studying the manual.

"When do you plan on leaving?" asked Mister Hughes.

"Probably the 15th of May?"

"Good, that's what I recommend, and once you get to Whitehorse, come to the government building, and all of your questions will be answered."

"Is it easy to find?" asked Billy.

"Yes, it's the largest building in the north of the city, a parking space will be designated, yours is number 4."

John left, as Billy kept on reading, John got in his car, went to the airport and flew to Madison, rented a car, and drove to this secluded ranch, as the gates were closed and locked, he call John Junior, and he said, "I'll come down and open them, but, if you're their now, drive, dead east a mile, to a turn off, now it's a dirt road, but go left, for a ways, and turn to the north, and we will be on the right."

"I'll do that" said Mister Hughes.

Moments later, he was at their homes, and chose the right one, got out to see, a lovely lady, say, "Hi, I'm Kim, how can we help you today?"

"I'm John, from the Yukon challenge."

"Well then come on in, we have been expecting you?"

Kim leads John in, to say, "Care for a drink?"

"Yes, water?"

"You're in luck, we have mountain water."

She hands him a bottle, it was ice cold, as he takes a seat, John Junior comes in and sits, for John Hughes to say, "Here is your package, he slides it before them, and two credit cards, to say, "The red one is your gas, fill up before you go, keep a log, the green one is 5000 dollar limit, be sure to buy a wood stove, so you can cook on it, the only requirement is that you build a cabin, survive the winter, and be safe and in the end a cash prize, beside the steers you'll be taking anything else?"

"Perhaps two sows."

"Excellent, what of the prized goats? And any guns?"

"Don't think she will take them, the trailer is already crowded enough, as for the guns, we both have six each."

"Alright, then any questions?"

"No", said John, as Kim said, "Is there electricity up there?"

"No and yes, depends on what you bring, like a generator."

"What of plumbing?"

"Then again, depends on what you can dig."

"Make sure we have some shovels", said Kim now getting the idea, as she calmed.

"So when do you all plan on leaving?" asked Mister Hughes.

"Oh probably May 15th." said John.

"Good choice."

John Hughes left the way he come, thinking, "Two down two to go, he had looked over both of the two contestants, their rigs to see that they were ready, as he drove to the airport, and flew to Springfield MO, got out of that busy airport, and rented a car, and drove to Lamar, MO, the birth place of Harry S Truman our 33rd president., so said the sign and drove in to see it was a one street town, but after some directions, the Mushroom factory was 20 miles up north, near Liberal Missouri off I-49, and to an another locked gate, John called Brian, who said he would come down, and he did, to allow him to drive in, as Brian locked up his gate, and led, John in, and inside his cool operation, into a house, part ways in, to see a long trailer, with wood grades in plastic, to hear, "There coming with us, some of it, is more than a hundred years old, then depends on the treatment, the mushrooms grow, buts it's a 90 day growth, so what brings you here, interested in buying this spread?"

"No I'm with the challenge."

"Oh right, I thought we just had to show up."

"Well you do, but were helping you out, as he slides the booklet, over to Brian to sit, and open it up, as John sets down, two cards, and says, "Red one is your gas card, to us, and a green one, is a 5000 line of credit, use what you think you need, like a wood stove?"

Brian shakes his head, to says, "Yeah a wood stove, where can I find one of them?"

"Well depends on your trip route, Winnipeg, Edmonton, to name a few."

"So on the trip then."

"Yes, when do you think your planning on leaving?"

"Oh probably May 1st."

"Why so early?"

"Oh we want to take a vacation, and take our time getting there."

"Alright, remember, be at Whitehorse, before May 28th."

"Will do" as Brian went out with John for him to say, "Say you asked me if I wanted to buy this operation, do you get many offers?"

"Yes, about once a week, I had a prospector come out the first week, we were chosen to be on the challenge, but as soon as they got wind of some of the processes, and the cost, versus profit, I never heard from them again, Oh well", as he opened the gate, and John left.

Anna in Denver was waiting the discharge of Matt, but his advisors had other ideas, to go one more step, to actually suspend, his service, and after the challenge he could come back. He finally agreed, which started immediately, yet his back pay, leave time and bonuses, he still had, 22, 000 dollars, as his pay went to his deposit, in Denver. He flew out, on April 18th, called Anna, and she and Erick was at the airport, also coming into Denver international airport was John, as Matt, ran through the airport, he actually knocked John over, as he went through screening, with duffle bag in hand. At gate waiting was Anna, and her older brother Erick, smiling, when they saw him. He was out, as Anna lept into his arms, and wrapped her legs around him, to kiss him to say, "Your home, what happen?"

"Well about that, they gave me leave, for up to a year."

"Really, they can do that?" asked Erick.

"Yeah, I guess it's called a diplomatic waiver, as soon as the officials from the Yukon Territory got involved, they said it was a matter of national security and allowed me to go, then after this is done, I can go back in or simply get out."

"Hey what are you too doing" said Erick, getting his man time with Matt and breaking the two of them up.

The three walked ahead of John who was too far back to catch up with them, as a car was out front, it was another brother, James, driving, in a Olds, honking, he gets out to embrace Matt, and Matt gets the front seat, as Erick puts the duffle bag, in the huge trunk, as Anna sits in the back. The car pulls out, as John Hughes hits the curb. The drive into Denver was fast, as it was around noon, for James to say, "When are you going to make an honest woman of my sister?"

"I have, I honor her, and her wishes" said Matt honestly.

"I mean marry her, we Italians have to stick together."

"We will" said Matt.

"Hush James, leave my man alone" said Anna.

They drove, to Morrison, up by Red Rocks, as James pulled in, to a celebration, all for their beloved son, Matt, to include his large family, he got out to embrace his sister Emily, for James to say, "Hey, hey, hey, what about me Sis?"

"If my brother marries your sister, we would be in-laws."

"That is true, but can't a guy try."

They all laughed, as Emily, had her arm around Matt to say, "You did well on your last challenge, but only third place, come on, we need to get you out running more."

"So you're in town for a while?" asked Matt.

"Yeah, I don't fly back for another week, what is your plans, now that you're out?"

"I don't know, but maybe an announcement" as they gathered everyone, as he looked over at Anna, to whisper, "Did you tell them yet?"

"No" she said, modestly.

"Listen up, family and friends", as he went to see the hot dogs and hamburgers, another brother, Mark was manning the grill, to say, "How many would you like brother?"

"Two doubles, and the works."

"You got it, there is beer in that cooler, as Matt, took one, and untwisted it, to take a gulp, as Anna received a call, she said, "Yes, John who, as she tries to hear him, to say, "Oh yes, were out at my parents' house, here let me text you the directions, good luck, good bye", as Matt was calling for her to come, to him, he puts his arm around her as the women were all gushing, as this was the time finally, as both mothers and fathers came out of the house, on to the upper patio to hear, "Listen up everyone, Anna and I are going to take on a challenge", as everyone cheered, as one said to the other, "Does that mean they are getting married?"

"I don't know if that is what they call it nowadays." Said the other.

"We would like to announce that Anna and I are going away for up to one year, and after that we will make out our wedding plans" as another cheer went up, as every disbursed, for Matt to say, "That went well.", he took a plate with his big burgers, as Anna was swarmed with well-wishers, as Emily, who lived in Los Angeles, said, "Honey whatever you need, I'm here for you, have you chosen the dress?"

"No not yet," said Anna a bit caught off guard.

As for the parents, it was a numbers game, as her Pappa Long said, "It's clear cut, Henry, we will pay, for the entire wedding, and I know you want to be part of it, I'll tell you what, the first 100K is all mine, anything after its all yours."

"Alright" as they agreed, as to where it would take place was anyone's guess, but the Red Rocks amphitheater was a number one choice.

The group broke up, some as a new vehicle approached. John got out, and went to see a party was well under way, Emily and Anna, were going over knitting, under the upper patio, as in the back it was full on volleyball game, the boys versus the boys, cousins, it was a huge group, and in it was Matt, well loved by her family. Anna saw John, but it was Mark, who said, "Care for a burger Sir?"

"Sure, do you know where I can find Anna Long?"

"My sister Anna is on the porch, up there, were celebrating her boyfriend Matt's arrival."

"So Matt Michales is here as well?"

"Yes, he just got out this morning, I guess and he is here to celebrate his proposal to my sister."

Mark calls up, "Anna, this gentleman wants to see you."

Anna made her way down, to say, as John gets a hamburger, "Who are you?"

"Name is John Hughes I'm with the challenge, is there a place we can talk?"

"Yes, do come in, as she looped her arm around his and led him up to the house, and inside, and up to the kitchen table, where it was quickly cleared by a few nieces and nephews, for him to say, "You sure have a big family."

"Yes, 22 on my side, and 12 on Matt's, to include a few friends, give or take, so what can I do for you?"

"Do you wanna ask Matt to join us?"

"Nah, I take care of all things financial, while he goes out and plays." John slides over the binder, and gives her two cards, a red and a green one, to say, "It's a 5000 line of credit."

"So we need to pay it back?"

"Well no and yes, the object of the challenge is to find someone to make their area prosper, and is eventually willing to live there."

"You say live there, indefinitely?"

"Yes, and make it prosper" he was unsure she understood.

"Yes, but you said live there?"

"Well for only one year, then I guess move to other places, but we are looking for residents." She read, while he ate, and a niece brought him a soda. Meanwhile Matt was the life of the party outside, spiking the ball on Erick, the two shook it out. As the play continued. For John to look outside to say, "Does it make you wanna go join him?"

"No, he is the outdoor man, and I'm the indoor girl, I cook and he takes care of the outside."

"You will help him, right?"

"Sure, whatever he needs," said Anna, pushing the book back to John, to say, "I think I have the just of it now, so you're looking for a geologist, what is the pay?"

"Whoa wait, were not looking for a person to hire, it's purely by accident" he said sincerely.

"If it does come up, It will be steep," said Anna smiling.

He gets up to say, "So when will you be leaving for the Yukon?"

"Whenever my boyfriend says we are going?"

"Any idea?"

"Nope, you will see us there on May 28th, just like the binder says we need to be there."

John left, with binder in hand, and Anna plotting her next move.

Later that night when the festivities calmed down, her four brothers, presented the reworked jeep, with plastic top, and a roll bar, for Matt to be surprised, as he was looking it over, on the back, was a drop ball, ready for a trailer. He hugged them all, and the next day, Matt and Anna went trailer shopping, they went to a trailer place, as he was eying a really long one, as a sales associates approached hem, to say, "Hi my name is Steven, so what are you looking for today?" as he was eying Anna.

"I think I'd like that one?"

"What are you pulling it with?"

"That jeep?" said Matt.

"No, you can't the trailer would buck, and blow your transmission, No what you need is a 8X 10, single axle."

"So show me one of them?"

They all went together, to see a small, that had a ramp, for Matt to say, "Can I try it out?"

"Yes, lets hook it up, Matt went and got the Jeep while Steven made a play for Anna, who acted like she didn't hear him, as he just kept it up, till Matt, was waved off by Steven still smiling at Anna. Matt got out, and hooked it up, and then the pair got in, and away he went, drove around, backed up, and parallel parked it, to get out to say, How much?"

"1299" Steven said?"

"I'll give you 999, plus tax, as I can see the same one at another store."

"Wait a minute, I'll go check inside."

"Sure go ahead, then to Anna inside he says, "Do you wanna drive it?"

"Sure," she says, getting behind the wheel, deplaces the clutch and away she went it was smooth, as Matt went inside. He got it for 999 with his military discount, and he left, got in the awaiting passenger seat, as Anna drove, she took him over to a big box retailer, and took up two spaces, the pair went in. he first found a pillow top mattress, he pulled it out, as they laid on it, for her to say, "That will do it, but get one all wrapped up, a person came and helped them, and said it would be ready up front, next on their list was seeds, and something to put them in, so he and Anna, began to pull off, all kinds of vegetables seeds from exotic, to tropical, as Matt said, "How about figs?"

"Sure, do you like artichokes" asked Anna smiling.

"Yes, as the two went back and forth. Till the entire 5 gallon bucket was full, and put that in the cart, as Matt thought, "What to carry water in?", and put 9 more buckets in, then got to the plastic section and there was 4X 8 sheets of hard plastic. He got a cart and got 20 of them. He saw soft toilet seats and took two, then a shower head, it was a raindrop, with plumbing, to a gate valve, and to a ¾ inch pipe. All in all he was done, went to check out, when the clerk said, "Buy one, get one free on the buckets, so Matt took ten more with lids. The next day, he had the trailer, with the mattress up right, and went to an army surplus store, by himself, he parked outside, and threw a tarp over it, and used bungee to tie down, then went inside, he was looking for a canteen belt, he found one, a poncho, and then he saw the foot lockers, and purchased all ten of them, complete with an insert. He was excited, and then set them in to see that they all fitted, using the tarp he put it back on.

The next day, he was off again, this time to a sale, at a hardware store, it was on chainsaws, he choose three sizes, a five foot bar, and ten chains, a 4 foot bar, and ten chains, and a smaller limb saw, with 32 inch bar, with ten chain, and a 16 inch bar, with ten chains, with that single biggest noncommercial purchase and a military discount, they gave him a box of files, and a guide to sharpen them, also, off to the right was a stand, for Matt to say, "What is that?"

"Oh it's a stand for your chainsaw to cut wood planks, but it's more like 2X4's, as only 3foot diameter logs fit in it, you want that too?"

"Yeah sure" said Matt.

They put that in and two mix cans, and the total, which he paid for himself. Before he left, the guy said, "If you're doing some serious chainsaw work, you need a fording box?"

"A fording box what's that?"

"It's a box that has mauls, wedges, and all you need to work with wood."

"I'll take it."

"In addition, you might need an auxiliary kit."

"What's that include?" asked Matt.

"Long handled shovels, pitchfork."

"I'll take that too."

Later that week, Anna and Matt and her family was taking a trip to Garden of the Gods, in Colorado Springs, to take in a native American Indian show, once down there groups of people were divided into smaller groups, as Matt and Anna were with Grayhawk, a young warrior, and over to a nearby teepee, as both Anna and Matt had a great idea, as they went inside, as they sat with others, Grayhawk, had a peace pipe, and Matt tended to the fire, it was sure warm, and the wind outside seemed to be diverted, he showed of using the firewood as a wind block, as it raged outside, it was calm inside, after the major ceremony, Matt inquired from an Elder, "Where can I buy, one of those teepees?"

"Oh they are small replicators, we have larger livable one, some 20X20, and of course we can sell you one, can I ask, what will it be used for?"

"Well I'm going to the Yukon, and it will be used to house both my girlfriend and I."

"Then come with me", as Matt went along, to a huge truck, he spoke in native tongue and workers pulled it off, for the Elder to say, "20 poles, 20 feet long, there is a stirrup, and lash, I would recommend, placing, sticks, down, to make a raised floor, then cover, with carpet, 2-10X10 and a 2-10X10 linoleum, for bath and kitchen. Use only charcoal, no fresh wood, it will burn clean. To make charcoal, take the wood, burn it down, then transfer it to the teepee, as Matt was understanding now, he hands him a grand, they shake, as two men carried to the family Olds.

CH 2

The Challenge

I t was May 1st, and Brian Lewis and Lily white, were loaded, and pulling their long trailer, with seasoned wood, and a long greenhouse frame. There was lots of bedding and cooking stuff, all stacked in the rear of the overly weighted down, Jeep grand Cherokee, the two lovers left, from Liberal Missouri up to KC, then left to Denver, Utah, Nevada, to Reno, then to Sacramento, and then San Francisco, then straight up the coast. To Victoria BC, to stay a while and then a ferry to Skagway, then the first to Whitehorse, as they pulled in to slot 2. As for the Farmers, Billy and Laurie, all loaded up, and they were ready, for the nearly 4000 mile trip, it was the large truck and long horse trailer, and all the animals, their camper was filled with food and supplies, he had four chainsaws, himself, as he headed out of northwest Minneapolis, up to Fargo, then to Minot, up to Regina, to Calgary, up to Edmonton, up the Alaskan highway, to Whitehorse, to take number 4 slot.

For John and Kim, they got what they wanted in the end, and 13 head, of the finest black angus cattle, three were confirmed pregnant and 2 sows pregnant, they too had a small topper, on their truck, with a bed in the back, and bedding, their horse trailer was filled. As they left Madison, went up to Winnipeg, over to Saskatoon, then Edmonton, Fort Nelson, to the Alaskan highway, up to Whitehorse, and slid into number 3. All by the 20th of May.

Meanwhile, Matt had packed, and then changed it five times, Anna grandmother, gave her a plastic bag, filled with seeds, to say, "These are the family heirloom tomatoes." They kissed and said their tearful good byes, when they decided to leave, all ten footlockers were packed, as they went to fill up, at a farm co-op, gas station, he filled his five gallon gas can on the back, and went inside, to check it out, when he saw, 18 chicks, for 5 dollars, so he picked up the box, to say, "And six months of feed?"

Four bags were set out, he paid, and they carried them out, to the back seat, all four bags, and the chicks. They took to the north, to Cheyenne, then to Great Falls, Montana, switched drivers, and Anna drove, to Calgary, then Edmonton, Matt took over, and drove to Dawson's creek, where the weather turned cold, and they both changed into long pants and long sleeved shirts, then to Fort Nelson, and through the Rocky Mountains, on to the Alaskan highway. And in four days arrived in Whitehorse, on May 25th, and parked in the number one slot. The next morning, all went in, as the doors were open, to a 9 o clock meeting with the governor, they all sat, as he came in, for he was a native American Indian, he was nice, as he shook everyone's hand, as if they were all equals, to say, "Welcome to the Challenge, over here is a board, where 320 acres of land was equally divided, as each of you has a slot, so will the number one, stand and make a selection, it was Matt, who went around, to look at the topographical map, to look at all the different configurations, each had its own features, but looking at what was closest to town, of Beaver creek, he put his finger on the southwest corner. Everyone else agreed, for the Governor to say, as he hands, Matt a package, and goes to sit down, to show Anna, she looks it over, for "Number two?" it was Lily, who came forward, as she smiles at Anna, to choose the southeastern one next to Matt's and Anna's parcel.

"Next please, number 3," as it was John, and both Billy, to look at the board, Billy chose left and John took right, as the Governor, now said, "Please at this time turn in your two cards, as Matt, saw Anna pull it out, and turn them in to a distinguished woman, named Miss Tillwater. for them to be taken away, for the Governor, to say, "Now let's talk of this year's rules, we ask that each of you build a cabin, then make improvements, and dress up the area, for the ranchers, means fencing, maybe plant hay, maybe some outcropping for the cattle, and for the farmers, plenty of housing for your animals, because it could get down to minus 30, and with the wind chill farther downward. Let's see the mushroom growers, any farm animals?"

"Nope, were vegetarians." They both said proudly.

"Really, I hope you have enough vegetables then."

As the farmer and the rancher just looked at the two of them in disbelief.

The Governor, then said, "What of you Marine?"

"Oh just 18 chicks, and the rest I'll trap or trade for."

"Funny you say that, because in each year, a convenient store, with a hardware and feed store is available to you, to trade pelts, or those by a river, bring in some pan gold, or any other resource you may find, if you're a wood worker, build bird houses, the man and woman running that operation, will accept anything of trade, your money will be kept on account, and the one whom has the most when this is over, will be declared the winner. You all have your packages, any questions?"

"What if we want to go shopping, say in Anchorage?" asked Matt.

"Well I have never had that request before, but if it's done in a day's trip, I'll allow it, the only stipulation, is if its work related, like for instance the mushroom growers, if you drive to Anchorage, then we will allow it, the only way, all this goes away, is when someone gives up, and wants to go home, then it will be over, in addition we will have a team visit during the cold temperature months of October, November, December, January, February, and the rest of the months. In addition each of you will have your own satellite phone, we took the liberty of forwarding your current cell phone to this new phone, in addition you can use it to communicate with each other or to call for help, as we will give you support. Your point of contact will be Jake Wilson, he runs the hardware store, I belief he has a sale going on of the last of the spring livestock, and feed, be sure to sell him out," Miss Tillwater came back in, to hand them all a card, it was blue, with a note on each, Anna looked at hers, it was 10K, doubled the amount, as the governor, said, "Those green cards are worth double, on whatever you have left over. Matt saw 3K on Brian's, to shake his head, to hear, "You now have three days to get to the convenient store, check in, and Mister Wilson will officially get you started, to simplify I'd suggest you all travel together, it's another 150 miles, give or take."

Anna and Matt went back over to their motel, and cleaned it out, as he saw the other three couples, going over to the diner, they put their stuff away, and joined them, to sit at the round table, as Billy said, "So let's meet everyone, and tells us about what you do, on my right", "Hi, my name is Kim Locke, I tend to young animals."

"Hi my name is John Junior, Locke, I raise Black angus cattle, and as soon as we get to where were going, I have each one for you."

Everyone shook their heads, as it was Anna, who said, "My name is Anna, and I'm a geologist., "I'm Matt, a former Marine Corps scout, tracker." Over on the other side, was Brian, who said, "I'm Brian, and this is Lily, were gardeners, and grow mushrooms, like big portabellas." "I'm Laurie, a Vet, so if you need a visit call us, I have a phone, or on that sat phone, change to frequency 3 from 7." "I'm Billy, a farmer, I have almost every game animal I can have, as the food came, everyone had eggs, hash browns, steak, and toast except, Brian and Lily, it was eggplant in a tomato sauce, for Billy to say, "Where do you get your protein from?"

"Vegetables?" said Brian adamantly.

"You're crazy, when your burning 4,000 calories a day, you need meat, you'll see," said Billy, as the others were gnawing on their T-bone, Brian and Lily left, but paid cash, as Billy said, "I hope they're not the ones who put us out."

The rest finished, and each paid, and then went out, for Laurie to say, "If any of you girls want to ride with me in the camper, come along?"

All declined, as each got in their respective vehicles, as Matt fired up the jeep, and he had the littlest, by far, to the three others, he led them out, as at the window of the huge government building, was the governor, Jim Hickson, to say, "It was so hard, not asking that Geologist, for the job, as she was the only one to figure it out, right John?"

"Yes, sir, I believe she is looking for about half that prize money?"

"Oh, Imagine she is worth it, let's just see how they all get along, as we can wait for her."

Matt led the caravaners out, it was team 1, then in order, was Brian and Lily, team 2, then the ranchers team 3, and the farmers team 4. It was probably the most rugged hundred and fifty miles they ever drove, burning up the gas going up, and then back down, first place to stop was a place called Champagne, in the foothills of the Rocky Mountains, it had a gas station, it was a welcomed sight for the big trucks, as for Matt, he was in awe of looking at Mount Logan. And according to his map was the highest peak, at 19,850 feet high, and another pass they would have to climb. The temperature was a paltry 40's, meant put on a jacket. He took off, and over, to about 25 miles more, to Haines Junction, a once known place for trapping and Indian trading. It had a convenient store, and a fur trading store, and a hardware, and an all levels school, population, 200, as they were at the base of the enormous mountain, they went down the long road, to see, "You've just crossed into the Kluane Indian reservation, and on the right was a long huge lake, that stretched for 25 miles or more, and in the distance a pack of buffalo, endangered, and on Indian land. Matt drove on, down the undulations, caused by the massive mountain, as now it was a river, churning on the right, and then it went away, as the sign said, 25 miles to Beaver Creek.

Matt and Anna were first to the convenient store, as Matt filled up on gas, Anna went in, she saw a frizzled out white haired woman, for her to say, "So your Anna Long, how was your trip?"

"Good."

"Look around, anything you need, like a fire pit stock pot?"

"Sure" though Anna, but waited, for Matt, who came in, to say, "Hi ya Miss how much for the fill-up?"

"It's all on your card, as Anna produces, as Anna places the stock pot on the counter, for Matt to say, "You need that?"

"Why maybe I do?" said Anna.

"Well get it, but I have something similar."

She put it back, as the lady said, "My name is Rita, The next thing you will go do is see my husband at the hardware store he is waiting."

Matt and Anna drove around to the back and parked, to see at least fifty homes, with windows, to hear, "All abandoned, but if you see something you want, I'll put it on your account, so your number one, come in, you get first crack, at what we have to offer, as Matt held the door open for Anna, with a credit of over 10K, pretty much everything is available to you." Matt came in to see Anna, all over a cast iron claw foot bathtub, to say, "Alright, how much for the tub?"

"Going rate on line 999, but for you being number one, I'll give it to you for 500."

"Sold, as he pulls out his money, to hear, "No, all of this is on account, as Matt looked around, they had everything, from pots to pans, utensils, as Anna was looking at the Dutch oven, but knowing she had all the kitchen stuff she needed. Then over to gourmet coffee roast, for Jake to say, "I import this myself and grind it, and roast it, in an oven, it imparts the flavor."

"I'll have 20 pounds of that" said Matt.

Next to that was walnuts, and other seasonal nuts, Anna chose half the bag, then it went up to the preserves, any kind, Anna chose five, green tomato relish, blackberry, blueberry, apricot, and peach, then over to a whole counter dedicated to teas, they went past, next was rain water barrel's they chose two, at 130.00 each, next up was the stoves, and Matt chose a box wood, wood stove, long, like a barrel, to a pipe up, for

200.00 to see a round parlor style, to a big barrel, but passed, next was cabin plans, and the book section, Matt walk right on by, into the hardware, to see oil lamps, and chose four, but at the book store, Anna chose candle and soap making, and then in that area loaded up on supplies, they went to odds and ends, like a whistle, a flint starter, gold pans, got Matt thinking, then on to swings, free standing and a slider, seeing her eyes lit up, to a tune of 120.00. Then on to the music department, guitars, violins, banjos, fiddles, going back around to see the tub, and accessories, wash boards, she took one, looking at the pails and the price he was happy to have the five gallon buckets. The hand pumps were interesting, but he had another idea, a high wheel garden plow, he passed, the rest were tools, for Matt to see the others coming in, to see the board, posted, as in the following;

Pelt for exchange

1. Fur seals, 1000
2. Artic fox, 900
3. Grizzly bear, 800
4. Caribou, 700
5. Elk, 600
6. Mountain lion, 500
7. Wolverine, 400
8. Brown bear, 300
9. Mountain goats, 200
10. Deer, any, 100

The above is for only reference

Matt looked up on the list for Jake to say, "Depends on quality and if everything is on, but some of them don't apply to you, unless you go deep in the Yukon river, some of the seals have been spotted as far north as in Dawson, and in some places such as White river, is a salmon spawning grounds like right now. Come with me to the feed store, I have a few items remaining, they all went outside, to see four snowmobiles, brand new, with a trailer, for Jake to say," 2500, each plus 500 for the trailer, they all took one. And inside the feed store, where there was game of all sorts, thinking about his chickens, these were 20, as Jake said, "Share as you like, 5 each plus a rooster, they all raised their hand, except Brian and Lily, who went back into the store, as next was geese, ducks, grouse, and a homing pigeons, all four of them, for Jake to say, "You have to build a platform, for which those need to fly too." They all agreed, as next was pigs, four each, for Jake to say, "Now over to the rabbits, we have a breeding pair, of new Zealand whites, the largest, as Billy passed, so Matt, said "Sure", as the rabbits went to both, the rancher and Matt. Lastly Jake said, "I have feed for all the animals, hay bales also, the last thing I have is two steers hanging, each a half side of beef, but you need to place it high in a tree, all for 500."

Matt took one, then though of trapping, to say, "If you don't mind, I'll take the others, there was no one to refuse. Outside, Matt, saw a bunch of siding, to say, "Hey Jake how much for the siding?"

"All yours for 50."

"You got it" said Matt.

They went back inside, as Lily had all kinds of stuff, but they were limited on funds and spent all they had, Matt used his own money to cover the rest, Jake allowed it to happen, for him to say, "Why don't, we go up and follow me to each of your camp places, as first we will go to number one, then, on to 2, then 3, and finally 4."

They loaded up what they could carry, the farm animals stayed behind, and followed Jake out, across the road, up a dirt road, that bordered the Alaskan border, straight up, as Matt followed, seeing the land was still hilly, it was as if a berm was beside them, but it opened up to see a river, then he turned to the right, onto another road, over a bridge, and he slowed, to a stop, everyone got out, to see a clearing on the south side, the dirt, had minerals in it, as the clearing was evident, something was there. For Jake to say, "Gather around, last year a cabin was here, pointing to the open lot, but behind us is where its best to build your home site."

"Yes, Sir" said Matt, as he saw cameras were everywhere, Matt and Anna, left there rig, to get in the truck, and down some ways straight over a bridge, for Jake to say, "This is still your parcel, and it goes, up, to a waterfall, which is where the Kluane reservation stops, over a ways, to the open lands, and they stopped at a hill of sorts, for Jake to get out, to say, "This is number 2, notice the high point, great place to build." Brian and Lily left their jeep, and got in, as they drove a distance, to a road, north, up a ways, crossing several streams, while driving, Jake said, "This is all of your parcel, as this is your last clump of trees, which to build with, up a slight hill, and down, toward the river, he said, "This branch is the Yukon river, parcel 3 has this one, starting about here, you all see the fencing, it has great grazing land for the cattle, all fenced in, as he came to a turn, to see more of the huge river, as it was down below them, as they came to a stop, all got out, for Jake to say, "This has incredible views, but your source of water, will be Beaver creek, its continuous source of water will keep you refreshed, see that site, was where a cabin use to be, they tried to harness that stream, by creating a water wheel, but it is all gone now."

"Or a wind break" said Matt, showing John Junior, a wall, he agreed. As John left his rig, as all got into the truck for Jake to drive to the last one, like he did the last nine times, to stop, about a mile down the road, to number 4, a Northwest parcel, with a strong river, in the distance, for Jake to say, "Yours is the longest, but widest, about a mile over is the white river."

"And again, another wind break upfront" said Matt, Billy agreed, as they got back in, and drove, to their place, and parked, it was spacious opening of trees, plenty of grass, for the animals, his source of water, was too far away. He got stuck, but had a dilemma, where to capture water, and quickly, the four rain barrels would help, Jake and the group help pull Billy out, as he stayed on the rocks. Everyone else got back into Jakes truck, and turned around, and went back to number 3, where, he let off, John and Kim, and then, turned south, and then, west, to number 2, for Brian and Lily to get out and then lastly, to number one. Where Anna then Matt got out of the back seat. He watched Jake go. They still had two days before the start, so on freq 3, Billy called a meeting at his place, Matt agreed, to pick up Brian and Lily, he off loaded his feed, to the trailer, and box of chicks, and unhitched the trailer, on the road. Everything was still, yet the sound of rushing water, so he and Anna, drove off, past the home site, down east to Brian's, he had unhitched, and had a frame already going, for his greenhouse, as a frame stood tall, Lily was carrying plate glass, up, for Matt to stop, and on the bank, to get out, to say, "We were to wait two days?"

"Who cares if we get a jump on this" said Brian.

"You sure have a fierce wind here" said Matt.

"Yeah that north wind, is demanding" said Brian, putting in the below glass, instantly making a difference, for Matt to say, "Billy has called a meeting, just come up with us, and afterwards, we will all come down to assemble this altogether."

"Oh alright, hey Lily, were going with Matt, just close up the jeep." She did that, to get in the back, as did Brian, and off the small jeep went, back on the road, which was wide, then around the corner, Matt noticed metal stakes at least ten feet high, as he drove north in a head wind, to cross over a bridge, and then up north, a left hand turn, past the ranchers, who let off their cattle, to graze, past them and down the road, to number 4 parcel, and drove in, all got out, to see a BBQ, was up and running, for Billy to say, "What if we meet every Sunday, to mark the 52 weeks, at each other's place, so 12 times, and were through, so Matt what were you saying about a wind block?"

"Well once you set in, and decide where to build your cabin, I'll come in and set in a wall."

"You got a deal, what do I need to trade?"

"Nothing for now, let's help Brian out with his greenhouse, "Sure let me unhitch the trailer." Billy was eager, but not John, he was out searching tree limbs, but Kim, was game, so with Billy, Laurie and Kim, they all followed Matt down to Brian's and Lily, all three vehicles pulled up, while the men went to the slight hill, to help Brian, already well underway, it was Brian barking out the orders, while, Matt and Billy, assembled, the remaining frame, Matt noticed how powerful the wind was here, but once Brian placed in the plastic plate, instantly the wind was deflected up, the greenhouse was huge, probably 12X 80 feet long, with three doors, two on the ends, and one in the middle, Matt and Billy finish the last frame, and set in a door. Billy attached the spring and chain, while Matt helped the girls, carry more of those plastic pieces, and seeing Matt was there, Lily and Anna, went to their Jeep grand Cherokee, to fix some lunch. Laurie continued to bring up plates, with Matt. Billy, set the other door, set the spring and the chain. As an instant wind gusts tore open that door, but Billy was able to catch it, to say, "Brian you may need to put an inside lock."

"We'll do."

Lily and Anna presented the team with peanut butter sandwiches on whole wheat bread, and a bag of chips each, for a drink was iced tea.

Around a make shift table, in the greenhouse, it was nice, 70 degrees, for Brian to finish first, to say, "Next we have the counter boxes, they are all on the trailer, and one by one, Matt and Billy brought them in, through the open door in the middle. Each one locked in, and an arm came down to support instantly a row was forming, giving about 8 feet of width. This went on for another hour, till they were down at the door, and that's when Brian said, "That's enough, who wants to help me dig?"

Both Matt and Billy, said, "No thanks", to hear, "Come on boys help a guy out?"

Matt collected Anna, who was getting attached to Lily, as she got in the jeep, they said their tearful good byes, as Matt backed up, and drove off.

Both Billy and Laurie left as well, for Lily it meant, pulling out the seed starters, while Brian went on to digging, just west of the door.

Meanwhile John was doing a bit of collecting on his own, he gathered up large enough branches, using a little chain saw, he fashioned notches, and used a hammer, to drive in the six foot branches, about 3inches in diameter, at an angle, in a semi-circle, direction, to keep the herd in. Kim arrived back, to help him, to hear, "So where did you go?"

"Help out Brian and Lily, did you know they have a huge greenhouse, and is allotting space for us to start some vegetables?"

"That's great, can you tie the ones I already put in?"

"Yes John."

Meanwhile, Matt and Anna made it back to their flat piece of parcel to the southwest, for Matt to say, "I'm gonna drop three dead trees, so stay back."

"I'm just gonna, collect some dirt, can I have five buckets?"

"Yes, I need to use five for water" said Matt.

"How about I take the jeep to the bridge and get the water while you drop those trees" asked Anna.

"Alright" said Matt, as Anna, counted out, ten buckets, and took five lids, and some rope, got in the jeep, and drove a ways, to an open part, and a bridge, she stopped, to survey the fast moving water, she tied off the end of the rope to the handle, and tossed it on the other side, and it filled up, and was able to lift it up, it was about ¾ full, then did the same for 3 more. Then the last one she used to top off the rest. Then placed a lid on each of the four, the last one, she got it pretty full. Now with the other buckets it was getting creek sand and rock, she went to the edge, she took off her boots and socks, seeing her trousers were going to get wet, she took them off, and then, with five buckets in hand, jumped down in the cold water, easily, filling the bottom, with gold filed sand, and small rocks. When all of a sudden, she heard a chain saw echo, as it screamed, and then, the sound of trees come crashing down, Matt took the dead ones down. Then limbed them up, he set those in a separate pile, and then began, to cut up the huge logs, about 5 feet in diameter, in 18 inches apart, it went fast, once done with one log, on to another, he dropped it, and then did another one, with both on the ground, he limbed the second one, then cut it up, to the last one, he limbed it, then cut it up, all were about 120 feet long. Now it was on to chopping the wood, using a block, he rolled them out to the ground and begin to chop, and then add a wedge, it was hard work, but it was fast as it was dry wood. Anna was back with the jeep, she got out, as she saw the entire south lot full of down trees, and in the middle was Matt, blasting the wood apart with each swing, Anna, undid the top plastic, and folded it up, to pull out a five gallon bucket, and a ¼ full of sediment, and said, "Matt, look we have gold."

Matt stopped what he was doing, to go see it to say, "Maybe later, we can go panning?"

"Nah, but if you could build be a ladder, in a sluice box."

"I think I can do that", as he went back to chopping, about halfway there, he cut up some kindling, and started a fire, and put some chopped wood, in it, while Anna was putting some black soil in her five buckets, then dropped in five tomato seeds each. Took one bucket and uses a ladle to scoop out the water, and water them in. then went to the kitchen footlocker, and found plastic wrap, and sealed the top, using some bailing wire, she tied them off, using her small utility tool. Her next chore was to till up the field, with the long handled shovel, while Matt finished the chopping. As each block burned the greenness and smoke out, it was on to stacking the charcoal, next to the fire, that was where Anna helped out, he set a line, and began to stack dry wood on the west side, instantly noticing it was a wind break, I took it up to eight feet, and then due south, it was working, the middle fire was calmer, for Anna to say, "If you could help me out, I found a large piece of limestone?"

"Sure let's go get it", with that Matt drove, to the spot, near the river, but said, "Hold on, and drove over the bridge, to see where the road bends, on in the field was red rock. Matt got out, and walked over to it, with sledgehammer in hand, struck the top, it broke free, and hit it again, till it broke free, then took a chunk, and saw the vein, he took un upswing, to break off some more, thus opening up the hole, he knew he would need to dig this out for a quarry, he got back in to say, "Is that enough?"

"Yes, this will do fine" said Anna.

The drive back was nice, as Anna said, "What do you think of our property?"

"It is nice, I just wish there wasn't so many bugs."

"Maybe, you ought to build a bat cave" said Anna.

"A bat cave up here?"

"Yes I notice bat guano, back there, and if you were to build them a place they could eat and rest after a days' worth of eating."

"How do you suppose I do that?"

"Well first you need to be off the ground say twelve feet, then using a plank, to knock out the cold, and a network of branches to hang onto, and you have a bat cave."

"Interesting, I guess I can figure out that one."

"Well don't think too hard on it, it's really simply, build a wall, twelve feet high, then place in a catacomb of branches, then put a plate on the front, and they will live in the overhang."

"How will you attract them here?"

"Don't worry about that, I have a plan,." she said.

With a shovel in hand, he scooped up wet dirt, to form a pile, then stood on it to smooth it out, and then in the middle, I dug out a two-step, down pit, taking that cue, Anna was mixing up, burnt ashes, crushed limestone, and lava rich soil, to make a mortar slurry, she with My help, poured it in the middle, as I used a shovel to spread it out, to form a circle, with a flat one side, next I set up a fire in the middle of the pit, and kept putting on wood, it was roaring, but it cured the mortar hard, next using straight smaller branches, I began to place them, on the platform, from the fire pit out, ten feet long, tight in the middle, to a apart towards the outsides, using the mortar, it was spread over the branches, for a flat surface, all the way around for 22 feet. While letting that cure, Anna placed burning wood on it to help the process of curing the mortar, Matt was off, to his longer 5inch wide poles, 20 feet long, 22 of them, he lassoed a rope around the top, and secured it, in one motion and with Anna's help, up went the frame, Matt spread them out, to form a solid frame. Next was the bed, using some cut blocks, He cut at three feet, and notched them out for a support, then using, poles, He split in half, and in half again, He built a frame, then on one side, affixate four more planks, turning it over, He put on the foots, and nailed them in, lastly it was ready, as just in time Brian and Lily arrived to help out. Brian took on end, and lifted it up, and over to the side where it was going, when, the mortar set, a piece of carpet, went down, cut into place around where the bed was going, then to where supply was on the other side, also a piece of linoleum was set down, and nailed in place, all to form a circle, and the excess was cut away, by Matt, as Anna was using the outdoor fire pit, to cook up some soup, as Matt went to the trailer, to take off the footlockers, Brian helped out, to the teepee site, and set them on. Anna set them how she wanted them, in a stair step method, her two cooking lockers near the front, on the linoleum. Next up was the bed, it went on, and the mattress, on top of that it fit perfect. Next was the poles, as each person grabbed one on all lifted at once, and carried it five feet, to set it down on the edges, they lined up with the branches going out, I lashed them down to hold them in place, next was the canvas, I got it, rolled it up, to have an opening, using four poles, I fashioned a arm off of it, so each person had a side, as I went around, putting, a portion, on each end, then at the last moment I did this, and I said, "Ready lift", and in one motion, the canvas went up, and in the back, I had his, on the rear, as the rest fell away, and around the poles, Brian, was pulling it out, and down, in the stirrup, of the pole, it became taunt as I went to the front, to see, it was straight, the front flaps, were open, as I walked in to somewhat of paradise, it was warm, and out of the wind, it was large and nice to stand up, as I went out, to see Anna had dinner ready, a vegetable soup, each had a bowl, and some warm tea. Brian looked like he was staying around, so I said, "Let's go into town, I need help with a bathtub?"

"Alright I'll help out" said Brian.

I kissed Anna, who said, "Oh I want to go."

"Alright, let's get this cleaned up, and we will all go."

Meanwhile at Billy's fight number one was on full alert, Laurie was ready to leave, him and go home, for Billy to say, "No you will ruin it, just play out this year, and if after that your free to do whatever you want?"

"Really you'll let me go?"

"Yes, I realize it was a mistake, in doing this, but were here let's make the best of this."

"Alright what do you suggest?"

"Let's plow the field, and grow a huge garden" said Billy.

He broke out a small wheel plow, she held the handles, while he pulled it along., row after row, after going 20 times, it was a seed a foot, in the water line, know he had some pipe, he put it together, and with Laurie's help, all the way, south, about 400 feet, to the river, where he stuck it in, and water was flowing, and then Billy had an idea, where to build the cabin, he went to his trailer, got his chain saw, and went into the forest, and began to drop trees, about 3 feet in diameter, he limb them up, and then that's where he had a problem, he was stuck, he went out, to see Laurie, trying to keep the animals apart, to hear, "Can you go to Matt's and see if I can barrow his jeep?"

"Yes, sure", she was ready to get away from him anyway. She shut the camper door, she backed up the truck, and down the road she went. She thought about rescuing Kim, but drove right on by, seeing them outside in the rain, putting up fencing. And drove on, to a turn south, and past an outcropping of cattle, south, to another turn, past the empty camp site of Brian's, and over a bridge, to Matt's and Anna, and no Jeep, just a Jeep grand Cherokee, she got out, and went over to the teepee, it was nice inside, so much so, she crawled into their bed, after a bowl of soup, and went to sleep.

Meanwhile at the store, the four got out, as Matt refilled his gas can, as Rita called out for Jake to open the hardware store, he did, as they all looked at the huge claw foot tub, Matt could barely budge it, let alone the others, but with some moving experience Jake, lifted it up, and placed a dolly under it, to roll it out, to the awaiting trailer. Jake used a tie down cable, to secure the tub to the dolly, it helped going up the ramp, it stopped on the end due to the plywood, where Jake asked, "Do you want any more plywood, I have twenty sheets?"

"Perhaps", said Matt, going in with Jake, to see them, as the bundle was attached to a rope, and up above that was a block and tackle, to hear, "You can't have that, it helps me load and unload?"

"Alright, you got another, I could sure use it to maneuver this tub in place" said Matt.

"Well I do have a larger one, but its massive."

"I'll take it, as he looked it over, it was massive, as Jake said, "Lash three long poles together, say, 20 feet long, about a foot in diameter, tie off a dangling rope, then hang that, and you can winch up anything, and move it 20 feet."

Matt, helped take it down, and into his trailer, he securing the rear ramp, as he was thinking now he had a way of how to move the tub once we get there. They all shook hands, as Matt picked up his siding he earlier bought. They all drove back, not before each got an Icee, they arrived, and Matt backed up the trailer all the way to the teepee, as the others un-did a side, and rolled up a portion, then in an instant, Matt took three 20 foot poles left over, tied them together, to form a tripod, and using his block and tackle, secured it to the tub, and with Brian's help, hoisted the tub upon sung it around, and winched it down, to the edge of the wood, floor, then in one motion, one side was up, and then the other, it worked, as Matt saw Laurie all curled up, to set the tub where he wanted it, undid the harness, and off came the dolly, and the rope, as both girls discovered a sleeping guest.

Matt went quickly, to attach a drain pipe, and snake it down aways from the teepee, it came with a plug, as Anna and Lily were first to try it, using all the water they collected, it was pretty warm, twenty five gallons later, it was bath time, as the flaps went back down. Matt and Brian went back to the jeep, and took the empty, buckets, for Brian to say, "How did you know to get five gallon buckets?"

"We use them in the military, to sit on, and haul things with, so I just got twenty."

"Twenty, but I only see ten?"

"The others are off to the side, why you want them?"

"Sure, can we, we would forever be in your debt."

"Then I guess, we will see you here every day around 1."

"Yes, I guess so."

CH 3

The journal, day one

May 30th 2004

It's still two days before the official day to start this challenge, a bit of a recap, the farmers, Billy and Laurie are apart, she lives out of the modern camper, while, he is in a tent, later I will be going over to help him pull logs, with the jeep, as for the ranchers, John and Kim, are putting up fencing, which they are supposed to help Billy.

For Brian, to make Lily happy, he is over here every day now, as for us, I keep thinking about what Anna said about the wall, and it makes sense. So this morning I'm going to thin out all the 3 foot diameter trees, I have about forty acres, to the south, and to the White river, so I took the big chain saw, and began to cut, using a cloth tape I got from Anna's sewing kit, she was up early, and onto a new project, weaving branches together for cages, also I must tell you this, it rains, the last two mornings till about ten, and then it is soaked, so what we have planted is still not up, she found I had a roll of sheeting, she took it out and covered her beds with it. On the ends, she used big rocks to keep it down. Two issues she was nagging me about, the bathroom and the shower, I told her I was working on both, but as soon as I fired up that saw, she was out of there, and off to Lily's, as tree by tree fell, I was opening up the acreage, to see Mount Logan in the southern distance. I stayed away from her field, she and I planted in my sleep, but it's over, as tree after tree went down, it was opening it up, thinking only take what was needed, and with the need of 34 trees, I stopped, began to limb them, and set them aside, using my tape measure, I marked out fifteen feet long, and cut, and kept that up, for the next cut, those forty logs, or so, would net me, about 320, so I kept those to use on the outside wall to be the biggest, at the middle was 20 feet long, using my tripod, I lifted them, on to a three bar brace, as they lay up three feet up from the ground. I carried them back to the camp using my jeep. I was experimenting with the logs. I used wedges from the fording kit, I drove them in, and just like that I split them apart, able to lift them freely, I carried them, to the inside of my wood pile, for a floor, as I laid them face up. Now I had an idea for a massive wind block, and use the logs, as a wall. So I took out the shovel, and began to dig, a hole, it was fairly easy to dig, down a foot, then it was big stone filed, then it was hard compact, at three feet, using the tripod, I choked the log, and pulled it up, into the hole, to stand at twelve feet high. Then the next one, while still holding it, I back filled against the other one, this went on for three more. Then using the split 20 footers, I laid them split face up, to make a floor, and tie in the wall, then another one, gave me 4 planks, I notched them in, next was the inside wall. I set up the tripod over the inside and dug a ten foot trench, then using the thirteen footers I cleared the outside wall, and began to set them in, up to five, as it was now fifteen feet long, on both sides, it was straight, so then I moved the tripod, back over to the braces, and set on a 22 foot log, and with some wedges spit apart the log, I did two that way, then moved the tripod, over to the beginning, and picked up the logs, drug them over and up, I set it on the end, and used twist nails, ten inches long, and drove them in, it was on the west edge side and over hung, two feet on the inside, as it was inverted two feet, 12 to 10 in the middle. I did this for the remaining three, instantly I had a shelter, it was about twelve feet long. I thought about what Jake said about the plywood, after that and just twelve feet, I was spent, but ate a protein bar, and a piece of meat, we had stored, and I was back at it, actually the digging was better than hauling the logs around, but it was, now, with the tripod, to finish the inside log. An outside log, two spit up for the flooring, and two down for the roof, it was a slow to go, but level, and was forming a dry place to go, and on my way, sometime later Anna had come back with Lily, and the two would make mortar, and stuff them in the gap, between the outside west wall, from time to time, I would go get more limestone and put it on her pile, one of ashes, as we kept making charcoal, to using the ashes, to limestone, sand, and hard clay, in addition, Brian came over, and he began to nail the logs together, we had the west wall was going up, I dug, both trenched, fifteen feet at a time, with thirty feet done, we were nearing halfway. I was spent, but when the unexpected rains came, we got inside and we were dry, where there was mortar, all other places leaked. When it let up, we went back at it, I built a scaffolding unit for the girls, to get on the roof, to seal it. About five gallons per several lines, of mortar. The girls were busy, and about halfway, I marked out the rest of the way, still about another hundred feet to the tree line. We had plenty of logs, I unloaded the trailer, and I took off the plywood, and the plastic, all 20 sheets, and stacked them up on the inside. I was thinking of doors.

Brian and I left for Billy's it was a bit past noon. We arrived at his place, with tripod in hand, and set it up, and unhitched the trailer, to see the truck and camper, still intact, for Laurie to come out, to say, "Hi Matt, do you think it would be possible for me to take a bath?"

"Sure," I said. As I looked her over.

"Thanks" she hugged me.

She backed up and drove, past us, for Me to unhitched the trailer, and back in the jeep, and across soft terrain, all the way up to the tree line, and hopped out, with choker in hand, I set the line on the end, and hooked to his bumper, and dug deep, yet, it came, as I and Billy were a team, and drug the logs, to the homestead, it was one after another till, all 26 were there, and it was at closing of this day, to see the camper wasn't back, to say, "Why don't you come over, and have some grub?" I asked.

"Alright I will do that, what is that thing?" asked Billy.

"Oh my tripod to lift up the trees."

"Wow, can I use it?"

"That's why I brought it but I'm taking it back, but don't fear, I will, bring it back, tomorrow afternoon."

Brian and I hooked up the trailer, and set the twenty foot long poles, three of them and block and tackle in place, secured it down, and backed up, and we three left. We passed the ranchers still doing fencing. Around the corner, down, then right, and past the greenhouse, and over the bridge, to stop at my south compound, for Billy to be amazed, to say, "Your building a fort, cool, can you do this for us?"

"Sure if you help out", as Billy went to the dry part, to stand on the edge, to say, "It's warm in here, and you have a teepee, cool" a makeshift table was constructed, as soup, and cornbread was on the menu, inside, Laurie was asleep on the bed. Billy chose not to bother her, and ate outside with us and the others, as Anna said, "Honey, Lily and I finished the halfway mark, maybe we can finish the rest of the wall, if you help?"

"I'm sure with Billy's help, we can."

That night, everyone slept in the teepee, Laurie and Billy on the carpet floor, Lily and Brian on the other side and us in the bed.

May 31st Sunday 2004

Day 2, it was everyone up, and it was Anna, getting dressed, to look out and it was bleak, a monsoon of rain, was soaking everything, it put a damper on the mood, but not Billy, he was raring to go., dressed, Anna made a hearty breakfast, for all six of us, eggs, beef, and potatoes, and the rest of the bread, for toast.

We were wearing our rain gear, and wet boots, same as the girls, all three of us dug the remaining trench, to make 100 feet. Brian and I was setting the logs, while Billy and

Laurie went collecting large rocks to fill five buckets, however they used our drinking water buckets. For a bit of good news, Anna's tomatoes, emerged. She set them, in the light, which the huge trees were blocking. Then it was us on the south side, with Brian's help, the inside went faster, as I did the outside, I dug as the rain just kept falling. For the girls, it made it easier to find the cracks, as both girls, were on the west side roof, they patched the roof, as the logs were the tightest ever, on top, with Billy's and Laurie help to the end. It was lunch, and there was enough soup and cornbread for all. I washed my down with tea. Billy was amazed by this outside wall, that was all he talked about, doing for his place, but I told him it was for storage, he just had to see it to believe it, the turn was quite simple, as we had all the logs ready, and talk about easy, off the wind side, it went twice as fast, by dinner, we were just about done, with another hundred feet. With the roof on, it slanted inward and was being sealed. The next big thing was a massive roof, over the entire open space, as the rain was something fierce, so I mapped out 7- 5 feet in diameter trees, and cut them down, and cut it to twenty five feet long. Using a measurement of twelve feet apart, 7-5 feet holes deep were dug, to close out another day, we finished up the soup and cornbread.

June 1st Monday 2004

Our first official day active, but for video reasons, they edit, our progress, and then show it to a live feed. Day 3, the half back side was done, and this morning, twenty five foot logs went in to seven different places, they were straight and secure. On the top I notched twelve foot, 3 foot in diameter poles, across the span, and because I like working with 3 foot diameter poles, I split them apart, as did Brian and Billy, and the tripod lifted them up, to set down, it was cool, looking at the first log down, to the slanted top roof, to touch down, about halfway on the west side roof, then another one, Billy was on top, driving in the nails, it was wind swept, all the way across the 80 feet span, all twenty seven of them. Set in place, hammered down, it was done by noon, and Billy stayed up there, to begin the patch of mortar, from the stand point of sheer spectacular, it looked amazing, there was hardly any wind from the west, and for forty feet it was dry. He went quickly, and we went to the other side, and finished putting in the logs, both outside first, then the floor, to the end then the inside logs, it was fast to go, to no wind, the rain even tapered off, I like to dig, and so did Brian, and Billy he like heights, bragging how his will be the coolest fort.

We moved the tripod to the middle for the roof, split logs went on, at a rapid pace, inward, while other were dragged over by the jeep, this hundred feet, was easy in comparison, as the floor settled in as the ground was settling, it was dry, the ends were tricky, as, it was tapered, from the high to the low, in the corners, and a rain barrels caught all the water, as a barrel was on all inside corners, but it was the final application of mortar to the south side, which, next was getting dark. Another meal, of fresh soup, and cornbread.

June 2nd Tuesday, 2004

Day 4 all we have left is the other side of the wall towards the trees, and the other side top roof, also on my limestone travels, I discovered an old growth of cedars, and it was nice, a patch of about ten acres, next to white river, where some were down, I went to work, cutting 18 inch blocks, then loaded them, in the trailer, and took them back, but stopped, and turned around, and went down to the hardware store, and parked, Jake was in the back, for I to say, "Jake a word, please."

"Sure boy, what do you need?"

"How about those windows and screens?"

"Really, have at it, most of the houses have been gutted, so how far are you along,?"

"Oh about halfway." Said I.

"Really, what is this day 4 for you?"

"Yep, as I used my crowbar, and took each window out, to get twelve, and said, "Do you still have that plywood?"

"Yes."

"Load it up." I said.

With that done I was off, and back to home, crossing that bridge was a welcomed sight, that top looked powerful, as I stopped, and turned in, to the log area, Anna was in her fields, seeing her crop was up. On the top roof was Billy still patching, Laurie was making mortar. She appeared to be having fun. Instantly I was offloading and had a window in hand, the first place was the west wall, and the windows, going in forty feet, I used my chain saw, and cut out the opening, next I set the new window in, with mortar, it was a bit loose, but the outside shingles, will firm it up later I thought. Then ten more feet down, another window cut, and in with another window, and mortar, later cedar will go up and around it. Next I moved the logs around to the far east side, as Brian dug the line to the street, I dropped the logs in place one at a time, with Billy's help. To the end, then next was logs, Brian had split apart, with mine and Billy's help, the split logs, were notched and set face up, they were set quickly, and evenly, as the ground was drying out, next was the logs, going in the middle, from south to north, it was fast going as all the logs were there to place. The next thing I did was set in three specialty built racks, and I laid 6-25 footers, on them, to set aside for later to rest and dry out for seasoned firewood. Then it was onto the roof of the outer horseshoe, I cut to fit the south east roof, inward, as it was Brian who set the split logs all the way to the end. Behind me was Anna and Lily mortaring. Then the remaining, were 55 feet long as they were placed up to Billy on the open top roof over the teepee. He, who hammered them in place, all the way down it was Him and I, working to the end. Next was mortar over this side of the top roof. All the while the girls, mortared behind us, as I got down, and Brian and I cut shingles, it was quick, as Billy, took up a bundle, thank God the upper roof wasn't connected, I used the tripod to lift it up, in sections, to put, cedar on the roof to the inside roof. I was going fast, as was Brian, but this would end our day, mistakes learned, and the next job, would be easier. Billy was fun to be around when he wasn't being funny, I can see why Laurie wants out, it may be over before its at our first review. I know I can't talk with her, let alone socialize with her, as I continued to drive harder, with the shingles, the girls switched to helping me out, as the entire west side inverted roof was done. Next the girls, were mortaring the west wall, and around the outside wall. We finally, all ascended on the top roof, it was Lily, Brian, Billy, Me, Anna, and Laurie, going from the bottom of the west side up as the wind was to our backs, at 18 inches a row, spanning the split logs, to the top, it was fast moving, over lapping the other, up to the cap, where we cut to fit the top. And that day was over.

June 3rd, Wednesday, 2004

It was day 5, I want to emphasis, the days are 20 hours long, and this was no routine day, I started out the day, digging the latrine, all ten feet down, then used bricks made by Laurie, Anna and Lily, while Brian went to collecting more limestone, and cedar. Billy was my go between, them, as he would set them down for me, I had a bucket of mortar, which I put on the sides, leaving it open below, I quickly worked the sides, all the way to the top. Using plank boards, I made a 10X10 shack, and a box over it, to set a toilet seat in place. As I framed in the floor around it, with planks, of 3 foot split boards, I used a window, and set that in, for the gaps, it was mortar, then lap cedar, to a the roof, which was, plank 3 foot tree splits, to a mortar job, and topped with shingles, a custom plank door was built, with hinges I brought, finished by noon. Next was the east side top roof, where I used the tripod, to lift up split logs to Billy, who put them on, biggest too little it was calm day. Billy hammered them in, going from the south to the north, over the entire complex, to the front, with all logs used, it was Brian helping out. I went to work on the shower and wash room, in a far southeastern corner, where the rain water collects. I cut planks, of cedar, to form a box, 5X 5 and a bottom, to set aside. Then I started the frame, and used 3 foot poles, as piling to set in the ground to raise it, in a

20X20 in the southeastern corner. Then using plank's 3 foot splits, to lay flat side up, and pined together the floor was laid. Then, to the rear, where a collection box, made of cedar, was set just below the floor, and a spare pipe was added, and a trench dug to the latrine, from the cistern, again another mistake corrected later, to place in a floor, with openings, in a 5X5 area, the upper box in place, above, and a shower head installed, with a stairs going up, to put in hot water, and that's where that box heater fire place comes in, set in the north east corner, a pot, to boil water, is place, a plank split 3 foot bench was built by Brian, it almost seems like they both want this place. Then it was the front and side walls went in using cut ends, of 3 foot logs, cut at 20 feet, to a top of ten feet. I used my saw to measure and cut out a front window, and a door. This roof has a trusses and a gable, as a stack pipe goes out between the roof, and further up to the top roof, yet to be mortared, then planks of logs were set which has two sides, as there was enough room for Anna to mortar that roof, after a long time, shingles were added. Lastly we all went on the east top roof, with shingles, Brian and I cut, and laid out, as we all drove them in with roofing nails all the way to the top, with a little detour, around the stove pipe, I felt how warm it was, to get another idea, as I would use later, all the way to the top, then Brian, handed up a twenty foot, five footer in diameter split, for a top piece, Billy nailed it in after I mortared it in place. As Day 5 comes to a close, with a nice hardy meal, of soup, and some beans, and cornbread. Our place was nearly done, and tomorrow it was off, to the farmers, all of us.

June 4th Thursday, 2004

Day 6th, and for the first time camera's got to catch what is going on, as I was up early, putting in the windows, with stringers, and mortar to fit, while Anna made a marvelous breakfast, fried potatoes, and beef. The caravan went to Billy's and Laurie's, Billy expressed he wanted a fort, with turrets on the ends, to view the river, and a spacious courtyard. I said "First I need to mark the outside wall with 5 footers in diameter, fifteen feet long, some 33 of them, and 3 footers, and this time it was an old growth forest close to the ranchers clear cut property, and I was dropping them like crazy, and finally this is where John pitched in, as well as Kim, both strong. Anna, Lily and Brian went collecting limestone, and gravel from the stream, those ten buckets were returned, as we needed many more than that, I marked the logs, and cut them as I needed. Billy, limbed, John, choke set the trees, and drug them out, as Laurie drew out the floor plan, with sticks, taken about 300 hundred yards from the river, also Billy wanted a roof over the entire fort, with an awning in the back, and one in the front. Out back was were the pens were going. Laurie was really into this whole thing, so much so, she barrowed our clear tarp, and covered her field, it was still windy, so after I spent cutting down some fifty five trees, I took a break, to Laurie, having a BBQ, a charcoal grill, was hot dogs, and hamburgers, it's also her first encounter with vegetarians, as both Brian and Lily passed, as they got in their jeep and left, much to Laurie's disappointment, to hear from Anna, "We'll let them go, you know they are vegetarians?"

"No I didn't, next time I'll have a eggplant burger."

"They're gone now, so have you given any more thought of leaving" asked Anna.

"Well to tell you the truth, I know how it all means for you and Matt, so I will stick it out for the year, then I'm leaving."

"Sorry to hear that, about you wanting to leave."

"Oh, I'll stick it out, besides Matt is here."

"Oh yes about Matt, He is mine," said Anna defiantly.

"I know, don't worry, the thought hadn't cross my mind" said Laurie.

"So when was your last encounter with my man anyway?"

"I think it was just before he went to Sicily, I just couldn't put up with him gone all the time."

"Just makes the heart grow fonder" said Anna mocking her choice.

"It does indeed, but he has you now, and if I know one thing, it's not good to cross a Sicilian woman."

"I'm glad were on the same page" said Anna.

"We are, besides he loves you way more than he ever loved me" said Laurie smiling, as she held her tongue. Outside I was setting up the tripod, as the first wall, was going in along the front east side of the drive, where Laurie's garden now had plastic over it. I went on a digging rampage, and the front left a space, as I dug a twenty foot trench, and one by one fifteen foot, 5 foot diameter logs, went in, five logs later I was done, sealed back up, as Anna and Lily with Laurie's help mortared both sides. I pined them in with nails, up top and down below. On the opposite side of the road, another trench was being dug by Billy, down to twenty five feet, and I positioned the tripod, and set the first one in but Billy came over to wave me off, to say, "Matt, I want it at twenty feet. I looked over at him, and the piling, to winch it back up, and thinking, "Why am I even here, being ordered around like this. But I did see everyone helping thinking twenty feet does he mean a twenty five footer?, as I said, "So how high do you want the roof?"

"Oh twenty feet?"

"Then were gonna need a twenty five footer."

"Ah right yes?"

I went to the yard, and showed John which one to pull over, he did that in regularity as I positioned each one, and one by one they kept coming, all the way to the end, and then at the corner, I wasn't thinking now, as I stopped to see the huge mistake I made. So I stopped, and backed away, to say, "Now what?" to Billy, he also looked up, to say, "That's alright."

"How, where is the snow fall going to go on a flat roof?"

"Oh sorry" said Billy.

"Is it in front or in the back, the angle or slope you want?" I asked.

"I see what you're saying, I guess just like yours."

"So what is this anyway?" I asked.

"A car garage, for the camper" he said.

"At twenty feet high", I exclaimed, when I came up with a brilliant idea, taper it back to 15 feet, that's a five foot drop, so I yanked out the last twenty five footer, and went and told,

John to bring, the five footer diameter, at eighteen feet, he did and I fix the correction. It was 50 square, and ten of those, we were there, at twenty five feet, about 7 in the middle, to support the problem now was matching them up with the sides, "Shit" I said, "Another mistake", I was ready to give up and go home, as I dropped the first one in, and that was it as Billy, didn't dig out anymore, till the outside, and all of those was 25 footers, the same dilemma as the other side. It was ten of them. Now with a top cap in place, split rails could go on. At 55 feet long, from the top, with a five foot overhang. The first two looked alright, we then built scaffolding to fifteen feet, to use a chalk line to cut off the gradual five feet, that was probably the most difficult cut I had ever made, and a lot of no do overs ever again. This sucked in all the wrong ways, but the rest of the roof of 3 footers with 16 up, and the ends to contend with, as I used my big saw, to cut the line, then another took its gap. Then we had to break the scaffolding all apart, and take it over to the other side, to set it up all over again, I went up there as darkness was nearing, to hear, "Vegetable soup and grilled cheese sandwiches, with macaroni and cheese." I cut the line all the way down, then added the last board, it was positioned and nailed down it was strong. I ate with my suppose group, Anna, Lily and Brian, while, Laurie, Billy, Kim and John went first. It was night and we were driving home to call it quits.

June 5th Friday, 2004

It was the morning of day 7, a huge carport was in place, not really visible, I was joking, this thing was an eye sore, totally out of place, but oh well, it housed the truck and camper and today is the castle, but what he wants doesn't fall into what I want, I saw the huge ten foot gap of nothing to suggest, to Billy, "Lets, put up a floor about half way down, for a floor and set your bales of hay in there".

"Good idea go ahead, it's your show any way" said Billy.

I had Brian with me as he dug, the supports, down to five feet, and we set in fifteen footers for support, then using the tripod, set in split 3 foot diameter logs, on a log platform, to make an open floor, all the way down, Brian nailed them into place, they were face up, to make a crude floor, but now the carport had a dual purpose, later I would make a staircase, going up, as it was still early, as Anna and Lily arrived later, with trailer full of limestone. Anna gave me some chipped beef and fried potatoes, it was a phenomenal breakfast. I sat around, for her to say, "Don't you have to go?"

"Go where?" I said being coy.

"You know back to work?"

"Nah, I think I'll pass, I'd much rather look at you."

"You should not, he is counting on you, besides he was nice enough to help us out, and get a roof over our heads, the least you could do is support him on that?"

"Maybe your right."

"I know I'm right, but everything will be fine, just say your sharpening your chains, on me."

So I eventually went back to work. But Anna said something to me about seeing John and Kim in their field, so I hopped in my jeep, and left, to go down the road a ways, to where the ranchers, were in their lot, using sticks or something, so we drove in, and parked, shut it off. We got out to see John and Kim, trying to decide on a nursery off the bedroom, for I to say, "So what are you guys up to?"

"Just trying to figure out our log cabin, any suggestions?"

I looked at it, to say, "So you want a three quarter face, it is possible, but what are you gonna do, in ten foot snow drifts?"

"What do you mean?"

"Well it gets to minus 30 below, and lots of snow blowing, the reason I built a wall around the outside of my place, was to have a place in the dead of winter, to work out, chop wood, and make some furniture."

"Oh I see, then we got this all wrong, can you build us your lodge?"

"Sure", just then Billy shows up, in his truck minus the camper, gets out, to say "First off I want to apologies, for my bossiness, Laurie said, I might of scared you off."

"It was for me, that is why Matt is here" said John honestly.

"So let me say, sorry, and I might of overstepped my boundaries, would you Matt consider, coming back, if anything, to build a compound just like yours?"

"I'd consider it, but first, John you and Kim, begin to dig out a trench, and make it 100 feet long, that still gives you 10,000 square feet of working space, remember it's not about form and fitting, it's all about practicality, and usability."

Anna and I got back in the jeep and backed up, then turned around, and took a left, and down to the carport, as Brian was hard at it, putting in the front wall, of the castle at about fifteen feet high. It was a slow go, till I got there, where Laurie's eyes lit up, as we drove into the huge carport, where the camper sat on supports, Laurie stepped out, to greet us, to say, "Bout time you guys got back here, my husband was about to have a coronary."

"Sorry, I had to give Matt what he has always wanted," said Anna smiling.

I was with gloves, over to the tripod, and Billy was in the trench, I set the next 5 foot diameter log, checked the line, to say, "About a foot off."

Billy threw more under, and again I set it., and then we were off, some 50 feet, or ten logs, to the end for lunch. It was Lily who cooked for all of us, eggplant rolinitini, or stuffed with greens, I ate mine, but the others, like Billy, Laurie and Anna, had trouble, so they ate hot dogs. After lunch, we stayed where we were at, dropping eighteen feet long logs, and five foot wide, quickly filling in the line south, all twenty logs worth. To stop, as Brian and Billy went to splitting 3 foot in diameter in half, could be picked up by two, so they begin to lie, the split face up, only to see the rains let loose, it was a heavy drencher, for me to point out, sections at a time, Billy agreed. so we carried the tripod, back to the front and the inside trench was a creek, it was muddy, as this time it was a thirteen footer, and it was small in comparison, as 20 foot split 3 foot in diameter poles, were having the bark taken off, and wedged in half, by Brian, I was on the scaffolding, next to the wall, where one by one, I nailed them, as I cut the top of the wall, to an angle, all the way I went, as each half log, fit perfect, it was Anna looking cute in her yellow poncho, and gloves working the new mortar, between the first two, while I set three, instantly it was dry as we kept this going, to about 75 feet, we turned the construction to the middle and set in the thirteen foot long five foot in diameter poles, and that was it for the day. All the mortar used up, Anna and I went home.

June 6th Saturday 2004

It was day 8, we got off early, as we thought of the animals, were supposed to pick up, so we went over to Billy's, it was sunny, and John and Kim were there, as the middle was done, as a big opening was left for doors, it was weird, as we set the rest of the thirteen foot long poles in the ground, next was the floor, and the back walls, they were leveled, like the east side, was done, from the split logs, were able to make stringers, it's about a 2X2-3 depending on who splits it, and a wall was constructed, also I had a gift, three windows, which I cut out, the outside wall, and with mortar, set in the first one, about head height, next was about ten feet apart, and then finally, in between both of them on the inside, I cut a window, it went in, it was nice. Then it was back to the outside wall, big logs, twenty five feet long, and five feet wide, they were a bear to handle, all 20 of them, but John was there to muscle them in, and the whole south side, went in, as Lunch was called, some twenty logs, it was pinned in by Brian, while hamburgers and hot dogs was served. I finished fast, and was helping to pin, while Lily and Anna, took ten buckets, to the river for more gravel, sand and small rocks, Laurie helped too. Kim helped carry the buckets to the mortar making place, Billy wanted fireplaces, in this back area, made of rock, and brick, Anna brought her form, and all four girls were putting the mix together, and into the molds, then turned out, and set in the fire pit, to cure and bake. Anna kept up the fire by using wood I chopped from a unusable log, it was too gnarly, the last side or wind side was the west, but it really didn't feel like that at all, as it was pretty calm, in comparison, we had plenty of logs left over, but stormed to the finish, as the floor tied in, and was flat, but a long way to finish, the roof, on the back side was 20 feet to fifteen, and the sides, was fifteen to ten, it still looked hokey, the roof went on fast as we laid the logs, split from north to south, following it around, inward to catch the water, that was the side roof for the top roof, we had twenty footers, going east to west, as split twenty footers, with the inside notched out, laid over the distance, next was the fifty five foot, split 3 footers in diameter, first on the front side, or to the north, using the tripod, we placed from west to east. I was on the outside when, Billy stop me, to say, "I want to build look outs, so 3 footers, split in half, to make up ten feet sat on the wall, then support were nailed in, before even sealing them, to then using the stringers, we all four built walls, with window cut outs, talk about a waste of time, for the rest of the day, while the girls, sealed up the rest of the front top roof. We went home, I was eager to help John.

June 7th Sunday 2004

Day 9 what I thought would have been a great day it was a light rain, Anna and I were in our rain gear, in new clothes as our others were soak, from three days ago, but we got back out there, in addition, I put the canopy back on the jeep, all this rain is tiresome, as at night we park the jeep in the garage. Thinking about that plywood, but set that aside, as we drove up to Billy's two front turrets were being constructed, using stringers, then Brian started on the split 3 footers in diameter, by ten feet long, they were hauled up, by John, and I got up there and affixate them to the side, and using a board for each row, for the roof was a simple strut up and a split for the beam, as I worked my way up about eight feet, you could see John's spread in the distance to finish for lunch, at lunch Billy said, "What day is it?"

I said, "I think it's Sunday?"

"Really, we should celebrate, get dressed up."

"Whoa wait, hold on", and hold on we did, as two trucks pulled up, and it got crazy now, as John Hughes from Whitehorse emerged, to say, "Can I get everyone, over here, as everyone stopped what they were doing. We assembled, to hear, "The idea of the challenge, is you build yourself a cabin, not a castle, it was supposed to be you, battle the elements, not the clan, this challenge was to see you have a struggle, not having Matt, build this for you, you have 358 days left, to impress us, while I'm here, it's advisable, those you hire Billy, you have to pay for their services, and from what we see on our camera's this is another, Matt project, like his homestead, where some helped him at, but not on this scale, so Matt what do you feel it's worth?"

"I don't know?" I said.

"I do, a dollar a square foot," said John.

"So you have a wall, fifty feet, and a carport, fifty by fifty, and a castle 100X 100, that comes to 22, 550. You owe, Matt, and all the other workers, looking at Brian and Lily leaving, in their Jeep grand Cherokee, and then the Locke's, John and Kim, as Miss Grant went into the camper, and talked, while, I hooked up our trailer, and Billy helped me with my tripod, and got in the jeep and left, sometime later, Anna found out, Miss Grant is a psychologist, determined to work on Laurie, to get her to quit. We got back, and in some anger, I went to our suppose homestead, to the north of the road, to our property and began to drop trees, one after another, till I clear cut at least five acres, and the winds were at it again to the west, to the east, also Billy and Laurie had to come up with a way to pay off their debt, by the end of the challenge, and for Billy, was split all the 3 foot in diameter logs, himself, and wait our secret return to finish his roof on the south side, all the rest of the logs would go to us, he would deliver it to us then Jake would be summoned, to evaluate it, to give them credit. For I was sorting logs, by value. In the first area, was the 20 foot wrap around horseshoe, like the south compound, and a floor, while Brian laid low, I was working out to set the logs in the ground, I have to tell you this parcel slopes down in places, from the road, but where I choose, was perfect flat and level ground. My goal was sort out the first 47, making the north compound 140 long by 120 wide. the fifteen feet tall outside wall and ten feet for the inside, giving us some head room, when I was sorting, I still had time to chop wood. The day slowed way down, as Anna was with me all the time, she was collecting rocks, in our ten buckets, and it was back to gathering water in five not so marked up buckets, using a magic marker we put drinking water only, and a number 1-5. To the south of us, Anna was doing her 25 plus chores, like making charcoal, for the teepee, among other things I could not see. I began to dig out the perimeter wall line some 140 feet x 120 using the five feet in diameter logs cut at fifteen feet, to form the outside wall. For the inside it would be ten feet tall. Then in the middle, was twenty foot poles, split, and face up, just like the south compound. I set the first log in to the north side with the tripod, and steadied it with 2x4's, it was a lone log in the ground, at a level fifteen feet high, I stepped back to admire it, and then to visualize a two story middle buildings, on each side to hold the split top roof logs. A barn in the middle was planned. So I was off, one log at a time, a five foot in diameter, cut at twenty feet long, it was drug by the jeep, to the tripod, and hoisted up, and into place, next to the first one, for all of the world to watch, all by myself. Anna was in the distance picking up rocks, bringing them over, to dump by each log in the ground. As for Billy, he was lost in the castle, all visible work stopped, as even at night, new cameras were placed, still no one was around., as for the ranchers, this was another interesting pair, they went back to their original design, for a ¾ face front, using, a 3 foot log, as its guide. For the vegetarian's, sand was being moved from the greenhouse, out, along the creek, but it was a slow go. As for us, I put another log down, cross tied it in, to make three, I didn't know if I wanted to lay the split floor next, and then the inside pole, which was still 5 feet away, as we were fifteen feet in, when the trucks came by to stop, it was John Hughes, and Miss Grant., she took Anna aside, as John said, "What do you plan on building?"

"Oh a larger version, of that place over there" I pointed to our place to the south compound, as John was quiet and went over, to see it was locked up, to shout back, "Can I have a tour?"

"Sure, as I went over, and unlocked the main door, and opened it up, for him to see a thing of beauty, since the last entry I put in windows in the washroom, I set in a wall of three footers, at ten feet high, and cut two doors, well actually three, so I opened it up for him, for him to instantly see the teepee, as he walked over, on top of branches we laid for a soft walk and dry up the dirt, to it, as I opened it up for him, he was marveled, at its simplicity, the lineup of water barrels, "Aw shucks, I forgot to write that down", for the six small water barrels, and the two larger ones, I showed him, our shower, and then where our greenhouse was going, to the latrine, and finally to the rabbit cages for which I caught two, be it two boys, to a door into a rather warm place, where the trailer was, and wood piles, of chopped and stacked wood. To hear, "So you have fire wood for the winter?"

"Yes", only for him to see, the cedar planks, to say, "You have something here, in these planks?"

"Yes, I have about a five to ten acre lot of old growth, I dug up forty trees, and planted them over by the water's edge by the bridge."

"So your now a conservationist?"

"Yeah, you could say, that, it interest me, to rebuild and propagate our own natural resources, by placing those trees there I cut down the potential for flooding."

John shook his head, and went out, as I closed it back up, for John to say, "So why lock it up?"

"The bears around here are something fierce."

"Well you're in luck, on your property you can kill them to defend yourself, and that goes for anything else, but if you happen to come across mink or otter, they are prized, and propagate them, and they are worth 10K each to the state, on a release."

"Really, I will keep that under advisement."

"Oh I know you will, good luck."

They left, as Anna came to me to say, "All Miss Grant was trying to do was get me to quit, I told her to get the F-ing off, I told her I was loyal to you, where you go, I go, regardless of any conditions, so did you want me to mortar, the first four logs?"

"Yes." I said impressed with her.

Dinner was close at hand, as I put the fifth log in place, giving me 25 feet set, as Anna, washed up and went to get two bowls of soup and cornbread, we ate together, right in that field like a picnic, it was nice, afterwards, I went on the attack, moving and bringing more logs over, till I had ten done, that night we crashed into bed.

June 8th Monday 2004

It was day 10, and we were for the first able to lie in bed, I held her, as we cuddled. She then said, "You look tired, care if I give you a massage?"

"No, go ahead."

"Well you have to get undressed?"

"Really where is this coming from?"

"Well I'm practically your wife, am I not?"

"Yes, I guess, you are" said I sleephisly.

"Well then undress", as she pulled off her pajama top, to show her well-tanned body, and her amazing set of breasts, for her to say, "Go ahead and touch them, their yours to play with if you like, I just pulled off my shirt and rolled over and put my head in the pillow, as she got up, and sat down on my back, and scooted down, and began to rub my back with lotion, when all of a sudden, we heard a voice, say, "Oh Anna, it's me Lily, can I come in?"

We both just froze, and then off went Anna, as we heard, "Come get up lazy butts, both Brian and I want to talk with you both?"

Instantly I was up, quickly getting dressed, as was Anna, but I did get a good look at her new bra she put on, to yell, "Hold on, you just woke us up." I said with some authority.

"Alright we will wait," said Lily, in an apologetic manner.

Moments later we opened the teepee flap, as both Lily and Brian came in, as Lily hugged Anna and then I, it was a bit awkward, but I quickly got over that, as, Anna said "What's up?"

"Brian and I want to hire you to put up a wind barrier to the north, then to build a shelter to house our mushrooms."

"Sure, I can get started today?"

"Great, in exchange, you get 50 percent of the business."

"Wait I thought I already had that number?"

"No, it was a quarter, but we have been sending you more than that" said Brian as he hugged me out, for Anna to say, "How do you know each other?"

"Oh when he responded to a cry out for help, when he was dating my sister, Daphne."

"So how is she doing, these days?" asked I.

"Oh you know, married with three kids, in Kansas city, she still talks about how you broke her heart, but since then you pumped in 100K, and instantly in six months Matt recouped that amount and triple that, at a quarter share, and now this, so what do you say?" asked Brian to Me.

"Sure, let's go" I said, as I led Brian out, to say, "And that's why I thought this would be a perfect place to grow mushrooms, seeing I saw a fellow Marine, did that in a bunker I was in, the cool temperatures, make growing mushrooms, suitable, instead of, the hot, humidity laden Missouri."

"Well we will see" said Brian, helping me to load up my trailer to my jeep, and on it as I lowered the ramp, to be straight, we loaded with the tripod from the field, and, 13 foot 3 foot wide poles, ten of them, and I knew I would need another ten later, and the tripod, once loaded, Brian went with me, while he left his jeep. Lily wanted to take a bath, but Anna suggest a hot shower instead, and they went and did that. I drove over to Brian's, and up, around the front of the greenhouse, as the winds blew, I was getting sandblasted, as I pulled in on the bank, it was good dirt to travel in, so much so it was easy to walk on, up above was the hill, the greenhouse was on, as both Brian and I carried the tripod to the top, set it out, and with shovels in hand dug, 3 feet down, in sand, and some dirt. As he continued to dig, the straight trench, I lifted up the first log with the tripod, and set it in the trench, it was straight, as both Brian and I places rocks, around it, enough so, that I got the second log, and set it in, it was wobbly, due to the wind, but on the other side, it was calm, as that was the side I was standing on, as each log came up, one after the other, but something was wrong, the logs were going down further, till I said, "Wait, the sand isn't holding the logs, we need dirt, or rocks as a base."

"Alright what do you suggest we do?" asked Brian.

"Find some clay or dirt we can put in the hole, as I was holding at five, as another mistake was before me, as I yanked out each of the five, and set it aside, then four, and then three, to two, and latched, on the five remaining to get out of the trailer, to free it, as Brian was off, to the ramp up, digging, to say, "I found dirt, with limestone in it, it should do the trick."

I latched down the first log, and jumped down and got into the jeep, fired it up, and drove the thing around, and up, and to where Brian was digging, I stopped the trailer beside him, as he started to throw dirt in, as he dug, I helped with my shovel, we were at it for an hour, till it was part way full, then got in the jeep, and back over to the east side of the greenhouse, I kinda wish it wasn't there, as it blocked where I need to go, so I pulled out my phone, and dialed up Anna, whom was sitting in the teepee, to hear her ring tone, she went through her stuff to find it, to see it was Me, and answered it, to say, "What is it now darling?"

"Can you bring up the ten buckets and yourself, I have but a small problem, and could sure use your help, will you come?"

"Of course darling."

"When will that be?"

"Well we just finished bathing, and all lotioned up, all for you."

"Enough of the games, come up and at least drop off the buckets."

"Yes sir, right away, Bye" she hung up on me, as I put the phone back on the charger in the jeep, to figure out how to move the dirt to the hole, in the meantime, I went down to the stream, to collect stream rocks, and with shovel in hand, unearthing them, one by one, and throwing them on the bank, my work boots were getting soaked, but I just kept on working, by removing the rocks, the water level went down, digging some of the dirt out, showed speckles of gold, thinking it would be nice to walk back what I have, but only in my hip waiters." After about an hour, Anna showed up with the buckets, and seeing me, in my condition, went back, and got me dry socks, and my wet boots. After I changed, it was lunch time, Lily had a hearty root vegetable stew, and fresh baked bread, we all ate on the tailgate of the Cherokee. After that it was full steam ahead, as the bucket brigade was in place, by Lily and Anna, as I held the logs in place, as they put buckets of dirt next to the poles with rocks, till the last log was in place, all ten. To call it a day.

CH 4

A new lodge for Me and Anna

A new day was upon us, it was June 9th 2004, day 11, and in the early morning light, Anna and I was loading the other ten logs, and tripod, to head out, this morning we had a bit of dried beef, and the rest of the fresh bread Lily made. We went to Brian's, and up and around the other side, to stop, both Brian and Lily emerged from inside the greenhouse, I got out, Brian quickly went over and helped us out with the tripod, to hear, "That was the first night, it was calm, your wall really works."

"Wait you slept in the greenhouse? I asked.

"No, under it" said Brian proudly.

"What, how?" I was puzzled.

"I dug it out."

"Show me" said I, as Brian and I set the tripod down, and went to the east door, went in to warmth, and then to a set of stairs down, to see a lower level, for Brian to say, "What do you think?" as I looked around, it looked like a mobile home underground, but with sand walls, it was about fifteen feet down, with about seven feet of head space, my first thought was bring in some split logs, and support the sides, and ceiling, for him to say, "Isn't it cool?"

"Yeah, but your next to a stream?"

"So there isn't anything damp."

"Not yet anyway, I don't like this, all you need is a really good down pour and you're a swamp" looking around, to see him digging a well, to the left, for him to say, "That's going to be our latrine."

"Come again, are you crazy, not where you live, the methane gas, will burn you alive, no you need to move that elsewhere, well let's see the rest, as he showed me a 16 x 40feet long room, and a slab in the back for their bed, a double pillow top, which seemed new, all I can see it massively caving in, to say, "You need some supports down here, immediately, then place plywood on the ceiling, in case of a cave in, no Brian, you outdid yourself this time, it's a mess."

"Well what can you do?"

"Run on out of here, as I made it up to see Anna and Lily going down, as Lily was just as proud of it" I just shook my head, in disbelief. These two were in dissolutional land, as I made my way out. I was now looking at the place they were digging, and thought maybe, "This place might do, for a cabin, across the side with a roof spanning the distance. When Brian came up to me and says, "What you thinking about?"

"Oh nothing, let's get this dirt, so I can be on my way" I said in a statement. The next ten went in easier, and all I could think about was that underground place they live, is all gonna come crashing down, do I help them to support the walls or what, only the answer will show itself later. We aligned the rest of the poles, even, at ten feet high, the great thing about the tripod, is the maneuverability, of the rope and chains, and the weight was distributed by the block and tackle.

With the last log in, Anna and Lily went along, patching the makeshift mortar, into the north side gaps, while I and Brian lifted off the tripod, and moved it south about ten feet from the greenhouse. For me to ask, "So where is your real cabin going?"

"I told you, it's down below."

"Alright, but you're gonna have to get Jake Wilson's approval, as per the rules for this challenge was for you to build, a cabin, not a underground cistern, and expect to live in all that dust, and grime.

For the rest of the day we argued, I took Anna home to the teepee.

June 10ᵗʰ Wednesday 2004

It was day 12, and I was back home, working on our 140 foot outside line, with five in, another 23 or so to go, as I already had all of the outside wall logs ready, and for some reason it was sunny, with little or no wind, but it meant I could go faster, at about halfway at lunch, when guess who comes to visit, Brian and Lily, with a peace offering, of some mushrooms, Anna took them to the teepee, for Brian to say, "When are you going to town?"

"Oh I don't know, when I'm through here."

"How big will this one be?"

"Oh about 120 X 140 I think."

"Then let's get going I want to help you in exchange for some lumber?"

"What do you need?"

"Well I was thinking about what you told me about supporting the walls, so maybe it's a good idea, you know to protect Lily."

"Or make an above cabin, like the rules say."

"Alright what do you suggest?' asked Brian.

"A long cabin, with access to the greenhouse, the other to the mushroom beds."

"If I agree to do this, will you help me out?"

"How much do you have?"

"What mushrooms?"

"No money, to pay us, for the labor, like John Hughes said, "I need to be paid accordingly", laughing was I as we went on to finish, the line, 140 and some odd feet, it was straight, as next was the 120 foot inside, of 24 logs of ten feet high, five foot wide, and five foot in the ground, the trench was being dug by me first, then Brian to level, Anna and Lily had rocks ready, as the jeep, drug them over, by Brian, to where I hooked them up, and drug them to the spot, and lifted them up, these were easy to maneuver, as I said, "Let's try to get this done by dinner, and with that it was a push, and all 24 went in. It was dinner, and it was vegetable soup and dumplings, we stopped and ate, and drank tea. After dinner, we had some light, and on stands I set the 3 foot diameter, by 20 feet logs, at the top was 2 and 7/8 wide and at the base 3, as we split them apart, once we did that, Brian and I installed them, for the floor, leaving twenty feet on either side for the turn starting with the beginning, and with two down, we used the tripod, to put more on the racks, while I and Brian split the logs, and then set them aside, we needed about forty. Which was about 34 split logs. We were done at dark, Brian was ready to go, while Lily wanted to stay, as she convince him to take a shower, so I thought it was time as well, so we went to the shower, and took a five gallon bucket of water, into the pot, as the fire Brian built was working, till it was hot, as I walked it up the stairs, to the top, and poured the hot water, in the cedar box, with some left over water, all in all twenty five gallons, Brian was first, as I said, "Water on and soak, lather up, and rinse, as for your clothes, soak in that other tub, and then wash with soap, and then we will rinse with our remaining water. He did it, then I and then our clothes, as we had water left over.

June 11 Thursday 2004

Day 13, it was another sunny day, which meant bugs alive, I was covered in a long shirt, pants, and boots, a hat, and a bandana. The floor went down rather easy, especially, when I notched the support standing logs, so that the floor would be supported. Next was the roof, for another 34 of twenty two footers, and after lifting all them to the racks, I needed seventeen logs, again it was fast, going, set a wedge in, at the bottom, and one ¾ way, and it just splits, it that easy, as I worked the logs, Brian was on the splitting part, by lunch the roof covered the distance, twenty feet wide, with two feet inside overhang. Then we moved the tripod, and began to set the west wall, of five footers in diameter, and began dropping them to form the outside wall, the split twenty footers, went in the corners, was cut to fit a square, and the most crucial piece was the middle pole, which was five feet in diameter, it took up space, yet the floor was solid, as the trench to the south was dug, by Brian, as I set them in, all the way down. I nailed down the log on the outside wall, while, Brian was on the scaffolding to nail down the inside, it was fast going, while behind us, Lily and Anna mortared the gaps, we went down to the corner, whereas that was tricky, turning the corner, so we stopped, I had some more windows, so at twenty feet in, I used the chainsaw and cut out the frame, then, using a stringer, set the window in place, with mortar. It was nice, to see out, going down thirty feet, for one more window, about chest height, this one was snug as the mortar oozed out, as I cleaned up the excess, and wiped it off, and then it dawned on me, build some look out, as that day was done.

June 12 Friday 2004

It was day 14, and the rains were back, but for us we had the east side done, and although the roof was yet to go on, but that meant speeding up and setting all the logs in place, and in that corner was tricky, in that I used split logs, cut at an angle, from the end, it tapered back to the support log, and mortared, it still had drips, for the most part it was dry and working. So we went to town the four of us, to get more windows, and twenty sheets of plywood, as Jake said, "I still have your animals I want to rid them by tomorrow?"

"Come on, give me at least another week" I said, pleading to him. He agreed, as Brian asked Jake to come take a look at his underground place, to see if it passes, he agreed, as we loaded windows on the trailer with the plywood, as while they talked, I went snooping, to see each house had, a sliding glass door, I came back, to see Jake to say, "How much for the sliding glass doors?"

"Depends on how I can fill that hole, or if one of you would like to come and disassembled the entire house?"

"How much," I asked.

"1000 a house said Jake.

67

"Done", I said it first, while Anna and Lily were loving the convenience store. For Jake to say, "For the 12 remaining houses, you can have anything, you see fit, plus I will give you 1000 a house. Credit of course, and for the 38 remaining, I need taken down as well."

"Alright, but I won't start on it till Monday, or later" I said.

"I'll help too" said Brian.

We all four left, in the jeep, and back to our house, and went back to work, setting in the last of the west side roof, we then mortared the west side roof, then shingled it, from, inside to the top of the line, for an end cap, as we did this over to the north side, all the way down, to the end. The horseshoe on the west side was done, well except the doors. They went home, when Jake arrived, past us and onto their home. Meanwhile, Anna and I finished off the dinner and dumplings, and for a treat, I fired up the generator, and we watched satellite TV.

June 13th Saturday 2004

It was day 15, I was going strong, with these fortified meals Anna was making, even to put some in a thermos, for lunch, I and Anna moved the tripod, to the outside edge, and the trench Brian dug, as I started up the outside line on the east side, working my way up the hill, even it was only about a foot higher, which meant I dug a little deeper, I did it all it was slow, but it was what I loved, one at a time, I just kept counting down, there was a system, each log, I would, notch below, and force in the twenty footer, face up, it was pretty flat, but the sheets of plywood, I laid on the floor of the horseshoe, made the horseshoe easier to walk, as I nailed it down, at least, as it took 13 sheets per quadrant next to each other. And just like clockwork, Brian and Lily arrived, but it was Kim and John instead, as they parked to admire the work, to say, "We will give you three steers, for you to build our log cabin?" asked John.

I said, "Sure" for John to say, "You know Billy and Laurie have running water". That's when it gave me a good idea, to build my own raised water cisterns here for us, and at the log splitting, I used sections, to form a box. using a frame from cutting five foot cut logs, I hoisted them up, and moved over into place, all four of them, then using five foot half logs, fastened them to the wall, then, tied off, another, realizing I can do this any time, I stopped, and went back, dropping more outside logs, to fill the trench, while John and Kim looked on, eventually they left, as the day ended and the entire east wall was set.

June 14th Sunday 2004

It was day 16, and a suppose day of rest, but with it being sunny, I moved the scaffolding, and began to nail the top together, then the bottom of the outside, there was still plenty of logs, and just like to the south, it was back windy, making dropping the logs even harder. I was courageous, in my efforts, and showed why I was a Marine, and I was on the inside, with the last wall to go in, each log went in, the below ground was easy to dig, inside, our compound was over twenty, stumps, that I had on fire, burning with dry wood I had built a fire on each one. The smoke helped kill the bugs. It was a slow go, as this side was a pain, I had my back to the wind, and finished up the line to the end. Meanwhile Anna was making up more mortar, and applying it to the gaps, the wind dried it faster, but with wind, there came the rain, the rain dampened everything. It was lunch and I was happy with the results, we had stew with dumplings again, and some fruit tea.

Brian and Lily came over, to say, "The wind break is nice, it keeps the wind off the greenhouse, and calms everything behind it." We are digging out the earth to get below frost line, and down eight feet. I went to Brian to say, " I would drop a post every 12 feet, to make up a roof, and ten foot outside walls. He suggested make it square, I said, "I'll put a pitch on it, then a thought occurred to me, build trusses. Do the ten foot all the way around, and then truss it, then roof it, brilliant" I thought, as I was now working on the inside of my compound, by dragging all the rest of the split logs, inside especially the 3 foot in diameter split in half, to go on the roof, and the twenty two 3 foot split logs, Brian was a maven, a few minutes more, another two, he put them over, while I used my saw, and notch the log, and slid the corner floor in, it was fast going, as the rains worsen it, this was the worst weather I had ever seen. I couldn't put the roof on fast enough, everything was wet, I was dripping wet. Anna was soaked as well, today ended in a mess, we all went to the shower, and each took our time, helping one and another, but kept to our own privacy. Afterwards we changed into warm clothing. First done was Anna, who went out and started dinner, then it was Lily, who helped her, then Brian, and finally Me, and Brian helped out me. We were done, and hurried over to the teepee, the above roof was nice, it kept the inside dry, but you could still feel the wind. A soup with buttermilk biscuits, earlier, Laurie dropped off, a quart of milk, it was goats. It tasted good, I and Brian ate to our hearts content, then they left and we went to bed.

June 15th Monday 2004

We awoke to day 17 refreshed, warm, and feeling good, it was also sunny, but everything was damp. Today was all about getting the top roof on the northern compound, with the roof on the east side all hammered in, and the outside sides, mortared. Anna was inside the compound, and her whole operation, a pile of limestone, ashes, river bed pebbles, and this fine dirt. From where I was at, her garden was doing great, the corn was up, it led the pack, I used the tripod, to maneuver the split logs into place, the scaffolding was moved around, to assist me. I was on the north wall, next to the water cistern, down to a gate hinge and decided to cut a huge hole for a door, to go outside, it was about 4 X 4 size, the above logs stayed in place, I affixed the hinges, to a split pole made of 3 foot diameter, and it fit snug, I always had my rifle close by, as I opened it up and pushed it open, I saw Anna in the field getting the rest of the buckets it was as if I was in a movie, she was picking up some stones, when all of a sudden, a huge grizzly bear, roared up, and stood, then ran across the field, as Anna was clearly the target, I found my rifle, took it off, safety, set it up, and fired at the head, as it was bounding towards her, my single bullet was to the head. He stumbled then fell dead, as she turned to be mortified, as I was out there, comforting her. The bear fell a hundred yards short of her, I left her to field dress the bear, as I hung it by the tripod, to skin it, and dress the meat out, I knew I needed a smoker, so by using the split poles, I built the smoker next to our teepee in the south compound, and from the rafters I hung the meat. The inners were taken to Anna who took the rest of the day off. I tanned the hide, by pinning it up, and scraped it free of skin. On a split pole frame, in the south compound. It was nice being out of the rain, as it started up again, so I decided to stay close, and chop green wood, I used my med saw, and cut up one of the six resting logs, into 18 inch blocks, then split them. It was nice to know I had a dry place to stack, them, but also knew I needed a wheelbarrow, in the lieu, I used the jeep and the trailer and drove those logs to the inside of the northern compound, it was clever of me to have it 20 feet wide, as it was nice, as I chopped the wood. In the south horseshoe, I had split logs, and an idea came to me, by using a stringer, I could attach, them together, to make a pipe, so I divert to that instead, besides I have all winter to chop wood. Using the twenty foot sections, I made 100 feet of square pipe. It was lunch, as Anna called it, it was fried heart, and fried bread. She told me the rest was in the smoker, which also was keeping the bugs at bay, the whole lure the bats to us wasn't working. That afternoon it rained, curious as to see what Brian was up to, we went over to see them, with plywood, and split logs, jeep and trailer. We got out, to see, some progress on the depth of the lower level, but still aways away. I knocked on the greenhouse, Brian came up, to unlock it, to say, "It's sure cold up here as we are living it up, underground, and Jake said, "It's fine, his only concern was the spring runoffs, but that they are passed, so we should be fine."

"Well I brought logs and plywood for above your ceiling."

"Great, I know it will be a piece of mind for Lily."

I off loaded, then cut the logs to ten feet, and took them down, using the flat side against the wall, it was fast go, and the inside roof, it was plywood. I worked like a banshee, while Lily made up some fresh bread with peanut butter and jelly spread. I stopped to it, in a few bites it was good, then went on working, I framed the bedroom, with a ceiling, an oil lamp illuminated it, it was warm, in the living area, it was drying as the wood stove, heated the room, the smoke stack, went up, through a hole, along, the logs we put in. I had a little left, to make a bench, with a back. So our visit was done, we had dinner, of soup, and fresh bread, and tea, everyone held a plate and sat and ate. I and Anna left and went home and went to sleep.

June 16th Tuesday 2004

It was day 18, and it was warm, sunny, little or no breeze, and it was making mortar time for Me, and Anna was on the roof, patching the cracks, after I had three buckets up, it was time for me to build a log cabin barn, using only 3 foot diameter logs, I set a frame in the center of the horseshoe, the first floor was the feed store room, it had an entrance, to a three room design, right up next to the upright logs, I notched the corners, using the 20 foot method, ten on either side of the great door, it went ten feet high, till lunch, as Anna said, "I have a smoked liver and onions, I want to fry up, I said, "Go ahead it sounds great." I then used the split logs, for a second level floor, but, from the ground floor, in the middle I used a stairs method to the top, and the top was going to be all hay bundles, Jake mentioned, hay was available from his feed store, at 10.00 a bale, I also knew I needed to take apart those houses, for the wood. Anna brought me out a delicious looking plate, of fried liver and onions, and a salad, of baby corn stalks, and kale, which she said, "It grows like a weed here", with an oil and vinegar dressing, I ate it all up, for her to be impressed with the layout of the barn, it was simple yet ruggedly built, I didn't mess around, as I was always moving faster, using the saw, and cutting the logs, I had still about 15 logs left, until another clear cut. Anna went back patching the horseshoe roof, using some water testing if it held or not. And by looking under, to check her cracks. Lunch to dinner was about eight hours, and that was when Brian and Lily showed up, and went right to work, Lily helped Anna, who still had still some of her liver leftover, for her to say "Don't touch that its liver and onions."

She did anyway to feel a surge of energy, to say, "This is really good, Brian you must try this, as the pair of them ate the rest of, her plate, and wanting more, for Anna to say, "Sure, we finish this and I'll cook us some more up, and that was there last days of being a vegetarian. Especially the way Anna cooked, was beyond anything I've ever tasted, it was spectacular. I used the tripod, to maneuver the second floor of the barn on, we used half planks, to assemble the floor, around the two sides, allowing a place to walk up the stairs, as usual I cut a window on both sides, and used a stringer to help support it with mortar. Brian was by my side, and Lily by Anna's, she was like a sister to her. The second level was cut on the ground, and then nailed into place, and set, as the wall went up quickly to ten feet, then I used a twenty foot 3 foot diameter log, that we took an end off, and another edge off, and finally, one more to make it three sides, and span the top, at twenty feet high, then using, half planks, I hammered them, on the top pole downward, on the barn, the front second floor, I used my biggest chain saw, and cut a huge front, opening, and get my last block and tackle I got from Jake, to the outstretched beam. Its ropes were held by Brian. I kicked the logs off, and used a stringer to fortify the door it now had a way to get the hay bales up. It was nearing dinner, and we used, the tripod, as a crane, by setting it on the roof, of the barn, it was at an angle, from a set gable, going east to west, and pulled up the split logs, and I hammered them into position., it was a fast go, the barn was about done, when Anna called dinner, I was determined to finish it, and shingle it tonight, but as Anna told me, she wants to seal up the cracks first, as we took our plates, and went back out, I ate and in-between bites, moved the scaffolding, for the two girls, and we worked into the night. Till even the lamps weren't helping, and we went to bed, Brian and Lily slept over.

June 17th Wednesday 2004

It was another sunny day, and the day was the 19th and the bugs were out in force, we dress to cover our heads, with bandana's, it was back to the roof of the barn, as Anna and Lily, placed a layer of mortar along the cracks, I was on the other side, doing the same, about seven logs, total, and we were done, as handful of cedar planks, came up by rope, I set them along, and began to span the logs, starting from the bottom, and working my way up, overlapping the next line, and all the way up to the top, it left a gap in the middle, perfect I thought, from a larger roof on top, but the span was about fifty feet, so I had a brilliant idea, build 20X20x80 feet houses for the animals, leaving about a 20X20 to the east for a field for them to graze. I also saw that the sloping horseshoe roof had no gutter, to a rain barrel, so that was my next duty, using a sliced off end off a 3 foot in diameter end, to nail up to run as far as possible, then the next one I butt up next to it, all the way down at an angle. Next I got down, and measured off the whole east side, animal houses, then went to the other side, to do the same, and now I had my outline complete, as I set in sticks, where they were going, and its distance, when Brian joined me. Together we had a system, Brian hauled the cut twenty footers, by 3 foot in diameter, over to me, we used a saw guide, and sliced off the ends, we set each log in place, but free standing, on its side, at about, 20 feet from the inside wall, and 20 feet south of the inner northern wall, to make it free standing but lying on its side, it was a box, and each log of four went up three more feet, our goal was 4 to make it 12 feet high. Next was the another one, as I tied it into the first one, we worked fast, to finish four set structures, we had little log about a foot in diameter, and dug a fence line, at the top, to six feet showing and two foot deep, we put rocks, and mortar in the holes to fill, that went fast.

This went fast because we were out of the wind, and it was dry, the last thing we did was set in the front wall, on the south end, to the end of the structures, Brian dug a trench, I moved the tripod, and set in five foot in diameter, ten foot high, all the way next to the structure, which meant ten logs, filled that gap, I was able to finish, by back filling and top nailing it in place. I was on to the structures themselves, each had a front and back door, and a window up front and a window in the back, also a fireplace, built on a free standing set of split logs, to form a cradle. With a solid floor, about two feet wide. Each room had a solid wood split log floor. I put plywood down, for the top flooring. It was solid, as each large room, had something different planned, the top north room, was for the chickens, as I built a nesting box, from siding, as Anna and Lily, set in the bricks, to form up the heat box, and to the planned second floor, which I told her I would incorporate for the guest rooms. Brian was also a good furniture maker, and built the doors, for each structure, both front and back, it was taking form. Lunch was called, it was fried liver and onions, and fried potatoes my favorite, we all ate together, as the next construction was the next level.

Brian and I were laying down, the split log floor, for the second floor, starting at the north, next to the greenhouse, and working our way to the wall of 5 footers., using 3 foot diameter split logs at 30 feet long, to have a five foot walkway on both sides, to set, and with the plywood, I had, I laid it down, to cut holes for the chimneys, from down below. Anna and Lily worked around us, for ease of getting to the second floor, I built a stair system, up facing the north wall, to a pilling support landing, and then up to the second floor, as thinking, "I would have everyone at some point, why not build a lodge to house them?"

The logs, were laid fast, as one by one, the flat side was up, for the stair system, to include a landing, in front of the greenhouse, and Brian was a master, but I was there every step, in using the med sized chain saw, with the guide, it went fast, and we had the most day left, we were fast, and this was fun. It was pretty fast to ten feet high, as we viewed the

3 beams high, to where the roof line would go, and stopped. I realized the next thing I needed to do was set in the middle poles for the top roof.

So next was the roof, below the top roof, I built up the logs higher in the front, and a little lower in the back, at a good angle, then laid thirty footers, split 3 foot in diameter logs, over the frame, as then I used 55 footer, on top of that to the top main roof supports, to see if I had the right angle, and it was true, so Brian hoisted the rest of the thirty footers, as I laid them down. Then using the hoist we continued all the way down, to have all the logs in place, using a sledgehammer I drove them together, then nailed them in, and they were even, all the way down. We used the scaffolding, on the highest setting, to fill the roof with mortar, as it made it easy. It was sturdy, as the girls worked on that my next focus was on the open yard, so both Brian and I dug a channel, from the west side to the watch tower. With five large logs to go, both Brian and I enlarged the trench, my other concern was the front line, and gate systems, to keep out unwanted animals, especially the wolf's, which run in packs, we had a sighting early in the morning it froze us. But they left, and we continued to work, the trench was dug, but which log to use, I like the 3 foot diameter, the best, over the huge 5 foot diameter, which holds better, the weight, that's when it hit me, I'm going to build a watchtower. Basically a stair system to the top, housed in a box, and use that roof to span the rest of the way, to have a top beam. The construction part of this, was fairly easy, build steps, in notched out, planks, it was fast going, but realized I didn't need to enclose it, up to twenty feet. About four sets of stairs, and four platforms. And that was it for the night, as Brian asked, "When are we going to demolish those buildings, as he was looking to the south?"

"In due time, first I need to finish this place" I said.

June 18th Thursday 2004

It was another sunny day, overnight rains, watered the garden at the angle of the opening on day 20, of 365. I finished my climb to the top, now how do I support a beam, no more steps up, and I was still short to the top, the platform was five feet wide by that, and it needed, reinforcement, as I made another mistake, as I was in line with the fence line, so I got down and dug a five foot hole deep, right beside it, and moved the tripod, and then set it up, and hoisted up the twenty five foot long 5 foot in diameter log, it went in straight, a beam was next, to sit on it, it went up there, and we hammered in place, as the end was within reach, as Brian held it, while I was on the scaffolding. It was a slow go, as the next one, at 20 feet was dug by me, that's when Brian said, "Say, if we have other five footers at twenty five feet, why don't we place them at the base, of these stairs, to form up a support structure to the beams."

"Good idea, alright, let me put this one in first." Now I knew I was wrong, and doing this all wrong, but went along with it anyway, and Brian stayed where he was at, to hold what he could, as the winds picked back up, and we were swaying, as I jumped down, and began to dig, a square around him, as on the outside, I measured, and it was a perfect five feet deep, and set in the first twenty five footer, five feet in diameter, it went in, and married up the beam to its top, as Brian, hammered in place, I went and got the next one, then hoisted it, it went in, next to it to make a ten foot support, as Brian hammered it together, and finally, on the other side, another five foot in diameter, to twenty five feet tall, like a telephone pole. Below the women squeezed in rocks, to support the base, now Brian said, "It's sturdy now, looks like one more in the middle."

"Yeah I'm on it", as I dug the last hole, it was easy, yet firm, a few big rocks, but still went on, till the bottom. I spread it out, and checked the measurement, and then drug it in, lifted it up, and straighten it, till it slid in to stand, I got up the scaffolding, and centered it, then hammered it to the beam. It was lunch, and I knew what and by smelling it, I knew what it was, and went to the outside table, to see fried liver and onions, again, this time everyone ate it. After lunch it was the front wall, and especially, on the west side first. About four logs, at thirteen feet long, by 5 feet in diameter, it was fast going, for forty feet, when I stopped to go to 3 footers in diameter, for five feet, for one door, and around to the other side, five feet, wide, and ten foot tall, to do another forty feet, I then cut my two doors, out, as they lay off, as next was the animal housing complex roof. Anna told me she wants two bedrooms, a huge kitchen, and a dining room, into her TV room, then a living room. So I went to my logs, and took in the twenty foot 3 foot diameters, and began to lay out a frame, notching them, the semi blue green wood was nice. I left enough room for a snowmobile, as the first logs set the foundation, next was the split logs, that Brian was working on. In the kitchen, was where she wanted the root cellar, so that's when I went digging, along the frame, directly under the kitchen, I dug, and so did Brian, as I knew our next purchase was canning jars, her five, or say twenty five tomatoes plants, have buds on them, it is her baby. They are at the top of the bucket. Meanwhile, we just dug, till it was about half way, and it was time to quit. Brian and Lily went home after the last of the liver we went to bed as it began to rain.

June 19th Friday, 2004

It was day 21 and it was raining again, I mean a gully washer, everything was wet, up north, on the south, we still get a few drips, but the amount of water over flooding the drinking water is incredible, we put on ponchos, and both of us went back to the house assembly, as I set a huge tarp over us and used the tripod to put the logs in place, I used the chainsaw, to cut, and notch, the walls went up, slowly, as I was the one working on them, as I took the split 3 foot logs, and set them in, facing up, as my supply was running thin. So that was what I did, and it was a slow go in the rain. Brian and Lily did show up, and helped a bit. But I knew what I need to do now, it was time to clear-cut again, I had about four real places to do that, over by her garden, south of the south lodge, and north of the north lodge, or, a ways down, near the valley, of the river split, but it was rocky, at places. So with tape in hand, I cut down 3 foot diameters, in the rocky valley. Some fifty trees later, and called it a day.

June 20th Saturday 2004

It was a new day for day 22, it was still raining, but today, I was using my winch, and pulled out trees, some, twenty feet long, cut to make walls, the clear cut opened my inside valley to the north, and that of Billy's property, in the distance, as I strung line to them, my winch pulled them in. and on my trailer, which I took home, my tripod, pulled them off, and hoisted them up to the racks, where, I was ready to cut off two sides, to fit, to make a wall, the first was the outside walls, for a long retanguaral box. Up ten feet. And that was my day. Just a note, some things I do may take several days to do, and I just put down what I seem to do every day.

June 21st Sunday 2004

It was still raining on day 23, but it was a light one, I did find out that the barn was dry, which was a good thing, and with the entire outside walls up, I began to work on the west side of the complex, one door at a time. The place closest to the walk up tower was the carport, then the kitchen, a dining room, and then a living, I still had some 40 feet to go, but left it open, I was thinking of a fire pit, on the end, like a blacksmith's place, but also a bathroom. With three doors in front, and one on the side, I knew I needed hardware, as it was Sunday, I could get the rest of the guys, to help out next week, it was on to windows, each room would have at least two windows, front side or back. For the bedroom, on the end, I cut a south window, looking out into the carport, set it in with a stringer and mortar, then to the west, and in the middle of fifteen feet, it went in nicely, as I knew a wall was going up to form a 15X15 room, with a walkway, next room over was in the middle of 15X15, it would be our room, close to the kitchen, one in the back, would wait, as I did two on both sides of the door, same for the dining, and living or TV room. In the back of both of those rooms. I was wondering what happen to Brian and Lily. So we cut out for the day, and took another load of planks to him, Anna went with me, as we drove over there, and in the valley was Brian, with something in his hand, as we drove up, to see Lily was cheering him on, as he had a wild boar, on the run, he had a bow and some arrows, his aim was way off, it was somewhat comical, he trying to kill a boar, although at a closer glance, it wasn't a boar, but a wolverine, or badger, it was something, I felt for my 45 Cal pistol, on my side arm, but it was a good laugh, as he was scrambling, he fell several times, and then in the stream, and for the first time I got a view, of the canyon, to the south, as the river, roared down it, and towards them, it was nice. The wolverine was getting away, as I pulled out my pistol and fired a shot, it dropped just like that, for Brian to get up to say, "Thanks", for I to say, "So what have you guys been up to?"

"Were you worried, we didn't visit?" asked Brian.

"No, just missing, not seeing you're there to help out" said I.

"Hear that Lily, they miss us?", he turns to see Lily is gone with Anna, for him to say, "Alright, it's just the two of us."

I was already, down in his shelter, constructing the next wall, and floor. I was pulling in custom 16 foot planks, an setting them down, to raise the floor, and tie in the wall, in and around the wood stove. And then in was Brian as we made fast work of the project.

I said, "I think I'm ready to tear and salvage some houses. I was thinking of asking the others."

"Let's go" said Brian.

Brian and I went together in his jeep, and down the road, turned left and up the road, where the valley, allowed us to see the various streams, to the ranchers property, and low and behold, John had a shack, he built. Out in the middle and was working on a barn. Kim was right there every step of the way. For I to say, "Yo John, can you help out in town with the demolition of fifty houses, and all that we can salvage?"

Kim agreed as she led us in and showed us, the littlest cabin, a bunk, a fireplace and a bench, that was it. It had two doors, and it was damp inside as the roof leaked. As it started to rain now, and we stood on the inside as the rain came in, it was getting everything all wet it was a shame, their bunk, their possessions, it was truly something awful. I felt bad for Kim who was in despair, as she looked at me, to say, "I don't think how much longer he can take this."

"How are you holding up?" I asked.

"Oh just as strong as ever, you know me I'll be there to the end, so have you though up an end game, yet?"

"Nope, Brian and I are having too much fun, and after next week, I'll come and build you a very nice place for you to live."

"You mean it, as she came at me and gave me a hug and a kiss, just as John stepped in to say, "What is going on here, with my woman?"

She turned to say, "What did I say about personal boundaries, I'll hug and kiss who I want, and you or any other man will say anything different."

"Yes, sorry" said John a whipped man, for I to say, "I was just telling Kim how I would come a week after next and knock out a place that will withstand the snow and the weather. All in the hopes that you come and help me out on a demolition job, as it is more a salvage than that, so what do you say?"

"Alright I guess, I could use some help around here, sure you can count me in, when and where?"

"We will all leave my place tomorrow morning, and work till sundown, for as long as it takes, there are fifty houses that need gutted, wood salvaged, and windows, set aside, especially glass doors, which they are mine, but there are some windows, so during the day, you collect and take with you, I'd bring a trailer if I were you."

"I will, what of Kim?"

"Bring her along too, Anna and Lily will be there."

"Alright, we will see you tomorrow."

I went around and got into Brian's jeep, as he got in backed up and headed left towards Billy's place, it had been 12 or 13 days since I last saw them, and it was nice driving in, to see the castle, and the lone look out, as we parked in the massive carport, got out to see Laurie first as she was delighted by what I built for them even though it was incomplete. She led us in to a total remodel, from leftover 3 foot logs cut in half, to makeshift walls, and in the middle using a bucksaw, was Billy, who seemed upset at me, for not completing the work, and he said "No", as he was running hot, the roof was yet to be done, for me to say, "I'll tell you what you help me out and I will come back and finish my job here."

"Oh alright, I couldn't stay mad at you very long, Laurie has said a lot of nice things about you."

"She did, did she, well I hope all true, so tomorrow at around 0830, come to my place and then we are going to salvage some houses, under my direction, the big glass windows are mine, and some of the windows, but the floor, carpeting, and roofing is all available, just bring your truck and trailer."

"Will do, sorry."

"No problem, he stopped as we went back out, I commentated, "You know we should really finish what we started."

"We will next week" said Brian.

"Indeed we will" said I.

We got back, to Brian's, and it was I who skinned out the wolverine, taking out the inners, which was a gamey meat. As I dressed out the pelt, it was coarse to touch, as Lily made a root stew, and fresh bread, we ate in the underground house, after wards Anna and I went home.

CH 5

A discovery and riches beyond belief

I t was early the next morning June 22nd Monday, day 24, as the vehicles with trailers, all left our house, and drove, out, over the bridge, and then due south, to the makeshift town, of beaver creek, and over the road, and down a street to the fifty or so odd remaining houses that stood, I gave each of them a section of houses as from the furest to the closest. Billy and John were the furest away, then Brian and then I. As they understood what to do, all by the watchful eye of Jake Wilson. I went in and saw carpet, overhead lights, sheet rock, and then thought, "Whoa, let's take the siding first. So I went outside, and began to rip the siding, off. Down to a set of houses each of them took a different approach, Brian was taking out the windows, as they were the most fragile, a huge dumpster was provided for the excess, both Billy and John were tearing off the roof, together, till the rains came, and were forced, inside. Brian had all of his windows in his jeep, his sliding glass door, was taken and all four of us lifted it off, and over to my trailer. Brian was eager, to lift out the rest, so one by one, we went to every house and took our time and extracted each one and then onto my trailer with two- 2x4 dividing each one. Lunch was served by the girls, at the convenience store. I ate with Anna, and Lily with Brian. It was a hearty beef stew chili or so what Rita called it, plus a loaf of homemade wheat bread, Lily made, she is a superb baker. We broke this up to go back to work. The rain quit for a brief moment. I went back to what I was doing, ripping up the carpet gently trying to salvage as much as I can. In walked Jake to say, "Boy you sure have a jump on the others I think you're gonna win?"

"What did you say?" I asked.

"I said, I think you're gonna win?"

"Win what?"

"This, the prize?"

"The prize, non-sense I don't even know what you're talking about?"

"Really, I think all a long you knew you could do this but now you had to find the right people to do it, take John for example, you have him wrapped up, he will do anything you say to him, and his girl is quite a looker as well what is your connection to her" said Jake smiling, only to hear from Rita, "Jake leave that boy alone, he has work to do."

"I'm keeping my eye on you" said Jake smiling using his fingers to point at his eyes back at me.

I looked up and he was gone, I was using tools I found in the garage part to peel up the carpet, as I thought, just then my phone rang, outside in the jeep, I went to it to see it was my friend Vic, from the Marine Corps, I answered it, to say, "What's up buddy?"

"Oh, I was thinking of taking some leave and come visit you up in the Yukon, what's it like up there anyway?"

"Well right now, its pristine, beautiful mountain, and lots of water" I said.

"Good, good, I talked with Paul Nelson and he wants to hunt bear, when is that season open?"

"September 1st, to November 1st."

"Fine fine, how are you holding up?"

"Good, I have Anna with me."

"Really that hottie from Sicily you met?"

"Yep and she is gonna be my wife."

"Does she have a sister?"

"Yes four of them."

"Wow, cool, is there any chance that they could be up there in September?"

"I don't know, I'll ask Anna, so when do you want to come?"

"Why do I have to make an appointment?"

"No, but by the rules, I must put down times and dates and purpose" said I.

"Alright then it will be the first week of September, and it will be Me, Paul Nelson, and Russ Hamilton. And our purpose, is were hiring you to lead us for an expedition, and guide to getting some bears."

"Your limit is three each, as for me its unlimited, as their already on my land."

"Cool, cool, see ya, I'll call you a week prior out."

I knew tracking bear isn't too hard, and I had the weapon to do it. I continued on, as I had the rest of the rooms, carpet up, I liked the subfloor, next I went onto the roof, to tear up and off, tar shingles, it was a mess, but I used a tool, and scraped them up, and off down below Anna picked them up with Lily. I worked fast, and by the end of day I had one done, completely disassembled. We all left around seven, stopped at my place, and offloaded, the six sliding glass doors, and four rolls of carpet. Each of us had something, but mine was the heaviest, Anna and I went in to take a shower, and set our clothes in a wash vat, full of soap to soak, but I'm a fraid we will need turpentine to get this tar off. After the shower, we went in for some dried beef, and corn biscuits, and tea. Then to bed.

June 23rd Tuesday 2004

It was before the sun came up, I was in fairly new clothes, Anna was up, making potatoes, dried beef, (Bear), and it was good, and from our chickens four eggs, yes you got it and a pair of roosters, we took the animals last night and put in their pens, which could be dinner tonight, well actually, one of them if they don't shut up. It was day 25, and we all hooked up with each other and drove into town, and onto each of our houses, but it was I who said to those waiting to go, "Make sure you pull out your windows, the stress of the building going down, will pop them out, in addition make sure that all the carpet is pulled."

"What carpet" said John.

"Never mind carry-on" said I.

The morning was all about window removal, and to the other house I went, while Anna, opened up the area around the windows, as this next one had no carpet either, just fake hardwood floors. I went to the other house it too had the same, thinking I lucked out with the carpeting. So I went back and Anna and I removed all the windows, as we saw Billy and John working together, and just like that Brian was helping me, and it went faster, way faster, till lunch, when we ate that phenomenal chili, and for the first time we saw a little VW bug vehicle, pull in, a guy get out, he eyed us all, to get gas, as we all ate, he paid cash, to say he was going to Anchorage, I told him, "It's about two hundred miles away. He paid and took off after a great lunch, John said, "Why don't we all work on one house at a time, after we fill each trailer up, we take off and off load it, we were all in agreement, it was fast, as first it was Billy's place, he took off the roof, and the sub-floor plywood, and on the ground was Brian and Lily, taking off nails, and saving them. It was I, John and Billy, pulling off plywood, there was lots of it for subflooring, on top of the split boards, next was the trusses, as we all had sledgehammers, it was easy work, as next was the ceiling, and supports, as we all got off, and took a wall at a time, the siding came off and was stacked, as crowbars were used, to tear it apart up a ways, then ladders were used courtesy of Jake Wilson. As the siding went away, it was just a shell, of framing, we three went to the top, and took out stabilizers, and got off it, and on each corner, hit the brace, it was by all three of us, it buckled, and sag down, to where it was open season, as Laurie, Kim and Anna carried them to a pile, while Brian and Lily removed the nails. It took us a mere two hours to get that 40X40 house down, these small 800 sq. foot houses, were easy, as we went to the next one, as we were a machine, off with the top, and then the siding, and then, the supports, the most important things like toilets, and plumbing was below, yet to get, but kitchen cabinets, and sinks, were pulled first with the windows, but there was no other appliances. With Billy's house clear, it was sub floor, that Brian, Lily and the three girls helped with, once a corner was up, the rest was easy, stand on dirt, it went fast. Till the whole structure and concrete block gone in a pile. What Brian and girls did was amazing, but we almost had John's houses down, as another pile was growing on the opposite side, where empty houses used to be. As that house was down, we three went at it quickly, hauling 2x4's for Brian and Lily to take out the nails, as we went onto Brian's houses, as the rain came, but it sped up our progress, as we had the roof off, as it was near dark. We drove home, and went to sleep.

June 24th Wednesday 2004

It was day 26, and we went back into town, and we had a system that worked, as John's places was next to be cleared, it was Brian's lead, on how we did the salvage, and began to put it on Billy's side, everything was out of it, as the siding was next, then, the stabilizers, as we dropped it, then all eight of them, next was Brian's, he was fast, and we all worked together, till lunch, when the last was my 12, the bigger of the rest, as the roof's came off, then it was the siding, and then back up for the sub roof, plywood. It was as if we were wrecking machines, we generally don't like to skip lunch, but when it comes to destruction, and sorting it was our game, this was a day to remember, as we had all the houses down, plywood sorted, as night was upon us, so we left, loaded, and now agreed to come as needed.

June 25th Thursday 2004

Day 27 Anna and I got up, and off loaded the trailer in the south compound home, it was sheets of plywood, all 200 of them, I took to the south side, I was constantly thinking, "Do I have enough seasoned firewood?", I looked around the corner to see the five remaining logs left I placed before sealing it up, and was satisfied. Also on that side was four garage doors. I went back to my trailer, to see Anna stacking

2X4's, against the wall, I collected her up and we went back to the town, we were the only ones, as we loaded another forty sheets of plywood, as Jake appeared to say, "So that was fast all fifty houses down, and now you carting off the remains, do you know you saved the Territory over 25,000 dollars, with this removal, and another ten if you take the concrete remains?"

"I don't know, but ask Anna, as she appeared from the jeep, for Jake to go talk with her, she agreed, and he left and came back with a hammer drill, for which he said, "This will cut through that slab, there are 12 of the fifty left. Then I could use the road, for deliveries", she later told me, that concrete will be nice, to add to her current mix, so I agreed, but I wanted to get all the piles home, as we made five trips by lunch. We had lunch with the Wilson's. Anna cleaned up the dishes, as Rita said, "Boy you got yourself a strong hard worker, you need to marry her, you know to make her feel very secure."

"I already have, and told her I was committed to her, as she is for me, but I wanted her to think this through first, before committing to me long term."

"That's just it boy, she has, any women in this state of mind, is crazy enough to get here, and we haven't had the worst of it yet?"

"No we haven't but there progressing further than we had seen anyone" said Jake.

I just went back over to the jeep, and began putting 2x4's on the trailer, there was a lot of them, enough to fill it full, then used a strap to tie them down, we both got in backed up and drove to home, when I noticed something was weird, it was a bridge, we were on, as I drove up the highway a mile, got out, to see a towering waterfall, just before, and then I ran to the other side, and then saw a ravine, but also trees that blocked my view, as I went back to the jeep, got in to hear, "So, did you find what you were looking for?" asked Anna.

"Sure, you" I said as she shut up, as I drove home. We off loaded in the garage as I backed it in, and took everything off, it began to rain, we drove out of there, up onto the road, and past out the bridge, and down the road to town. We loaded plywood next, as the rain soaked everything, including us. Another forty sheets, and 2x4's and we were set, we did this for the rest of the day, till we were done, as all the houses were gone. The rest took their time. On that last one we just backed it in, off the road, and parked. She went in to start dinner, while I looked over my next job. We ate and went to bed.

June 26ᵗʰ Friday 2004

It was day 28 and were at home, in the south compound, she wanted a greenhouse, and I wanted to make her happy, and with a chainsaw, and 2x4's and nails, it was first a frame, about 3 feet high off the ground, I tapered two by fours upward to about eight feet to form sides, with two doors, on each end. I worked fast as I can, as I had a 4x8 sheet of hard plastic, and set in for the slant walls, along the 2x4 frame, using a drill, I pre-drilled the holes, then used a screw gun, I had in my auxiliary box, and a set of inch and 5/8 screws. It was two sheets long, about 15 feet x 8, and did the other side, then it came to a top beam. Then on both sides to form 4 feet wide, I measured the plastic sheet and used a diamond blade glass cutter, and cut it in half long ways, this was tricky, as I had to crawl, up and hung over as I drilled and screwed in the top, then going backwards, and then the other side, till I was done, it was working it was warm inside, as the plastic kept it warm, and no drafts, there was enough light coming in, but I built two lamp holders. Next was the working benches, out of 2x4's, about waist high, when Anna walked in to say, "Say, this looks really nice, only put them half way, the other space will be on the ground, I guess if you want, say, build it up about two feet and then back fill it with that dirt, out there, but I want to mix it with moss, I'm going to collect later, care to accompany to the valley?"

"Sure, I could be your defender" said I.

"You could be, but I need a collector too?"

"You know I'll do anything you want" said I respectfully.

She left, as I did what she told me, and quickly, I knew I needed a wheelbarrow and the feed store had several, but went on working, when Brian stuck his head in to say, "Hey what are you up to?"

"Just putting the final touches on Anna's greenhouse."

"Well from here, you did a nice job, but what about the air flow?"

"She'll just have to open the door."

"No, I mean constantly," said Brian.

"I don't know, I'll build her a fan."

"A fan can you do that?"

"I don't know, till I try, what say on the roof as wind comes in it will be diverted down, oh but the only problem with that is I have none, except if I put it on the roof, but then it will compromise that," said I.

"Hey I have an extra fan on my west side I'm not using, I'll give it to you" said Brian.

"Alright, are you going now?"

"I could, anything else?"

"Well actually, could you go to town and get a 12 pack of beer, and over to the feed store, and he has two wheelbarrows."

"Sure, but I have one, you can borrow, but if you like I will do that for you" said Brian looking at me.

"Great, and don't forget the beers, I want to party tonight, its Friday night and it's party time."

Brian shook his head, and left, as I finished up the greenhouse, and now it was the dirt, as I came out to see the over excited Lily, who hugged me, to say, "I just found out."

"Found out what?" I asked.

"Were having a party?"

"Yep, it's about time huh" I said proud, as Anna even hugged me, as she said, "How much more do you have?"

"Not much, maybe some grow frames, you know like the brick mold."

"Yes, that would be nice, good thinking, for that I may reward you later, if you know what I mean?"

"Do I, right on."

"Actually if I knew you would be this crazy, ask me anytime, I'm all yours" she smiled as the two walked back to the teepee, she was talking like she was putting on a show for Lily, but why? I went over to the door to the wood shed on the east side, it was warm, and over to one bucket left alone, with a lid on it, I picked it up, and took it back to the greenhouse, to open it, to see any and every seed imaginable. But left it at that, as I made another huge mistake, where do I put the fireplace?", I was beside myself, for this oversight, as I saw the wall, only five feet away, at the back door. Not having a fire place was an oversight, but then a thought occurred to me, make it two feet up on the east end. So I went out and found Anna, with Lily, to say, "Hey, honey can you make some bricks?"

"Yes of course, how many do you need?"

"Well enough for the greenhouse, right now I'm building you a frame, so that you can line it with bricks for your fireplace."

"Alright, then are we going moss digging?"

"Yes, just as soon as Brian gets back from town."

I went back inside the warm room, and thought of the tin pipe I collected earlier at the hardware store, using my ladder, which was free standing, I went up to the roof, used my drill, electric, and with drill bit, drilled through the wood, outside I went with my small chainsaw, and up a ladder I had left on the east side, I got up on the roof, then over, to the big roof, it was solid, and the cedar was nice, to where my, drill hole was, using my chainsaw, I went down center, then X it, then begin to cut out chunks, as I was able to get it before it fell, as I pitched it, it was cool up there, as the wind, was definitely up, but also for day 28, Anna's garden has tripled in size, that minerally enriched soil was sure working." I thought, as I finished the hole, but made a mess of the cedar, but it was an easy fix. Besides a little water coming in is better than no heat at all. I went down, and got the pipe, to see Anna, to say, "I'm just about done, do you have any mortar I can patch with?"

"Yep, in a bucket across the way".

"I'll go get it" volunteered Lily, as Anna sent her. I went back up and sent the pipe back down it was snug, I waited, then heard Lily, I went back to the ladder, as she handed it to me, as I said, "Thanks."

"No Problem," said Lily as her man drove up and parked on the street, she went and helped him offload two wheelbarrows, and a case of brews. I quickly patched the pipe, then used cedars, in and around, and then another layer, about a foot, to cover. I went off, with everything, and then, around and in the courtyard, to actually feel no wind, it was nice, so I went back to the long pipe, as it came down six feet, and two feet at the top, I was still short, but the box, I built was on a platform, that I knew to extend up to support the bricks, as Anna first stack of 12, was set for me, I lined the bottom, and the sides, I build up the sides, but realized I needed mortar, so I took them out, and smeared some mortar on the bottom, laid the bricks in, to form a bottom, it was nice, then the sides, I stacked them on their sides, on mortar, down six, and I was done. I put the lid on, and set aside, to go out and see the gang, for Anna to say, "Let's eat first."

We all sat down to a vegetable soup, and a fresh greens salad, not my favorite, but the vinegar and oil dressing was nice, with crack black pepper and sea salt. I ate two bowls as did everyone else to finish it off, each of us had a beer. Anna cleaned up the dishes, as Brian volunteered his Jeep, so in went the wheelbarrows, and five empty buckets and shovels, as Anna held a sickle and she handed me a carpet knife, with a curved blade. We drove on the road, as to where the trees were gone, to an open valley, earlier I had clear cut the valley we were going to, we had on mud boots, as it was marshy, which meant mossy. I was first out to the south, with bucket in hand, as Brian was tasked with the wheelbarrows, Lily was always with Anna, she was like an older sister to her. She deeply loved her. Anna was a very strong woman, and I knew it, and marriage was on the horizon, but I was waiting the right moment to ask, as I felt my pocket for the ring, I purchased, on base, before I left." I was easy at this, pick up a piece of moss, and pull it up, and cut off the base, and put it in the bucket, I looked down and saw something shiny in the creek, I picked it up, and put it in my pocket, I was in the stream, pulling and digging more, and the same thing, a piece of gold, it was all over this stream, but as I looked up I saw a moose, big antlers, grazing down aways, I kept to myself, as it did it the same, and on this day, it lived another, then something did occur to me we were on a flood plain, it took about three hours for me to fill my buckets, as for the others one bucket each, and back to the jeep, my pocket filled with gold. But how much?"

Brian took us home, we got out with our wheelbarrows, and wheeled them in as they went home. We locked everything up, for her to say, "I have twelve more bricks done and baked."

We both went to her fire pit in the center, it heated about a 20x20 area, it was nice, as she used tongs to extract the bricks, we got from the hardware store. Next we set them in the wheelbarrow, I wheeled them over, and, un-did the mortar bucket, and stirred it up, and put on a slab on front, and along the sides, I set up each one, but as soon as I got a whiff of those bear ribs, it was sweet, I grouted the bricks, and cleaned them up, my half bucket was complete, as my work netted me a curve top, I was mortaring bricks together, at an angle, to close in the top, to form a box. Then with three bricks, I was done. I went in to the teepee and smelled the ribs, to say, "That sure does smell good, I hope we don't get attacked, wild animals are all over this place."

"Don't worry, I'm sure you will protected me."

"I will indeed", as I went to the wash room and cleaned up, and set in a fire, in the stove, another pipe I need to vent up.

I went back in, to the teepee, it was warm due to the fire, of charcoal, which burns clean and minimizes on the sparks, yet the upper flap was open, she had the meal about done, looked like beef ribs, and salad again, with fresh homemade noodles. I put my hand in my pocket, to grab all the gold pieces, and set them on the make shift table, of double footlockers, as I sat on my bucket, for Anna, to reach over and snatch the ring, before I could reach it, for her to say, "Yes I will marry you."

I was at a loss for words, wrong place, wrong time, as she got up and gave me a hug, to say, "This is what I've been waiting for all my life, yes, I will marry you, as she was overly excited, as I held her, she calmed, for her to say, "What's wrong?"

"Oh nothing."

"Then why didn't you give me this earlier?"

"Because I was waiting".... As she cut me off, to say, "I knew the moment you took my hand and we went swimming in the ocean at Taormina beach, for you to come along and swept me away."

"But it was different for me, I was a loner, and you and your sister, well were topless."

"In Sicily, were all topless, or simply nude, we respect our bodies, so now you get to have me."

"Well about that."

"What's wrong now?"

"Well about that, I find not much interest down there if you know what I mean, well what I mean to say, lets finish this, and we will see how the rest goes."

"No, from now on we do this here and the right now, I've waited four years for you and now I want it and I want ten babies myself." We counted out the gold nuggets to be twenty five pieces. As I ate those scrupulous ribs they were fabulous. I was full on greens, kale and spinach. As she threaten the greenhouse would give us greens year around. We went to bed, as I cuddled with her and went fast to sleep.

June 27th Saturday 2004

It was day 29, and brick production is at an all-time high, she wore the ring, around her neck, tied by cordage we had, until we were finished with what we were currently doing. We were on the other side of the greenhouse, completing the remains of the fireplace. I agreed with her I would take her to a romantic place, where I could get on one knee, and propose respectfully, or so she said, "But from now on, this body is for you to touch as you freely want and so desired, but respectfully. We were done, for lunch we had ribs leftover, and the smoker was about cleaned out, except for the carcass, which was brittle, I used a miter saw, to cut into smaller pieces, as Anna extracted the bone marrow, and saved it for a soup thickener. I built a sledgehammer box, which allows me to crush the bones, then with mortar and pestle, Anna is able to grind them into very small pieces. I needed another animal in the smoke house. Before we left to be on this great adventure, we were all given a unlimited license to kill anything on our property, within reason, and record, as such, so that we can keep track of them, and in their respectful hunting times, as deer was year-round, for us but high during now, so I went back to building the fireplace, in the greenhouse and it was brick upon brick, in a one foot box, up six feet, to finish, I grouted it professionally, and then started a fire, to set back in the cradle, it instantly heated up the place well, as it dried out the mortar, it was done. I had other things to check on, like the rabbits, we had a litter, it was ten, and mother had a fine diet of bagged food, combined with bear meat, and bone meal, the blood was dried, and stirred till it was dry. She added both the blood and bone meal to the dried moss, and rich dirt, to form a mix, for each frame I made, on a foot by foot plywood, frame, actually I could make pots, with one foot 2x4's on a one foot plywood square. I still had to attend to the pigs and ducks and geese now living in the north compound, we were on something with the feed we made up, as we used every part of the animal, Anna was the butcher, and that is what her family did for generations, I liked to tan the hide, we used the brains, to tan the hide, its composition, gave use the right enzymes to make it work, to dry soft, as I had a tanning knife, it was a bowed half round, and made sure the skin was off of it. So I finally grabbed my Enfield, and went east, to the woods, where I don't know probably, 200 deer were feeding, and shot a 12 point buck, I went over as the herd, went away, and kneeled down and grabbed its legs, and slung it up and around my head, and got up and carried him back to the compound, went to the smokers, and hung him up, Anna was there to assist me, as I had snares for its legs, she went to work, by opening it up, and allowing the blood to flow into the blood box, as she cut it away, to harvest the internal organs, the heart, the lungs, liver, kidneys, their intestines were short, lots of venison on the deer, as she cut out the steaks, in inch by 4 strips, and as I started the fire, from outside, using hickory wood, it was an excellent smoke wood, especially, when I would throw some water on it, as I got a lot of smoke. After an hour Anna left the front to say, "It's all set, the hide is all yours", she smiled, as I undid it, to see the array of meats, all hanging, some had a rub or seasoning on them, as I opened the flap all the way, and hurried out of there, and took the hide to the shed. We generally like to do things right away, like I, tanning the deer, with its brains, as its mush, but leaves the inside remarkably soft as it dries, I use a stretcher, to pull it as far as apart as I can, till tension, then twist the rope even tighter, using my small utility knife, and twisting till where I want it in the frame, once done I set it aside. Little jobs is what I do every day. And this day was the wheel barrowing of dirt to the greenhouse, which is done, and next, was bringing in the dirt. With Anna inside, a small fire was going, she was at it with bucket of cool water set aside to temper, till she dip a small amount to each seedling. As I packed the wheelbarrow full of soil, I came in with and dumped, on the left or right sides of the greenhouse, as she combines all of those ingredients, in a bucket for later use. For her to say, "One more and I'll be done, thanks."

I did that and went back to another project she wanted me to do, put in her herb box, set on the west side, of the south compound, between the two doors, to the horseshoe shed, I dug in the soil, and formed a semi-circle ring, and I used the bucket of mortar, and set the brick in mortar, about a brick high, I mortared between it, and created a wall, time for lunch, as I went in, to see liver and onions, and oh it was so good, amazing as she deep fried them in oil, and seasoned so well, also a fresh green salad, with kale and rocket(Arugula), and oil and vinegar, also on the plate was tomatoes, sliced and seasoned, for her to say, "I find this meat to be sweet like berry sweet, do you wanna after lunch go find this patch?"

I said "Yes, I will." As the meal was fantastic, as she put it up and cleaned the dishes, we went out, as she wrote a note to Lily, "We are out in the woods, picking berries, wait or go home, Anna."

We took two buckets, to where I killed the buck, and sure enough there was others, babies, and doe's, as we chased them away, to see brambles, of multicolored raspberries, blackberries, and gooseberries. Off to a bush that had currants, it had but one red berry, as all the others were ate off, for Anna to say, "If we dig that one up we can propagate it, make for a great jam."

I went back to the compound to see Brian drive by to stop and pick me up, to say, "Where are you heading?"

"Well back to the compound, while I left Anna in the woods."

"Then I'm getting out" said Lilly, exiting the jeep, and into the woods, she was calling out her name, for I to say, "If she doesn't just scare them off."

"Who, whom are you talking about?" asked Brian. "Just drive", I said. We stopped at the south compound for the available buckets, and inside was a artic fox, pregnant, as she was trying to get comfortable, on the plywood, I found a blanket in the jeep, and laid it out for her, she crawled up on it, and sat down, she was wounded her left foot was off, she curled up, and waited, to die, as Brian and I watched as she gave birth to five, pups, and died, and right then and there I had to clean up her carcass, as I took her to the front, where I skin the game, I opened her up, as the blood dripped into a box, everything was salvageable, heart, lungs, liver, and kidneys, all other set in a plate for Anna to cleanup, she had very little meat on her, enough so it was used as bait, and into the bait box, and into the smoker, as Brian just watched. It was over soon enough, as I set her carcass to dry, and tan her hide, it was worth about a grand to me. Well minus her left leg, which was gone. I stretched her out, as Brian watched on, later we went back, and I told the story to Anna and Lily, whom was heartbroken over it, to say, "Where are those 5 pup now?"

"In a box, we will have to nurse them back to health, today is Saturday, let's make a run to town, to get five bottles, I think the convenience store has them." Said I.

Later after picking, and digging up some canes, she bundled them up, and carried them out, as I had found their roots systems, to put them in buckets, as I said, "Lets clear cut this part to allow the brambles to grow further, as all the trees do is protect them, but also with that, I got an idea, what about, if I limb up the trees to about ten feet high, and then the deer and us can get to them, without taking the trees down."

"I'm O Kay with that" said Anna, so Brian and I went back with two buckets of berries, and two plants, to the greenhouse, and a red currant bush. And got my two chain saws, it was like an awakening, when the lower branches came off, it immediately opened it all up and that was on twelve trees in that area, it was right, as the wind blew in, the place was nice, the sun shined in, oh yeah no rain, for a while, it seems, as we picked to our hearts content, another bucket, which meant there was still, maybe, 50 plus buckets, who knew it went back for aways, my goal was just to open it up, and let the brambles grow. We left filled of berries, and a new place to cultivate, back at the compound, for Brian to say, "When are you planning on finishing the north side compound?"

"Oh in due time, why, what's the rush?"

"Well about the mushroom plant?"

"Oh yes, alright, so tomorrow is Sunday, so let's do it then, I'll bring my tripod, and digging tools, and let us make a warehouse, what about a row of a house, next to the front and that of the rear?" said I.

"Oh I see for the trucks, or an airport for mail pickups, good idea, we have space on the lower"…said Brian.

"I was just kidding, it will have to be just trucked out of here to Anchorage, some 200 miles away," said I

"Or flown, if I can get someone willing to transport them for on-line orders."

"How many so far?"

"Well Charley, Lily's brother is still filling orders in Missouri till November, then it's all out here."

"So we better get going, and build that warehouse", said I as I led him out, and we took his jeep, and went back to his house past it, to an out cropping of trees, it was vast, and close by, as I took my tape, and a band of yellow, tree marking tape, and measured out 3 foot diameter trees, and five foot diameters, and it was like we were thinning out his old growth trees leaving about 20 some odd trees. At about fifteen feet long, for the walls, and most of them looked 120 feet tall and 3 foot diameter, and about forty of them, equally towering. That night we went back to our south compound, and ate like kings on the buck, it was good, seasoned in berry sauce, as for the rest, Anna and Lily made into jams, jelly and syrup, for use now. The girls took the jeep to town for the bottles and five gallons of milk, and picked up some formula. They also picked up some pectin to fortify the berries, and canning jars, to seal them up, the meat was divine, as both Lily and Brian tried it, they ate what they had on their plates, we ate on the new table, made of plywood and benches, it was easy, to build and a table cloth was over the top, the girls on the east side, and we men on the west, it was nice, and not much draft, as they left, and oh yes, a kiss and a hug from both of them, was weird, but I went along with it anyway, as we told the girls of our plans tomorrow.

They all agreed with us."

June 28th Sunday 2004

It was day 30th of 365, not bad, two compounds in play, south finished, and now working on the north, but today work on a warehouse, Brian's and Lily. It was sunny, and actually warm, but not for short sleeves, as it was still powerful mosquitos country, but just recently there wasn't as much, I don't know why. We loaded up the jeep and trailer with all we needed, to include mortar, and pieces of limestone, she had some chopped wood, to use to burn, for potash, we were ready, we locked up, and as for the cubs, the box came with us. We drove out to Brian's greenhouse first, off loaded, with Anna, and her stuff, as Brian was digging the posts for the middle, I waved at him, to dig the trench, as I went to his old growth grove, and myself fired up the really big chainsaw, and began to cut down the marked trees, it was a mad dash, the five footers in diameter, at 120 feet plus came down in a flash, I was cruising as I went from furest to closest, as I thinned out his area quickly. It was coming on upon lunch time, but I kept on going, till I had, all 30 big trees down, and all the little ones down as well. I took a break, as Anna and Brian came to my rescue, it was now a deer's paradise, as I cut the trees at a foot off the ground, the chains were sharp. Then after a thermos of delicious soup, beef stew, and jalapeno pineapple cornbread, which Anna told me they had a shipment come in at the hardware store, and the dumpster is gone, there is a check for Me at the feed store, but was put on my account, oh another thing, Jake wants us to take the animals feed we purchased?" said Anna, sitting closer to me than usual, on the log as I ate, and drank tea. She smiled, to put her hand on my leg, for her to say, "Is this a perfect place, for you to propose to me now?"

I said "No", and with that, I fired up the chainsaw, and began to cut the five footers in diameter in lengths of fifteen feet, for about 6 times, and all my marks were the work of Brian. Anna and Lily, were dragging as I was cutting, the two girls were choking the logs, to be pulled to the site, it was and the rest of the day's work, we stopped at night, and went home. Lily took the cubs, and was going to feed them three times a day.

June 29th Mon 2004

It was early morning, and it was day 31, and Anna was giving me a back massage, till she was through, then we got up, and she made an elaborate breakfast, she had a loaf of Lily's bread, and made French toast, then toast, and potatoes, and dried beef. With a gravy. It was energy building and good, we drove to town to collect up what we had left, as Jake was ready, for him to pull me aside, to say, "What is your play here boy, you're the first to ever come down here so much, and for you to stock up on your supplies, what gives?"

"I don't know really, maybe we like to see the two of you, "Well about that, If you do win, then we will be gone?"

"Oh that's a shame" I said, eyeing the buckets, to say,

"I would like all of them."

"Sure you would, and there for me, to pack up all of this."

"You don't have to do that, I'll buy this entire place."

"Really why would you do that, some of this stuff is outdated and for show?"

"So what, I'll tell you what, price everything out, and I will pay for it."

"It's not that, we work for the Territory" said Jake.

"What's that?"

"Yes, every year we come here and set up our trailer, the one in the back of the convenience store, and around November 1st were out of here, and back to Whitehorse, as the snow will be 20 feet high in places, and that goes to around April 1st and we come back, if there is anyone left, you survive that period of time and you all have won."

"Then what will you do?"

"I don't know, travel?"

"Listen why don't you come up for a Sunday feast, around 1 pm, this coming Sunday, as for my animals feed can you keep them one more week?"

"Ya, where do you want those buckets?"

"In the trailer" as we all three loaded them up with lids going in the backseat, to say, "Before I forget, I want 600 bales of hay, I think I calculated that right, I think I could use 900, oh just give me 900, what is that cost?"

"About 12 dollars a bail, which I can give you a discount, it is about 10K, plus or minus."

"Do I have that on account?"

"Yes and much more."

"Then make it happen, oh and by the way, do you have access to a portable saw mill?"

"Not really, but there is one in Whitehorse, a mill, maybe they have one, I could call them, ?"

"Go ahead and make the call."

"Alright I will, anything else?"

"Nope that about does it" said I

"And the lady?" asked Jake.

"Nope" said Anna, getting in and we took off, over the road, and on the gravel road, and of all the trees, lots of them, as we turned, and crossed the White river, I thought I need to set out a box in the river, as we drove past our place, it looked so dignified, as we drove on, to Brian's, I let out Anna, and all the buckets, and took the trailer with me, what I liked about it, it had a front wheel, to sit level, as we loaded it with the tripod., while using my jeep, as Brian did that. I worked the tripod on all cut logs, in place, all five of them, then hooked up the jeep, and took them to where, we were going to drop them, first place was the west side, or wind side, the wind was pretty fierce, as we were on a rise, excess dirt, was set aside, as Brian dug four feet, down, in the middle, as that cause a problem, with the five foot log in diameter, any further we will strike water, another mistake, as we are going to be insulated. I was beside myself, on this error, but Anna suggested, "Why don't we concrete the poles in?"

"Because it's only a foot deep" I said.

"Ooh" was everyone's response, to see the dilemma now, for Brian to say, "Let's just bury it up a foot."

"Because, it will be loose dirt, instead of packed, and which will hold in place," said I

So Brian went off another ten feet out, then began digging the five foot wide five foot deep trench, it was easy diggings, but one major problem, water, on Brian's property water was everywhere, until we either can dig out a channel, we will just have to put up with it, and sure enough at three feet, Brian struck water. Then it became a mess, he easily got stuck in the mud, it was a sopping mess. I went back to cutting and measuring logs, to be cut, and just on cue it began to rain, I wasn't so much affected by it, as was Brian, he was in a trench, for which he allowed it to flow, it was aggravating him.

That went on to lunch, as Lily had hot vegetable soup, and fresh baked bread, and the fresh berry jam and hot tea. After lunch I went back to my sorting, and dragging with the jeep, Lily took half the buckets as plant pots, while Anna helped out, as the two shared stories and ideas, Lily announced that what was ours is yours, then she saw the ring, and she was gushing over it, asking, "When will the wedding be?"

"After the challenge" said Anna.

"Great I'd like to come?"

"Of course, you'll be the maid of honor," she hugged her and said, "Your my best friend, and kissed her, so said Anna to me later. I didn't care that much, they were doing the best that they could, with what they had.

I was now cutting my marks and sorting them, all 20-fifteen foot long five feet wide was ready, using the trailer, I carried five at a time, to the west side, or what I like to call, the dry side of the proposed warehouse. Using the tripod, I set them in, using rocks, forced them in together, till all five were in, then I crossed nailed them in together, scaffolding was constructed, and I was able to get to the top. The wind was blocked. I cross tied the top together, below was both girls, finishing the burial, and stabilization of the five poles. I took the tripod with me, and I was off for five more. Anna made the measurement, to make sure it was straight and on line, later I came back with five more, set them in individually, and now a wall was set, I tied them in, and left, to get five more, I laid each of them in, as Brian was there to help, as it was day over, for them, but I wanted to get the last one, and I did with Brian's help, I parked the trailer, I was gonna unhitch it when Brian said, "Take our jeep, by now we trust you", and with that I drove Anna home, and after a supper of dried beef and roasted potatoes, we went to bed.

June 30th Tuesday, 2004

It was day 32, and it was the old hat, get up, get water, have breakfast, and we went back to Brian's, the western wall was up, I admired him finishing it, next was the top cap. It was Brian and I carving out a section of the log, and placing it on top, to bind the wall. For young guys we worked fast and efficiently. Next big issue while Anna and Lily patched the wall, with mortar. Was the water issue to the east, with shovel in hand, I showed Brian the trench I wanted, and where, it was about twenty feet away, and as I dug, water popped up, but it was to become a drainage line, and at the bottom of that hill, it was working, as I went one way, north, he went south, on the other side of the three foot waterway. It was about a foot deep, and the flow, was pulling water from up top, down and out. For Lily to yell, "Its working boys." The next thing I did was not stealing, but I took several buckets with me, and scooped up the heavily graveled road, and filled them up, then carrying them to my jeep, I drove them to the trench, and poured them in, and continued till the length of the 100 feet was dry. Then we dug the line, five feet wide five foot deep, the logs went in on the east side. Next it was Brian's turn to fetch logs, per the rules, at five at a time, just like I showed him. Then he got his trailer involved and he could carry fifteen, only problem he got stuck because of the weight. So he went back, to my trailer, and used the jeep, till he was able to get out, he then set his trailer aside, as he brought the logs to me to set. On each trip I went back to sorting and cutting lengths, for the ten poles, five feet wide, and 25 feet long, several trees took care of that. But before I cut them, a thought occurred, Brian dug down four feet from the level line to gauge, and I would need to lose a foot, four foot to cover, so 24 feet long, as I only got 3 per tree, so four trees, took care of it, as this day was ending, thinking hey I missed lunch., but we had dried beef, and bread.

CH 6

Camera's everywhere, some spying is going on

July 1 Wednesday, 2004

It was day 33, and I got up and noticed off the teepee pole was a camera, and got up and went outside, to see more of them, but went back in, and quietly dressed. I woke Anna had her get dressed, to point to the camera, she nodded, as I went out, to see overnight, the whole compound was wired up, as I thought why?, or maybe it was to get to us in a better situation, well who cares, we all signed waivers, so let them film away. We ate another fine breakfast, and we will be off to Brian's, we loaded up, and left, with all animals fed. We arrived at Brian's it was sunny, as we worked hard to finish that east side wall, Brian and Lily were digging out the trench, as it seemed like the water was less and less, as I thought we were in the heart of the summer, the heat index rose to 85, and we were in the morning, we worked on, as we all dug out the center poles went in and down by lunch, it was dang hot. Now came the issue of the 55 foot span to the ends both north and south. I suggest some storage towers, on the corners, say 20 x 20, all the way up to the roof line, and leave the middle open to the growing, thinking of the water when it rises. Brian finally agreed with me, but it was interesting, because, of the concept, all I was looking for was a center support. A room, of many levels, in the center. So it was decided on, four poles set in a 20x20 configuration, to form this room, we used split logs for the floor, which had to be modified to cover the distance, about, fifteen feet, each, 3 foot in diameter was split and set in. It looked good, now was a set of stairs up to the next level. Then by using the split five foot in diameter to support the 2nd floor to the center in it was brilliant. So the 3 foot in diameter was split in half was used as a wall, all the way up. Next I set his plywood down, to form a sub floor it was about 20X20. We took the siding up about seventeen feet, we set the frame, and inside the pole structure, all the way up, and set in a support platform. About halfway down I set in another floor, they were the 3 footers in diameter split in half then notched in, then using the plywood Brian had, I cut to size for the floor, then we worked on the top, to angle the roof line, it was about eight feet to the top give or take a foot, as I set braces in to the center pole which was south of us. In addition, he wanted a window, looking out, so near the top, I cut it out of the massive 5 foot in diameter, framed it in, and set the window with mortar in facing south. Inside was nice, and breeze free. Next was the other side, near the middle, as lunch came and went, but I was used to working, that was till Lilly called lunch, then it was vegetable soup, with eggplant floaters, and fresh bread. After lunch, it was back to another support, as it was the east side room corner north, using the four pillar method and the wall, it seemed to work faster, as all we did was set in two poles on the end, up to the top, it was coming along nicely. Brian liked the window theme, and the outside wall, facing east was cut into a five foot in diameter, and framed in, the window was set with mortar, and drilled in with screws. Lily asked me to do that to the south, so I went back as Brian was bringing the logs, they weren't that heavy, for guys like us. Next was the support on the east side, two more poles, set in, a floor, as this was the water side, I cut an east side window for that north east room, I called them side supports, I framed it in, and then set another window in, with mortar.

Then cross screwed them in. a lot of light came to that room, I think Lily was hoping it would be for them. The room was huge, by comparison to anything else they had. That's when Lily came to me and said, "I want another room like this one, but on the south line, then next to it a double garage, over to the southwest. I agreed, and as poles were being brought up by the two trailers, and Anna drove the jeep and Brian doing the other, he received the news, he was somewhat devasted, as He were having fun living under the ground. My next adventure was the building of the south support wall, and rooms Lily wanted, as I saw her floor plan, two huge rooms, and a large garage. I was a machine, in cutting the logs to form up a 20x20 frame, in two sections, one for the bedroom, and the next one for the kitchen. I laid a split log floor, and then set in a plywood for the floor, next was the walls, they went up fast.

Brian came over to see me cutting out two doors, and a window, He saw it coming together, as he went into the room, I put up the plywood, and framed up a bed, and he changed his mind, as I cut a door, and hung it, it was pretty nice, next I took split logs, and began to make a roof, as they all asked why?" I told them in case the top roof leaks you will be protected. In addition, Lily wanted a second level, so at about the 8 foot mark, a second floor, of about half way was constructed, leaving the rest open and plywood was laid on the floor. Using the saw, I cut out the inside wall, to be large opening, I then added three other sides, all the way up, to form a wall. As it was getting late. We went home and that night it rained.

July 2nd Thursday 2004

It was day 34, and Brian and Lily had a dry place to sleep. I felt good as I got up to a gully washer, it rained something fierce, as we got up and hurried over to Brian's, as we approached, to see a literal river, coming to us, their whole place was under siege, we got out to see Brian and Lily exit the jeep, it was around 50's degrees Fahrenheit, and cold, I could see I had issues to contend with, but this was a loss, as we went and saw the greenhouse, was flooded, and the room below, it was bubbling, as I said, "Well I guess you found a spring?"

"How's that?" asked Brian.

"See those bubbles, that indicate a spring, and it's all dug out so you'll have fresh water year-round, great for getting and collecting water, this driving rain is for the birds, come to our place, we drove back, and they took warm showers and changed, the interesting thing was we were dry, Billy told me later, his castle was a mess, it leaked everywhere, so they went to the camper, John and Kim, built themselves a nice log cabin, and kept warm, it was a bed room, kitchen, and dining, and the other room was for work, or chopping wood. So said Brian who visited them. We were outside to see that storm go on by. Water was everywhere but not in the south compound, I also saw what I needed to do across the way in the north compound, build the second level as rooms to give the top roof more support. It was late we had a light lunch, and so we called it a day. I went in to the south horseshoe, and began to work on a trap for gold, till dinner, we ate and went to bed.

July 3rd Friday 2004

We woke up on day 35, to a disaster, outside the compound, most of her garden was trampled, and that's when we realized it all had to be inside, the rain and wind was fierce, and damaging. We salvaged what we could, and let the rest to the animals, we fight off every day, but not in the compound. I shoot a squirrel a day, or a raccoon, those I can use their meat for trapping big game, as the smoker could literally fit, five deer's, or a huge moose. We went over to a bigger disaster with Brian and Lily in tow, to see some of the logs were still standing, as all the structures were in place, I said, "Let's go, all we can do is build, and that's what we did, I finished the front southern building warehouse, and then, took it up to the top ridge line just below the suppose top roof, and added a roof to both rooms, and then a concrete patch down the middle, of all of the logs for the roof about 7 split logs, 40 feet long. Anna made up another bucket of mortar, it was mushy until it sets and combines, then we stir it to make it useable, by adding tempered water(Water that sits a day or so), in a bucket. I did this for two reasons, it binds the roof better together, and also to prevent seepages. With the roof ready, we applied shingles, from the southeast end, up to the slated roof. We were done, next was the top roof, as we hoisted up the hoist and tripod, on the sub roof, we began to set the 55 footers split, down, to form the upper roof. It was setting and hammering them into place, with three feet over, and one at a time, till all were set, hammered on, as Anna and Lily began to use the mortar to bind the south side roof. I used the scaffolding, to build up to the top, lots of light came in as we used 2x4's to bind the roof together underneath in rows of five. It was fast going, as Brian was setting the 2x4's, as we covered the entire distance, in that day. All we had to do was finish the north east side, to marry it to the lower roof, and support it. The day was done. And we went home.

July 4th Saturday 2004

It was day 36, for us it was the challenge, no big fanfare, except we had deer liver and onions, for breakfast, and washed it down with tea. We drove back to Brian's, as he and she was already up, and dragging logs to the ready position, on the lower road, which was higher than their place, an onto the ramps to split apart the logs, as we all make our own paradise, and for them it was here, they were easy to please, and I was tasked with finishing the other side and its inside construction, while, Anna was on the roof, patching with Lilly using a brush, down the split logs, as the roof sat nicely on the inside structures, I finished by securing those two together, and, then we hoisted up the shakes, I cut, enough for the entire roof, as each bundle was placed near the bottom, we all took an area of twenty five feet, and went up, row by row, overlapping as we went, to about 36 rows, I was flying, as was Anna, the other two not so much, as Lily complained about lunch, so she got down off the roof in the center room, as for the scaffolding we moved to the north side, so she left the rest, for us to do, see she was eager to get to her new kitchen, we used, the underground spring, as our water source up high, and we built a box, to catch the water, and using a pipe on the inside, we ran it up high, to the north side for a shower, and the other, along the wall, going down to the sink, and the drain went to a hole Brian was digging. She made us a soup, from vegetable, and we knew we would have to address at some point. Lunch was good, as the south side roof was nearly done, we had about 169 sq. feet of was roofing yet to finish, but I was already, on the north west side, finishing up the 20x 20 room, with a north face window, it was a pretty nice view, Lily finished her portion of the roof, Brian was hard at splitting logs. Anna was making more mortar to fill the gaps, of this part, while she did that I cut one window at a time, I framed it in, and then set the window, with mortar, and in it went, I cross nailed it in place, mortar was everywhere, Brian helped out with the roof, over the center 20x20 room, he told me he had plenty of time in the winter to frame in each room and put up shelving, and storage crates. I told him to stop dreaming and go get me more logs, to say, "Let's get this roof on." Lily announced she was done, I told her to help Anna, she did and all was quiet again, as I cut into the five foot diameter log, and it was a mess, but it worked, I framed it in, an set the window in mortar, and it went in as it binded, and I shattered the window, I pulled that one out, and cleaned up the mess, to make new measurements, for another window, and rest it and set the new one in, it was loose, and I filled it with mortar, it worked, it was nice. Now onto the north roof, but Brian had other ideas, as 3 foot in diameter which were 55 footer were being cleaned up, as I moved the tripod over near the top, pushed each one over to Anna, who help me set the outside, I went over to help set the first one, and drove it in to the north up to the south top, and it went fast, till I stop handing them to her, then Anna went below to make up more mortar. As I went to the northwest room. Then to bind it to the roof, which was another mistake I made, the north side wall should have been first, but we kept on laying logs to finish, with the roof done. I hammered it into place, as I adjust the logs, over with a sledgehammer to set tight, then nail down, just as straight as the south side, it was really nice, as Anna was up here, patching the roof, with Lily, it was a slow go, as I went down using a ladder, to the ground, I looked at that massive structure to marvel at its existence, as Brian approached to say, "This was a good idea of yours, now I can darken the inside room, and the mushrooms can grow." "Oh right" I said, not even thinking, as I assessed the north suppose wall, for Brian to say, "Looks like that will be a tough one?"

"Nah, just start digging in between the walls, and then there is the transition to the greenhouse."

"Yes, I need something to put in to make that transition."

"Let's build a tunnel" said I.

"Good Idea, as he went to the digging, as I went to the choking of logs. One by one I drug the huge logs over and up top I then moved the tripod, to pick up the logs, and set it in place, as Brian guided the first one, over, it fit snugly to the northwest corner, then he back filled, to secure it, as he moved the straight ladder over, so I could tie it in on the top, as below, Anna choked the next one, as I hoisted it up, and it went in with Brian setting it, the fifteen footers were easier to manage, to cover, the big five foot in diameter took up huge space, but it also shored up the structure, this took two more to then to seven to cover the distance. I was now at the middle of the greenhouse, and now it was the 3 foot in diameter, these little ones, took the distance well, and sat straight, as I went down and cut a 3 footer at an angle, to use as a top piece, to form the northwest wall, to the warehouse. Brian had cut the 3 foot in diameter, at fifteen feet for the other side of the door, we set them all in, I top capped it, as below I made a stair step all the way up to the door. Next was a roof, and for that I built a truss to sit on top, then it was 3 footer split in half, to make up the roof, it was impressive, and plus the light from the greenhouse illuminated the tunnel. The last of the five logs went in going to the north east side, the last one to go in, was a bear, we had to twice dig it out. It finally went in. Lily and Anna broke out a blue tarp, and slung it over the north roof, and over me, on the ends tightened it down to the greenhouse. It was nice, but not necessary, as I was working towards the top, as I was checking the angle of the top roof, to this sub room's roof, when I think I was close, I set it to the top. Lily and Anna, were climbing ladders, to see I had fastened that roof down, and now it was time for mortar, and a set of shingles, which the girls said they had that. I moved out of their way, to see Brian was laying the 55 footers over to the road as we are done. Brian laid out for the top cap, taking a 55 footer, I was on the roof, pulling the tarp off, and mortar was going in, so I said, "Anna, when your done there, come over here and set in some mortar."

She looked at me, to say, "There is another bucket made up, shall I go get it?"

"Don't bother", as Brian had it on the tripod, and swung up to me, I caught it, and began to uncap it, and smear it, on the gaps, the bucket went some twenty feet. The split board was nice, but I thought a five footer in diameter, split in half would be better, as Brian went and did that, took a twenty five footer five foot in diameter and split it in half, and then set it up to me, and it was golden, it covered over the top, nicely, and I cross hammered it in place.

While he sent me more, 55 footers, as I hammered them in place, across the top to finish, Anna was at the lower part of the roof, as all four of us joined in to lay cedar to the north roof, nailing them to form the first line we were hung over by five feet, and Lily, took it upon herself, move up further leaving Brian to finish her work. We put the entire roof on, I actually went the whole distance. The day was done, and everyone got off the new roof. Inside scaffolding was moved, so 2x4, could, be nailed in under the north roof in five rows all 100 feet long, to help tighten up the roof. We went home.

July 5th Sunday 2004

It was a nice warm morning, it was day 37, and back to Brian's to finish, when we got there, Brian suggested, a second floor, above the planned workshop and garages, and in the front an awning, some 55 feet, so I said, dig the holes where you want them five feet deep, he worked on that, as the whole place was lit up, as he was working early to tie in the finished side, with two by fours, straight, so now it was Anna making more mortar, and Lily, distributing into buckets, while I assessed how I wanted to build this, so on the end, was, the only place it was near level, and where the snowmobiles would go, and the trailer, it was 20x20, and began to build, a box, next to the wall, as I secured it to that, I took a thirteen footer, cut at an angle, to tie it in the front, and support the roof, it worked, and tied it into place, normally I would dig it down, but it tied it in nicely with the structure. Then the last top roof board went on, tied in and the girls began to seal the roof, that one had a split pole flat top, Brian made a set of stairs to the top, I cut the opening, and the rails to the garage door, went on, we framed it in, with a threshold, and side supports, for the additional logs, then the door, it was nice. We put plywood down, to finish. Next was the garage, on the other side of the opening, next to the support pole, that will make up the new wall, or so we seemed, but in fact, I put a log, on top with tripod's help, to cover 50 feet, to the wall, it worked, so it will be cut at an angle, all the way up to the roof, while below the logs are set in, by me and Brian and made easy work of it, as it was getting dark, we were done.

July 6th Monday 2004

Day 38 the days seem to fly by, but were also sturdy workers, as we got back over there, and today was finishing day, and up on sub roof, to seal the rest of the cracks, and then, each taking a section, we nailed down shakes, from the lowest point up to the crest, it was a fast job, considering the pitch we were at, and how easy it was, we made fast work of that, to the top, where Anna did the mortar Lily was cooking us something, I set the last piece and we were done, with only a few doors to put in., to the final end. As I saw, Brian, back out front, digging again, as I and Anna got down to hear, "I want an awning, across the front."

"Alright let's do this", as I used the tripod and dropped a five foot diameter, five feet deep to the size of fifteen feet tall, next to the building to the roof height of fifteen feet, and we did three of them, and three out front ten feet high, then we used three foot split rails, across the fifty feet area, actually it was 55 footers, as I put them up to the side, and straight down, it was fast and looked nice, as underside was 2x4's, to secure it as the mortar and then the shingles, it was a long hard day, as we were done, and now it was up to Brian.

July 7th Tuesday 2004

I made another mistake, and this one was difficult to fix, and I knew it, it was day 39, and Anna and I were back to Brian's, he was happy, she had running water, and a cold shower, now they wanted a fireplace. Especially in the kitchen. I was amazed how fast we worked, it was nice, I said, as I went in, as we were under the awning, as it was nice, and went in, to see he was building a door, well trying, and into the darkness, as he took me north to the light coming in, and I constructed a door made up of 3 foot in diameter split logs, and a 2x4, we were four feet lower than it, and the stairs made for an easy transition. Now we were done.

Anna and Lily mortared the wall, as Brian and I began to shingle it, along the gaps, but it looked odd, so, it was the entire face, up to the roof, and suggested doing the rest.

July 8th Wednesday 2004

It is the 40th day here, and it was extremely sunny and hot, the garden bounced back, and shingle cutting was at an all-time high, as I had a patch, and I was harvesting it, also, took a hundred sapling, and planted them, along the bend, by the bridge, it was open, and ten feet apart in all directions, especially along the bank and evidently, they were growing,

I noticed every time I cross the bridge the group is getting bigger, as I uncovered more saplings, and took them over to that bend, and planted them. Then from what I cut, I have about hundred logs cut at 18 inches, and now I have a tool, that cuts the slakes to a half inch, as they pop off, some on the end, end up as kindling, but the center out is nice, we went to Brian's and Lily's place to finish the warehouse, we first finished the front wall, and around the windows all the way up. Then worked on the west side first where the wind comes, and it howls, but not anymore, it is cool inside the warehouse, as Brian has started his mushroom plugs, and watering method, we all went to the east side or calm side, and did that, up to ten feet, it was lunch and we ate good, several fresh breads, Lily was loving that kitchen, it was warm and inviting, as she wanted a kitchen stove, it was Wednesday, so Brian and I went to town, to see Jake, he told of us, a camp about ten miles up, and that there was multiple stoves available, all we had to do was trek in and carry them out, I was thinking, everyone, should come, as we picked up more crushed rock, concrete slabs, we took back with us, we went back to Brian's, to tell the girls of the news, that night we went home.

July 9th Thursday 2004

Today is a group day, 41st, as Brian and I drove our jeeps, to a place called Lone gulch town, where it was once a silver mine, as the road was an instant drop, and it was bumpy, yet I was four wheeling it, over rocks, and up a huge hill, nearly on my side, as I trail blazed through the high grass, into a valley, and it was going good till Brian had a flat tire, so he pulled off, as we helped him change it, we went on, the two of us, as a road was clear, all the way up, and around, into a small town, or a huge mining shack, inside it had a potbelly stove, and then we went up to Victorian looking custom houses probably 800 sq. feet, the doors opened to a lavish interior of the 1820's lost and forgotten treasures, and there in the middle was the best looking heaviest stove I've ever seen, dated 1889, for me to say, "Wow", and for Lily to say, "I want it", both Brian and I looked at her, as if she was crazy, I went back for my tool box, while Brian examined the roof, Anna said, "Let's go exploring?" to Lily who agreed, I came back, with the jeep as close as I could, and parked at an angle, to see the kitchen door, to realize I need the tripod, but it was back at Brian's. "Aw shucks." I said, as Brian said, "The roof should be easy, have you a plan?"

"Yep, tomorrow I'll bring my trailer and the tripod, and we will swing it out and set it down on the trailer?"

"Brilliant, simply brilliant, I guess we should go then," said Brian.

"Yes, that may have to wait till the girls are done exploring" said I.

"Indeed lets go find them," said Brian.

"You go", as I went in, and took the potbelly stove apart, in three moveable pieces, each easy to handle, and then I bent down, and lifted the trunk, and fell flat on my face, I was doubled over and in a curled up position, with my back out, it was excruciating pain, I was done. A little time went by as everyone was searching for me as if it was a game, as Lily called out, "Matt are you there, as she stepped in, to see me on the ground, quivering, as she yelled, "I found him, and now it's my turn", as she bent down, to see I was out, she began to scream, to Anna, "Get down here, I think Matt maybe hurt."

Instantly she was there at my side, looking me over, to say, "My dear what have you done?"

"My back, it's out" I said in massive amount of pain.

She felt it to say, "I'd say so, it's all inflamed", for Lily to say "I have fresh arnica, we could put on that, as Brian said, "No wonder you popped your back, this thing is bolted to the floor", as Brian was wrenching it off, and then slid it away, for I to say, "Do you mind putting it on the jeep?"

"No problem," said Brian as he left with it, as both Lily and Anna helped me up, I straighten and I was in a lot of pain, both girls massaged the area damaged, to hear, Lily say, "I know what I can do to fix him, come let's get him in the back of our jeep."

"Shall we leave the other jeep?" asked Brian.

"No what about the rules?" said Anna.

"Then can you drive it out?"

"I can try, as she got in as Brian secured the stove parts, and top, Anna drove off, and to the left, instead of the right, as the way we came in, and for half of it I was being held in by Lily, it was bumpy, and at one point we went over a hill, and back down, and around, over a wood bridge, and guess where we came out?, behind Beaver creek, and to the convenient store, and not to arouse suspicion, Anna went in complaining of a back ache, so she got those pills from Rita, then Lily did the same as she bought some back support and also got some pain medicine, and bought some groceries, for Rita to say, "Please clean us out as after November 1st we are leaving, and this place will be close till Mar 1st. Anna paid with our credit card, but it was put on account and loaded up the jeep, as we all went to Brian's. Lily smeared this arnica all over my back, I took the pain medicine, and was out.

July 10th Friday 2004

Day 42 I write this as an afterthought of the day of complete and total resting, on their bed, Lily and Brian, I was out for this day, my back was severe as Lily said it, but cold water packs, replaced hourly. Anna was here but with Lily, Brian was digging his septic tank, it was brick building time for the girls, and I missed all of that as I slept this day away.

July 11th Saturday 2004

Day 43 was as same as day 42, it was sleep, on a comfortable mattress, with Anna by my side, Lily and Brian was up top, it was comfortable in there, and open windows allowed in the wind, but it was nice I was up a couple of times, to do my business in a bucket. Those plastic buckets are a lifesaver, so many uses. I was finally was getting better. I was up and out to see what Brian was up to, besides all the spores, the warehouse was cool, and free of drafts, it was a perfect environment, and each room, we built had a theme, so he was going crazy. I was feeling loads better till I saw Lily who was looking for me, for another application, she lathered it on, it did its job I was better, enough to go get her stove now. I let Anna drive, to town, and the back way to the Lone Gulch town, along the mining road, and up over a hill, and then straight into camp, she backed up our trailer, Brian got out and made sure the stove was unsecured, as I had help from Lily and Anna, setting up the tripod, and we hooked it on, it pulled it out and around it slowly took flight, as I lowered it down to the trailer, we closed up the doors, as I took the tripod down, and secured that massive thing, drove out, over the huge hill, and down into town, and back to Brian's, to his awning, backed in, to the door, and waited for Brian and Lily, that was a bear, but we walked it off the trailer, and into the house, up front, I cut a hole for the stove pipe out and up, through a space up front., Brian secured it to the wood floor, and it was set. We went back home.

July 12th Sunday 2004

It is day 44, and were staying home. I went across the road, to work on the north compound house, and the second story over our place, as I had the tripod, and the jeep, pulling cut logs in place at 25 footers, and set on ramps, to use wedges to split in half, it worked smoothly, then lifted them up, to build a floor, the thirty feet, giving five feet up front and five in the back, as it was log upon log to the top, some ten feet higher. Anna, she had a routine, she was up earlier than I, had breakfast ready, as I would fetch water, she now wants, what Lily has, fresh flowing water, after I get this side built and a top roof on, and then work on the whole water issue, as we had a huge truck arrive, it was all the hay bales, and another mistake, I was way over, as we loaded the upper barn full, to the rafters, and then inside the horseshoe, and then down to the south compound's horseshoe and that was quite a lot as it took it all with more spare room, bundle on bundle, till we were done. When the driver said, "That was ingenious the wrap around, especially draft free and warm inside, as we took all 900, well it actually was 1200, to fill the truck, so that's what I got. The driver stayed for lunch and it was delicious vegetable soup, dried beef, and the rest of the fresh baked bread, with tea. Then before the driver left to go back to Whitehorse, he said, "In all the years I've hauled up here, I've never seen an operation like this, your light years ahead of anyone else, especially with this lodge, and I dig that teepee."

"Thanks" I said. As he left, on came our friends right on time, Brian and Lily for a Sunday feast, as it was. Anna took Lily on a berry picking adventure, while Brian helped me to finish the walls to the roof, across our new home, for Brian to say, "Let's start on the other side, as the 20x20 rooms were formed, with a door on both sides and two windows, and a fireplace, to the roof. Anna put those in while I set her up a wall cradle. Work was about complete when, the next project was to set the stairs for the step up on either side, we used pilings to put in place, then stairs, cut into them, then a landing, up to the second floor, for the animal side it was before the greenhouse, and on the other side it was by the barn, but in front of it. Next was the top roof, so 55 footers were hauled in, and split in half and set by the tripod, all the way to the greenhouse, and on top of the 20x80, rooms, on both sides, I used poles on the roof, to make sure the top poles sat firmly, as I set an inverted flat roof on it, and that's when Anna appeared with Lily, and helped by mortaring the roof, as it was laid to the greenhouse leaving six feet of space and hammered down. It was all the way across the 80 foot span, to the watchtower. Then I went to the other side, as Brian set the other 55 foot long split poles, down, from the watchtower over to the washroom and stopped, hammered them down, leaving two on both sides alone. first on the house side I cut the places for the fixed sliding glass windows as skylights, then went over to the animals side and cut three openings over the pens. Anna was making her own feed from, blood meal, and bones, with fiber from moss, and berries, the 18 chickens I had, plus the 7 layers gave us 25, solid prospects, and one rooster, we were done for the day, as we had a feast, and drank beers, thinking of inviting others we did not. We partied late into the night, they spent the night.

July 13th Monday 2004

It was day 45, and Brian was up early with me as we fetched water, and then, went to work on the second story over our house, I was laying the frame for the second level, I was thinking of a trip to Anchorage, as it was 200 miles away, but knew we needed permission, but today was all about the top level over our house, starting over the jeep port, I realized I need to have a front support, and a fence, so we dug a five foot wide, and forty foot long, and began dropping in fifteen foot, poles, five feet wide, they were monsters, and instantly we had a front wall it was nice because it kept unwanted animals out, and the place safe. I put a top cap on that, to seal it up strong, also the second level sat on its edge, on the top roof, all the way to the horseshoe, where it stopped. Next was the split flooring, 30 feet long, notched, it hung over 5 feet in the front, and five feet in the rear, all the way down. It was lunch late, and it was vegetable soup, and fresh bread, berries, and tea. We worked late to the night, and quit, they stayed over, to another of the same meal, then went to bed.

July 14th Tuesday, 2004

It was day 46, and we were back on the log siding for the second floor, it went up in stages, four rooms were planned for on top of our house, each 20x20, we were doing each room at a time, enough so, at the top, we now had to contend with the top roof, like the warehouse, so in the middle off the barn, we went in twelve foot increments, about 7 poles, to the edge, with a top cap, and we were done. They went home.

July 15th Wednesday 2004

It was day 47, and somewhat of a harvest for our corn, as Anna, was pulling it up, the stalks were left to dry, for the animals. I went to town to pick up more supplies and with trailer in tow, to pick up more nails, and talk with Jake, to say, "Heard anything on that sawmill?"

"Nope."

"So what do you think if we took a trip to Anchorage?"

"For what?" asked Jake.

"I don't know, let's say a gift to our girls, for lasting 47 days."

"That's all you have been out here, a little too cocky for yourselves, I would think less on traveling to Anchorage, than helping your last teammate with his ricky house, you know he has no flooring, let alone picked up his pile yet" using his hand to show it was still there, and to say, "When will you finish the job you said you would", again pointing to the slabs of concrete."

"In time" I said.

"In time means it better before November 1st, is the day I'm gone and my wife will be shutting down this operation, you got that boy." He said in a rather cocky way.

"Sure, as I grabbed my feed and all and left. It was weird how he was acting. I got back, and unloaded the supplies, I picked up a aluminum horse waterer, and dug down 3 feet, and dropped it in the ground. Next was the rest of the animal feed for the winter, inside the barn, was the left over sticks and branches for building more rabbit cages. Anna kept track of the breeding pair, and the offspring, now at ten, strong and growing. The garden yield huge loads, of vegetables, and were taken down in our root cellar to rest, whereas I built bins, elevated to allow the air to circulate around them. There was huge onions, potatoes, and scallions, garlic also thrived. My new project was water piping, I used smaller one foot boards from trees, equal to that size, very easy to work with, I made a long square pole, of twenty feet, I used the chain saw to cut it in strips, then nailed it together, it worked great, to make this form of pipe. After lunch Brian and Lily came by and it was all hands on deck, as we finished the rooms, cut the front and back doors, to the balcony, next is the two windows per each room. It was the same, cut it out with a chain saw, frame it in, and set the window with mortar, till it was snug. Next was the door, I liked the barn door method so much, I did that with every one of them, I had four solid rooms, and a long 20x 30 room, I was thinking for the pool table. That room had three windows each, and two doors, no back door, I knew using littler wood for the railing. Next we set the top logs to the very top roof, and set on a 22- three foot split logs, at the roof angle, all the way down, this is where everyone helped out, as it was nearing done. We had dinner, then to bed.

July 16th Thursday 2004

It was day 48, and the focus was on the roof over the rooms and the top roof, the gap for the roof was 50 feet, but with the pitch, was near 60, as that was the new logs that were cut and split, starting from the roof of the barn, it was fastened and rode the roof down, to the second floor, and out to the horseshoe, it worked and one after one, the tripod hoisted them up on top of the barn, it was fast going, I nailed them down, I left the first three off, for the greenhouse, and started inward, same for the other side, as the I had another project to start, but this day was laying all the wood I cut, and Brian split in half. The day was warm and inviting, and the bugs were non-existent, as we discovered we had a pair of bats, in our make shift bat caves, we spread with bat poo on, to attract the young couple, at night they eat, during day, they sleep. One by one split logs came up, I nailed them down, and Anna nailed them down on top of the middle buildings, it went from open to closed in one day, we were done, had a hearty dinner and went to bed. Brian and Lily went home.

July 17th Friday 2004

It was day 49, and Anna and I were on the huge top roof, early mortaring the cracks, and that's where it all changed, for I had 6 huge sliding glass doors, so I waited till Brian showed up and we carried them over and then lifted them up on the roof, then using my saw, I cut it further out, the openings of these huge sky lights, over the animals side open pens and on the east and over the suppose planned orchard on the west, framed it in, and then mortared them in place, we then began to cedar the roof, it was slow going, as all of us worked and then after lunch it went super-fast, up to the top, on both sides, where it was mortared and a top cap, of a five footer in half went, to cover the 100 feet. We lifted six more split poles, to leave up there as we extracted the tripod off the roof, it was done.

July 18th Saturday 2004

It was day 50, and today, Anna made a spectacular breakfast, our deer was getting low, so I went out and shot and killed another 12 point buck., had trouble picking it up, but was able to get it around my neck, and up, as I took it home, to the south compound, and hung it in the smokehouse. Anna was there to butcher it, I took the hide to tan it, and stretch it out. I spent time tanning it, and cleaned it all up. Anna was done, and she had a fine soup on, of inners. She wasn't doing much baking, because she wanted a stove like Lily's, whom was ready to give it up to her, but both Brian and I said "No", as for our request, Anna goes to town every Saturday morning, only to find out, from Rita, the Territory wants those slabs taken up, immediately, so she came back and told me, I told Anna to wait here, till Brian arrives and I'll go crush them and collect them, so I went to town, and began to crush a slab, at the edges, and then using a crow bar, from my fording kit, I unearthed, them, and threw them in my trailer, it was slow going, and wished I had help, at lunch, I was full and sagging as I drove back, and next to south compound, people got to watch as I shoveled them out, into a pile, seeing Brian wasn't around, I took Anna as she left a note, I also had a huge open space up front of the north compound, that need to be filled, as I had logs left over, but overall it looked impressive, as we drove back, it was easier with two people, I would break up the concrete and she would load it. It took but a hour, and we went back, as we did this for the rest of the day into the night, we went home exhausted, and went right to sleep.

July 19th Sunday, 2004

It was day 51, and it was Sunday, but every day was the same, either it rained, which I was hoping for, or it was sunny, which was this day, as we had a spectacular breakfast, of fried potatoes, chipped beef with a gravy, eggs from our chickens, and toast from leftover bread, we were going out to the road, as Brian and Lily pulled up for Brian to say, "Where are you going?"

"You don't wanna know" I said comically.

"What, are you going to Anchorage?"

"No to town?"

"Oh, need company?"

"Sure what happen yesterday?" I asked.

"Oh we were way too busy to get away, and by the time we were through, it was around three, why?" asked Brian.

"We were doing this yesterday as well" I added.

"Oh, let's see what we have, you know it's Sunday?"

"Yes, I'm aware of that" I said.

"Well Billy and John invited us over for a BBQ, interested?"

"Sure, but help me out with this one little job?"

"Sure what do I need?"

"Your trailer, a pickaxe and shovel."

"Wow, now that sounds like some work."

"Ah not really, it will go fast."

We were first there, Anna and I, and went to work, from their trailer, Rita and Jake saw me and Anna hard at work, as you could hear Rita yelling at Jake to fix this, I didn't know till later, when he came out, to say, "Cut it out today, and just work during the week, now get out of here" as Brian showed up, and then it was Billy, and John the entire crew was there, as we tackled the problem, by dinner, as we invited the Wilson for a feast, we finished our task, and Jake said we all could go to Anchorage, but for only one day, and be back within the

24 hour period. We all went to Billy's for a BBQ, and for the first time in 51 days, they were eating veal, we brought the potatoes, as both of their crops was lost to the flash flood we had on July the 2nd, but not for us as we held a bounty, as for Brian and Lily they brought mushrooms, really big portabellas, and black truffles, they grew. It was good on the potatoes. All Kim did was complain, so I said, "Brian and I will come out tomorrow and fix you up right."

She smiled and was happy, as the castle was in sad shape, and needed repairs, the lone look out was a birds nest. As Brian and I looked around. Jake and Rita were charming, yet they said they didn't like to fraternize with the contestants, but this year was different. Jake announced "The snowmobiles are ready, 8 of them, 2 per each, and now does anyone have hides to turn in, for pay or gold?"

Billy offered nothing, as did John, Brian said "No", as I said, "Sure, I have a few."

Jake went over to Billy to say, "If I don't get your account caught up, your all out, as they took off, for I went to see Billy, who said, "I have till November 1st to pay off my bill to you or we are all out, so I said, "Say, why don't you cut me some ten foot sections, and haul them to my yard, for firewood, and what else do you have in trade?"

Laurie stepped up to say, "We have some goats to give you milk, three for say 5K, how does that sound?"

"Sure, but ask the boss, she'll be doing the milking" looking over at Anna.

Anna agreed, but said, "If these chevron's are prized, make it ten, and we will knock off 10K, and the rest in wood, what about your camper?"

"Oh not that, I sleep in that" said Laurie., "Just curious what do you think that is worth to you?"

"How about 10K" said Anna, as Laurie pondered that. As we all broke up and we went home, ten goats richer, and what we were going to do tomorrow, we bathed and dressed, and then went to bed.

CH 7

Help out those in need

Back in Whitehorse the feeds back were outstanding as it was the highest market share for any challenge, by far, the feedback was, "They are some of the hardest working people", and of the lodge, had the governor, answering questions, over the lodge, as he was un-aware of it, as a housing crisis was near, in the outskirt areas, asking for relief over outdated cabins, and on TV they see these 140x120 structures, being built, and look magnificent, as orders were piling in as to that was what communities wanted, and now it was up to John Hughes to answer them, via the governor, as to what to do, as Matt Michales had fulfilled every aspect the governor was looking for, and knew it was too early to call it over, but he needed to get Matt on board, with helping out the Territory and squash this all, it was turning into a real mess, and at day 52, it was almost all over so thought the governor.

July 20th Monday 2004

It was day 52, and we got off to an early start, as we collected up Brian and Lily, and drove up to John and Kim's place, a real bad situation, as we all got out, and was invited in, to a plain wet floor, that was a work room, then into another wet floor for the kitchen and dining, and the bedroom, it was worse, I felt sorry for Kim, John wasn't providing for her, as

Anna, had lost a tear, for her it was that bad, the girls took Kim back to our home, for a shower and a change of clothes, and a hot meal. For us men to sit down to talk, as I said, "What are you going to do with the cattle when the twenty foot snow drifts come in during January?"

"How do you know it will reach that high? Asked John.

"I've been in Alaska when January is here and it isn't pretty."

"What do you suggest then?"

"How about a 100x100 structure, and around it a house, with an awning and a deck, and gates on the front, and a wraparound house, and wood shed to the east or west?"

"Sounds good, how much will it cost us?"

"Well here's what we will do, price each steer at a thousand, and from the looks of it you have 16, we will help you to ten, but here's what we will do, keep them with you, and we will only take what we need."

"Fair deal, what do I need to do?"

"Find trees, that are over 120 feet tall, five feet in diameter, and mark them to be cut, next mark out three foot diameter trees, about fifty for each, and I'll come in, and clear cut them, and if you find a patch of redwood(cedar) then it will be a fine for you, in the meantime we will take apart your cabin, and make it right." We broke up, as we knew we need a new sight to do this, so we went further back, and laid out the plan, and Brian began to dig, while, I assessed the situation, as I took my jeep back there in his vast forest, it was thick at places, and super big trees, I uncovered a spring, which, I lined rocks around it, it was close to where we were going to build, as it was on a bit of a hill, I knew I need to build a box, and line it with bricks, I was a bad ass with the chainsaw, and took down a marked tree, cut it up, to workable length's, at about 6 foot, using axe and maul, split in two, to build a frame, I began to dig out, the front to make a platform below it about five feet up, I nailed the split wood together to make a wall, and then I had four sides and a floor, I assembled it on the platform, I created, first the floor, for it to run over, then the outside walls, and finally the front, and lastly the back, as I used a cedar plank, for the water, to flow off of, and into the box, the wood swelled and contained it, although it would take some time. Next I went cutting, it was a fiesta, as I dropped trees, one by one, until I caught up with John who was slow, as it was about lunch, and Billy came by, to help, he started to dig, I cut the logs as I needed them, there was so much here, that nothing was really even touched, the first trench on the wind side was dug, down five feet, and down ten of the hundred, and then Billy took over, as Brian took over the choking, and pulling logs to the site, at fifteen feet long, one by one, the tripod was set up, as the first one was dropped by Brian, and Billy was in the trench. It was fast going, as I was on a roll, as five logs were in, the girls came back with lunch, we stopped, to vegetable soup, chipped beef and gravy and fried potatoes, which we had an abundant of and tea. Already amazed by the huge logs in place I showed Kim the drawing and she was in agreement, so it would happen. I also told her and John of some other good news, she would be third to have running water, much to Anna's disappointment. After lunch, it was back to cutting trees down, while, Brian choked them, and drug them to the site, John slowed down from marking as I took over, as I was twice or third as fast, as him, as he was off goofing off, but Kim, came out and helped me out, and took over. We knocked it out, all the suppose trees down, for her to say, "How do you know so much about working with logs?"

"Lincoln logs as a kid, it's really simple actually, and you will have a dry floor, I just can't belief he didn't have that for you?"

"Oh you know he is a loser, but he was the best choice at the time."

"Oh I gotcha" said I.

I made it back to see the wall was coming in nicely, it was level, straight and in line as I took over the setting of logs in the trench, as the girls back filled the hole, the line ran south to north, to just about their old house, as we finished the 100 feet, or about 20 poles, those monster logs took up room, and then then scaffolding was built, to the top, and a top cap for that wall was nailed into position. as it was it for this day.

July 21st Tuesday, 2004

It was early as we rose, we heard rustling, in the courtyard, I was up, with Enfield in hand, stepped out of the teepee to several raccoons, three shots later, three were dead as the others scurried off, I set them up to skin them, and gut them, chopping up the meat to dry, as I set out their hides, and tanned them, before we left. The only reason we don't move to the north compound is no bathing and bathroom place yet. I'm still working out the details. We took off a bit late, but wasn't the only one late, as Brian was sore, and took his time getting up there, I began to set the next wall in, about a hundred feet wide, where another trench was dug, as John was in that trench, as for them they lived in the cabin till this new place was ready. I worked hard, dropping the ready logs to go in, as 100 feet was soon ate up quickly, to lunch as the wall was in, fastened down, crossed hammered, now it was to the middle where John and Billy dug the holes for the center supports, and the ten twenty fine footers five feet in diameter, which was huge. The idea of having a 10,000 square feet of space for the cattle made sense, especially during the heart of winter. Where they would have to survive, while living in the cold. Now in the open it may get down to minus 30, but in this place, probably just at freezing. The idea for the open end to the north was for the north wind, and a breeze would feel nice to the cattle as they went through the storm thought I, and a place to keep them safe. Then one by one the 25 foot five feet in diameter, so it was center first, then on the end, then in the middle, as we went to the dark. We left.

July 22nd Wednesday 2004

It was day 54, and we were at John's early, but not before a another spectacular breakfast, Anna packed a lunch, and we were off after feeding our animals, and cleaning up and today was the first day I drank milk, it was cold and good. We had found our water box stays cool, in the shower so we put the milk in that in an aluminum pail. I placed the next eight poles in the ground, we were ready for the roof to go on, 55 footers 3 feet in diameter split, which Brian was doing on rafters, and for the first two on the end took the longest as we used the scaffolding to support the tripod, as we used that to hoist a split pole into position on the roof, as I moved it down, to the very end, and nailed it down. I usually like to do one side at a time, but, seeing this was free standing and all that, I moved the tripod, up on the top roof that had four split logs in place on both sides, and the other in the middle. We were ready to haul up logs to the roof, it was fierce on the wind side, but steady, as after the scaffolding went into place, on the outside, Anna went on the roof, with Lily's help, the two were patching, with mortar, as I had, split logs coming from both sides, at five feet over, Billy was hammering them down on one side, while John on the other, it was fast going, I hammered them on top, it went smoothly to the middle, where we worked through lunch, as there wasn't anything for anyone, except us on the roof, Kim forgot it was her turn to feed the crew, as she went with Laurie to do something. About two hours later they returned with hot pizza, and root beer ice cream floats. They had four pizza's, and after the four of us ate, there was only about two pieces for each girl, and they were larges. We resumed work as all was forgotten, with Kim and I, as we rushed to finish, to the south, and at the north. At the end. I set it in place, and went back to see the progress of Anna and Lily, to the patching, as Brian instructed the men inside, on extended scaffolding, to put up 2x4's underneath to hammer to the roof, at five rows on each side, they were not happy, but neither Brian nor I cared, as it tightened up the roof. As it took the rest of the day. Anna and I left, and ate our stuff on the way back.

July 23rd Thursday 2004

It was day 55, and back at John's, Anna fixed another great meal, as we left, this time I had enough slates to roof his roof. We drove over there, as no one was moving, as I arrived, to see that the inside was still not done, as I went up, and took it to the length, nailing in the 2x4's it was hard work but needed to be done, before I cap it, as the mortar was still setting, due to the damp weather, Brian arrived, then finally, John, then Billy, as I instructed them to put down the shingles, first on the north side, as Anna helped guide them, as it went fast for the five of us. Till they were done, and went over to the other side, while I finished the inside rows all five of them on each side. Brian was tired of the shingle work, besides he got a nasty splinter, for Laurie to get out, it was deep, and he was gone awhile, as the other two were slacking off, as I went to the roof, to finish, as those two left. So it was me, Anna and Lily finishing off the roof. It took all of the rest of the day, that's how far off we were.

July 24th Friday, 2004

It was day 56, and it was Anna and myself there and the help no where to be found, as we finished the roof, mortared it and top capped it. And it took to lunch when Brian showed up, we decided to start on the home place with a trench we started on, out 20 feet we placed logs at the front, it was 3 footers in diameter, fifteen feet long, and with the tripod, we began to set them, from the proposed garage, it was 7 logs down, then split those 3 foot in diameter, upwards for the raised floor to make the garage floor, on the massive wall, we nailed in a split 3 foot in diameter. Brian dug, the rest of the way, to 120 feet and I choke and pulled them into place, then used the tripod to set in, and instantly it was coming together, although the wall, did need some support, especially when holding the roof, as it was 30 foot long 3 foot split, I hammered on, as it was smooth going. Anna grouted the roof, and sealed as I went ahead of her. We built a ten foot gate, and hung it with hardware, to see it open up, it was nice, on the other side we dropped eight more logs leveled and cross tied them together. As another gate was assembled, and hung, it to slid shut under the force of the wind. Inside it was nice as the day was done. I was beginning to think the Locke's just didn't like me, well John anyway. He was missing again.

July 25th Saturday 2004

It was day 57, and I know for a fact John was pissed off that we didn't help him out sooner, well he never asked, he just assumed I was supposed to help him out. Maybe he needed an attitude adjustment, I thought, beat the shit out of him, to get my point across, as Brian was here with me, as Anna stayed at home, with Lily. Brian continued to dig, the back part, as we needed a fifteen foot log long, by 3 feet in diameter for the rest of the house. John was there, by Kim's orders, he dug out their root cellar, something he wasn't too happy about, as I had the supports in place, as Brian had the logs on rafters, to split in half, I laid the 30 foot split rails up, on the roof and even, down the entire 100 and forty feet. Next was his left over plywood, from the house, as it went down over the top of the floor on the east side, to the rear and south was a place for the kitchen, where stairs go down to the root cellar. A wall, was placed, by using my chainsaw, and cutting off the ends, to be flat, it sat on top of each other, meanwhile, the bulk of the logs, were put in the ground as we went out 20 feet, turned the corner and up 100 feet. The remaining was up on rafters, to be split in half. John continued to work to level the logs on this side, while I was still putting the floor in. I finished this portion it was nice, as it was made as a box in the ends, and now, straight going up. When I got to the already made garage, I was done with the floor. That is when the roof was next, and where everyone pitched in, and split logs were being set coming from the roof, at the end, it was cut to fit, to make up the turn. I went back to laying plywood on top of the split logs, to form a nice floor, even it was nice. I finished the first load bearing wall, to put around the root cellar. I made custom stairs, down, to help John out. Next was the back wall, where I cut out a door, to get in. I fashioned a door, with hinges and a handle. The next project was the rest of the floors to the northwest garage. I was hoping it would rain, and no luck, so it was back up to the roof to make sure it was going in right. Brian joined me to put the roof on, with John's help. They set the thirty footers split

3 foot diameter logs, it was fast going, as it was straight, and down to the first load bearing wall, to close in the garage, two set of tracks were hung and the door went in place, it worked perfectly. It was the day. I went home, to a treat, a nice meal was prepared, and followed with a nice hot soaking bath, then a full body massage. And then I went to sleep.

July 26th Sunday 2004

It was day 58 I awoke to a phenomenal breakfast and Anna saying, "What can I do for you darling?" which I thought was weird, as she said her garden was producing well, for I to say, "I've got to go to John's to finish his house, so she said she would go, and got into her mud outfit, and we stopped off to get Brian and Lily, whom looked suspicious, over something, as we all four rode in the jeep, up to John's, and went right back to work as another hot and sunny day. Brian set on the roof, as I set in the walls, cross wise, building bedrooms up to the outer roof, on the east side, as Brian, Anna, and Lily were on the roof, it was Brian who handed the mortar up to them, via the tripod, it was fast going, to the two small rooms, then the shower and tub, was a platform raised, down to a laundry tub, like the swollen spring box, it was a laundry over flow, not hooked up yet. Anna and Lily were on the making of the fireplace, after I set the small foundation, she went to work setting bricks, and mortaring them in, with left over pipe, I pushed a section, up through a hole, I precut below, as Brian fished it on the roof. Finally John helped, when Billy came over, to help set the shingle to finish the roof, along the south side. He was impressed with the whole cattle configuration, but questioned the opening at the front. I told them I would close it but cattle need fresh air to breathe, and by closing this in, they would die, and that stopped that, besides a few fire places, may warm up the area, it was fast going now, as Anna was starting to frame the corner fireplace, for the master bedroom. I finished the kitchen walls, the two guys, were getting into the saw guide, and shaving the logs flat, then set in place, as a back wall went up, to eight feet.

Next was the kitchen fireplace, went where the door was going, for the 10 foot wide deck. I moved the door into the planned dining room, as the end was put in, Anna was there to set another fireplace, I set in the office inner walls, on the other side, then up from that the living room, and finally to the garage which was already done, it went faster than I thought, especially, when all four of us, worked on it. Now it was done. The last details was the roof shingles, and windows cut, as I had to place a window in each room, I needed to cut, while everyone else, went onto the scaffadollng, to lay slats, under Brian's direction, they began the 35 foot inward. While I cut the window in the garage, on the east side, to see the slide window, I used stringers to frame it in, and then mortar and set the window. Then went in, to the next room. Anna came to me to say, "They want an additional fireplace?"

I said, "So put it in, we have the bricks, right?"

"Yeah, that's right but they are so demanding."

"That's why they are greedy people, looks like we have one more day here, as I cut into the massive log, framed it in, and then mortared it and set it in, it set nicely, as bedroom 1 was done, it was time to call it quits. We sealed up our buckets, and we were off.

July 27th Monday 2004

It was day 59, almost two months, and was getting tired of helping others, but we got up and Anna made a marvelous breakfast, she said, "I need to go get more limestone, for the mortar."

"So let's do that first thing" I said. We were still sleeping in the teepee, but I imagine I will be told when we have to move." We dressed, and went out to another clear and sunny day. I drove out to the limestone place, a quarry, that was being dug out, as pieces of flagstone, broke off, and was loaded up, till she was happy, and we drove back over to the Locke's, and past their cattle. Drove in, and parked, I carried the limestone over to a cradle, which had some sides, so that I can crush the limestone with the sledgehammer. Once I was done with that, I went back inside from a door I cut to the south, John and Kim were both up, and organizing, she in her kitchen, and him, in his garage as Brian was over, and installed the new garage doors, as the roof needed to be finished, so they took to ladders to begin to shingle the roof, and John asked for an awning, or more like a carport like Brian's, so Brian agreed, and looked at what we had left, and set out stakes, as I came out and said, "Don't worry about that yet, lets finish your roof, and set the drains, and connect up the plumbing."

They all nodded. I went to the next room 2, and cut the next window, framed it in, and then set and mortared it in place. The next room was the shower, and laundry room, it was near dark, except for the lamps, fixed to the wall, there was a gap between the wall and the roof, for ventilation. As I saw a huge 4x8 glass, nearly the size of the wall, I conferred with Kim, and she wanted it horizontal, but the fireplace was in the way, as I said, "Its best in the kitchen", so I had Billy help me move it, in favor of two small windows on either side, it was nice, and the windows were vertical, to be positional to the shower, and possible bathtub later. Next room was a door, out to the deck, it was wrap around, as all others were on the roof, putting down shingles. I used my big saw, and before, I used a white crayon, and set where the door would go at, and went for it, it was like knife through butter, the cut logs fell away, as it was clean, I framed in the cut door, and set the hinges, and threshold, and then the door, it was inside, and then shut, to a door knob, and it was done. I closed the door, in the master, and went to the window, next to the door, I marked it out, and cut it out, instantly let in the outside, as I framed it up, and then set the window, square, and then added mortar to finish. Over to the south wall, a door was planned, but I thought where will the bed go, in the master bedroom?" so I went looking for other windows and found two small ones, even on the master room, to the south, I measured, and cut the first window, next to the fireplace, and then on the other side, where the bed would go, and added another window. Next was the kitchen, where the proposed pantry was going, and I set where it should go, then cut it out, framed it in, and set with mortar, into the frame. I remember her saying she wanted a shelf unit, below the window. Next I moved around the kitchen, and to the wall next to the root cellar, it was dark, with light, I marked out a window, 2x 4 feet, and cut it out, then framed it in, to allow the light in, I set the window, with mortar, it was done. Around the wall, was the cooking fireplace, it was huge, a window on both sides, I cut them, all at once, then framed them in, and then set them in, it was next to a door, that was left open. Then over to the dining room, another window on the south, next to the end and the fireplace, it was cut, and went in easy. Now 4 windows to go, as lunch was called. As Laurie and Kim came back from the store, with pizza, and beers. We ate and drank, and then it was every one helping me to set the huge glass, from what looked like a sliding glass door, minus the frame, just a solid piece of glass. I showed them where it was going, they agreed, I marked it, and then cut it, afterwards, it was solid, as I framed it in on the outside, using slats of cut wood, as a frame, and then, carefully mortared it in, and then cut pieces around it, to set and I said, "Wow, does that ever let in the light", it lit up the kitchen. Next room was north on the west side, was the proposed office, where a desk was at, I cut the hole, and framed it in, and set in the window. Next room up was the living room, the floor was nice, as they used all of their plywood. A box or fifty five gallon drum wood stove, was next, so I cut a window, and framed it in, then set it in, this is where the front door was going, they had a larger than life solid oak door, which was huge 5x 7in half foot with knocker, as I framed it out, I cut it open, then framed it it allowed all kinds of wind to come in, till Billy and I set it in, and it closed. Last was the garage, which, was open, and a floor, which had plywood on, as they set the rails, while I marked and cut out the last window, framed it in, and set it and mortared it into place. While door by door went on. The next thing I did was set the gutter, and where it would flow to, as barrels were set, only to have Kim come to me to say, "Matt, can you come into the kitchen?"

I followed her in, to see four more windows, for her to say, "You forgot four?", she left as I saw it was in the five foot diameter logs, and I had 4x4 windows, I have to say, this was the hardest job I ever did, as they were going to be in the center of the logs, now that was a feat, but the really bad problem was the constant bickering from them over how high they wanted the windows, till finally they agreed, and marked them out, then using the big saw went straight in, then over, then up, and over, pulled it out, to see it was clear, I stepped up on the cradle, and used my foot to kick it out, it was stuck, so I went around, and on the inside which was nice, to see the problem, and using my big saw I cut it free, then did a slice cut, to make sure it was free. It took me over 8 hours for four, as much time as the entire 18 other windows, as it was actually starting to get dark, as Kim told me I wasn't done till those windows were done, as the breeze was cold. So into the night on some dried beef, and fresh bread, a bit toasted with peanut butter and jelly, I set in the first window, it was in but kinda weird, then the next one went in easier, as the same for the last two, we were done, and picked up our tools, and tripod, and left. I was mad at the way she talked to me, as so was Anna.

July 28th Tuesday 2004

Finally able to relax, we were done, well except for the flooring for the deck, but I didn't care as I asked Anna if she wanted to go exploring, on day 60?"

She said "Sure just as long as I get some running water?"

I said, "Yes Dear."

We had a filling breakfast, and we dressed in our hip waders, and took our fishing poles, we set out, past her garden, and around it to the red wood patch, and to the fast moving stream, of the White river, and I helped Anna across, and to the other side, as the water was coming from everywhere, as we made it to the middle, then I saw how it turned in the bend, to think, "That is where we need to put the pipe in, and take it to the camp, as we climbed, up and around, to see somewhat a lake, built by beavers, I had my rifle, slung over my back for protection, as we went further, up and back, it was going in a ravine, as hills were on both sides, we went a ways, as we went up, as the walls of the canyon rose high, we were in a deep ravine, not much of anything, except, we were on Beaver creek, according to my map, as the White river, was over aways, but still on our property, Anna was all over the gold nuggets this far up to say, "Look Matt, all around its gold."

I looked and it was fun just picking up the pieces, as we stayed in that part till lunch, easily filing a bag of burlap, with nuggets. It was fun, and the water was crystal clear. But it also meant wild animals, of all kinds lived there, up on the upper shelf, was a large moose, over a ways, was a bear, it was like we were at a zoo, but down in the front, in a creek, observing this spectacle, it was amazing, I sat and watched the animals interaction, as it was a neutral free zone, between two great beasts, while they were playing in the White river, which had the strongest runoff, and waterfalls, I made it up on the other bank, to see another stream, not as violent as ours, but in the distance a drop off, and another huge waterfall, as I looked at my GPS, to determine it was on the property, all this time, Anna was still picking up visible nuggets, I stood, thinking of how to get the water to camp, as for lunch came and went, I had a chunk of dried beef, which I ate half, and gave the other half to Anna, hoping to catch a white fish, but it eluded her, when I looked up and there was the bear, ready to attack, and from that moment to when I pulled around that rifle, to my shot, it fell dead at her feet. She backed away to the bank, it was huge, easily 12 feet in length, I field dressed it right there, as I cut its legs from its body, it was easily 2000 lbs., I was working, with Anna beside me, as we set aside everything, for me to say, "Let's go get the jeep."

"Wait one of us needs to stay here" said Anna

"Then who is going to get the Jeep?" I asked.

"I will, so you sit tight, I'll follow the river around, and go get the jeep." I was against it, but we had no choice, as I took off my sidearm, and she put it on, we kissed, as she was off,

I stayed to see the flies were forming, I buried the blood, as I took each piece of the inners to the river, to wash the blood off, meanwhile, Anna went through the woods, right to the south compound, and down a side, to see the jeep of Brian and Lily, they were walking all over calling out Anna's name, till she snuck up on Lily and said "Boo" she fell over in fear, dropping a loaf of bread. Anna laughed at her, she picked it up to say, "Hey that isn't fair, you scared me, what are you and Matt doing?"

"Oh we went exploring, on our property, why?"

"Really what did you find?"

"A place to pipe water to me, so that I may have running water", as she sees Brian, coming from the north compound, to say, "Hey where is Matt?" only to hear a rifle shot in the distance, for Anna to say, "Hurry up, he needs help, as she was emptying out the trailer, and placed in some shovels, to say, "Get in, do you have any waders?"

"No" they both said. For Anna to say, "In the horseshoe is a pair of wade boots, as Brian grabbed both pair, as Lily was in the back, and Brian in, she took off, and around her garden, as another rifle fire went off, she drove off, and splashed into the river, and kept on going, onto land, and instead of the river, she took the ravine up, to the next level, through grass, and up, and on the same part as Matt but, climbing up, and onto that surface, coming in through a flat lake, which she opened, to create a new waterfall, across it to stop, as another ravine was in her way, down, it to the other side was Matt, and four wolves, laid out, as I was skinning them, they left behind four cubs. Lily rounded them up, and with a rope tied them each a harness and tied them to a tree. Anna came running to me, as she slowed to see the carnage, four wolves, a beaver, and a woodchuck. I was waiting, as she hugged me and kissed me to say, "You're alright" for me to say, "And you brought guests, as Brian was there to help, with the animals, it was as if he already knew what to do, the bag of gold, was taken, by me to the jeep, which was in a serious mess, it was stuck, for Anna to say, "But I wanted to get to your aid."

I put my hand up and she was quiet, while Brian loaded up the meat, I had to turn the jeep around, not because I can maneuver better and that the meat will be safely up, than down, using my winch, I undid it, and found a tree, and set it around, I got in, activated it, I was in neutral and it pulled me up, then stop, set it in gear, I went up and undid it, I retracted it and got in, as the meat took the back and front seat, Brian, Lily with four cubs, and Anna walked down the other way, as I drove the way she came in, to see a huge problem, through the river and bank, so I stopped at the river, and undid the cable, and went over to the tree, got in, and allowed the winch, to pull us through the water, up the bank, on the other side, I unclipped, retracted and got in, over the river, through the redwoods, and to the south compound and took the meat into the smoker. And then set the fire, and took the hides and began to assemble them on stringers, the carcass was cut up, and set aside, I allowed the smoke to preserve the meat, to make later into meal. The group came back as Brian held the rifle, and back in, for a feast that Anna and Lily went into prepare. Of venison, some bear into a hearty stew. From the teepee, she carried out to the table, to us while we waited. They had dinner with us, and enjoyed it who knew, vegetarians would eat beef?" later they left.

We went in to retire.

July 29th Wednesday 2004

It is day 61, and the day is already warm, muggy, and again no bugs, "Nice" I said to myself. I went into my shop, opened the inside doors, and began to put the stripping together, to form a small box, it was 20 feet long by a foot, and took others, to be another 20 feet long, I estimated I need about four hundred feet from the stream to the compound, the issue will be the turn, to the shower, and greenhouse. And then to the teepee. I now had 100 feet, which is 5 of them, I also needed ramps, to rise the water level up, that distance, I would need two each for ten, from small to high, and through the woods, bend around slowly, to the water box. At lunch they came over, to say "Hi, and Whatcha doing?"

"Putting in a water supply for Anna."

"Oh right, because Lily had one first" said Brian.

"Yes, because Lily, then Kim, and so forth and so on". I said comically.

They had the rest of the hearty stew, being kept in the root cellar, in the north compound, while I figured out, what to do with the sink, and moving the bed, and tub, let alone a wood stove, plus oven, hence the trip to Anchorage. Still waiting approval. I built several cradle of logs, so why not build a wood box, as the wood will swell, to seal the ends, so I built a box, using wood, 6x6x6, x 6 high, and built it on the above platform, under the roof, using a saw I cut into the side of the eastern wall, in the horseshoe. And ran the wood pipe, all the way across, to the water box. It was set, as I went out, the wind had picked up, as I went to the line, it was a little even, as I got to the stream, but the angle was too steep, into the box as I checked it several time, so I went to the source, to see the water fall, and then connected more pipe, for another 100 feet. But the grade up was steep, as I had Brian, go up, and he said, "I think your cutting this way to short?"

"Then lift it up, and we'll add another piece," said I handed him up two pieces, using screws, he tied them together, then set in the water, using big rocks, he submerged it. Water was coming out every section, all the way in as the box filled up, as it slowed, to a trickle. I went back out to see the line had severed, to where it goes down, and slightly back up, to where a ramp needed to be higher, so I built that, set it under the bow, and it straighten up, to put the flow back on, I actually need some type of gate valve, because the water ran over it, and was causing more problems. Inside the bathhouse the water was everywhere, as I opened the door it was seeping in the soil. It came to me I needed a drain, so I cut a hole in the west side hole, in the top, and set in a measured pipe, about 5 feet, it cascaded over on the greenhouse, whereas I quickly made a box, using 8 footers, as a frame, it was two feet by two feet square. It was eight foot long and I affixed to the wall, as Brian helped me, and underneath it, I laid two pipes, one to the greenhouse, and the other two line one out and the other to the teepee. It lead out and one around, and out, as water shot out in the ditch out front, which instantly I could see another problem, I now had to build bridges over the fast filing up ditch, back inside the teepee, I needed to cut the floor and Anna came back to say, "No you're not, put something outside, and that I can dip it out."

"Yes dear" I said, as I went back to the shop, to begin on another box, it was about 3x3, feet and 3 feet deep, I then dug out the line, to set in in the ground, I dug out the box, and set it in halfway, and then set the dirt in around it, not to cover it up, and we did this all the way, to the fence, speaking of fence, I still need to finish the other, in the north compound."

Lunch was served, it was vegetable soup, with fresh bread.

Outside We heard a truck pull up, I was up first, and went to the fence to see it was John and Kim, get out, they had their trailer, in tow. He said, "Matt I have a surprise for you helping us, three cattle, two girls and a boy."

"That's fine, but what about you keeping them with the rest of them?"

"Well there is feeding them and the amount of hay and so forth, so they are yours now", he hands me the rope, for him to say, "Now I do want that rope back, you hear?"

They got back in, and drove off, towards town. I looked at Anna, who said, "Allow me to take them off your hands." She took them, and said, "Looks like you better build them a pen, or the wolves will get these too." "Indeed I had a surprise to contend with and some pretty bad neighbors, so we finished lunch, then Brian and I went across the field, to see the lush grass, and east of the north compound I made a few marking for a 100 x 100 area. Brian started to dig, while I went along the forest north, and marked the 40-120 plus large long trees, to be cut, then went up a hill a bit, toward the White river, as it cut into the banks, but noticed, where it would be nice, to put in the water line, and run it along the bank, into the northern compound. So I went back down the hill, to say

"Wait a minute, now that all the trees and stumps are nearly gone, we could plant this field in our own alfalfa, it's about five acres. I went back to see Brian was a digging machine, he was almost down the front line, I still had massive 5 foot trees cut at fifteen feet long, using my jeep and trailer, we moved the tripod into place, and loaded the five logs, and drove over on the turf, to Brian, then set up the tripod, and lifted one at a time, and set in the dry ground, as it was fast going. With those five in it was a fourth done, as I went back to do it all over again. Brian finished the five foot wide trench to the hundred feet. Then turned north, as the ground was going down, some, and now that was a problem, as I had set another five logs in, I saw Brian, easily ten feet lower than I, so either the logs had to be twice as long or go with the contour of the ground. Remembering in Alaska, during winter training last year, when it snowed it covered everything, and everywhere. The same goes for the animals, they need a spot, that they are safe from predators so I said to Brian, as he continued to dig, as I was calculating my next move. But in the meantime, I set five more logs in place. As it was getting dark and 20 hours of sunlight was fading. We went to bed.

July 30 Thursday 2004

It was warm already as it was day 62, and the plan today, is finish the confines of the pen, as the young steers slept in the middle tied to a pole. I and Anna went out after another hardy breakfast of dried beef, and potatoes, a staple diet up here. Anna mentioned to me, to build a perimeter fence around her garden, please. I said "Yes dear", just as long as she doesn't keep on pestering about that satellite TV. With so many logs around here, it was such an abundance, I was going north to thin out some of the trees we needed. For the top I finished the south part next to the road, next I stair-stepped the length's by having a long stringer on top for a level, going up to the top point, and then start going down to the north. I cut to the exact, with five feet in the ground, it was Lily and Anna burying the logs, with huge rocks collected.

It was level, all the way up to the middle, with twenty in the ground to make up 100 feet on the line, it was the size of our fort. I made the turn, and the first log was 20 feet, or twenty five feet total, as it went in, it was mammoth. As I set up the scaffolding, to tie it in, and hold, as we worked it back, it was hard, as we passed by lunch and on past dinner, we stopped for chipped beef and fried potatoes, and a flat bread, after that we were done, Brian and Lily went home. We went to bed.

July 31st Friday 2004

I woke up late, as it was day 63, and it was sunny and warm, it was late, as it was around noon, Anna wanted to go to town. So we loaded up, and I drove the jeep in with trailer, I parked it in front of the feed store, as she went in, to see Jake, I went to another concrete pad, to begin to break it up, inside she bought feed, to ask, "What have the Locke's bought if any?"

"They made their hay purchases" said Jake.

"Can I ask how much and what they paid?"

"No, but I do have it right here, as she saw, 600 bales at 2.00 each for 1200, but their waiting to fill the truck before they can send it, for her to say, "I don't think we paid that low how come?"

"Because that is rock bottom, and with that you get the dry hay, and what you got was the most expensive, alfalfa" said Jake.

"Speaking of alfalfa, we wanted some seed to grow our own."

"Doesn't work like that, it takes years to build a good crop, but if you insist I'll spare you a 55 pound bag."

"Will take it, plus oats, and barley, can we grow them all together."

"Or separate, it takes five clear cut acres each, and plant each in each own field, separate, then harvest at separate times."

"Or all at once?" asked Anna.

"True or all at once, so you have Alfalfa, oats, barley, what about wheat?"

"Sure, we will take wheat, and any cotton?"

"What do you think we live in the south?" said Jake.

"I was just asking" said Anna, who also picked up rabbit food, chicken, and then off to the side was a press, for her to ask, "Can we take that?"

He looked over to say, "That old thing, it's a grind wheel for flour."

"Precisely, but what about bones?"

"Like animals?"

"Yes like animals?"

"I'm sure but I do have a coarse stone wheel, I'll add, you still have credit, so you're alright, as I can see your man, doing what he is supposed to be doing."

"Leave him alone, now, where are we at, I saw you had linens in bolts."

"You are about 38,000 plus ahead."

"Then on your next shipment of hay, We will fill the truck, with another, prime hay, at 10 or the highest."

"You got it Anna, that same suppliers carries oats, and wheat to blend into flour, or I can get you large quantities of flour?"

"No that would be cheating, we grow and eat our own, besides were not big eaters, so a little goes a long way. She sees a shower head, and the plumbing to go with that. Then some tarps, and finally a thick plastic sheeting. To load up, and get some help, for Jake to say, "Go into the convenience store Rita would love if you said Hi?"

"I will, take care, as the jeep was loaded, she backed up, and to the trailer, as I set it back on the jeep, and continued to pick up pieces, as she went into the convenient store, as Rita lit up, to say, "My second customer today, so what will you have a fountain drink?"

"Nah, not interested, just to say Hi, and we will be off, as she saw a gambit of processed foods, then hugged her and said goodbye, as she went out, then remembered what Matt needed, and went in and picked up a jug of mix for his chainsaw. Rita wrote it down, and Anna was gone. She went to the jeep to say, "Come on Matt let's go, I have things to do", so I got in and away we went. We got back, to see it was full force, trucks were there, it was Billy, and John, who has since changed his tune, Kim, Laurie and Lily, were making mortar. I got out, to see the north line was complete, and now going south, whereas I told everyone to stop, as I explained to them, I was putting in the fence, as I explained let's put in the center poles, all seven, as I helped her off load, they dug the holes for the thirty footers. Then put up the scaffolding. Then it happened a visit from those in black Yukon vehicles from the territories, and it was John Hughes and Miss Grant. They exited with a team of experts, which was everywhere as I stood with John, whom said, "So I see you have improved this area, what of your plans to work for us?" he said so blatantly.

I said, "What did you say?"

"You know come work for us, as a conservationist."

"I'd have to think about that one, as I watched them go all around, for John to say, "Let's talk."

I walked with him as I saw Miss Grant, talking with the girls. Except Anna who was off loading. As we went into the horseshoe, as he looked out the windows, to say, "So your prepared for winter?"

"Yeah, I have enough right now, except enough meat."

"Well I have to say, your farther ahead than anyone, ever, and this lodge is blown up on the net, and the government's office has over 2500 plus requests, from all over Canada, your wilderness lodge, is featured all over the world, with just that alone, you solely have won this competition, but the governor wants to see how the rough weather affects all of you, I had a request, that you all would like to go to Anchorage, is this true?"

"Yes, to get a wood burning stove for my girl to cook on?"

"Yes you could go, but then forfeit the challenge, give your list to Mister Wilson, and just like the hay, you can have a stove, as for the sawmill, I know of a company well only one, who has a portable, it will cost you 10K, paid up front, I will have them, sharpen the blades, as I can see you really don't need it, your chain saws are working fine, as another person found John to whisper something, then leave, to turn to say, "Alright I will grant the trip, 24 hours, after we leave, you all travel together, and the challenge will held in limbo, till you arrive back, get all the stuff you need, then bring them back to Mister Wilson. Then you can pick them up in a week."

"Alright, so what you're saying, all of us use our own money?"

"Yes, if you can?"

"Yeah we have no problem, with that" said I confidently.

"Well for you have a credit of over thirty thousand dollars. I could have 10K of that in cash or carry."

"Alright, we will leave tomorrow, bout how long is the trip?"

"Probably 250 miles from here, about a four hour trip, good luck." I almost sensed something was up, for him wanting us to go, but I was suspicious, as all the work stopped I told the others, as some wanted to ride with others, but I told them, it was each in each vehicle, so they went to town and filled up, Anna did the same, and noticed a tire was wearing more than the others, and had Jake change all four, that took some time. She watched him, to say, "Why is Mister Hughes back up here?"

"You don't know do you?" said Jake.

"That's why I'm asking you" said Anna.

"It's all because of your boyfriend, who knew?"

"Who knew what?"

"That he could build those structures, he said, "You know he has done more than anybody in the last sixty days, than anyone, let alone, build three well four other sites."

"So what does that mean?"

"To me it sounds like he is a clear winner."

"What are you saying?"

"Just that in the will, that bestows the winner, all of this acreage some 90,000, and all of Dawson range, as this was once all of Rick Dawson's property, when he died, he asked the Territory to find a conservationist to keep his land and minerals safe from corporations mining efforts, so thus for the last 10 years this challenge was in place, now it's over, they have a clear winner, and the challenge real effort was to find that one person, whom could live here and protect all of this, after this in November I and Rita will be off, to retire, somewhere warm." Anna just kept quiet, as Jake did a great job, he even straighten up the top, to fasten it up correctly. Anna finished the detail work, as she was off with trailer in tow back to me. The others agreed to do the same, and would be here at 0500, so that night, they all left. We went to bed as Brian and Lily stayed the night.

CH 8

Anchorage is windy, we like it at home.

It was 0500, we left off, as a group, it was August 1st Saturday, 2004, it was day 64, as we took off, I was impressed with the new tires, all off road, as we took off in a formation, all the way to the paved road, and we went north to northwest, on hwy 1, we drove an hour to Tok, and then south on hwy 1, with about hundred and thirty eight miles to go, so really only about three hours tops. Meanwhile it was as if an army descended down on all four of our properties, each group on a mission to assets if we are ready for the winter, as John Hughes over watched the group, as one reported, "Sir, he has a rear to the compound water source."

"I can see that gusher, out front, but can they survive the winter?"

"I believe so" said Miss Grant, each of them has enough space and is built so nicely it appears it will be a fairly easy chore".

"Do you foresee any problems?"

"No not right now, both of their compounds are stout, not to mention the stock pens, its clever, to build roofs over the areas, and gives them 16, 800 sq. feet on the ground and 4000 sq. feet on the second level, plus another 10,000 across the way, not bad, we heard from your friend, they could have a saw mill out tomorrow, as ordered" said Miss Grant.

"I want this here for a gift to them from us, to him."

"It will be taken care of, oh one more thing, when I took the women's psyche evals it seems each had a special fondness to Matt, do you think that is a coincidence or there is something more to this?"

"Don't read into that, the guy is a stud, who knew he would build all that he did, and cleanup these yards, these are the most beautiful structures I've ever seen, as he took a picture, of the north compound, to say, "This is going in on our tourism site, this is really impressive."

As someone called out, "The transport is on its way."

"Now were in business, make sure you document everything and we will be off, and I will leave two behind to make sure its set in on the west side of this compound, understood."

They all nodded as a helicopter came in and off he went going towards Alaska.

I drove towards Anchorage, as I pass through four mountain passes, as we were going downward, only to think that we would be going upward going home. The road was solid, and we were all traveling at a good pace, overhead a helicopter flew by, as I drove on into Anchorage, and that's where we all went our separate ways, we all agreed to meet up at eight to go back, on the outskirts, I and Anna we were going to a junk yard, our phones all pointed us to one, as we pulled in, it was just opening, its doors, we drove in, got out to see an old timer to say, "So Jake sent you two?"

"Yes, we were looking for a wood stove modern, as he points to a white one, propped up, he said "Its 2500 cash."

As we backed away, for him to say, "Oh alright, I won't gouge you 2000."

"I counted out our money, and paid him, and they forklifted it onto the trailer, and I tied it down. It was nice, it had a double oven, and top stove, a warming box, a place for a tea or coffee pot, and a long stove pipe, I was eager to go search, and she let me go, as she was also searching for other stuff, I came across a wash tub, and several other water trough's, and some piping, and water connections, and he was generous as what he was charging us, as all of that stuff fit in our trailer. She found tools, like rakes, and a hand plow, several wheel barrows, a table, with fold up legs, a kiln, and a sewing machine, she asked for a yarn and fabric shop, and the old timer pointed us in the right direction. We paid another five hundred and we were away, we were loaded, Anna was happy. As for Brian he was off to a freight carrier, and struck up a deal, to transport all of his mushrooms, and was given the appropriate boxes in a crate, that was set on his trailer, Lily called Anna to see where she was at, Anna answered, "To the yard shop, for bolts of fabric." She gave her the address and details, as this was where we were at a crossroads, as I wanted something else entirely different, but Anna said, "Please come in with me, as we both went in, as she had bolts of yarn and I was the suppose carrier and 2500 dollars later we were done, we put it all in the back, in plastic as it was all sealed up. Just to see Brian and Lily arrived, smiling, as she took Anna aside to show her her new winter outfits, for Brian to say to me, "Whatever makes her happy, so hey, I got us a carrier, they will come up three times a week, starting first of September, and if this doesn't work out, I read in the local paper a 250 acre parcel is available for 100K, do you want to jump on it?"

"Perhaps, do we need a warehouse, to work out of?" I asked.

"Wait you mean transport them ourselves to here and then ship out?"

"Yeah like at the airport," I said.

Brian looked dejected as Lily said "Don't worry, I'll model these for you, when we get home."

"It's not that, I made a huge mistake," said Brian.

"Well then let's go fix it", as I waved goodbye to Anna to say, "Honey, Brian and I have to go fix something, I'll catch back up with you in an hour," she waved me off, so the two of us went south, to the west to the airport, as flights flew in and out, and over to the manager, and I and Brian went in, to see Bill Arthurs, public works manager, he came out to say, "How can I help you fellows?"

We both looked out of place, to say, "I, We need a space in which to store and ship our products, do you have anything?"

"Yes three hangers on the back side of the airport."

"How much a month?" I asked.

"Nope it's on a yearly basis, plus you have access to all the shipping containers and movers."

"How much is that" I asked.

"20,000" as I looked at him, to say, "So if we give you 20K, we get a hanger, plus access to shipping, I say let's do it?"

Brian was stunned, as Bill said, "Allow me to show you which one, for me to say, "Does it have access to truck deliveries,?"

"Yes, allow me to show you" as I and Brian and Bill left, just as the girls showed up, apparently they were right behind us, then someone saw Anna to recognize her from the challenge, and then they were indentated as there was so many questions, then someone from the airport came to their rescue, and led them to a room. While Bill drove us the long way around, to say, "See this is all new, yet, you will have a cool or warm cooler, and freezer if need be."

"Nah, we need a place we could get it to 50 degrees moderate temperatures" said I.

"Sound like your growing mushrooms."

"In fact we are" said I.

"Your joking right?"

"No, why" I asked.

"Just last week, a mushroom company showed some interest but was waiting, to see if an off-site location, was better, now if you sign this deal today, you have full exclusivity to the airport, unlike that other group."

We shook hands, as he showed us the perfect location here on the end, I used the credit I had, as we signed the deal, for Yukon Mushroom Organics LLC, to use this space, it was 100x100, ware house and a front counter for selling, directly, as we were going to be in the chamber of commerce, and in all the upcoming airport's special listings. We left with keys in hand, going 50/50 in this venture. I collected up the girls and I still had some money as we went to the mall. Brian, went back to that carrier to re-worked the deal with the carrier, and it saved him thousands. Anna and Lily went shopping at the mall, I went and got another pair of boots, this place was packed with a lots of young people. I was more preoccupied, at the arcade, and playing pool, for a kid to say, "That table is no good, if you go to east street club, they have all kinds of tables."

"What's wrong with this one?"

"Oh nothing its worn, we are trying to sell it for 500?"

I said "Sold", and counted out five hundred, I liked it when I hit a ball it made a clunk noise it was great, we carried it outside to my already loaded trailer, and set it down, as I cleared a space for it, we hoisted it, and it sat nicely and they used plastic wrap to wrap it up, everything pool sticks and all. I took a tarp, which Anna bought, and over the entire thing, and used tie down straps to secure it. Then went back inside, as she was in a book store, a twenty five book high so far, near a register, in this whole store was maybe, four people, max, as Anna said, "Honey find something you like, I looked around, I wasn't much of a reader, although there was this book, called Parthian Stranger, now that seemed interesting, and it was a series book, I got all 21 books, and brought them up, and set them down. She paid using her credit card, which was her Daddy's. We were off, as I said "Anywhere else?"

"No, I think I'm done, say honey when will the satellite TV be up and running, as I said "Batteries, Ah Shucks, and the chainsaws, to see Brian and Lily meet up with us, for I to say, "So how much room do you have left in your back of your jeep?"

"I have the back seat and cargo space?"

"I need both, can you put the yardage in your back seat" I asked Brian, which he did. As we went from the mall to an auto parts dealership as the three of us went in, I met with Stewie, the manager, and told him what I wanted to do, he said, "You'll need twelve batteries, set in parallel sequence, to a transformer, which will hold your energy, then a converter, from dc to ac power, as it was 120 each for 12, and cables and wires, so it was about 1500, he told of us where I could go to acquire the transformer and a generator, but it would be spendy, we arrived, at Mountain Energy, and met with Tom, whom was a genius, as I had all the batteries in the back of the jeep of Brian's all sealed, for him to say, these generators produce the lowest amount of energy, 10K each, but gave me a schematic on what to build, as he did that for a lot of home owners, and the transformer is also 10K, which I was now over money wise, but Brian and Lily put their money in. Then after that we went to the assayers office, and took our five pounds of nuggets, they were weighed off, 5 pounds 2.35 ounces, @ 1 troy ounce was 1000.00, we ended up at 43,351.60 cents, but after they came back to say "It has no flaws, it pure, meaning found in the wild, it went up to 1106.96. Our pay out was 47,986.71, paid in cash as the Guy said, "Where did you find it at?" I looked at him to say, "On the Yukon river."

"Oh" he said, as we left, as it was getting later, way past any food reserves we had left, so we went to a local diner for burgers and fries and milkshakes. I asked for a phone book, to find a hardware store, that sells chainsaws, so when we were done, we drove over to this place, ready to lock up, just before five, I went in, to see the line of chainsaws, I chose five more, and ten chains each, a box of files, he threw in helmets and ear phones, and chaps, to a total of 1500, I paid cash, we left to go back to the mall, as I dropped off the jeep and trailer, I took the other Jeep with Brian and we went to a home improvement store, I got boxes of long nails, to screws, curtain rods, for windows, to blacksmith tools, oil cans, tool things, and gate kits, for big gates. A couple of helmets, needless to say, I filled that Jeep grand Cherokee, as Brian drove off, he actually had to take me out of the store, as we left, he said, "Do you want an ice cream?"

"Nah, not much into sweets" I said.

"Oh this ain't sweets its yogurt."

"Yogurt, Oh all right, as we went through dive thru, our trailer climbed the curb, and took out a bush, as he ordered two banana splits, with everything, to ask me, "You want anything to drink?"

"Nah" I said, as he paid, as the trailer made a noise, as it took off for Brian to say, "It's through now, and handed it to me, as I looked at it, and my first bite was a bunch of good flavors, he drove out of there, causing a bit of more trouble, as he ran over another plant, leaving, and over to the mall and the other jeep, it was overloaded. We parked and at 6 pm when it was closed the two girls were ushered out of the mall, and I got out, to give half of my split to Anna, who was excited, as she got into the jeep, and we were off. We made it to the outskirts of town, to the freeway and parked. At just around eight, it was Billy and Laurie, we got out to see their finds, it was all animals, and a horse. Weird I thought, to say, "So Laurie did you go to the mall, as everyone looked at me, for her to say, "No I didn't, Billy needed more animals, and just like that John and Kim arrived, we all went to see more cattle, and some equipment, and then loaded up and took the slow trip home.

August 2nd Sunday 2004

It was early and back at Beaver creek, we all went to the loading dock to offload, each had a block of time, into the feed part and when we did that, we ended up working the rest of the day breaking concrete pads, and set it on my trailer and Brian's, as we took several trips, up, and dumped it next to the south compound as Anna was ready to build a brick factory, and do some pottery. This day was shot. But it got done finally. Brian was in speed mode, as Charley had finished out the last of the orders, and filled a cargo van, he sold the place in Missouri, and was heading up, but along the way, collect certain trees, with chain saw in hand, he cut them as needed, he was taking his time coming up.

August 3rd Monday, 2004

It was day 66, and each of us went down, to claim what we bought, it was the animals first, on Monday, and Billy, and

Laurie, while Brian and I were still finishing the roof details on the animal pen, as I was setting the split logs in place, Brian was throwing them up using the tripod. John felt bad, so he was there too, helping to set, choke and drag them to Brian, who sets them up to me. We set the logs, north to south, as I saw it first then said "What the hell", as there was a saw mill, on the eastern side of the north compound, I was anxious but had to stay on the roof, as I waited for the logs, then hammed the long nails in, it was nice. Those long nails were hard to find. We found out from Billy, we were last to get our Anchorage stuff, probably on Thursday. Next to go was John, as he was happy, he left, as lunch was served, mine was set in a basket, with Anna and she went up on the roof via a ladder and we had lunch together, for her to say, "So how long were you going to hid this from me?"

"What are you saying?"

"About the mushrooms."

"Oh that, not much to tell, during the Marines, I ran across this guy Brian, from a friend of mine, who introduced me to his sister, who said her brothers business was failing, and could I help out, so I met him, and saw whom had a struggling business in growing mushroom in Missouri he wanted to make me a partner, I helped him and gave him 25,000, he then put 100,000 in my bank account, so now were here, and we have a place in Anchorage airport, and Lily's brother is coming up as we speak with a cargo van, to run that operations, with his girlfriend, soon to be wife."

"Anything else?"

"No that's it baby, it's just you and I, so how do you like the water in the south compound?"

"O Kay, now you need to get it to the north, so we can move in."

I said to myself, "Always something, Aw shit, maybe get rid of her?" I thought, as she was done, and took out her mortar bucket, and began to patch the cracks. I continued to set the boards, it was over hanging five feet, as the north side was done, on that end we put a gutter, on the ends we, turned it upward, and led it to an angle, to a catch box, then down, and Brian cut into the log, and stuffed the drain, I went to the other side, to align the new split logs, the wind cut through but that was perfect, it was warmer, my plan was for four fireplaces, as the last split log was in place. I waved off Brian, whom took it inside, I went down a ladder, and was inside the sloping pasture, I set a stake where the fireplaces would be at. As I went over to my new saw mill, it was good, two lanes for logs, to make beams and planks, but I knew I needed a roof over this, I looked at the pen, and the frame, so I showed Brian what I was going to do, is bridge the gap and in close all of this in, from the pen to the compound, and slope it down, to the gutter, it was five feet up off the ground, with a top walk, next to the blade, and the motor house in front enclosed in a room. A top cap kept the blade safe, as we drug in twenty five footers, to assemble the south part and to the feed bin, by elevating it to two feet, off the ground. Then by using poles, to nail together to the wall, at ten feet high, then to the other side, at 100 feet distance to cover, plenty of room, to divide this place, while Anna worked on the animal pen's roof, Brian was bringing in more logs, to the north, where I went back to the animal pen and was building a ramp of sorts, to level out the surface, as that day was done.

August 4th Tuesday 2004

It was day 67, and it was John and Kim still getting their prizes from Anchorage. Anna was still fuming about the mushroom business, because breakfast was dried beef, and day old bread, I was in the dog house, but that was just a ploy, as Lily arrived to save the day, and told her if they didn't have my money the business would be dead, so he saved our lives."

"But why did he keep it from me?" she asked.

"He didn't, he told you when we built the warehouse, don't you remember, and you were cool with it then and what now has changed" asked Lily concerned.

"Well the way it happen" said Anna losing the battle as Lilly just left, to help out, I set 3 foot wide diameter split board up, and then across the hundred foot gap, but had to set in a halfway support, to keep it from sagging, we had a chain from those bikes, we found in the junkyard to make a ganty crane, so I built the support underneath, as the last of the roof was in place, it was ready, it was level downward and the split logs in place, nailed in, but it was sagging still in the middle, so next was center supports, at twenty feet apart, Brian dug the holes, as I used the tripod, to lift up one side and set it in the middle, then one outside of it, then one on the end. Up to the front, I hoisted it up, and set in a pole in the middle, then lastly one on the end, as all were about the same height, as I set it down, then we hammered them in place, using the scaffolding. So much to do, now with all this upcoming water, especially from this sloped roof to the north compound. For where to put a cistern, I cut a corner out of the edge of the north east wall of the north compound, set in a support, then built a frame with spit logs, all the way up, and in front of it a set of stairs, I then had Brian send up me ten foot split logs, notched, and first built a square frame to sit on, and nailed in, as the walkway was covered, then a floor, was set and sawed off, to form an opening to walk up, and now the outside logs, to go into place, shaved on the ends, it went up quickly. To form up to eight foot walls, Brian moved the scaffolding over to assist me, on the lookout, a window was scheduled for every side, I cut them out individually, then framed them in, and set it, and mortared in place, one at a time, till all four was done, it was higher on the south as it was lower to the north, and split logs, were placed on top, and the split logs filled the gaps. It was done so was I. I went to the teepee, and it was empty, so I went to the north compound, and there she was, in her kitchen, cooking away, as the white stove was delivered, and set up, without me knowing, and the bed also was moved. She said, "Hi Honey, go sit in our dining room table, dinner will be ready shortly, as Lily will help me", as I took a seat, so did Brian, as the table was also something we picked up, for I to say, "Who helped you all to do this?"

"Oh John, and Jake and two other men, brought up some of what we needed now", as I ate, it was, fantastic, even Brian raved, how much it tasted so good. Lily was impressed as fresh baked bread, and butter from Billy's. It was jam, from the store. I finished and went out to look at the sawmill, then to the new pen, and the awaiting logs to be put in, to form a pond of sorts, inside the pen. Next was the pen doors, made of split logs, I formed up a frame, six feet tall, by ten feet long. Both Brian and I screwed it together, then lifted the heavy gate, and set the hinges on the log, but that didn't work, so I had to box in the log, to provide a flat surface, it work, as it slid in and catches it. Next was the further one up, and I did the same on the other log, and affixed it going up, to lock in place, for the young steers. Meanwhile they were on the lower pasture, the next project was the fence line. We cut the remaining logs, into five foot sections, and dug a quick hole, and set a post, then five foot sections, and then another post, I used a top cap to stabilize it, it was crooked, but working, for the rest of the day.

August 5th Wednesday 2004

It was day 68, and for the first time we slept safe and sound, in our bed, in the north compound, it was nice, calm, and peaceful, we rose with our regular time, 0500, or so, I was off doing my chores, like feeding the animals, cleaning up each pen, and collecting eggs, in a pail, I drop them off to the kitchen. My next big thing was to finish the fencing, and also the weave, whereas I take a branch, and feed it through the fence vertically. Brian showed up early, to tackle the fence. Lily brought early morning gifts, it was fresh bread. We ate a hearty breakfast, as the fence was next, then it was up on the pen's roof, to shingle it. Anna and Lily went up on the roof, to finish mortaring, while, I and Brian worked on the fence line, we turned as we needed to go back up the line. From where we were at, I could see a valley, and in the distance that castle, this part was a gradual decline. Anna had mentioned to seed the open acreage, but first we needed to clean it up and burn a few stumps, which I put gas on, and set a fire, under a root. While taking my saw, and cutting it up. Brian was alright doing the fence alone, as I cut and had more posts and timbers set for installation, going back and forth, so many things to do, so little time. Anna and Lily finished the roof, now it was time to shingle, I set the scaffolding, up at the south side of the structure as it was only ten feet tall. And set on bundles, I had more slats cut but aging in the south compound. I collected them up, and we were set, Brian was half finished with the fence, as we took a quick tea and sandwich break, then it was starting, as we all laid the first line, and worked our way up, hammering them in, and working our way to the top. We went to lunch, and beyond, as it took all we had to finish the north side. I got down, and collected more bundles, and took them out as Brian and Anna were ready at the north end, they were up some twenty feet, and off the roof five feet. I used the tripod to hoist up the bundles, in place, all in all I had over forty bundles, but knew I needed double that, and went to the north compound, and saw my redwood blocks, I just cut last week. I split them licky split, it was fast going, as 25 to a bundle, I use hemp to tie it off, and set aside. I heard my name called, by Anna, I said, "Yes Dear, back here."

She arrived to say, "Everyone's waiting, to start laying the shingles, how about you?"

"Nah, I have maybe a couple more hours here."

"Alright I'll tell Brian and ask him to go back to the fence, that was a good idea to weave those branches that's what Lily wants to do."

"Fine let her", as I went back to splitting. It was nice to be in a draft free area, I had all the doors open, I knew next I needed to finish the bathroom and shower, and run water to us. Over the next couple of hours I finished what I had, I swept up the remains, to take in for her stove. She had a pan of water, or something boiling and I went out to retrieve the slats, and take them out, and down to the pen, and its roof, to set the bundles on the scaffolding. We gathered our counterparts, and took to the roof, it took us four hours, of constant work, but we finished. Anna went to tend to her garden. For me the next project was to fence that outside pen in. She went off, Brian and I went to load on the top cap, all the way down, 100 feet, with mortar, Brian helped, till we were finished. We got off that roof, and had some shingles left over, and took down the tripod and scaffolding. Anna suggested doing the walls, while Brian went back to setting in the fence. I was torn, between clearing a field, and plowing it to, wishing I had a tractor, also I had more trees to drop, for winter, enough to fill the side, as tall as I can make it, so using the jeep, I would pull already cut up trees, on the ground in front of the north compound, was all the logs. So I choked them and drug them under the side supports, one on top of the other, till all 16 were done. Next was back inside to work on another cistern, on the north west side, cutting into the horseshoe roof, corner, I set up supports, then stopped to think about Brian, and went out to the north part, to see he was on the uphill side, as I lent a hand, and it went fast now, up to about twenty feet to the pen. We sent that post down the furest, at five feet, it was to hold our gate, we finished putting together. Brian collected up Lily and they left, Anna and I had a good dinner, and went to bed.

August 6th Thursday 2004

It was day 69, and it was our turn, to go get our supplies from Jake, a proud man, stood and waited, as it was documented our new stuff, as we loaded on our trailer, everything, including our pool table, as it all fitted, we stopped by the store, and got some more gas, and filled our five gallon gas can. We were off, and back home, I backed it up, and was happy there was no fence. We off loaded, I had the pool table and waited for Brian, he wasn't around, so I went back out to the field, and began to hand plow about a quarter of an acre of the five acres, till I had fifteen rows each, and two huge stumps, I kept the fire up, and would use the chain saw, to continue to cut it up. Next was Anna happy with my work, and planted the first field with Alfalfa, while I went across the road, to map out the garden, or eventually go spread, the broken pieces of blocks from the slabs, and set down, for

Anna brick factory. I had over 24 things to do daily. My next big thing to do was cut planks, with my saw mill, I uncovered the blade, and went into the motor room, went through the sequence and started it, I set the gauge to the thickness, and set the lift, and log fell in, and a chain bucked it up, as the blade cut, it was hard manual labor, as the log was stripped, cut up, and stacked neatly on the end, I precut my length's so I had this pretty well under control, it was loud, as that diesel, powered on, the hour gauge indicated its working time, after seven hours, I shut it down, sawdust was everywhere, just as Brian and Lily pulled up from town, for him to see all that sawdust, and he wanted it, so we would have to figure out a way, to ship it. I then got him to help me lift the pool table up the stairs, and into the open room. We pulled out a ball and leveled it, plus I had a level, so we were good, went down, when Brian said, "When do you wanna do your big doors?"

"Not till later, I have to do so many things, and need that space, why don't you go home and off load, and I'll see you tomorrow?"

"Tomorrow Charley should be here."

"Oh right, your brother-in-law."

They took off, as I went back to building the cistern. I lined it with split logs, and it was done, I went out to see another project the fireplaces and the pipes through the top roof. We had all the piping now. Also where to put the transformer and batteries, so my northwest turret, I moved the tripod over, to rest close to the northwest corner, then I used the big chain saw to cut into the roof, then fashioned a set of stairs up, on the inside, to the roof, as I set a frame for that, 10x10, then added split logs, for the floor, I used 2x4's I precut, and framed up, a wall, with vertical split logs, nailed in, leaving a slit, for the transformer to breathe, next was the batteries, all connected, and a meter, to measure its wattage, to a converter, and regulator, to a box, then I ran small cable line to all the rooms, to set up a box for each room. This was labor intensive, but electricity was one that Anna so desperately wanted. I let this day go, as we had some leftovers, and went to sleep.

August 7th Friday 2004

It was day 70, and another dry sunny day, as that is what it is early, I have my chores, and Anna has hers, then we come together for breakfast, I went out in my shop, and began to build traps, not to trap fur, but to catch more rabbits, as they are our staple, milk from the goats, herding the others into the big pen. No water as of yet, for the pond. In the feed bins we carried in five gallon buckets, I put a broken up hay bale in each. With three feeding daily, and pasture land, were okay for the winter. Today marked the heat wave, and still no insects to speak of, maybe a fly, because we have bats officially, as told to me by Anna, whom has seen their remains, and when she isn't inside she is in her garden. Today I finish the transformer room, and the boxing of the stairs down, and firmed them up. Then went to the middle of the west side horseshoe, measured up to nine feet, I set up a frame, for the generator to sit on, and a output shaft, there was two versions that were interchangeable, I took the tripod down a aways to the middle of west side of the north compound, I cut a hole, with my small chain saw, in one of the vertical logs, it instantly let the wind in, and howled, as I went inside to slide the generator in, and the output shaft was visible, as it fit snug, then I pulled it out, and began to finish the stand, to allow it to rest on, by cutting half split logs, to fit together, and against the wall, yet it fit perfect, from where I was, it would be at 9 foot up, which meant I needed to build the windmill next, eight feet long, and 18 inches wide. The frame was crude, but, practical, as it was like a star. I used the tripod, to erect it, to the shaft, a hole was made, from the slats, brought down to it, to be a box, and it fit perfect on the shaft, then a washer and then a nut, I tightened it up, as I had a pipe hold it in place, but once I let it go, that inverted boards spun, and I had a windmill as I let it spin freely. I went back to the transformer room and put a sloped roof on top of the turret, nailed it down, as I saw the windmill going, it kept a good pace. I finished the turrets roof. Then took the mortar bucket, and filed in the gaps, then placed slats on top of it, in the distance was a cargo truck, un-marked pull up. The guy got out to say, "Mister, wait is that you Matt?"

"Yes it is, Charley?"

"Yes, do you know where the warehouse is at?"

"Yes, follow the road, he has the next place, over the bridge."

"Looks like you could use some help?"

"In time, your sister is awaiting your arrival, see you soon."

The cargo truck drove off. I moved the scaffolding over, and finished the roof with shingles, as it started to rain, eager to see if my rain box worked, I walked the roof, to the mill, to see it was opening up, I took a ladder down, as Anna had made good use of my planks, and built a maze of garden boxes under the tall roof, in the front, and was using wheelbarrows filled with dirt. As she was planting her existing crops, to see me and say, "Until I can have you build a fence around, then I need a center pole, to drape my plastic sheeting."

"What of the snow?"

"We will just push it off, when it occurs, so can you help me out?"

"Yes, right away, as I took a wheel barrow, and dug up, some broccoli, setting each plant in there, it was really raining now. I slowly took them back undercover. The wind was still blowing, but the plants were protected, as the root system was pretty well established. Being up here and all. It was easily 10 to 15 degrees warmer under the tall roof. Then it was a crack of lightning, and a boom of thunder, to hear for miles, as the clouds open up, and it takes its time up here, as it will move an inch a minute, pelting the ground, with lots of water. The cisterns, were filing, I had a top drain, for overfilling. I was curious about the pen, but, decided to dig the latrine instead, it was a dirty job, as it was supposed to be in a room by itself, but the rain, was everywhere, while I dug. Anna had dinner ready for me, I washed up, the best I could, and sat down, as outside, was the cargo truck, and then Brian and Lily, as Charley came in, to see us, and meet Anna, as he introduced to us his girlfriend, Tiffany Brant, "She is going to run the store, while I make the trip", for him to continue, she met everyone, when Brian came in to go over the plan, he said, "The cargo van is loaded up, and now we have enough for a month, so it's working, and by next month double this order, as we ramp back up."

I agreed with them as they left, and so did Brian, Anna cleaned up the dishes, as we then went to bed.

August 8th Saturday 2004

It was day 71, were at home, all of her crops, have since been moved, and the rain is good for our crops, we just put in. Anna has been having fun grinding up the bones, and combined with the blood to form a fertilizer, which she is applying, not much for a breakfast. I ate dried beef, and hardboiled eggs. My drink of choice is tea. Lots of fresh cool water. Today is all about the water traps, I build a box, using the planks I recently cut and a sliding ladder inside, that moves with the current, a screen of rabbit wire, to allow the water to flow out. The front is open, to allow huge water in, and flow out. I took the finished box out, it had skids, as I took it to the corner, at a curve on the White river, and set it in the current, using rocks, to set on the skids, to see it was alright. Water flowed in, from the bottom, to the front. The box was secure, as I pushed the ladder, all the way into the river bed, and left. Another box I was working on was the trap box, the animal would walk in, and is stuck from inside, till I release it. I was building them at twenty a day, in my spare time.

Also from the planks I prior cut. Those planks came in handy for fixing places. Also I need to continue to dig out the latrine, Anna has bricks ready to line it, using a ladder down, I was at the fifteen feet mark, leveled out, I had Anna hand me the bricks, as we set them down. As the day was done. I cleaned up and went to bed.

August 9th Sunday 2004

The next day was day 72, my priority today was build the bathroom, and pipe in fresh water. After a superb breakfast, I went to task finishing the latrine, by smearing the bricks with mortar, the entire wall, and front back and sides, I climbed out, and took the ladder with me, to begin to build a platform of split logs, face up for a floor, then a box made of 2x4's, then planks to cover them up, then toilet seats, two of them, also a plank wall, for privacy, as the roof was set, and the outside room enclosed with some windows, it was a small room, with its own door. Done. Now was the vast shower and laundry room. And a drain outside to a septic tank. Yet to build, but I will. I was getting more and more comfortable, with the north horseshoe, thinking I should, build doors, for the inside pens, to the horseshoe, and able to transfer to the larger pen, so I outlined each door, and cut it open, and then another, framed them both in, and set a plank door with a barn door style, a upper and lower, using a double hinge to set in place. Next was the water line, as I was building the five hundred feet from stream to compound, a straight shot, I had it all laid out, along the tree line, along the bank, to our compound, using a chainsaw, I opened the gap, and stuck it in, to dump into the northwest cistern, then using an over flow, diagonally across the room, to the shower room, where it went in at an angle, this is where it went to a wood box, then with piping, I placed it across a pit for firewood, down to a shower head, below I built a raised box, with a run off, to a huge log 2x2 x 4 feet long, log box, it was raised, as a drain went to a lower one, then under the floor of the horseshoe out, using a pipe, in addition the water from the cistern, went to the laundry boxes. From the shower head, I t'd it off, and ran a line, all the way to the kitchen, to the sink, then set a drain pipe, along the inside of the walls, and into the laundry, as a sweeping y connected the two, and went out. This was working great. I set the lines up outward, and all connected, and the inlet pipe in, and the water flowed. I ran back as it was a water works, inside the shower room, as water overflowed everywhere, but calmed a bit as I worked out the kinks. Then I lit a fire for the pipe, to heat up the water, for the shower head, and the sink. It was one type but was nice, as Anna said, "I don't need hot water at the sink", and I diverted it from the pipe, straight to the water source. This took the rest of the day, at night we both took showers, and of the laundry she loved it, each vat had warm water, soap to wash the clothes, then I added a window, to let light in, and a door, with a knob on it. She was first, then it was I, apart thirty minutes, it was refreshing, as I pulled the handle and got a dash of hot water, then, dried off, as I was done. We had dinner and went to sleep.

August 10th Monday 2004

It was another warm muggy day, the sun was out, it was day 73, we were at home, a lot going on, last night I couldn't sleep, so I assembled twenty catch boxes, and Anna and I are going to follow a trail, and set the trap boxes along the Stewart's river, all the way back up, to the series of falls. We set out, one by one, we set the trap with dried bear, and set it down, covered it up and set it. We walked the path, and every so feet till we ran out and went back and ate breakfast, of eggs, fried potatoes and fresh bread, also we saw her old garden tore up, under wandering animals. So I had a choice, do this now or hear about it later. I chose now, as she went to her greenhouse. It too was half finished, along with twenty or so more projects, so I picked and chose, today it was a fence around the old garden, using three foot in diameter logs, I dug the trench, five feet down, for ten foot tall logs, each was fifteen feet long. I used my tripod, to set the first one. She indicated she wanted two exits, and at least at ten foot apart, and an inside roof, around the wall, and a four support logs, so she can put plastic sheeting over it. I was easily moving along, to a dimension of 100x100. I stopped halfway in the front, to go cut down some more trees, limb them, and cut to size. I was a machine, to look back to see Brian, ready to help, to set the logs, and as I choked them, the tripod, helped out, as they were drug into place.

It was set and put in rocks, as the line was straight, in addition I told Brian, "Anna wanted an inside room to do work out of, but all the way down. He shook me off, as he just dug and set logs, smaller than the five footers in diameter, a little more shaky also, but I secured them, and moved the tripod in as other logs went in easily, to form the side by the road, and then to the cedars, it was ten foot high, as we were lining up logs, and standing them up, in the dug trench, it was work and we were doing it. The last of the logs went in, and we were half way done, to call it a day. Brian came in with me, and we sat down to an amazing dinner, lots of root vegetables in a cabbage soup, with dried beef, next was some fresh baked bread, I put butter and jam on mine. We ate in silence, as Anna was happy to show off her new waterworks. I knew I had a few more things to do before I was done. As Brian said, "Were scheduled for our first delivery tomorrow, what do you think?"

"That's great, and when you pay me that 20,000 back, I'll be happy." Said I.

"I know we will make profit, as we have no overhead, we have the land, the water and the timber, and the rest is mother luck" said Brian.

CH 9

Lots of predicaments to handle

It was August 11th Tuesday 2004 day 74, we were at home, well not really, it was a day of collections, first it was to the limestone quarry, to make mortar, and more redwoods, for shakes, then to the valley to collect moss, and pick up gold nuggets, "I think I could pick up nuggets every day, and salmon as the migration season has started, and with that the bears. The little ones I don't care too much for, it was the big grizzly bears, and with rifle ready, we cut and took out layers of moss as the whole valley was filled with it, it was good dried to absorb and retain moisture as we added it to our feed mix, and garden soil and if we have to eat it as a daily source of good fiber. Anna was wanting several hoses, to connect to all of this water I have dammed up. So Brian let Charley know, and on his drive back up, via the net, he brings them to her. He is up here three days a week, delivering things we need, and picking up the orders. We spent the early morning collecting moss, and gold nuggets. I was thinking of building a sluice box, it was on our property, and there was so much gold around. But it was as if there was danger everywhere, as the bears were out in force, and wandering the waterways I hurried Anna along, to keep her safe, I had a pant pocket full of nuggets, I escorted her to the jeep, we turned around, and went home, it was a good thing for the bridge, as that's where the bears go. We got back and there was so much to do, as I offloaded the limestone inside where the next building was going, it would be her factory, digging the trench was easy, choosing the right logs was next, as I went scouting, my goal was to cut all the trees down south of us so that we can see Mount Logan, as now the brick factory was going to be a simple 50x50 structure, with a road base of concrete. Brian was over, as was Charley whom wasn't traveling today, to help set the 3 footers, in diameter in five feet leaving ten feet tall, she wanted a door on the front for both sides, and later Charley told me he knew of a place in Anchorage and would be able to bring them on the next shipment up here, I was fast at setting, as Brian was fast at choking and bringing them to me, I hoisted them in place, it was easy going, and straight and level. We broke for lunch, as a truck and trailer came up, I immediately recognized the driver, he got out, and came around, to say, "I have a delivery for a Matt Michales is that you?"

"You know it, what is it?" I asked.

"Your enriched hay, made of alfalfa, at your price, some 600."

"Whose is the rest going to?"

"Oh it says here, John Locke."

"What is his grade?"

"The rock bottom price of a dollar a piece, but it's just hay, dry at that, it may mold, if he doesn't keep it dry, so where do you want all of this?"

"Probably in the south compound."

"You know your all over the TV."

"How so? what did I do?"

"Look around, you have a huge lodge, and no body as long as I been hauling up here, has nothing close to this, I'd be proud of just that, maybe you ought to, bridge this gap, and then you would have this huge road, for all your logs."

"Maybe I will, good idea."

He had a forklift, to offload us, as all five of us carried them in, to the very south of the south compound, horseshoe. He helped out, but the water in the ditch prevented that, but I got on the pallet, to throw over to the opening, Gary was impressed by the vastness of the place, and how easy, we took another 600, bales, as we were done, I showed him where to go, for him to say, "Your pretty set, with 1800 bales."

"Yes, it's only the beginning, we still have the salmon season, bear and grizzly, and then the snows, and spring, he waved me off, as he drove on, thinking of what he said, "Build a place over the road, and connect all the buildings, looking over the configuration, south compound is lower than north, so what to do?" as I was over helping the others carry in all the bales, we stacked them up. It was day over, as Brian and Lily left, for Anna and I to shower, and wade in one of the pool, it was nice, as I know what I needed to do tomorrow.

August 12 Wednesday 2004

Day 75, and after a phenomenal breakfast, and cleaning up after the animals, it was onto the roof, where four split logs were at, I carefully moved two of them over our wash room and into place, then drove in nails, to secure, I had a bucket of mortar, to fill the gaps, then it was on to shingle that part of the roof. I left two up there on the other side for the greenhouse. Also, it was time, to cut out holes for the stove pipes, using a pop rivet gun, I made pipe, using 4x8 sheet I got from the junk yard tin. I used the chain saw to make perfect holes, in the logs, I sent the pipe down about half way, and then the other side, by the end of the south compound, as another four went in and so did lunch. Below Anna threw it up to me, as she wanted to join me. She eventually found a way, we sat together, looking over the vastness, for her to say, "Who knew you were a wonderful builder my home feels so good, my sisters and brothers will love it."

"When are they coming up?"

"End of September after your buddies leave."

"What do you think of a cover over the road?"

"I think it will be nice, especially going over to the south from the north, you know we have our smoker, there, and if it's true we get 20 foot snows then covering this will be nice." Said Anna.

171

"The pottery and brick factory is about done, but first is your old garden grounds."

"Yeah good, for now, but come winter it will be another storage space."

We finished a nice portable lunch, she got off the roof, as I was cutting more holes for the north compound I got off, and went to make up the sheets into pipe, I bent the ends riveted them, and sent them down, all in all 24 points, of entry, using mortar, to seal, and shakes to finish, while Anna finished the northwest side of the chimney to the roof, in the north compound. She finished the brick box all the way to my pipe, for the rest of the pipes, along the north west side. Then moved to the rooms on top of us, to connect to each pipe. As we got down and had dinner, and another shower, we went to bed.

August 13 Thursday 2004

It was day 76, and the hot of all the summer had to offer at 88 degrees, but 78 with the cool wind factor, yesterday, Charley, brought Anna three hoses and fitting, using gravity, each hose has some pressure, yet able to move the water around was a good thing. Water was everywhere, and after the chores, and a another phenomenal breakfast, it was another project, using planks from my saw mill to make slats to finish my windmill, and its five points, big long eight foot, points, in a curved, slant, it took all day to modify it and into the night. Brian left early as he drove the saw mill all day and was dirty, the shavings were collected and he took them home.

August 14 Friday 2004

It was day 77, still hot, and calm before the storm, Charley was up early, as he dropped off us some hardware store fittings, as he said, "It was an auction, and I bought all of this for four hundred, all in boxes, I offloaded them to the north horseshoe, realizing I needed to cover the road, Charley was off to Brian's, for some reason he really liked me, no idea why?" I asked myself, setting the boxes on shelves, and then into to frame the greenhouse the door was well cut, and affixed, the open boxed stove, as I connected the stove pipe, was under the log roof, as it fit, then the next pipe and so on, till that was for five on this side in the second floor rooms, and then, to the back wall on the northeast side, in the animal pens, up a ladder to the top roof, as I attached the lower five. We had lunch, afterwards, with gloves on, it was opening up the inside doors, to get the wood, for each fireplace, that took all day. Even when Brian came over, we were still setting out the firewood, he helped out, he said, the others want to get together on Sunday."

"Sure, we can go together" I said.

"Well they were thinking, here."

"Alright better clear it with the boss" pointing to Anna, for Brian to say, "Ah right." He went up to her, and asked, she said, "Why not", and shot back to me, to say, "We can have a deer hunt" I agreed, as she was gardening, and digging up potatoes, which grew like weeds here. I and Brian went back to dropping logs, as I set them in to the old garden, and with the tripod, we set the above logs, we did that for the rest of the day.

August 15 Saturday 2004

It was day 78 and I finished my chores, and it was onto the completion of the north compound greenhouse, next to the large logs, I built a frame to allow the plastic sheets to rest, I drilled it into place, same as the other side to form, the roof, to capture all that sun, the walls were made of split logs up three feet from the ground, and a bench, a screen door on the end, to get in, but it was basic, and easy to put up, 8x 16 feet long, the east side was a covered part, for tools and stuff some 4 feet. Also the door to the horseshoe. Done. By lunch Brian arrived, to help me drop logs to finish the brick factory, we used the tripod, to set the across beam, to tie in the sides as Anna and Lily filled the gaps with mortar, we set in the side logs, going west to east, at twenty feet, and same on the other side, I liked one in the middle but it would get in the way, so I took a fifty foot log, and sent it over to the sawmill, and cut out a corner, then while the diesel was still running, I cut planks, and 2x4's, and some beams, for my next project. After taking out all the trees that lay in wait, I shut it down, Brian collected the sawdust, that's when I came up with the idea to build a catch box. It was nice I enclosed this, especially from the wind. We all went back to the pottery and brick factory, the roof was going to have 35 footers, front and back to cover, the roof, I cut two fifty footers, like the top, and was able to place, along the front and back top, then the newly cut in two logs, 3 feet wide, went on the back side roof, and with a 5 foot overhang, it was nailed in place, as I did four, it was 14 more to go, as Anna and Lily showed up with mortar in buckets, and was hoisted up. She climbed up a scaffolding on the south side, she told me a bombshell of some news, "I want a wood floor."

"I said, "Come on, really, so late in the process?"

"That's what I want, besides it should be higher than the ground anyway, listen honey, how about, half, like the back half, so I can use my kilns."

"So where are those going?" I asked.

"Don't worry, I and Lily are going to build those."

"Sure, go ahead."

I didn't doubt she couldn't do it, but we were all a strong team. Log on log was lifted into place, I nailed them down, I had noticed it was actually getting a bit colder, as the winds definitely picked up, but kept on working, I hammer the log in place, sometimes I would notch them with my little saw. But we were moving right along. We finished for dinner, of Lily's vegetable soup, and cornbread, she put pineapple from a can, and jalapeno's, which I was surprised, but she said, "It was all for me", and Anna would have to put up with it. Brian told me Charley was changing his drive days, to Sunday, Tuesday and Thursday, as Friday is our biggest sell day."

We finished the south side, and it was mortared, Brian and I split shakes, for this roof. It was getting late, Anna had assembled two brick stands, for fire kilns, a super-hot and hot, with a lower trap door, to get the ash out. It was time to make the outside greenhouse, as Brian and I threw over the top the plastic sheeting, and took a 2 x 4 to set the plastic, to be secured, then we got cleaned up, we all took showers individually, Anna chose to soak in her bikini outfit, she gave Lily a pair it was too big for her. It was nice being up here to bathe daily or as we want. They spent the night, in the spare room, on the floor, we had carpet, in sleeping bags. We took our bed and went to sleep.

August 16 Sunday, 2004

It was day 79, we had lots to do, as it was raining, not soft but a gusher, but we all slept in, it was warm and dry, water rushed into the ditch, and into the river, we rose, and Lily and Anna took care of breakfast, I was like a fireman, and stepped into my pants and suspenders, and put a long sleeve shirt over it, I lathered up the insect repellant, around my neck, face and back of my hands, I knew the roof over the brick factory was the priority to finish, as I dressed in my boots and rain gear to hear, "Where are you going?"

"Out to do my chores" said I.

"I don't think so, look its dry out there."

"Ah so it is."

"Now take that off, and help out around the house, our guests should be arriving soon."

Brian cleaned up his room, and we went out together, first to the wolves puppies, they were getting calmer and calmer, and loved the attention, next was the pigs, I moved the boy out, and into the big pen, they were getting huge on what we were feeding them, the lower door was open, to allow them out, I swept the floor, while Brian refilled the bin, then turned on the hose, and put fresh water, in the water pen, till it was full, in the back run it was mud, and Brian wetted it down, as I showed him what to do. Next was the goats, which were in the outside big pen, each had a collar, as I got 7 to bring back in, for Anna to milk. Brian wanted to, but I moved him along to the chickens, and the geese and ducks, had a small plastic pool to wade in, as for my young eighteen were full grown, but we still had a steady stream, of eggs about 5 a day. But today was 12, I collected them up, while Brian set in the alfalfa hay, in their boxes, as I scooped the feed we make up for the chickens, I also opened the lower door. I took the eggs in to Anna to hear, "Wow, that is a lot." As I presented her a larger one, from our goose I said.

"Wow, maybe it's the feed plus the hay."

"Or the backyard? And its calm environment".

"That reminds me can you make a worm box?"

"Is that for fishing?" I asked.

"It could be, but for the feed, chickens go crazy over them."

"As do birds, shall I make an aviary?"

"Would you Honey?"

"I'll add it to my list." I said respectfully. And into the barn, I went which was nice, as rabbits, were multiplying, we once had, 2 now another litter, we are at 22, and growing. I scooped up the litter, into a buckets, Anna had me drill holes in it, as I packed it, and then took it over to the center of her raised garden, and took the hose, and filled it full, and went back in, for another, as I did that same, and it too had holes, and set it in the middle, and filled up the bucket. The hose was working good. The rains let up outside, for a bit, as we waited, I went with Brian, to the horseshoe, and first it was to connect the power to the generator and then continued on my windmill, the planks, were set in at an angle, till I actually had six points, because as it moved it was lopsided, so I modified it again, it was actually ready to try, Brian, and I carried the frame, outside, and we assembled it, as he and I went over to get the tripod, and then carried it over, I knew now, a bridge was next, in the future, as we set it up, and then hoisted it, and set it on the shaft, and then the washer, and finally the nut. One by one, the planks went in, and we tied it down so it wouldn't move, but as more slats went in, the harder it was to control, it, we let it go, and did the bottom, several hours went by, as we were finished, I used long skinny bolts to tie it together, I stood back to admire my work, as the ropes couldn't hold any longer, and busted free. And it spun like a propeller, instantly we had light, and electricity. Anna was delighted, as the first thing she did was turn on her satellite dish, and all her channels, she couldn't wait to see me to thank me, but, I and Brian was back over to the brick factory, and working on the front, I set up the tripod, and using my jeep, Brian pulled the split logs in place, I went on the roof, while Brian handed them to me, as Charley and Tiffany drove up, they parked on the road, while, he said, "Can I help?"

Brian looked him over, to say, "Can you help deliver logs to Matt?"

"Yes, Sir", he said. While Brian went to choke, and set the rest of the 18 logs, one by one, it was slung up to me, I place them in, and hammered them into place. Charley was eager to help, as he was a worker, it went faster than I expected. I had the roof on, then mortar buckets were sent up, it was the worst job ever, painting the mortar between the cracks, we let cure, then it was the shingles, first the west or wind side, all the way up, the three of us, to the top, then the east side, from the overhang up, row by row, to the top, done, then the top cap, mortar, then the logs, split, by 3 foot in diameter. I hammered it in, and tied the top together. I rechecked the sturdiness, so I yelled down to Brian, "Start digging a hole like your house five foot deep, as soon as that occurred it was Charley, in the hole, as Brian stepped off fifty feet, then one pole at 3 foot wide went in, first was the fifteen foot long, and once set, and rocks in the hole, it was 50 feet in front, and two logs, went down, with the supports in place, we had two split logs, ready for the side rails, and set, then I had to shorten the other two to fit in-between, and nailed in place, then one by one, 55 foot split logs, were slid under the roof, a bit, and down, it was fast going, as we skipped breakfast, for lunch, as it was Lily who drove to visit the Locke's and the Holmes, family to tell them to come, for lunch, and dinner and a few games, so bring your rifles."

We were stacking as fast as we could. Till all of them were up there, I nailed them all down and crosswise into each other, as it was one job I didn't like was mortaring, it was the least part to do, I liked, it went on good, as it binded and filled, now that was tedious, as I got help from Charley, and Brian, as the rains picked up, the great thing about rain, is that the mortar loved it, as it spread better, but that was it, as it stayed where we put it and it sealed up, it was good. Inside the north compound a radio could be heard, it was Anna and her satellite was blaring away, in those woods, things could be heard for miles. It sure helped the day away, as it gave weather updates, it said it would rain and it was. I set a back stop on the end, which instantly the water ran off. To the sides, Charley had a shovel in hand, to dig a quick trench to the ditch, out front. As Brian did the same. On the other side. As Anna called lunch. I was starving, yet muddy, so was Charley and Brian, who saw Lily drive up with guests, she was yelling at the pair of them, I ducked into the shower room, took a quick shower, and changed into some clean clothes. I appeared to see the four others, to take a seat as Anna and I helped her, serve our guests, it was a frittata of sorts, as everyone had a portion, for she also had fresh fried potatoes, and loaf of wheat berry bread, it was a hit. I sat with Anna, at the head of the table, Anna to my left, as Lily was on my right, and the two dirty boys, Then Kim, John took the other end, with Billy, Laurie, and Tiffany. We ate, while Anna said, "Alright listen up boys, this is a turkey shoot find me some game to include ducks, geese, so we may have for our meal, in addition, while you're out there, collect as much gold pieces you can find, in the form of nuggets, afterwards, we will count them up and weigh them, the most and the heaviest, gets to choose the others losing." We were off, after I got into my boots and rain gear, and took my Enfield, fully loaded, and two magazines, on my holster I clipped them in, and I handed Charley another rifle, as we were off, to the peat valley, where it was open season, as they were on my property, and thinking of what was right, I said, "Be careful there are many bears", so we saw ducks and geese fly off, and the shooting began, till it was over, each of us, had two, as we took them back. Set them on the table, as Anna had her knife ready, all ten, as we went back in the peat valley, but I much rather called it gold field. I was bent over picking to my heart's content, that was till a grizzly came out of nowhere, and as John had his back to it, so did Billy, it was in a full run, as I stood in their path, aimed, and shot, for John to say, "Watch out, I could have went deaf", as he turns, to see the bear, drop and slide to his feet, as he high-stepped it out of there. I checked it, I motioned for the others to go, as it was other bears moving in, as Brian ran back and got the jeep, and tripod with Charley's help, and I stood guard, as the jeep arrived, John and Billy walked back. I hooked the huge bear up, on the hood, as the tripod was useless to me, and had it sitting on the hood, as my winch kept it in place, as I drove backwards, to the south compound, and the three of us, carried it in, to the smoke house, hung it by its neck, and arms, as Anna smiled coming in, to do her work, as she said, "Now how much did you get Matt?"

"Oh enough" I said. As I felt my pockets, and then said, "Well maybe not enough."

"I'll have the hide ready to tan, if you can wait" Anna said.

"Sure", I said, as I went around and pulled it from the carcass, she cut the neck, and around the legs, as it came to me, I used a knife, to carve off the rest of the connective tissue, as I left to take it to the back of the horseshoe in the south compound. That is where I set it on a stretcher, for its legs, then arms, and one to its neck, Anna dropped off the brains, as I squished it, and used my hand, to rub it in, till, it was all gone, and the inside was a pearl color and had equal softness. I let it alone, while the other men, were showing off their piles, on the serving tray for each. Charley looked like he had the most from John and Billy, Brian got over there, to show, his findings, and then finally, it was I, I had the most by far and second was Brian, the rest put all of theirs in the same pile, and Lily separated it, as I placed mine in a bag, for Billy to say, "What would it take for you to come finish my house?"

"A week or so" said I.

"So listen, what if I were to collect the gold in your fields, then set it in bags, could I pay you that way?"

"Sure, but I think you paid us off with goats."

"No, what I meant was for you finishing the house."

"Sure I'll be there tomorrow."

"I'll come too" asked Brian, to say, "What did I just volunteer for?"

"Were helping Billy to finish his house tomorrow."

"Oh alright, just come by and get me", as Lily says, "I want to go too, will Anna be there?"

"I don't know, since we finished the brick factory, she will be there, help me Brian load up the trailer, I guess we could go over there and scout trees, wanna go Charley", he jumped in, with tape in hand, and we drove out as both Billy and John were amazed about the electricity, but what grabbed their attention was the fireplaces, and went to each one to stoke each fire, it was fascinating to them, what I had done. We got over to Billy's farm, to see it needed a better roof than the tarps, and he did mention a back, frame like what we did for the brick factory.

A front cover for the animals, so I showed Brian what we would do, as I marked the trees, and counted out what I needed. I parked the trailer, and we drove back, passing Billy, and John, in the moss valley, thinking about the moss, I slid to a stop, to say, "Hey, can you collect up some moss, and still pick up nuggets?"

"Yes" said Billy, coming up for the six buckets I had, and he tried to hand me his handful of gold, for I to say, "Hold on to it, take it to Mister Wilson, an pay off your tab."

"Will do, thanks."

I drove back, and pulled in through the open gate, and into my carport. Brian and I got out, to see it was near dinner time, we sat, and talked with Charley, who wished he could stay out here, but Brian told him he needed to go back tonight, so he said, "Lets off load the doors, which we three went to the cargo truck, opened it up, and pulled out the aluminum doors, and a double track system. As we used ladders, to climb up, at the south compound first, to attach the doors and affixate with a drill and large long bolts and nuts, it was huge, all the way across, except on the sides which I need to fill in, then each door went on, and then the other, it, slide nicely, a chain and lock, went around to secure it. Next was the north compound as the two remaining doors, each one had a special fit, what was interesting, was the open gap on top, shall I leave it alone, or place some glass windows up there, and to the sides, Charley said "I will go to a junk yard and pick up 16 windows to fill those gaps."

"Sure go ahead", as I was trying to feel for that cash wad, as he put his hands up to say, "No, I will buy them for you, as you help everyone else out, it's the least we could do for you."

"Thanks" I said. A pile of topsoil, was next to the entrance, in front of that was a drainage to the ditch. Thinking about that bridge, I put it on hold, as dinner was called, and went over to a serious feast, as Laurie mention to Anna, "We have some homing pigeons, and if you could build a place for them, we could send messages back and forth."

She agreed, as she said, "Matt, Laurie wants us to build a bird house, can you do that?"

"Yes Dear" I said. That was the end of the day.

August 17 Monday 2004

It was day 80 and it was warm as a group of helicopters, landed on our road, and for Anna who stayed behind, to fire bricks, and build her two kilns, was a government entourage for the governor, Jim Hickson, exited the deluxe helicopter, he was in amazement over both structures, both north and south, to see smoke from the brick factory, and he and his group, came over to say, "Hi Miss Long, where can I find Matt Michales?"

"Oh he is out helping others north of here, at Billy's and Laurie's Holmes place."

"Alright I will go up there, what do you think of our place here?"

"Oh it's nice we have electricity."

"Electricity", are you joking" asked the governor.

"No well not today as it is calm out there, but let me show you, I think Matt said we have an 8 hour charge, as she went out and showed him the windmill just standing steady, and then went in to show him, the transformer, converter and the battery bank, Jim was marved at all the cut wood blocks, of fresh cedar, and went around, and out, to see a water cistern, to say, "You have electricity, water flowing, and everything you need, including TV, I'd say, you were set for winter, especially these lodges, it is simply amazing how he got the wood up there."

"Matt said it was the matter of principles, and leverage."

"Indeed it is, alright, as the governor was stunned by all the ingenuity, it was amazing, as he exited and got in his used car, Jake brought up for him to use, and drove, past the open valley to see a lone figure, with a rifle, and several buckets, and then past the warehouse, as the vehicle slowed, to say, "Who is that guy, to build such incredible structures, no I say, He is hired today, and put down a million we will pay him, we will assemble a crew around him, building these lodges, make it happen Mister Hughes."

"Yes, Sir, he is on to something", as they turned and to the north, to see the glimpse of the roaring river, below, as they turned, to see, multiple structures, and over to a massive castle, for the governor to say, "Now this should be his place, as they drove in, he got out, as I was on the roof, setting the logs, as Brian was handed them to me, for the governor, to go up and onto the roof, to say, "So your busy, How would you like to do me a favor?"

"Sure what is it?" said I.

"Go as my representative and build a lodge for the Kluane Indians, near Lake Kluane."

"Sure, but what about the challenge?"

"We will work around you missing."

"So just me, or can I bring my girl, and he will want to go," pointing at Brian.

"Hold on, are you saying you want the rest of everyone?"

"No, just Brian, Lily and Anna, the rest can survive on their own."

"Alright, I will allow the four of you away, for a week, can you build it in that time?"

"Sure, but I don't know how long, it will take, the soil could be tough, but I will go now" I said getting off, as we made quite good progress, and reset the tarps, as we loaded the tripod, and Brian hitched up the trailer, I had my saw, as we followed the governor, as Mister Hughes drove, we went past John's, then south, then west past Brian's and then stopped at our place, where Anna said, "She would stay", and so did Lily. She packed us some food, as I grabbed, two big chainsaws, and we were off behind, the governor, because of the right here right now approach. Mister Hughes, drove on out, I admired the view, and of the gorge, as we got onto the highway, and went south east, for it to say, "Kluane state park 70 miles. An hour later, we exited the state park, to a world under the highway, where everyone had a cabin, as they came out to greet us as we drove right by, and down to the lake, and the game reserve. We parked and got out, as the governor, went to see the chief. At a larger than average house under the highway. Mister Hughes fetched us, Brian and I, even before, we could take measurements, we entered, we took off our shoes, my boots, and walked in to see everyone around a table, there was plans laid out covering that table, something out of my league, for me to say, "Sorry I can't build that, I build, on what is around me, like the lake, I would need to build a base, then a wing on each side, what of all the buffalo?"

"They take cover under the bridge" said a helper to the chief.

"So no to a pasture home, does this place get lots of snow?"

"No and yes, depends on the year" said the chief.

"He wants the two of you to take a purification with him in the lake" said Mister Hughes.

I said, "Sure, how bad can it be?"

"Well I will tell you this, it was bad, I might still have a cold, we went out to the lake, stripped down naked in front of the whole tribe, and slowly walked into near cold water, submerged ourselves, it wasn't so bad, Brian and I did it, the chief wanted everyone, including the governor, and his aides, like Miss Grant, it wasn't so bad, kinda like a pay back. Then two young women were assigned to us, or this build, we both said, we were taken, but it was explained to us, it was for our comfort, as all I thought was that teepee, and how ironic if I showed up with that, no we were going home every night, as they lived a outdated life, the only one with electricity was the chief, and all the floors were dirt, like John and Kim's place, as we saw how they lived as I was trying to get my body warm, we went in and smoked a peace pipe, to finalize the deal, it was near dinner, I had our rations, but we ate with the tribe as the governor left, by helicopter. Mister Hughes, said "The governor ordered us up a crane, which will be ours to use", I thanked him, as he left and said he would be back in a week. I waved him off, and was shown by Little Hawk, a female guide, like me, how they lived, all under the bridge, and not in the elements, I said, "Not to worry, I'm putting you on that lake, besides, I saw, three or four waterfalls, and little streams, to gather from, while below, was the buffalo, grazing the field, I asked Little Hawk, "Why don't you all cut the field for grain?"

She didn't understand. But spoke English, it was hard, to understand, she said, "The land is sacred, we go to Haines Junction to trade, there is a Indian exchange just for us."

"No what I meant was grow your own, and raise what you need how many in your village?"

"Seventy five total."

"Alright I can work with that, thinking of my layout, the same principals, we were led by the lady of the forest, a young girl by the name of Aileena as we ended up on a tract of forest we can cut the logs from, about a mile north in a valley from the lake, she stood guard like we were invading her land. We still had light, and I went to work, in the theme of five footers in diameter, for the base, and three footers in diameter for everything else. This went on till night was close, then I went looking for the base, I located the perfect spot, by some old thick oak trees, Little Hawk was fierce with the men, as the chiefs assistant, she led the men to dig, with long shovels I brought, at the exact place I wanted at the exact depth. She spoke their names but I wasn't listening, as all other tribe members hid from us. Brian was choking and limbing the logs, I came back up and went back to cutting the logs, I was rocking it, in to the night. Later I packed up and Brian and I left, for home. He stayed the night at our home, as we had a huge meal, then a nice shower and didn't say another word and went to bed.

August 18 Tues 2004

It was early morning, and we were up, a hearty breakfast, and both Brian and I were gone, to the Kluane tribal lands. First to greet us was Little Hawk, looking disappointed, for her to say, "You don't favor us?"

"Yes, why?" I asked.

"You didn't take with you the girls chosen for you?"

"We are married already, and our wives wouldn't accept that?"

"How do you know, did you ask them, besides their your servants now, as a gift, so you must take them?"

"What of the men?"

"Oh no, they're the chief's personal workers."

I was trying to put a spin on it and realized, a visit to the chief was in order, so I said, "Allow me to see the chief?"

"Right now he is bathing with his wife."

"How do you know all of this?"

"I'm his personal assistant, just then two new girls showed up, to say, "We were the new ones chosen, to serve our master."

I recognized the lady of the forest, she had a mean disposition, and wasn't very nice either, looking at them I knew neither could really help me, so I said, as Brian left to go to work, "Alright I will take these and those, why not, I don't want them to feel non-accepted."

"Can you Little Follower, go tell the others?"

"What did you call her?"

"Oh, she is called Little Follower, and I think you know the lady of the forest?"

"Yes", I said, yes indeed I had a plan, for all four of them, to say to Little Hawk, "Can you ask the chief where if any I could dig, to make bricks, prefer along the bank, to dig out the rim, for the lodge." She left as I got my chain saw, only to see the more humble Aileena, just standing there with her arms crossed, she said, "You're not like the other men, who just want to lie with me, why are you so different?"

"I don't have time, I need to work" I said, not even looking at her as I walked away, but she followed, all the way to the site which was under full assault, as we clear cutted, what we needed, and from that to reveal a small river, but inverted, as the branches were in the way, I immediately saw, what she could do, and sent her over, to clear them up, then, Little Follower came back with the other two, for me to stop dropping trees, to say, "Does anyone know English?"

"Yes Mister, we all go to school and learn some of the ways, for we are ready for marriage and how do they say, procreate."

I didn't know now what was in store for me, but I went along with it, to say, "All right, clean up the branches and put in a circle, then find rocks, and put around it. I thought about digging a pit, but I didn't have time to waste, and went back dropping trees, I counted them out, and knew I was close. I dropped two more, into the lower ground, below the water was pristine, as I saw water lilies, the girls, continued to work. Then I looked up as another stood on the ridge line staring at me, she had long hair, and a huge smile, I made my marks and cut the logs in two, three and four, the lower limbs were gone, due to the vastness of the forest, there was still trees left, as they were out of view. Then noticed another figure on the ridge, it was the chief. I stopped what I was doing, and made a bee-line up to the ridge, to see the chief, who said, "Stop, your invading my sacred land."

I stopped to say, "But I was seeing if I needed to drop anymore trees."

"Then you're allowed come up."

I went around, to the top, to view, I counted out a patch to the right, below the ridge, to hear, "Thank you for accepting my gift, now you are truly a great man, unless you want my daughter?"

I turned to see her to say, "I know it's not in my best interests to refuse you, but I'm no chief, nor anyone special, for I am just a man tasked with helping you have a safe and comfortable living place to live."

"I understand that Mister Matt Michales, I do understand who you are and watch you on our TV, we have electricity, but we are poor to afford much more than that."

"Look around Chief, you have resources, and all that lies within."

"What are you saying you could help us out?"

"Sure, that's what neighbors are for."

"Then I'll take you up on that, if you have a moment, I'd like to soak, please come with me". I followed him back to the village, behind them, as the young girl, named Ramie, kept looking back, every so feets, till we arrived to the chief's main house, inside I had to take my boots off, and it was a bit modern, as it had a kitchen, inside the women wore practically nothing, to include the daughter, my comfort level was way out of control, as the chief took me downstairs, to see a crude hot tub, not vented, for me to say, as I saw him pull off his clothes, and get in, to the jets, of course I had to join him, as I removed everything, as we relaxed, it was nice, but it was stale water, unlike my pools, the water kept flowing, for me to say, "I will incorporate this in, my drawing."

"Good, good", as he called down for his wife, she appeared naked, as she presented him, with some wine, and a food platter, for I to say, "What do you do when guests are around?"

"Cover up, but you are not a guest anymore, you are family, and you now get the hand of my daughter, you are my son now."

I was stunned, I almost had tears running down my eyes, only to think of what Anna would say, let alone of being waited on for the Chief to say, "I will tell you for over twenty years, I have been petitioning the government to have them help us build a new community center and place to live, each time they send us some help, just long enough to build our 15x 15 shacks, no running water barely some electricity, as just then I saw his daughter, she was naked, and realized she wasn't as young as I expected, for the chief to say, "Ah Ramie, he has accepted you as his wife."

She was ecstatic, and came over to embrace me for the first time, she almost looked like Anna in almost every feature, we broke apart as tears were flowing, for I to say, "See I made her upset?"

"Oh no my son, she is filled with happiness, she feels like a great man is before us, and now we merge as one big family, she wiped away the tears, to literally run up the stairs, for the Chief to say, "Now what is your plan?"

"Well with the lodge, it will be about ninety thousand square feet."

"Are you serious?"

"Yes, plus a dock for the lake, do you stock it?"

"No, we have salmon now till November."

"Yes but what sustains the lake?"

"What do you mean?" the chief asks.

"A lake needs, frogs, water lilies, which I just saw one, it needs heat and shade."

"Well do what you think it needs."

"Then what of the lands?"

"How so, what do you mean?"

"You're not from here are you?"

"No, twenty years ago, we were living on the coast, near Mount Elias, and in a land swap deal, we got over a 100,000 acres, plus the lake, but it's because, beavers dammed it up, we even have this, we also got 2000 head of bison, and 200 reindeer, but most of all the reindeer is gone, due to the wolves and grizzly bears, we still get invaded."

"That's alright I will help you out with that too, now what of the men, if you have seventy five in the village, where are all the men?"

"Most are sick, and too weak to do anything, it's the women who do everything, and of them we have over fifty, the problem we have is we have to many of them, that they outweigh the men, besides, what to do with them is the whole another issue."

"So when this is done…"

"Oh this will never be done, your family now, I'd give you my wife, if that says enough on how much I am in your debt."

"But that is this, I will do it anyway, you don't have to give me your women, I'd just do it for the bison."

"You and everyone else", as he got up, and left, he was upset. His wife reappeared in the nude, for her to say, "Do you mind if I join you?"

"No, be my guest."

She sat, and said, "Awani means well, if he could he would give you all of those girls, they are a nuisance, but we need organization, do you have any suggestions?"

"Yeah, go out in the fields, and cut all that hay."

"I think me and the girls could do that, anything else?"

"Start a garden."

"What good is that when it will snow in a month?"

"Because I'm going to build you a massive greenhouse, on the open side, and a massive place to raise some reindeer."

"Really that was our staple diet" as she came forward and hugged me, to say, "Now you are family, for I am yours as well, to command" she broke it free, to say, "We need help, socially, physically, and mentally, this move twenty years ago, devasted us, we went from 200 strong to about fifty weak."

"We'll all that is changing, I'm bringing in reinforcements, and we are going to support you", as I got up, and got out, Ramie appeared to towel me off, and I dressed, as mother and daughter left, I went up, with my boots on, and out the door I went, but downward, towards our site, where Little Hawk, was screaming at the men, I saw her, to say, "I spoke with the Chief, and I say, "Let's get the men out of their cabins, and down in the field to work."

"We could do that, now that you're going to be the chief's son, what do you ask of me?"

"I need a pit dug, on the bank, and put firewood in it and start a fire."

"I will, what can I call you?"

"Matt."

I was off back past the chief's place, it was dirty and soon knew why, as the outhouses were full, of flies, it was pretty bad. I also knew that bathing and clothing was the low part of their needs, right now it was shelter, then a sustainable growing center, or two, we had our work cut out for us, I like the whole horseshoe thing, but needed to get going, as the logs, were laid out, in the distance, I saw, a group of men and women, out and were cutting and slicing the wheat. They too needed buckets, or tarps, as it was now clear why all of this happened, as I helped Brian put the tripod in the trailer, and hooked up the jeep, I drove it down, past the highway, which was calm above, it was go time, we set up the tripod, as Brian took the jeep back, and off loaded the trailer, and thus started to haul the big, five footers in diameter, massive logs, they were swung up and into place, as I checked the depth, it was flat, it is always the first one, it was soon apparent the massive logs were useless, and had to switch to the 3 foot in diameter, but was setting the five foot diameter five feet down, and then equal, as the ground was pretty flat as to where I was at, but butted up against the hill, 100x100, was my guide, as piling went in first, next was the dock, I almost wanted to drain the lake, to get all the clay out, that did give me a good idea, there was so many things wrong, I had to try to fix them, I had four diggers, as I had the tallest, a guy named Mike, or as I call him, he loved my maddox, or let alone tools, the five foot pilling went into place. I stepped back, to say, "It's time to go home, and tell Anna, we had ten poles in at ten feet high", and rocks found, in around them, Sadu, was another who filled them in as we left with trailer and drove back. Anna was happy to see me, as Brian I told of the incident, so she and Lily, were going home to get most of all of their vegetables, for tomorrow, I sat her down, as she said, "What's wrong?"

"Well I may have gotten myself in a pickle."

"Tell me is it another girl?"

"What, how did you know that?"

"I see it on your face, what is it?"

"Well I'm working for an Indian tribe, and for the work I am doing the chief wants to give me two workers, and his daughters hand in marriage." She looked at me, to say, "When is the wedding?"

"What are you saying your bailing out on me?"

"No on the contrary, it would be nice to have others around to keep me company, as I look forward to Lily when she gets here, as I have so much to do, so yes, I would welcome others, and if this chief daughter and I get along, we will see, about this whole arrangement, so shall I go with you tomorrow?"

"Yes," I said as I ate a hearty meal, and showered apart and went to bed together.

August 19 Wednesday 2004

It was day 82, and all seemed alright as Brian drove his jeep filled with vegetables, and kept our secret safe, to the Kluane tribe, which is where, Anna took charge, and directed Little Hawk, into storing the wheat, she threshed it, on tarps, they had no real means of storing, so our first barn would be our first project after the lodge, and Anna was appalled by the living conditions, as they needed a good meal, but after checking the conditions, she had to hold her hand to her mouth it was that bad, so she checked with Little Hawk, to ask permission for those pretty sick, mainly men to come back with her, for a good shower, and first aid, it was agreed on, and ten men piled in the Jeep grand Cherokee, as Lily and Anna, went back, as I thought, "Too bad, the Beaver creek city is gone, oh anyway", as I went back, to setting the floor, as I needed cut piling, to hold it up, as each 3 footer split, was a welcome sight, as it was a dry spell, so all of this bank was firm, but I can only imagine, when it rains and snows, this place that the floor was going down, was the main part, the wings are getting the pilings and a roof, log by log, went down face up, being it was raised, in the middle was a pit, with a fire going. I couldn't believe they didn't have a chainsaw. The floor was square along the back where I had Mike and Sadu, digging the trench, three feet down instead of five, it made a difference, the surface of the floor was a good place for the tripod, as the jeep hauled them to just below, and set on skids, as some of the other two, Timu and Realize, shoved them towards me. It was a real work in progress, the wall went up, it was impressive to see it straight and level, it took about 68 logs to fill the back wall, and double that for the floor, as I knew plywood, would fill the floor later. As the day was done. We drove home, I had the two girls Anna chose. Anna also had spent some time with the chief, as she whispered, "I accept her, she will now go off, and prepare, she asked me to be the maid of honor, and I told her yes," said Anna smiling at me. In the back seat was number 1 Little Follower, named Nina, she was a worker, and loved to please, to seek positive reinforcement, always, we got back to the home, with trailer, as Anna told me, they bathed them, and soaked them, applied some arnica and aloe on them, their strength is back, as some wasn't as bad, they were chopping wood, and stacking it as Anna cranked out the food, with Lily, as she showed Nina, to the lodge, she loved it, and then the animals, she was overly excited about the color of chickens, and of eggs, she was skinny, and probably under nourished. She ate, an then was Anna assistant. That night all was calm for me to take a shower, I did notice all the fire places were going, as it was warm, and for the first time I saw a bat eating it was fat, and I smiled, I went to sleep in a good place. Anna later joined me, to say, "I was doing a good thing."

CH 10

Meeting new friends and a work force

It was August 20 Thursday 2004, day 83, and although we left the men of the Kluane tribe there at our compound, we both Brian and I and the girls, went back for the rest of the tribe, whom wanted to come, meaning fifty or so, as some had to stay to help, but the girls took back as many as they could, the chief of course stayed, with wife Susannah. The daughter Ramie, was off with the Elders, in the mountains preparing for the ceremony. I was in action with my four guys, setting the floor beams of split logs, and connecting them up, across the middle was the 4- 25 foot tall logs. They fit into the ground and around the main part. Now to protect the newly laid floor, a split log roof, was going up, even before the walls went up, as we were on scaffolding I built. The four men were all over the structure, we used the tripod, to set in the frame of the twenty footers, they were massive 5 footers in diameter, and instantly set the main frame in place, as the first top beams, went across. All four were in place, nailed in, and set, and just like that a roof, was being laid, across the back to the front, inverted on the ends, to catch rain inward, but it was along the back row, to the front 20 feet long, square as I cut them on the floor, and they went up to the poles, to be laid out as on the roof. It needed to be done today. While Anna, taught the tribe manners and respect, as directed by Nina, who oversaw them. Anna was back to make mortar, she brought with her the Jeep grand Cherokee, the mud buckets made up. As she noticed the lodge was coming around, as the roof, was noticeable, split logs laid, from the top, to the sides, some 55 footers, split by 3 foot, as I was doing this on my scaffolding, while I checked Mike's work, it was good, I first thought about drainage, but my concern was the roof, over everything, as the back wall was sloped down to 8 feet in the front.. As in the middle of all this number 2 girl was presented to me, her name was Hailey, she seemed nice, as she camped out with all of her belongings, till Anna finally arrived, she spoke to her, as she put her stuff in the Cherokee, and was helping, onto the roof, as she showed how valuable she was, I think of them more as Anna's sisters, as she worked. I was now still laying the above roof, as it was 55 feet, to the lower, I had, the lower crew, stuff, the gap with mortar, as I cut off the edges, as the main roof was nearly done, the walls, were 3 footers in diameter, split log construction, with the ends off, so I could stack them, as for the other workers it was off to the second part housing for the tribe, and onto the wings, as this day ended quickly, but the roof, was nailed down, and next was finish of the mudding, as we all went back to our lodge, it was busy, some 60 people, we had dinner with, and a discovery of epic proportions, all the cedar blocks were cut into shakes, as I showed one how to do it, and all was on it. Some 400 hundred bundles. We loaded as much as we could, then went to bed smelling good.

August 21 Friday 2004

It was day 84, and both jeeps and trailers were loaded of slates, of cedar, we got there, with ten men's help, and only five hammers, I had enough small nails to drive them in, so some used rock, or so I thought it was limestone, and another discovery. The tripod was hoisted on the roof, and bundles were sent up, as I showed them what to do, as for the back wall, to its roof, down towards the main area, and the above roof, from the sides, I knew I needed a gutter, the cedar was laid, and hammered on, then up to the highly slanted roof, where five of the men started on the bottom and worked their way, along in rows, while, my focus was on the wings, and my four diggers went, as I showed them as the tripod was moved to the east side first away from the lake. The ground was a marshy flood plain, and soft digging, so I used the five footers in diameter and they went in, it was measured 100x100, as I hooked off the remaining structure, I added a back wall, 5-25 footers by five feet wide, in, as the day was done. The lodge roof shingles was complete and ready for a top cap, it was mortared in, and a five foot in diameter split log, 2-50 feet long was in place, as 100 feet was laid nailed down and the top roof complete.

August 22 Saturday 2004

It was day 85, and we went back with more shingles, and to do this all over again. Another dry day, meant, construction on the wings, with a tie off to the east from the main part, to where the new greenhouse was going, 5 footers in diameter was the norm, as the 100 x 100 structure took shape, 2-20 x 20 x 100 were under construction, with the logs ends cut off, then laid down to form a foundation, then 3-foot in diameter were split and a 30 foot floor x 100 was laid, then it was Mike and Realize, laying the walls up, as I had instructed them to do, as five others were helping out.

On the west side, or bank side, another wing was being assembled, off the main part, where a 4-25 footer, by 3 foot in diameter, went in, and the work went fast, to the 100 foot mark, on both sides. The lake was another issue, as two streams were diverted by me, it's my job every day to ensure the water stays away, meanwhile Anna and a crew of men came with her, to dig out the clay, in and around the front of the lodge, while Brian and I kept dropping huge logs, and choking them to the lodge. This time for the front dock, and to the front another 100 feet, of dock as the poles went in leaving about six foot up to hold the deck, and then cut 20 footers to lay, to form a flat dock surface, all the way down, to a turn, where we went in front of the east wing, to the edge, and out of the water, or marsh. Next we took the remaining, and did the same for the west side, along the bank, it was level all the way out to a hundred feet. We were done and went back in that forest had plenty of more colossal trees to work with, the plan was quite simple, as all work stopped for lunch. Anna had a big stock pot of vegetables, and the workers ate that, while Brian and I had our stash of dried beef, and leftover wheat bread, the workers didn't care that they ate the food all up, nor did I. I had a deadline, to have this constructed and all I have is one more day. So I chose to drop in the center poles, across the west side as the east side was almost identical to my north compound. Two sets of structures 20x20 five rooms each for ten per row, and ten on the other side. We each took a turn at the tripod, which was the handiest tool I had. Brick making was at an all-time high, as Anna had her men digging out a bowl, along the front of the lodge, then stirring the batter and then set in a form, let stand an hour, turn over onto several ash pits, and the fire sealed them, then the bricks were carried in, to the main part, which was vast, as the bricks came in, and set in on the floor, to begin the outline. Two massive open pit fireplaces. I went back to my construction on the east wing, as, poles were cut on the sides, which we had to split earlier, and used my chainsaw guide, each 24 foot log, was swung over and placed, I had my chain saw and Mike and Sadu helping me, and with Brian was Timu and Realize. We went fast, as by the end of the day, we had the frame for the both sets of houses, for both sides a total of 40- 20x20 x 100 feet long, I was just laying logs, as I would later cut doors and windows, two each. We stopped at near dark, well it's still actually light, but it was time of rest. I took Anna and our two girls with me and Brian had the girl workers, as we went back to my lodge. Anna helped Lily fix a grand meal, but it was I who ate first, with Brian, we had Nina and Hailey at our table. Also Little Hawk and some of the men went deer hunting and came back with several, to feed the men and women, it was a celebration, as Anna was actually much nicer to me, for some reason, maybe, she knew I was getting married and she was jealous. I ate to my heart's content, Little Hawk, came in to say, "We like your pen on the other side, can you build one for us?"

"Yes" I said not looking up, for her to say, "Your probably the strongest hardest working man I've ever seen." She left as it was quiet, as it was brief then talking resumed, after my shower as I was first, then Anna, and Brian and so forth, everyone went to sleep, Charley brought up more mattress's from Anchorage, for them to sleep on during the week. They were all happy, and so was a couple of girls, as Nina came to me and spoke up, to say, "What she meant, Little Hawk, would have forsaken her husband, to be in your favor."

"I see, but I don't care, I do what I have to do." And then I went to bed and to sleep.

August 23 Sunday 2004

It was day 86, and I got up, and dressed went out, to see the animals were well taken care of. It was Nina and Hailey, fetching wood for the fireplaces, and it was like having two sisters around. They were the real workers, as I got my gear together, as Brian arrived, he said, "Boy, it's nice to have help, both of my girls you lent me are strong, and proficient, especially in the greenhouse, as he handed over a bucket, to Anna, who took them in to make a stock pot of vegetables and he held up two artichokes, to say, "This is from us to you, enjoy". Brian and I drove to the Indian lodge. But coming on it I saw the crane on the highway, then we exited, to a flood of trucks, all lined the drive, we got down to the end, to stop, as almost forty men, were staring at the structure, as a guy named Rob, introduced himself as the general contractor for the governor, and he said, "It wasn't supposed to start till this Monday, but I can see you got a head start, so tell me what you need, as you're the point, and the governor did tell me to follow your lead."

"I have to finish the east side structure, to the roof, then put the roof on, then mortar it and then shingle it" said I.

"Well you're the boss, I'll allow you to work, just tell me what you want my men to do?"

I said, "Let's go have a meeting?"

As Rob gathered his men, we went into his shack, it was crowded, as I said, "State, your positions", It was the crane operators first, which I said, "If you have walkie talkies communicate with Brian, general carpenters, I need you in the east wing, do you have any plywood?"

"Yes" said Rob.

So I said, "Have them put that down over the face up logs, if it's not straight level out the floor, we will notch the logs, I need inside help, electricians run your wire, plumbers, I want to work with you, I orchestrated the crew, as I was hands on, an architect drew up my plans on the fly, and the whole crew executed it, as the main room center was the place everyone convened on, following my lead, I set logs on their sides to form walls, passageways, and rooms, up to a second story which split logs were laid, insulation put in was complete. Then it was windows were added, furniture makers, made beds, each had a fireplace, we were all working as one. Rob told me it was 24/7 till we were done, the crane was faster, as it set the top poles in place, over the west side, as I had the tripod over on the east side, as a bundle of split logs, were laid, masonry men filled the gaps, and the roof was on, and shingled. Inside each room, two windows and two doors, each had a balcony, or on the ground floor, a walkway. Room by room it was completed, to give the tribe 80 beds, or four to a room. I checked on the east wing, it was near complete as it was relatively easy, as it was as fast finish. The electrician tied in all the power, the whole place was lit up, all the plumbing was in, with a drain going to a huge septic tank. Well that's not true, wastes from the toilets went directly to it, as the showers and sinks, went to a vat to be recycled, although water pressure was down, Rob wanted me to build a water tower, above, to get pressure, as I could divert two streams, into it. While I and Brian left, to go home, the crew continued on all three places, I had to call it a night.

August 24 Monday 2004

It was day 87, and I and Brian was up early, I was on the saw mill, cranking out planks, the Jeep grand Cherokee, and trailer, was getting planks, as I cut 2x4's, for inside framing, while I did that, several helicopters, landed on the highway, above the Indian tribe and the governor was driven down, he saw firsthand, the massive structure, in all of its glory, and men were all over that thing, as Rob ran over to him, for Jim to say, "Where is the boss?"

"He went home."

"Goddammit Rob, I told you work for him."

"Yes, I told him that, he is still the lead, nothing has changed he went home, to use his saw mill to make a water tower."

"Your joking, seriously."

"Yes governor, seriously, shall I show you around, this guy is a serious large construction builder", the governor looked at him, as he entered up some stairs, to see a vastness of wood, to the ceiling, as lights were being installed, to say, "I see supports what of rooms?"

"Well, Matt, said he wants to construct this as the gathering place, and thus offices for crafts and welfare."

"Good, good, I wonder how much he has in all this?"

"I don't know but from one estimate, it's over a million dollars, of some materials, which we used from the land, but electrical, each room, to the appliances, I have to say, this is all impressive."

"Alright, can you send someone up and get Mister Michales?"

"Yes sir" said Rob telling someone else that, as Jim said to John, "He is on to something here, as they walked out front, to say, "I gave him a week, and this is what he did, this place is huge probably over 100K feet of living space, as he walked the dock, and over to the west wing, undid a latch, and saw the men back filing the dirt in the open space, between each room which was 20x20, and impressive, as each room had twin bunk beds, for a family of four, then went out, only to see pilling going in, for step up to the second level, using a tripod, as he was over along the dock, seeing the lake being dug out, and over to the east wing, marveled at the ingenuity, and practicality. Anna and her crew arrived, as she went to work on the two main fireplaces, the governor stopped to say, "Anna is that you?"

"Yes Governor?"

"Where is that man of yours?"

"The last I saw of him was tearing up trees, and making planks, and 2x4's, they should be down here, shortly."

"Good I want to have a word with him."

She went back to work instructing the masons, what she wanted, as she got the news, they were having all the modern luxuries, and conveniences. The electrical was going in the main room, huge windows, went in, front next to the fireplaces, the governor was impressed, as the west wing, was going in and as he stepped out, he was on the dock, as below him they were digging out the shallow bottom.

"Simply impressive" said the governor, as crews, were hard at work, and that's when I arrived, to get caught up, as we had lots of planks, and 2x4's, and as I was to lay out the wood water tower, it was the governor, I looked up to say, "Sorry I didn't get it done in the week, so many things to do."

"That alright boy, come take a walk with me."

I got up and followed him to a nearly cut field, for him to say, "We need someone like you working for us, you have demonstrated, your capable enough to handle, yourself, you have made improvements, you're a conservationist at hand, I have had multiple inquiries into these massive lodges, and from other parts of the country, so I ask will you accept the job of lodge builder for the Yukon Territory?"

"Yes, sure, what of the challenge?"

He kept his mouth shut, but went on to say, "I will pay you a million a year, plus expenses, and I will allocate 20 million for this lodge project, I hope to net much more in revenues, so when can you start?"

"I guess I've been at it a week now, but do let me finish this lodge and decide after my friends are coming in first of September."

"Alright, we will work out the details later, but in the meantime, I'll have a check for you about 83,000 so let me know, and I will give you a list to get started on."

I raised my hand, as he said, "Speak freely."

"I do accept this job, but if you could, allow me to finish this, can I have my right hand, Brian,"

"Sure, what will his pay be?"

"The same as mine?"

"Nope, maybe half at best that is what Rob gets."

"That's fair." I said as he was walking away from me, and into the truck, as he drove off, as I went back to laying out the tank, I chose square as it was easier to put together, the tongue and groove was created by a master carpenter, as it was 20x20 and my goal was 80 feet tall, each 20x20 board was glued together. I went working on the base, 4-5 footers in diameter at ten feet tall, the above crane moved its position, to help set the logs quickly, was set down, in the ground up ten feet, it was solid, the streams, ran about 40 feet higher. I was watching them build the platform, 20 x 20 x 20 feet tall, with stringers to 80 feet tall, the tongue and groove was working, the day ended, with it a quarter of the way done, but what was done, a greenhouse duplicate, of the east wing, to the west, and the main inside was nice, plywood down, plumbing was going in. I went home with Anna who said, one of the fireplaces was done, and it was nice.

August 25 Tuesday 2004

I woke up thinking, I was a millionaire on day 88, which proved it would happen over and over again, as I knew my 50 percent stake in mushroom organics llc, was topping a quarter of a million and half of that is mine, the gold collection in the valley by Hailey and Nina is also growing. They want to set traps along the White river, I agreed to make some small box traps. Brian and I went back to the Kluane tribe, and to see the lodge nearly complete, both wings were done, and off the lodge was the two greenhouses, using the last of my Plexiglas, was installed, on the roof, as the carpenters planked the sides to form it up. The roof went down to about seven feet high, the Plexiglas gave me two rows of 8 feet, it was weird at first, but then, I saw its advantage, it was hot in there, but will be effective. All men converged on the inside of the main house, where a two story 16 room apartment complex, with a bathroom in each across the way was showers, and bath in the old fashioned style bath house way and tubs, and laundry, in flowing tubs, 10x10, 2 feet deep, some conveniences was hard to understand, but was there for later, the front dining was big, in the middle was a courtyard, but I instructed the men to build a jump into a water place, with split logs, as I diverted some water into a trough, and it flowed to that spot and flowed out both sides, into a 8 foot pit, with a ladder, a platform to jump off it was about 20x40 inside dive or jump pool. We used logs to finish the rooms, and fireplaces were set in. I fabricated a smoker, while the work progressed. It was another day as we went home, I told Brian the news he was hired he was delighted.

August 26 Wednesday 2004

Day 89, and the lodge was about done, the final, awning was set out in the middle and on the wings, the electric worked, and the water flowed, like nature, plumbing was in, all the beds made, and assembled, more mattresses were on order. The inside main room was spectacular, even the hot tub the chief liked so much, was cleaned up and set in his place, he took the lower room, with his wife, and the next room over, I cut a door for him, he was the only one with carpet, the rest was linoleum. Even the back room, which was 40x 200, huge, I cut blocks for them to bring in to split. We were done. It was now onto a small barn for the crops cut and need to be stored, so on the back of the main house, it went in for a two story barn, pictures were taken, and a total was added up, it came in at a million 2. For me it was a flight to Whitehorse, in a helicopter left by the governor, with a pilot. I was present for the wedding between Ramie, and Mike the tallest of the tribe, young man. It was nice but Anna tricked me into thinking it was for me, but she told the chief, it was actually for me till she set him straight. I was at the tribe who had a landline, and made the first call to the governor's office and talked with governor, he was elated, but also by the large mortgage, they owed, at 1.2 million divided by 360 months, is a monthly payment of about 3500, or a buffalo, to the state, but I had my own plan, as they moved into their new accommodations. In the greenhouses, Lily showed some of the girls, what to do, the hot side and the cool side, which was the west, I had Sadu, the chief of the fields, as I put in a second massive barn, it was 100x100, as the crews continued to work, while others went home to Whitehorse. The hay was stacked in the top part, as I made a call to the supplier instead of Jake and ordered another 1200 bales of alfalfa hay, at 10K and put it on my credit card, then, I needed to fence this in, with 3 foot in diameter logs fifteen feet high, as the crane was useless, we used the tripod was what worked and the crew was there, it was massive as the diggers dug, and also a backhoe, dug, which cleared the way, along the hill, it was probably 1000x 2000 or at least for another week, the last thing I did was break, the dam, and the streams again, flowed, into the half dug bottom about 6 feet deep, to about 200 feet out. We were done, and Brian went home. I took the jeep, to the gas station, and got into the helicopter, and sat up front as it took off to Whitehorse, an hour later, it landed, it was nearing, 1 pm as I went in, I was grubby looking, but didn't care, but Gladys, the Governor's secretary did, she swept me into an apartment, and said, "Shower, change into some nice clothes, prefer a tie, and then you may see the governor."

I did as I was told, and cleaned up nicely, even shaved. I went out as she was waiting for me, to be introduced, as I was swept into his office, as he said, "Ah you made it, Matt Michales meet my secretary Gladys, Gladys he will take over offices 212-214. Come walk with me, the buzz around all of this has got me to wondering will you build me a mansion of this nature?"

"Sure, whatever you want?"

"I like to hear that, because I have the crew waiting, but first let's see your office, as we rode up in the elevator, I didn't know when to say it, but now was any as I said, "Mister governor."

"Call me Jim."

"Alright Jim, was the last I spoke, as the doors opened it was mayhem, of those surrounding us, as we were let through to those rooms, massive room by size and height, for him to say, "I wished we knew you before, I would have had you build these impractical offices", as I saw tables and desks, to each division of the building. For him to leave me to Rob, as another lady named Anneillea Tillwater, gave me a packet, to say, "Welcome you are the new senior planning and building officer, in the envelope is your check, I am the assistant to the governor and comptroller, anything you need and also you need to staff, as you like, we have a pool of secretaries, you can choose from, but its best you choose your own." She left as I said, "Calm down, quiet please, Rob, catch me up on the governor's mansion?"

"Well were waiting, your expertise, and direction, it sits on a cliff, and he wants to incorporate that, also we have an order for a mall, to house all the shops."

"Send the architect out to draw the mansion using logs."

"Will do, when do you wanna go out and see the site?"

"Let's go now" so Rob and I went down to his car, and drove out and a ways up a hill, to an open site, where it was the chosen spot for the new governor's mansion and grounds, as I got out to see it was quite breath taking overlooking the city, forests all around, a perfect place, I said, "You have a shovel?" I got one from him and struck down it was rocky, for me to say, "This one will be a duzy".

It was getting late as we went back, for Rob to say, "The next project is up in Old Crow, an old outpost of people along the Porcupine river, they get there supplies from Fort Yukon in Alaska, but seek us to build them a lodge, similar to the Indian lodge, but with some cover over their entire operation, to the train station."

"That reminds me we need to send a decontamination team to the Kluane Indians, and dispose of all the contaminants and left over buildings."

"I'm on it, and I will oversee it being done."

"Thanks", we got back, time enough for me to see the governor, for me to say, "A word Sir?"

"Yes Matt, what is it?"

"For the debt on the Kluane Indians, I'd like to give them my pay."

"No out of the question, they have 100,000 acres, and plenty of buffalo, not to mention gold, so they can find a way to pay it off, besides, in their petition, they specified, they had that amount of reserves, I'll accept anything from pelts to hides, gold to whatever, oh that reminds me, I need a geologist, know one?"

"Yes I do, it's my girl Anna."

"Great, next time bring her along, for I have a job for her, oh and one more thing, we need to update your place, do let me have a figure and I will, fund it, did Miss Tillwater present you with your check?"

"Yes, but where do I cash it?"

"Two places, here in this building, and at our credit union, your choice, and lastly I don't expect you to be here all the time, but do check in with me once a month or two."

I took my check down, to cash it, Miss Tillwater was there, to cash me out, as she then took taxes out, with taxes of 40 % I came in at under 50K, in a professional satchel, I walked out the front door, across the street was the credit union, a Miss Jelville Grant, said "Hi, how may I help you?"

"My name is Matt Michales, and would like to set up and account", I showed my driver's license, and she took a picture of that, to say who do you work for?"

"The government."

"In that case your tax exempt" as she counted out the amount, to say 49, 800 cash. Do you want any back?"

"No" as I got the receipt, and the passbook, she said, "Where do we send your visa card?"

"The government building across the way, room 212, attn. myself, thanks", I walked over to the helio landing, where my pilot was waiting, as I got in, and off we went, an hour later, we were on the other side of the gas station in beaver creek, as I drove the jeep home. Anna had a nice meal, the tribe was all gone, but the chores were caught up, as I said, "Guess what honey, the governor has hired you to be the territory's next geologist."

"That's great, now finish eating you have a big day tomorrow, so let's get some sleep."

"Yes dear." I said going to sleep.

August 27 Thursday 2004

It was day 90, I was at home, doing things like building several bridges, while, the helio flew over to us, seeking us to go, so Anna and I flew into Whitehorse, and onto the big government offices, I led Anna to Miss Tillwater, who looked up the job, to say, "I imagine senior one, your pay is quarter of a million, oh wait, here is the memo from the governor, it says, "Half a million, so about 41, 666, as she cut it to say, "Do you wanna cash that here?"

"No" I said, as she said, "Alright". As I led Anna up and over to her office she had a few students waiting, I went on to my offices, still abuzz with workers, for I said, "Find some work or I will have you digging trenches, or matter of fact, all of you just standing here gathering a paycheck, take a truck, up to the governor's proposed mansion and begin to dig, a five foot wide by five feet deep trench a hundred feet long. "I'll have John Hughes", whom was just standing, "There to help out there to supervise." The place cleared out, as I was going over the projects, to see it was Old Crow, in northern Yukon, then Teslin, Watson Lake, Keno Hill, Mayo, Pelly Crossing, Forty Mile and the Carmacks. Each presents lots of challenges, but it was the mansion first, as it must be a priority as it says so, so I better get up there and supervise the crew myself, as I went down to motor pool, and to see all of our stuff, and got a monster truck, it was big, and wheelies to ride the train tracks, it was a specialty designed big truck, and got in, to see the crane, as I said, "Seen the operators, have them come up to the top of the hill for the new governor's mansion."

"Yes sir" said the fleet inspector, as I drove it out, and up the hill to see some standing around, to hear me say, "Let's get going dig." I watched as everyone waited.

"Were working smart, were waiting for a backhoe."

I took off towards the backdrop and forest. With a new tape in hand, I marked trees, for excavation by me, 3 footers, and 5 footers, I noticed right off, these woods were not as gifted as ours, the timber was maybe, 2 in a quarter at best, which meant another approach to this, the governor wanted a towering roof, but I would need twenty five footers five feet in diameter, and most of the trees were at the most 55 tops, which meant a lot of little ones, at the top. I went for it, and began taking trees I marked as I went using the gear on the truck, and a nice chain saw, it cut like going through soften butter. I out worked this lazy crew, when I realized I need my four diggers, and it would be honorable work. So I left that crew still struggling, and went back in, and dropped off my saw, to maintenance, they sharpened the chain, as I went back upstairs, I went over to see Anna whom was in all kinds of paperwork, so I got out of there, to see Miss Tillwater, who said, "You have room to hire, shall I post something?"

"No I got a handle on that."

I went out to the pilots offices, to get my pilot, only to find out he went hunting, and would be gone, so I asked for another, but said "They were all out, till night, so I went back in to see the governor, who Gladys said was busy, so I went back up to my offices, try to think what to do then an idea came to me, my buddy Paul Nelson is a combat helicopter pilot, maybe he could show me, then I could get around. I pulled up my phone, to call him, it went to voice mail, as I said, "Paul its Matt, just want to know when you're coming up?" I slid it shut. I went back to work, when the governor stopped by to say, "Matt you had a question for me?"

"Yes, what would be the possibility if I could have a helicopter, and fly it myself?"

"Well, sure, they are all yours, we have five, as for lessons, you would need to go to Anchorage airport is the only training place, shall I set it up for you?"

"Sure Mister Hickson, if you don't mind."

"I don't, it would be nice to have an additional pilot, plus I'll add another 100K to your salary, most people are up here to collect a paycheck, but not you, you're a worker."

"Thanks governor for the nice words." I said.

"You're welcome, oh one more thing you need a secretary?"

"Yes sir." I said, as I dialed up Gladys, for which I said, "Can you post a job opening for personal assistant, to me."

"You mean secretary?"

"Yeah, secretary."

"I'll have four up there this evening, when are you planning on leaving?"

"At five" I said.

"Oh right because of the challenge."

"Yes."

The rest of the day I went back out to the site for the governor's mansion on the hill, it was still in the same shape, so I suited up, helmet goggles and earplugs, and another saw, and spent the rest of the day taking down the logs, then measuring them, and cutting them, the suppose diggers became my chokers, and began to haul logs to the site. The work was slow and although it was close to five, I went back in, dirty and went to a room I was assigned, for day visits, I took a shower and into cleaner clothes, Anna brought. I went upstairs, to see four women of varying degrees of age, I said, "Ladies I will be with you soon, as I collected up Anna who helped me to interview them, and she chose one, we notified the governor, and it was a young girl named Karlotta Damia. She immediately went to work, as she was an organizer, from the stack of in papers to a cluttered desk, all was cleared off, as clip boards went up for work orders, it was 530, we just got word our ride was here, as we went out, into the helicopter, and we flew out, as I instructed him, to fly to the Indian reservation, he did, as he landed outside the door, the whole of the tribe was there, to greet me, as I went in to visit Chief Awani, and Little Hawk, to say, "I need Sadu, Timu, Realize and Mike, to come dig for me?"

"Yes it is granted, the chief would also express his gratitude for this spectacular place, and of the cleanup of the cabins."

"Tell him he is welcome, so we will be by tomorrow, take care, as I went off, we were flown back home, set down, just outside the brick factory, to come up with an idea. The day ended with the eight of us having dinner. We went to bed.

August 28 Friday 2004

It was day 91, the helio was supposed to be here by 0900, but wasn't, as Brian was here waiting, and the radio had clear advisory, so I called, the governor, who said he was sorry, all pilots are busy, so we will see you Monday. I called back to the office and was patched through to my secretary, Karlotta, who said, "All work orders are being worked, for her to say, "This is the most efficient this place has ever been, so said the governor, and I said, "Good job, keep it up", and said good bye, she told the others, and I went to work in my shop building trap boxes, while all the girls went moss collecting, Brian stood guard. I took several box traps, for rabbits, and went up the line, and was in my wet boots, to walk the river it was the lowest ever, as we were in a draught, but knew that would not last, as in the middle of the north compound her crops, were up and growing well. So I took my jeep, along the well-traveled trail, and got out to check each line, as we are only trapping to keep, all the way to the trail head. To park, then it was walking in to the canyon. I went up stream, to set the last box, it went in to the sand, I went and placed rocks in and around it, the ladder went in the water, I was set. I went back, and into my jeep, each trap was marked, as I drove back, and into the north compound, while the girls came back loaded down, I told Brian of the new job, he said he was ready, as for Lily, she and the two girls were running the warehouse, food was plenty, as some was being stored. I also heard from my Marine boys, they would be up here on September 7th on the early flight into Whitehorse. I told them I would pick them up. With Kluane lodge done, and spectacular pictures taken, and put up, for tourism, it was on to my next project, gathering berries for the winter, so Brian and I went gathering with the women, we had four girls whom were like our sisters, as they were hard workers, we picked all morning, it was an adventure, we were across the bridge, near moss valley was a massive patch of blackberries. It was nice. Anna had said "I wish I had canning jars, and I said I would get some on Monday. That afternoon we all had a picnic, by the bridge, I was thinking, "Why wasn't the homestead, selected here, next to the bridge, with all the water, oh well, only to realize because of all the bugs."

After lunch we all went to the field, left of the north compound to slice the fast growing field, of wheat, alfalfa, oats and barley. It took all day. They were all over in tarps, similar to her vegetables. It was late, I took a shower, and went in to relax, and watch TV, and fell asleep.

August 30 Sunday 2004

It was day 93, It was truly a day of rest, as Anna sent a pigeon, which resides, in a place I built for them on the outside of the northeast lookout, they were a dirty bird. The bird was launched to Laurie, explaining it was a day of feasts, come one come all.

I was busy wood working, and keeping all the fires lit, because it was a gloomy day, and just like that it rained, and poured. We were all dry as the roof was solid and water diverted into water holding tanks, bugs were at an all-time low, we need to discover a way to keep the bats warm, through the winter, and ourselves warm as well.

Billy and Laurie showed up with John and Kim, it was a celebration of epic proportions, we had deer, elk, and bear, we had vegetables, and salads, and lastly we had, oatmeal raisin cookies, it was a glorious time, as each shared how they plan on making it through the winter, for John and Kim, their place is stacked and stored, the cattle love their new place, as do them. Billy and John finished Billy's house, and back area for the animals, and wanted to know when we all could go again to Anchorage, I told them, I was going the second week of September."

They all wanted to go, but I said it was business, as I told them of my job, and they wanted to work for me, which caught me off guard, so I said "Sure, why not", as did Laurie, she wanted to get back in the Vet game. We all ate to our hearts content, for me it wasn't much, just a sampling of foods. We ended the night in song and dance, as the rain kept on going, it was actually ten-twenty degrees warmer in and under that roof, it was nice. We ended with each hugging the other, as they left, and drove off, I knew I need to build a heavy gate for the front of the north compound, and of the place to go over the road. Brian left with Lily and his two helpers, Aileena and Mariam, as for ours it was Nina, and Hailey turning in after the cleanup.

CH 11

Meeting my friends, for the chase of bears

August 31 Monday 2004

It was early 0500 Monday day 94, as it was the same old thing, check the animals, collect the eggs, and we all have a hearty breakfast, all was secure, as it was still raining, our drains, were on full throttle, the wind was up, it was nasty, we all four, Myself, Anna, Nina, and Hailey checked the south compound, the animals, was well under our breeding care, down here and up there. We all four were soaked, realizing why a roof over that road was next. That was maybe 100 feet in the open, it was bad, harsh weather, Brian showed up for work at 0800, and at 0830 a helio landed, long enough, to load up our gear, I had the block and tackle, as the three of us flew to Kluane, landed, and four strong diggers, got in, we were loaded, and could feel it, all the way to Whitehorse which was overcast, but dry. Anna and I kissed, she went in to see her staff, I went into the motor pool, and got transportation, and took the diggers up to the mansion, where the backhoe, and crane was, the crew was ready, and found David who had the plans to the governor's mansion, it was complex, it called for three places for a basement, into rock infested ground to boulder size rocks, it was a mess, and the drawing was accurate as I agreed with it, I did make some final changes, I sent the boys, Mike, Timu, Sadu, and Realize in each hole to dig out the basements, with the other crew. Each group got down to a very low place, at a foot an hour to a total of five feet in five hours. I decided to drop the logs down to be the support, five feet deep, I had ten footers at about 4 foot in diameter cut, and built another tripod, even though I had a crane handy, the tripod kept it from swaying, like the crane did. Overall it was about the size of the lodge on the north compound. 140 x120, with three basements, and a 40x 200 log and rear storage. We set up ramps, for the logs, the crane hoisted, Brian oversaw the splitting, he was good, while, the 3 footers in diameter was cut for the floor, in the basement, then everyone got in the middle, where it was the main room, and worked, someone forgot to tell us it was supposed to rain, and instantly it opened up. Now we were all drenched and muddy. Realizing it was wrong to start there, it should have been the 40 x 200 structure first, as everything became water logged but it did allow us the opportunity to dig it out and finish the basement. We broke out tarps, using four twenty five footer 5 foot in diameter, we set it, I in the middle, with Brian and my four diggers laid out the huge tarp, it worked, as it was a portable roof. They finished digging out the basement, for the main house, the crane placed each of the 4-25 footers, five feet in diameter, in each basement, as the rain surged. We were official in the cool season, but we were able to set them in, and stretch the tarp out, as corner ones went in, to form the foundation. Next was the split floor, logs were notched and laid all across the bottom. The tarp kept some of the water out but it was just damp.

With the last of the split logs for the basement set on the edges. It was now the floor, it was 40x40, with some on pilings, to keep it level, and for the plumbers to do their work, we laid the logs in a pattern, allowing a set of stairs, up in each of the basement rooms. The diggers went to the chain saws, to use the guide, and we got another one, as the two teams, shaved up the precut logs, and sent them down, to form up the load bearing walls as they were laid horizontally. They were in between the supports. We were getting an upper hand, as the logs were placed by crane, ten times faster, as it was all logs now, being set and forming three distinct rooms, up to the main floor, I left 2 feet or so I could put in high windows, at the tops, to allow the light in. The next phase was the basement, as crews used rotary sanders to smooth out the floor, and insulation, at the top, also plumbing was done, and working their way up and in, and under our floor for three distinct restrooms, out to a septic tank, being dug 20 feet down and set in.

Next was the wiring, as electricians went at it.

For the main floor, it was split log upon split log, first was in-between the outside support logs went in, then 40 footers, 3 feet split, face up, to cover the distance. Night was among us, as we quit at 5 pm, My crew and Anna boarded the helicopter and it flew off, our captain's name was Dave Scott. He flew to the Kluane, and the diggers got out, and then us to home. We ate dinner and went to bed.

September 1 Tuesday 2004

It was 0500, we woke up to dry, as the rain past, it was day 95, did our chores, and kept the fireplace lit, the two girls, were continuing to forge, collect berries and nuts, as they found a rare walnut tree, it was called a white Russian walnut. Lily was canning jam and syrups, oats were shelled, as was barley, as they kept on working, we had a large number of eggs and had omelets of vegetables, and beef chipped in gravy with fried potatoes. Toast of fresh wheat bread. Helicopter was here, and we were off, to up to the Indian reservation, to pick up our four diggers, we were in by ten, and on the job site by eleven. We were setting the main floor, nail it down, it was crude. Next was the rotary sanders to smooth out the split logs, then a layer of plywood went down, level, out to the edges, where one layer of logs lie, actually, a grid was in place, with the exterior was that of all logs, but placed differently, than I was used to, and reason being it was David's drawings. The logs were all on their sides, precut by a crew, the ends shaved, as the diggers, were working on the back line up to the first level 10 feet high, we in the front line caught up with them as the carpenters were on the sides, till the middle caught up with us. Then the 1st floor went down, of 40 foot 3 foot in diameter, were split, and laid face up, as lunch was called. Brian and I went to a local diner, he had a burger and fries, and I had, liver and onions, actually two plates full and a chocolate milkshake. We got back up there, as it was around 2:30, pm and the next set of logs were going down, this time to 8 feet tall, for a second floor, as we raced to that level, the hardest part was the grand entrance and the split logs for stairs, as we worked till 5 pm, and stopped abruptly. Brian and I went back with the four workers, the governor's mansion was the priority and looking at it as it was 75 % finished. I was sure going to finish before the ground freezes, as some have said, "After the second week of fall". I listen to the locals, and knew I had only that time to compete the roof. Next up was the windows, for all the entire building and for the mason crew to come and do their work overnight. On tap was the six massive fireplaces, as we went home, had a good meal and went to sleep.

September 2 Wednesday 2004

It was day 96, but I knew the challenge was over, because, Anna told me, she had our deed, and 1280 acres of all the land, but the secret would last, as it was business as usual, with our chores, and I knew it would be around 11 before the helicopter would come, so Brian and I went looking at my traps, with my wade boots on, and up to the box, it moved, as we got closer, it looked like inside was a bunch of Otters. I could of just released them, but I recently read a manual, that river otter was extinct in the Yukon, I had Brian help me carry it, I pushed up the ladder, to secure it, and the front slide door, it was a box, all the way back to the jeep we carried it, and then back track to smaller boxes and sure enough rabbits, two of them, and lastly it was the second river box, it too had a creature inside, it too was suppose extinct, a mink. We went back to the south compound, and set them free inside, to the rear pens, for the otter, it was a mom and two pups, for the mink, just one, it shrilled at us, as it was vicious. We then cleaned out the box, and dumped it into a half barrel, and to my surprise gold, gold everywhere, once cleaned up, we took them back out, and reset the traps, and we were done. Brian and I went back, to the half barrel, and began to sift through it all, the discovery was all that gold, a lot was flake, but some nuggets, I began to sort, as I applied some water, and a makeshift ladder, to collect up the gold. Into a bag, it was a slow go but worth it. Next Brian and I went with Hailey to the moss valley, as she was cutting pieces. I was picking up gold nuggets, they were everywhere, so was Brian, the valley was huge, and some of it was on Brian's side, but that didn't matter anymore, as it was all Mine now. As for Billy and Laurie's marriage was cracking, she showed up in their only truck, to say, "Take me with you to town, I'm done?"

"Why" I asked.

"Because I want to be a Vet, not a house mate, can you help me out Matt?"

"What of our agreement" I asked.

"Fine, how much longer?"

"It is only day 96 of 365, 269 to go, it hasn't been that bad?"

"No I guess not, alright I'll go back." She said dejected. Seeing her that way, he knew it was not long before she found out to say, "Wait, I might have a job for you?"

"I'm listening, like what?"

"Like what you're doing."

"Sounds good when?"

"How about now" I said.

The helicopter, took, the four of us, and four more at the Indian reservation, and over to Whitehorse, got out, and took the crew to work, then came back, to escort Laurie upstairs to animal sciences, where a young intern was at a microscope, for I to say, "So where is your boss?"

"One hasn't been assigned yet" said the girl.

"Well now you have, here is your new boss, meet one Laurie Holmes, the two shook, for her to say, "My name is

Tina Wester, intern". I left them to get acquainted, as I went to see comptroller Tillwater, who said, "Ah any more hiring?"

"Yes a one Laurie Holmes" I said.

"Fine, what does she do?"

"She is a veterinarian."

"Seriously."

"Yes, why?"

"We just lost one, when can she start?"

"She is upstairs in animal sciences."

"Oh no, we need her in the field, upstairs is reserved for research, how much did you offer her?"

"I didn't."

"Good, I will" she said, rushing off.

I went outside, and into my vehicle, and noticed on a truck coming from the rail station with brand new helicopters, as I went up the hill to see progress beyond belief, the whole of the structure was up to the third floor, and the tarp was off, as split logs were going down on the roof, just as how I wanted them, as crews were all over that place. In a line were concrete trucks, waiting their turn, as the masons were hard at work, as they followed my plan of mortar on every log. I arrived, making sure the mortar was being used as filler in between the logs, if it needed it or not, as the whole structure was tighter. then the roofing crew, began to lie the tar paper, which I allowed them to do that, as the mortar was set, then the slats, of redwood, they found a patch, as the builders were getting in the groove of what I wanted, as Rob was acting supervisor, back from the job in Kluane. Inside the rooms were getting sheet rock, to tighten and quit the rooms, while windows were cut with precision, they used some cutting devise, as they went in perfect without any mortar. It was a call to lunch for me and Brian as the workers had their own schedule, the mansion was all but done, as the smoke came off the fireplaces. Rob came to me to say, "Were about done here, where to now boss?"

"Start digging the courthouse and feds center basements, and link them together." I said, as he was off, with the workers, whom were working three shifts, and around the clock, I left, as it was to all the plans now. At the end of the day, a truck brought Brian and the diggers to the admin building, where they went in and changed, I gathered Anna, and all of us, flew out, dropping them off, and to our place, it was 7 pm, still light, I said, to Brian, wanna dig and set some logs?"

He agreed, and we set two massive five foot diameters, at twenty feet, to the other side was ten foot high, we used three other poles to use as a block and tackle, which I literally have one with me at all times. So now we had four posts in each corner of the road, and two at twenty feet tall, near the north compound and two at ten by the south compound, we were done. I showered and had a nice meal and went to bed.

September 3 Thursday 2004

I remember what Laurie said to me, and now, she is knee deep in poo, pee and at the house and clinic of the late doctor Pilson, although he is gone, he had no one survived from his family, so the governor, gave her the property, in town, ten acres, a house and modern stuff, she was happy and secure. It was day 97, but the challenge was still going strong, in the editors mind. I guess there is so much footage, they are just keep replaying it. We went to Whitehorse, and took Lily and the two girls Nina and Hailey. they went shopping, at an outdated mall. I was still chief of operations for the governor's mansion, it too was modern, even after Brian divert a major spring, towards the residence, as he and Timu built a channel, as it deposited into a cistern, some 20x20 x 80 feet deep, slightly above the mansion, thus providing the mansion with its water source, and with an overflow, that, drained over, to a spectacular waterfall, as it hit a trench, and flowed through the city before emptying out in the Yukon river. I was everywhere around the admin building, it was so large, it had five levels, two underground, a vast parking underneath. From the admin building you could see the massive governor's mansion, and that's when I went into a meeting, to see others, and that's when the governor said, "This is what I think we are gonna do, create a theme park, up there, to include the federal building, and courthouse and park, all designed by, Matt Michales, please come up, I was taken off guard, but went up, to stand before fifty, to say, "Yes, once the governor's mansion is complete, it will be onto the court building, which we have already started and then the federal complex, to include a park, I stopped and whispered in his ear, "So that mean's planting of sequoias?"

He agreed, with me to say, "Were gonna try to replant the hill, with redwoods." Everyone agreed, and it was all agreed on and it was passed, and it was going to be so. I said to the governor, "Is this before or after the mall?"

"After of course" he said.

I left, with new orders, as Karlotta was phenomenal, in her abilities, and had my office running very efficiently, I went out to go to the mall, when I got there, oh it looked bad, some 50's themes, it was outdated and ancient, but there was a sign, it was moving, as I wondered why they were moving it, further out of town, where as it was in the alignment street wise to the admin offices, but on the other side of town, as I drove to the new location, there it was, a place not in line, with any progress, so I went back, to put up a fight, when the governor, agreed with me, and said it should stay where it is at, as I said, it can be lowered and have a upper, and some 500 feet long by 100 and a pool and slide, and make a water park."

"Are you joking?"

"Nope I did that for the Kluane tribe."

"Then draw it up and I will get it passed."

I went back upstairs, to sit at my overly huge desk, to draw out the amusement park, plus year-round water park and shops. It was huge, but the basement gives me twenty more feet of head space, as I designed a log run, and water park, in the ground, all recycling its own water, and helping each other, created a flume ride, of rapids down, and back up a again, we submitted the work to my architect David, as he put on the final touches, and it went to the territories parliament, it was passed, and set out on the net, for four designers of amusement type rides, and then I had to make an assessment of the total costs, for lumber I estimated 1.2 million, and water park the same, and the log ride half that, and all the shops, heat and air, to be 7.6 million to build. I took the estimate to David and the drawings, and he went to work, with my drawings, he put a price on everything, as bids were coming in, for a prespectious, so they can build the plans. I was done for the day, picked up Anna, as the governor pulled me aside to say, "Will you become a citizen of Yukon Territories?"

I said, "Yes, whatever it takes, just as long as you marry us, me and Anna" she smiled, to say yes, as the governor said, "Sure, you got a deal." As he was taking me out to the helicopters, to say, "You and Captain Dave will log hours flying back and forth, then solo, and then to Anchorage, for certification. You'll need your ID, in Yukon to do that." I understood and took Anna by the hand, as she released the ring, and took it off the cord, I inserted it on her finger, to get on one knee, to say, "Anna Long, will you marry me", she said Yes, and hugged and kissed me, as the others were showing up, including Lily and the two girls, each hugged us, as they two were growing a bit. With all of us in and me up front, I was given a manual to study, as Captain Dave took off, and back to the reservation. And then over to us, as Dave flew off, we went back to the slope roof, was ready, as in the road, we split logs on ramps, the tripod, lifted it up, on the edge, some 3 foot by at least a hundred ten feet, it was a fast go, I nailed them down, using our scaffolding and Brian was on the end, it was across the road, but still about twenty feet to either compounds. After each log was laid, all were tight. I was determined to close the gap and build a roof to each place, my focus was on the three bridges across the newly formed ditch, while Anna, Lily and the two girls, went up, and began to patch, with mortar. This was relatively easy, 2 massive 5 foot in diameter logs, laid down, to the fence and at the gravel road, for four places, then cut split logs, by 3 footers nailed down, with both garages having 20 feet wide by 20 feet long, then one in the middle for 10 x 20, walk way to the smoker, another 20 x 20 for the west side garage, level and it was nice, as it sloped up slightly, and then to the brick factory and a 20 x 30 as it was going fast, as night fell and we were done. And off, as Brian and Lily left, as I went to take a shower, and then had some dinner, and snuggled up with Anna, and we went to sleep, as I knew she wanted much more.

September 4 Friday 2004

It was day 98, and I was cramming my flight book, it was difficult, but with light, I was able to understand terms, and was ready, as Dave was there, as he quizzed me then we took off, he was hard on me, but knew if they had but one more pilot, meant less stress on him, so he was eager for me to learn. And I learned, he allowed me to fly, and it was a bit scary, but relativity easy, I was a natural, as I landed it, and then we exited, and on to work, up to the mansion, which was done, with the exception of the of some finish work. It was a dry day, well for the last four it was that way. Up on the hill, I arrived to get the official papers, as it was done. I looked at the assessment, it was all completed. The massive six fireplaces, were complete and going. The mansion had three levels, and in the theory of the White house, a hall down the middle, it was stout. Rooms were custom made, it was really warm inside, especially when the huge fireplaces were going. Next to the mansion was the parking structure, all three levels, made of logs, and was 100x100, the roof was on, windows on the sides, it too was study. It went together fast, and completed. It was nice it was all made of wood, the floor was made of plywood, and mortar. The back in level 2, was the wood storage, I did kind of feel left out, but that was in my own mind, as if it wasn't for me, none of this would have occurred. The platform was made up of logs, it looked spectacular, another issue that has come up is going to Old Crow, up in the arctic circle line. That is where the governor was from, a mining operation was on hold, as the last of their building, fell off the slope and all work has stopped. They need a lodge in which to repair and run and house the entire operation. I was in agreement I would go and assess it, a few said, that they would work tomorrow. I was waiting my friends arrival. I decided to take a helicopter ride to Old Crow. I waited for Anna, as my whole crew was here, and we flew off, dropping off the diggers, at their home and then up to our place. Dave said he would be there early it was a long flight, some six hours, a fill up in Dawson, then up and back. That night we finished laying the split logs over by the brick factory, and next was some railing, for the walk way and the garages, then it was on to shingle the roof. We went to bed.

September 5 Saturday 2004

It was early day 99, and the chores done, and the exotic animals, otter and mink somewhat happy, the roof over the road was nice, as now we can get from one side to the other, without getting wet. As I made the roof over, a simple, two logs set to the watchtower. Then I set in split logs some fifteen feet up to a top pole, on both sides, and the same for the other side, to the door at the smoker. After my chores and good hardy breakfast, I was in my shop, when the helicopter landed. I kissed Anna goodbye, and I went, with Dave, as we flew off, over the Dawson's range, up along the Yukon river, to Dawson. It was huge in comparison to Whitehorse, it was laid out in a fork, of rivers and the main machinery operation, also mining operation was there. We refilled, then we were off, over the hill crest, to where instantly it was cooler, and picking up the Porcupine river, and its many branches, and between several passes, around a bend, and into Old Crow. We landed at the suppose airport as rain was evident, the helicopter was escorted into a bay, to de-ice. We went in, to see where we needed to go, but it was I who was escorted to this secret place, as the guy drove me in, as he explained, that it was to mining operation west, for gold and silver, "It would be nice to have a roof, over the entire operation was needed", as we took the gravel road up for him to say, "Over all of this", as the truck came to a halt, I got out and met with an engineer, to show me, I drew up a square box around the operation, he signed off on it to say, "When can you start?"

"A week from this Monday" I said.

"No we need you now" said Bill, leading me over to a bank and down below was a set of cabins destroyed.

"Sorry I can't, but I will send up a crew to start digging."

"That's much better, winter, is only a few weeks away, as you can see we live out of tents, the sooner this is in, the more we can extract, and feed the government its riches. As he was referring to the governors land, and what he is tied to. "Holy Indian land used this land to mine, gold and silver, and along the way we hit copper. I was finished with my drawing, and he signed off on it, to include some cover for his vehicles, to extract and work the front end loaders, with plans in my hand and a signed off copy, I was taken back to the airport, as Dave and I flew back. We briefly stopped over to Dawson to refill, and back. It was a long day, I fell into the couch and went to sleep.

September 6th Sunday 2004

It was day 100, and I slept in, on the sofa, got up and realized everyone was gone, seeing the Jeep grand Cherokee, meant Brian and Lily was here, even the two girls who were the helpers they too was gone. Then around the corner, was the gang, it was like a parade of people, carrying food, some proteins, it was Billy, and John and Kim, for Laurie she was now living in Whitehorse, it was our last official party as the challenge was officially over, I keep saying that, but what's the point, especially if they are taping it, so I guess it's still on, and also saw, Laurie as happy as ever, for me to say, "How did you get here?"

"This morning flew in, as pilot Dave is going to Anchorage today, then he will come back and collect me up."

We all sat down to an incredible lunch, this Sunday routine was getting nice. It was our get together, for Billy it meant he was leaving to be with his wife, disappointed he let me down, I said, "Not to worry, the challenge is over, so if you wanna go, then it's up to you." Only Billy was going, as John and Kim were happy and was sticking it out, for now. Brian was in, so was Lily. As now that the land was claimed, I told John and Kim it was their property, do what as you will, just settle the debt with the Wilson's, and all would be forgiven. I especially loved the moss valley. And all those nuggets of gold. We ended our celebration, saying good bye to Billy and Laurie as they went home and packed it all up and half their animals went to John and Kim, and Anna and I, as they stopped by the Wilson's, and paid off their tab, and went towards Whitehorse. John mentioned he wanted to help out, so I said, "Be ready on Monday, as Brian will take you up north, wear long clothing and a jacket."

September 7 Monday 2004

It was day 101, and two helicopters came, one a transport and the other for me, it took Brian and the tripod block and tackle, chain saws, and equipment, and John, over to the reservation to get the four men, they took my teepee, in addition, Ramie went with her husband Mike, with supplies, up to Old Crow. Much to everyone's surprise it had snowed, just a dusting as it was bitter cold, Brian had his work cut out for him, with drawings in hand, he knew they were sitting on a plateau, it was crushed rock, on the left of the grounds, a proposed helicopter pad, complete with a small hanger, then where the cabins once was, was where the lodge was going in, and to incorporate that small office, at the end was a mine, it was set in a mountain, on the northwest side, that had train tracks visible, as it was car less now, as they went up north to a look out, and forests all around, John was me in theory, as he was tasked with taking the logs down, once Brian marked them, and the diggers dug a hole next to the entrance, for the 5 footers in diameter, went in the dugout five foot wide holes next to the entrance, apart 40 feet, the logs were 20 feet tall. A brace had to be used, to support them. Then another 20 feet long went away along the edge as another two went in, in a theme to provide cover for the front end loader while it worked the outer edge, as it was going to be in a stair step 40x40, as down another 40 feet another two poles went in, with the tripod, Brian measured more, as logs were drug to them by a massive forklift, as it was on tracks, but just as those pilings went in, and were righted, the digging crew was working solidly, downward to the train depot. Brian and John, were laying out the logs, on the ground, trusses were being built, to cover forty feet, stringers that held the trusses, were set in place by the large forklift, across the front of the mine, it seemed to work, as the top was at 20 feet, it over hung two feet. While they were there the mine cars were offloaded, into the front end loader, and then to an awaiting dump truck. To go, to the below train cars. But by enclosing the top means, faster production, and as for the teepee, it didn't help much as it was set out in the open. For me, I was in Whitehorse, for my flying lessons, and the start of my week at the admin building, I just received word, Brian made it safely. Anna was working today, and we both visited Billy and Laurie's new place, called the Pilson's ranch, Billy took that sign down, to put up Doctor's Laurie Holmes practice. As Laurie said, "Care for any food, Matt, Anna?"

We both said, "No, were not hungry." As we got a tour of their place, it was nice but outdated, as Laurie said to me, "Can you build me something newer?"

"Sure just after I finish the mall."

We went to the airport, only to hear the airplane was delayed out of Edmonton. I took Anna back to work, it was also the official day the governor was moving his operation up on the hill, into a well-insulated place, with spectacular views, he moved out and the feds moved in, and took over the building and the doors, which I meant, manning them, to allow only us in and no guests like there was any, it was weird, as I immediately knew I missed the governor, as we seldom get any visitors, it's like a city in a city, the governor still has a place here, but lives in his residence. Since then the request's for buildings are astronomical. Karlotta records all of them, and projections, I just got word, a plane was coming in, so I left, off the second floor down the stairs, out our own door to the motor pool. I drove to the airport, where a single plane landed and three men got off, hooping and hallowering, for me to say, "Calm down fellows", for Paul to say, "I had a helicopter shipped up, so I hope it's ready."

We went over to the aircraft bays, and sure enough it was ready, fueled up, and it was larger than what we had, as all the gear went in. We all loaded up, and just like that we took off, and went up to the challenge, and Paul put it on the road, to say, "What do you have here?"

"Just a few buildings, do come in, as I said, "Allow me to show you around, as we went upstairs, above our place, to show them the pool room, then four more identically looking rooms, for me to say "Choose a room upstairs here or over there", so they choose the animal side, and stashed their gear, and came back down, for Paul to see Little Follower, to say, "So Matt who is she?"

"A gift from a nearby Indian tribe."

"Really what did you have to do?"

"Build them a lodge."

"Your joking right?"

"No joke, what do you guys want first?"

"Oh you know, bear, we want the famed grizzly."

"They run in packs, we have a valley, they will be coming up for the fall showdown, first and second year salmon is running."

"So let's do some fishing" said Russ, as all stopped to see another girl, stunning in their eyes, came out to say, "Care for some dried beef?"

"Boys, this is Hailey, she too is a native like Nina, do treat them with respect, for they are protected Kluane native American Indians."

"Okay I get it, yes, were not here for a date, we want you to guide us in and around these places," said Paul.

"I will, what are you giving me?"

"Why the helicopter of course."

"Nice" I said.

"I told you I had, or we had a gift for you, especially when it came from my dad, he said, to enjoy it, only thing was I told him you were a search and rescue and this helicopter would come in handy."

So I showed them around as Russ was in my ear over coming back in the service, which I said, "No."

"Why not?"

"I'll show you later, but you must keep it a secret."

"Sure," he said, as I got out my Enfield, and they the same, and pulled out my jeep, the four of us got in, and went down the road, then due south, it was wet swampy, and all the way onto higher ground, I stopped, for me to lead them into the Mount Logan lower area, where the White river was coming from, and up to a perch, that was evident I've used before, to show them where the bears, migrate, and some huge ones, in the river now, before I could say something, Russ killed the first one, and then Victor the second one, and lastly Paul the last one, as we were on the move, down to get them only to pull up on the hill, to see it was a mass killing, as other bears came to feed on them, it was the last thing I wanted to happen, as bears were crazy, running all over, it was like a shooting gallery, left and right, it was a massacre, twenty three bears down, the river turned the color of red. As Vic said, "This is fun".

"How much fun, we now need to field dress them and get them out of here, before others more violent than these." Said I.

They agreed, and one by one we loaded them up. Till we had, the jeep full, then I made a drag, and for the rest, some ten, and we were off, to get out of there. We made it back, as I pulled up under the roof on the road, across the bridge, to the smoker, and brought in the kills, only to see Anna was back and ready to carve them up, to say, "Good shooting boys." She carved them up, and drained off the remaining blood. It took into the night, as I had the smoker going, good wet wood, makes a difference. That night we had leftovers, and mostly beef, from the bear. We turned in, the boys played pool till late.

September 8 Tuesday 2004

It was day 102, and now it was wild turkeys hunt, we four left early and into Brian's area, and beyond, into the prairie fields. Where the turkey's once roamed, based on their poop and tracks, I held a stick of sorts and began fanning the grass, when one popped out and was shot, then another and finally four more, as we carried them in, we were walking back when we noticed a bear of sorts running, then a few more, then all of a sudden we were running for our lives, as a swarm of bears were after us, Paul stepped in a rut and twisted his ankle as he went down in pain, as we all took to the jeep, I got out as the other were crying to get Paul up, I stood, and fired above Paul and once, twice and a third time, till the bears went down, as it lay before Paul, all others retreated, I wasn't too busy to pick up a gold nugget, and put it in my pocket. I field dressed the huge grizzly bears, saving the internal organs, and allowing the blood to slip away. We three carried Paul to the jeep, then each of the three bears, we tied the large one to the roll bar, upside down, and the other two on the hood, like I did this before. I got in and headed out, my first stop was Lily's she felt the ankle to say, "It's a pretty bad sprain, as she wrapped it in tight gauze, and placed arnica on it. Then told him to elevate and ice it, thinking now about the ice, to build an ice house, then a thought occurred to me, we won't need one, were getting a refrigerator and freezer. Billy is making his way back out here for the rest of his animals, and is bringing one to us. We got back and went upstairs and took Paul to his bunk, to rest, while, Russ and I field dressed the turkeys, the head and feet went into the grinder, as for the feathers, dried and saved, the inners were also saved, Russ and I hung the three bears, they were at the other end to the other, probably the biggest bears I had ever seen at ten feet long and wide. Lots of meat, in around the ribs, a favorite of mine, as I used a hacksaw, to cut up the ribs. The leg meat was tough, so I set that in strips, to dry. On some of them, I found a rub, and rubbed the meat. Meanwhile up in Old Crow, John and Brian were going gang busters, the pavilion in front of the mine had a roof on it, and they were setting shingles, as Brian said as he called to me, to tell me that next was the miners lodge and landing pad, I said I would fly up there, and check it out. Then I also got a call from Rob, they began to form up the walls, as the basement floor was in on the courthouse building, and the fed center, as equipment moved dirt. The governor loved his mansion, as he was fully moving in this week.

The rest of the day was rest, until dinner, when Anna was flown back as she was called to Whitehorse. It was turkey, fried potatoes, and fresh bread baked by Nina was an excellent baker, we all ate together, the boys went up to play pool, I went around, to stoke the fire's. there was no wind, so it meant little electricity, but we did have rain, I still think of this pavilion and why I did this, it's nice to go out and not get wet, water was everywhere. The last of Anna's plants were moved to the greenhouse, which was getting pelted from the rain. We went to bed.

September 9 Wednesday 2004

It was day 3 with the boys, day 103 overall, Paul was laid up, Lily came by with her two helpers, and redressed that ankle. While I took the others with me to check traps, all twenty nine of them, it varies due to what's inside, and what it is, I have another, prototype box ready, and put it in the jeep, I drove it out, with Russ and Victor, I knew where I wanted it, so we took it out in the river, and set it down, then we put rocks on the skids. I slid the ladder in the sand, and turned it, at an angle. The box was set, then up a ways to the first one, it had a guest, it was a mink, I had a bag, I took him by the tail, and into the bag, and tied him off, and hung him from the roll bar. Inside it was gleaming gold, a project for later, the next one up was way, upstream in the canyons. It was good three miles in, and to the box that was rattling, I opened the top to see two otters, it was two boys, so I took them by the tail, they were undersized, like muskrat, and bagged them, it also had riches beyond belief. I imagine it was what attracted them to the box was the glitter. I went inland along the jeep trail, and my boxes, it had two rabbits in them. Russ asked, "That makes for some good eating."

"I know, I have over 40."

"You joking?"

"Nope, I raise them, well Anna raises them, breeds them and takes out the males, for eating. We drove back the four miles to the road, with low tide, I can cross the river safely, and the river was flooded with salmon and trout, Russ got out, with pole in hand, as did Vic, who said they would be right here, as I drove up on the road, and over the bridge, all the way to under the roof on the road, it was nice, to off load the animals, into the cages, with water, and food, they were hungry, now thinking of the salmon, I grabbed ten buckets, and went back to the stream, to scoop up some water, I literally, was catching them by their gills, and into a bucket, with three it was easy pickings, as the salmon season was in full force, and up at the canyon fork, was the bears, as Russ came running back he spotted bears chowing on the migrating salmon. It was a fiesta. I filled all ten buckets, both guys caught three, and we were out of there. Back at the south compound I dressed some of them, as the others went in each pen, live for the animals, and for lunch, we visited Paul with a plate of pan fried salmon, and fried potatoes, and fresh baked bread, using the oats, it was delicious. He looked at me to say, "How do you do it, now with Anna, she is such a looker, I could spend all day just staring at her."

"Don't" I said.

"Tell me about this Lily, she seems she will do anything for you."

"Don't go there, it's all business." I said.

"Then what is it with the two girls you got from the Indians?" asked Paul.

"Actually it was four, and it was just that it was their payment for what I did."

"Let's fly up there and see this lodge, you are talking about."

"In due time, I need to fly up north are you well to travel" I asked.

"Hell yes, I'm nearly healed, that Lily is one fine woman."

"Enough" I said, she is a friend of mine. A little later Lily came by to check on Paul as she was innocent by that, but Paul thought it was special treatment to begin to flirt with her, as she sat on his bed, to redress the wound, she could feel his hand on her back. She turned as I watched, to say, "If you're going to do a back rub do it right, as she positioned to him, for him to be respectful. She finished so did Paul to hear from her, "Thank you that was nice, but it would have been nice to ask first, for I'm done as your healed, now get up and do some work, "Oh hi Matt", as she went by me, I said, "Care to visit Brian?"

"Would I, yes, when?"

"Whenever Paul gets up and flies us up there, as the two saw each other, for Paul to say, "I'll get my jacket."

We loaded up some supplies, as I was in front, Russ, Vic and Lily and Nina, had baked good, as the deluxe helicopter, lifted up and off, and we zoomed as Paul said, this baby has a five hundred mile range, basically my dad wanted you to have the best of the best, try it." I took the steering rod, as I said, "I do have a permit."

"I know and it shows, listen, fly, to the sides, and then I will give you exercises, up, level down, turn right turn left, push forward for maximum speed" he said as I had a little handle on it all the way up to Old Crow, we went fast as we set it down on a platform the crew built. As all worked stopped. As I shut it down, the boys secured it down. Brian and Lily embraced, then all were out in the near freezing conditions, as I walked around and back to the guys, to say, "This is fine, but I'm now here let's get cooking", as the diggers went back to work, I on my tripod, as the three watched me work, and dropping those big logs, took skill especially, twenty five footers, into five feet holes, it was level and straight. I went down the line, to the front and down the hill, and down to the train staging area, where we had four logs to the end. I then sent the boys up to start on the lodge. I myself was back up on the hill, and was having logs brought to me in the center by the large forklift. I marked them, the diggers dug the holes, hole after hole, as I had the tripod place the one, by the helio pad, and the small building. The next one was in-between the pole by the entrance of the mine. I kept a watchful eye on where the dump trucks traveled, they ran down the hill, as the lower yard was a mess, even with road base down, the water saturation point was too much. I put the four diggers down the middle, of the lodge to dig four holes, as I was setting, the other two others started to help out, Russ and Vic were choking the logs, and setting them in a spot, a little lower than the top, as trusses were made by Brian and John, whom was actually a very nice builder and set in place, we had a massive fork lift to help. With all the foundation poles in, it was securing them together, and using that huge forklift like scaffolding, we were hoisted up, I laid a split log cap, together held them in place, as split logs were the runners, then split logs went up and I nailed them in, being that high didn't bother me, it was like putting the puzzle together. It was tough work, as Brian took the other side, as Paul helped guide everyone. In the middle was the teepee, a warm fire was there but it was hands off to the men, as they had a tent of our own. It was told to me that when it really rains, that this place was over ran with mud, thus it's a mess up there now, so now I knew it what was next, the roof to go in next, as all the digging was done, now it was onto the log walls, just like the governor's mansion, all logs on their sides. It was a mad dash to begin to set the stringers so that the roof could be built. It was log upon log, ends shaved off, then set in-between the pilings, to shore up a foundation. It was one after another, as the whole grid was secure, then the split log floor was going in, as it was a hurry, as the weather changes in a minute, but it did tighten up the pilings, then the wall to the west was going in first, it was going in one log at a time, it was nice there was three projects going on at once, once I had the diggers on a task, they would complete it. I went back to the stair step with Brian, a front end loader, helped up, looking down was a sheer cliff, from all the logs, we pulled out as Russ and Vic who were limbing and choking the logs then to us, the diggers, were splitting the logs, and setting them down, as the middle was open for now, as the teepee was moved to the flooring of the lodge. The crew of diggers set the west wall of 3 footers in diameter, ten feet high, as it was closing down to dusk, we had a wall to set our tent to and it was a hot dinner of beef and potatoes and gravy, some leftover bread, butter and jam. We ate, while John was overseeing the building of the train depot.

September 10 Thursday 2004

It was a restless sleep, of only four hours, then we were back at it as the hazy day was over cast, we had section two done, it was steep, we used stringers, to help with our footing, as Brian and I went to the corner, it was a turn downward, split logs went up on the frame, as I nailed down one side and Brian the other, it was 3 footers in diameter, split in half were easy, 44 feet long, I hammered them in using the truss as support, it was a steep incline. While the diggers set the first of the south walls going in, The women got in the act of mortaring the west wall from the inside, as on the other side was a steep drop off, as we were on a massive crushed rock pile, some forty years old. Real concrete was made in the town of Old Crow, and delivered. Lily showed them what to do, to fill the line. John made a notch on the top board and set it there, as he was working on the middle support for the roof, as Timu and Realize were the split crew, as different length were divided. Some over to us, Brian and I and the rest over to John, Russ and Vic. Paul was with the other two diggers, cutting and setting the walls, as split logs were going back and forth, till lunch was called. We ate a hearty vegetable soup and fresh baked breads. After lunch, the inside grid was set, as walls were constructed to ten feet high. As for the split logs, we were on the stair step down. John was rocking, and so was the boys to finish. I was doing good as we went to dark, then a forklift took us down. As the day ended.

September 11 Friday 2004

It again was up early, but it didn't matter, it was blowing snow, it was cold, wet and we were halfway done, I was supervising everyone, as truss were being built on the ground, I had the roof going on as my main priority. All the walls were set, as another level was being worked on, not planned, but, as the pilling disappeared it made sense to have these as miners quarters, as they were set back 20 feet, as in front of them, 44 foot 3 foot in diameter, were split apart, and laid. Hammered down, it was a fast go. Then the mortar, over that west roof, to the entrance of the mine pole. On the lodge the next level logs were forty feet wide, at another hundred feet long, on the east side, it too was getting 44 footers, and the forklift was helping to set them, once the floor was done, then the east wall went up, in between the supports, to the end. Then on the roof line, it was I and Brian as the top pole went in, to cover the hundred feet, then it was the split logs, set on the north, I nailed the top, out 44 feet, to nail it down to the newly set east wall, it was fast going in the blowing snow. At 12 feet high, the east side wall was set to where Brian was placing the roof on. Meanwhile the boys and John took to the high stair step roof. The snow was sticking, as the miners were on a skeletal crew till accommodations could be met. I was working like a dog, realizing, this should have been first, as I also knew what I wanted to do, as I sent John and Brian for more wood. The day was turning into white out conditions, and snow was accumulating in places, I and my four diggers were now setting the roof, down the line I was on. This went on to the south, and we were done. Next up was the mortar, as it filled the gaps, as the girls, handed up to us men, while they were on the lower roof they filled the gaps, also sweeping off the snow. Next was the cedar slats which came by train, as it arrived with supplies was there, with plywood sheets, laid on the floor, next in was the wood stoves. Then it was all hands on deck, and onto the roof, as it was all of us, laying cedar slats, from the end, up the west side to the middle and from the east up to the middle and the second story wall. Then it was up fixed ladders, to the top roof, as we just kept going, to the top. As it was lunch, as we got down, for a line, we went in, as the lower box stove was going, as it was warm in there, on the first floor was a kitchen, as finally my support crew was here, electricians, plumbers, and Rob, as for me it was a time to rest. The snow was relentless. But after a hearty dose of cheeseburgers and fresh cut fries, we were back on the east side, as my crew of forty was sheet rocking it, plywood floor was down. Outside we were in a blizzard, the east side went on, over the wet mortar. We set the shingles, all the way up to the east wall. My guys were still setting the high roof, as they were down the hill. We set our ladders in, and started on the top roof. The top was done as dusk was with us, and all the mortar was used up, as the last concrete truck left for the day. The electrician ran line and worked through the night. It continued to snow, at least another five inches overnight.

September 12 Friday 2004

It was day 106, and we were still at Old Crow, our helicopter was covered and secured in a hanger, as the snow was everywhere, we were finishing up the last details of the lodge, as the roof, was catching all the snow, but it was melting under the heat of the stoves, as we had each wood stove going, the boys wanted to finish the roof over the train cars, some 100 feet, as did the rest of the carpenters. While outside it was freezing temperatures had yet to affect the boys. Everyone did a job, but I know the boys wanted to get out of there, as they fly out Wednesday, but decided to stick it out, and finish this. So it was just them finishing that roof, as cement trucks arrived, as too two set of four crews went up to mortar the roof, in front of the mine, and down to the train. The wood stoves were set in each room, on the second floor, with two bunks, the tube went up as I cut into the roof, instantly the fireplace warmed the inside, as each hole I cut, as a pipe went up, was sealed in mortar, and slats, around them on the outside. Twenty log stoves, or boxwood, stoves, in each room of two. There was bigger rooms on the main floor for the foremen, as four took the east wall, and on both sides, and in the middle was the meeting room, then the kitchen, and dining and lounge room, even a pool table, imagine that, set and level, a hallway went to the mine's entrance. Next up was the cutting of the windows, as my crew had that long stick, and easily cut out the window, for each room, cut the log, framed it up, in slide a window, it was done. As it was room to room, where the plans I drew up indicated where they went, and then upstairs, each room had a window, and a door, down a center walkway, similar to the governor's mansion. Then it was plumbing for showers, and the finishing walls. The last to do was construct a water cistern for the water to flow, they already had a pump house, on the river, and the pipe broke off, when the cabins, slid over, but there was no real pressure, so I and my fellow carpenters, constructed a water tower, it would sit on the mountain, and on the front logs, outside the mine. I showed them what to do, as I wanted it eighty feet long, but, it was forty, and quickly put together, as the frame was set in place, it was round, and we had some lasso ties, three to be exact as they finished that through the night. My carpenters were staying, to set on the singles, as we were done.

September 13 Sunday 2004

It was day 107, and we kept up the pace, all goods were off loaded, and the train was off, to change to coal, and silver. We finished the rooms, the conference floors, the kitchen, dining, and showers, as a water source was the Porcupine river, and pumped to a newly constructed water tower, its flow was serious. it worked, it was filled and circulated, all we had left was the shingle job, and just like the mortar, two crew of ten, went up, and completed the job, as another crew started at the train station, and worked up to meet them to take up the slope. The train stop was massive, 55 feet in both direction to cover, 110 feet wide, by 100 feet long, for the cars to sit under while being loaded.

September 14 Monday 2004

It was an all-nighter, and some was able to sleep in the second story rooms, as it was tight and smelled so good, but downstairs, it was as modern as it could be, as the kitchen was up and running, as we were all fed, as the foreman came to tell me he approved, and gave me a completion letter, signed by him, as he thanked all of us, he was extremely happy. The helicopter was pulled out and uncovered, as the women left, Ramie, Lily and Nina, Paul flew and Russ to our lodge, then back to pick us up. Brian and I finished the last of the details. As another train came to us, it was food supplies, blankets, and the miners, they raved over the accommodations, and went in happy. An hour later, with our tools we left and I flew back with Paul as he came to get us. As for my team it was a slow train ride home, or to the next job, the mall. There waiting for me was Anna, but we collected her, and all flew back to Whitehorse, I was supposed to fly to Anchorage with Dave Scott, who was waiting, I said my good byes to the fellows, Anna went to work, and Dave Scott and I flew my new helicopter. I made the airport, and was given a place at the school, and excused for my lateness, as the governor called them. Meanwhile Dave went in with the other trainers, it was school, I missed the morning, but caught up, as we flew, I excelled above the rest, due to Paul's military instruction, but kept along with it.

CH 12

Flight school, this is where I become a pilot.

September 15 Tuesday 2004

I survived the first day of my recuperation from the intense work, and living in the barracks, isn't so fun either, but hey it's a place to live, sleep and eat. It was a day of training in the little stingers, a two man trainer, that can do nose dives, but it mainly was for speed, the class was 8 total, as each of us has some distinction, some were already pilots, and this is a refresher. Some want to join the service, for either Alaska or Canada, either or, were all connected, and we all help each other, and that's what we do. First to visit me was Tiffany, from the factory, she offered up her house, as Charley was away on Tuesdays, I didn't t know what to do, as the school let out around three, some went to the barracks to study, while others went to town. We had to rent a motorcycle to travel around, as it was still damp from the last storm. I drove over to the warehouse, which was in full production for organic mushrooms, extremely successful operation. She waved to me, as I sat in the waiting room, till the last customer had left, for her to say, "Fabulous, so you'll come home with me?"

"Yep."

"Well then I will cook us a great meal, are you driving anything?"

"Yeah a motorcycle."

"Then, bring it around, to the first door, I'll open it up and you can park it inside." I did that, and went up front, to see her ready, we went out, and she locked up as it was 5 o clock. She drove to a supermarket. I got out with her as we went in and I got a phone call, it was from the governor, as he said, "Great job in Old Crow, the miners are raving over the rooms, the heat, and accommodations, especially, the roof idea, to the train depot, when you get back, I have a bonus for you, good luck on the school, I already heard your first in the class, keep it up, and thanks for starting the federal complex." I closed the phone up, as she was buying beef steaks, and potatoes, some milk, chocolate and other vegetables, to say, "Care for anything?"

"Nah, I'll have whatever you have." I said, as we went aisle by aisle. We went to check out, for her to say, "Lily told me all about you, and said, if there was anything I could do, I should do for you."

"She did, did she, then maybe a nice meal and some sleep."

We got to their house on a hill of sorts a nice three story building which was theirs, it had a place for the big truck and a garage for her car. I carried in the groceries. I was somewhat dirty, and she offered to wash my clothes, as I took a shower, then put on a robe, and she was a hard worker, I went to the sofa, turned on TV and went to sleep. She woke me for dinner, I ate while she talked about Charley, Lily, and how close they were to each other, and how, I was now the center of their world, and whatever I wanted. I kept dozing off, I asked her for the bed, and she led me to a spare bedroom, I fell into the bed and I was out.

September 16 Wednesday 2004

It was 0700, and the class had started, it was a relaxing sleep last night, as she dropped me off by 0630 to retrieve my motorcycle as I was off. The classes were stern, then we went out to fly, I log six hours, of defensive flying, then it was search and rescue, to finally precarious landing zones. As the day was done. 5 pm, I had many choices, but my interest today was the mall, its construction and details, as it was a super big mall, lots of shops, to think, amusement ride on the left and a water park on the right, I think, as I go back, and into the barracks, and found my bunk and went to sleep.

September 17 Thursday 2004

I woke with screams of those having to get up at 0600, as we dressed and were off to chow, it was palpable food, then on to some more classes, on rights and right of ways, how to fly distance, and in the afternoon it was a flight to Fairbanks, to deliver milk and mail, today was my turn, I was with Captain Dave Scott, we were loaded, as I took off, pitched it forward, for cruising speed, and flew at 1000 feet up, so said my altimeter. I spotted the wind currents, and flew underneath them, all the way to the city on the river, as it was the Tanana river, originates in the Yukon, and filled with riches, dredging crews, had at least 8 platforms on the river, as we landed at the airport, we off loaded, I did a safety check, as it was cold and blowing snow, as Dave came out with a pair of coffees, to hand me one, he said, "Boy all the news up here is what happen at Old Crow."

"What did happen?" I asked.

"They had some crew up there build a fortress, in and around their mine, and it's pretty spectacular from what I heard."

"Seriously" I said. As we did the checks in the cockpit, I radioed to the tower, they said to wait as a transport was in our direct path, so I waited till the huge plane landed, taxied, and stopped some 100 feet from us, then I was given the okay, to fly off, then I noticed a pilot it was Russ Hamilton he waved and came over, to say, "Boy your moving up in the world, hey have you heard, were all receiving a medal for freedom and valor."

"For what?"

"For what we did in Old Crow, the prime minister of Canada, is coming to America, to award ours, you'll get yours in Whitehorse on Monday, it was good to see you, now you can go back." He left happy, I got the okay and I was off, and turned around, then back on course, the flight time was about an hour ten minutes, depends on turbulence and rain, and this flight back it was snowing, but we cruised right on through, popped out over Anchorage, got word it was clear to land. I set it down, and shut it off. I now know I'm a pilot, and it didn't help that's all Dave Scott was saying too. I went in to a battery of tests, as there was two more days to fly, and the next person was off. I answered the questions as I knew most answers, it was fast as I finished, as that next person was back, it was about almost 6 pm, and it was another close of business. I went to the barracks, as Tiffany was looking out for me, as she came in, to say, "Can you come over one last night, I have a nice dinner planned".

I said "Sure" and went with her. She took me to her place, it was nice, as I waited for dinner, I was getting my strength back, as I watched some planes land and take off, as she handed me a hot chocolate, to say, "What are your plans, later, say Saturday?"

"Oh probably go home, and relax."

"That's a shame, we could go take a scenic trip."

"Nah, do you see the outside it's snowing, and by tomorrow some accumulation."

"That's all the reason to take a drive."

"I didn't know if she was dissolutional or what, as I said "No." and that is when it happen she kissed me, I felt nothing, as I broke it off, and said, "This isn't right, as I grabbed my jacket, and was out of there, I took to the streets and ran away, all I could think about was Anna, I ran, then hit a patch of ice, and fell back, and hit my head I was out, on the major road. I lay motionless, as the truck, which sanded the road, sprayed me, and then stopped to help me, as he lifted me up, and helped me into the truck, and by 9 pm I was in my bunk sleeping.

September 18 Friday 2004

It was day 112, and my actions earlier were immature, I was just taken off guard, by Tiffany's advances, but that would never happen, even for that lonely girl. I had a bump on my head, I was feeling sick, so I went to the medical offices at the airport, they discovered my brain was bleeding, and would require surgery, while my class all graduated, I was waiting to go to surgery. Anna had flown in with another pilot, I felt fine, but no one wasn't taking any chances, I went into surgery, to repair the fracture and stop the bleeding. Afterwards I was fine, as I awoke, to see Anna, Brian, Lily and Charley. Charley said "Sorry Tiffany couldn't make it due to the warehouse, or something," Anna kept pressing me, why I was out there, as I said, for a walk, which she didn't believe for a minute, even Lily was suspicious, as she was concerned, for I to say, "Look I lost my balance and went down."

"Yes, but why up there on that hill, it was close to Charley and Tiffany's house, as according to my earlier statement. Then Anna stopped, and Lily tore out of there. I could write down the dialoged but I won't, Tiffany confessed to her attraction to me, and I over reacted, all was forgiven, even Anna, but putting my own life in jeopardy, was a bit alarming to the two girls.

We all flew home in my new helicopter, then to Whitehorse, and then back home, I flew solo, the helicopter was put on sleds, and a winch on the jeep pulled it into the brick factory. And the doors were closed as a winter storm watch was on, as a storm was coming through. I showered and went to bed.

September 19 Saturday 2004

It was day 113, at home we were snowed in for the first time, as snow accumulated outside, inside it was warm, and dry. I got up and did my chores, and the great thing was it was roomy and dry, and the windmill was in full motion as it hummed in the wind, and there was places to go, and so many little things to do, Anna was here, and kept an eye on me, the windmill was a bit loud, as the electricity was beyond capacity, as lineman have since tied off the remainder, and it goes down a line the excess. A meter registers what I give, and what I take, and what is shared. Charley was up and held no hard feeling, for he reiterates that all she was trying to do was to show gratitude, that's all, it did however jump start their love life, so he was happy. He delivered us a brand new refrigerator and freezer which was given to Brian and Lily. All was calming down, as Brian came over, as I was on my saw mill, outside the snow was accumulating. Brian was on his snow mobile, and came over to park it, and help out with the planks. After I had enough, I used a circular saw, to cut into shapes, and began to put them together. I shut down the diesel, and went to assembling the boxes, I wanted to make 12 more, to go with my three. Since the challenge is over, Brian has asked if Him and Lily, and the two girls move into the south compound. We are building them a cabin instead of the teepee. But not till I finish those boxes. That night we had a feast, then I went to bed.

September 20 Sunday 2004

It was day 114, at home, I finished off the boxes and moveable ladders inside, and Brian and I in wet boots, walked the White river, setting in boxes every hundred or so feet, my three other boxes were empty of animals, yet filled up with gold. Now my smaller boxes netted rabbit, muskrat, and a sable, although a baby. All were taken back, put in cages, and fed and watered, then it was salmon catching time, with a net, and we took about twenty in with us, also another interesting thing occurred, in the White river, the spring, turned warm to hot in the winter, so we enjoyed warm water, and so did the migrating salmon, to live during the winter months, as they were here. We fillet the salmon, and seasoned and dried them. Days like this was memorable. We had a feast for dinner. I turned in early and went to sleep.

September 21 Monday 2004

It was day 115, on the ground was a foot of snow, it was clear, as I used the jeep, to pull out the helicopter, then drove the jeep back in, we all loaded up in the helicopter, with Anna in the back, Brian up front, as I did all the checks, and up I went and off to Whitehorse, outside the admin airfield, I radioed in my approach, they said it was clear, as I came in and then dropped down, got out to a fierce wind, to secure it down, then locked the blade, detached one, and put over a tarp, then fasted it down, and went into the admin building, first to see was the governor, he was elated, as he pats me on the back, to say, "That was some good flying, and to be top of your class." I was being led up to something, for him to say, "I'll have to say, I have some rather not so good news, they at the hospital did some blood tests, to reveal an abnormality, so if you could, fly back into Anchorage, for some further tests, I would be very pleased."

"I assured the governor I was fine, what just a little bump on the head", and now something is wrong.

"No, it's just a precaution, besides I need a physical before I can sign off on your new pay, also for doing Old Crow, that fast, another 100K, go see Miss Tillwater and get your check". I was a bit concerned, as I caught up with Brian whom was waiting in my office, as the crews were out in the cold. Some liked this better, as he followed me to the comptroller's office, to see Miss Tillwater, who said, "Ah come early for your check?"

"Nah, the governor, said something about a bonus?"

"Oh yes, for Old Crow, that was some feat, here you go, and who is your friend?"

"He is Brian Lewis."

"Oh yes I have one for him as well, and hands him 50K, for Brian to smile, as I pulled him close, as she said, "Care to cash them here?"

"No, I need to fly off to Anchorage, as I got Brian out of there, and across the street we went, to the credit union, and Jelville Grant, said, "Hi boys", as he presented the check, she cashed it out in its entirety, as I deposited mine, as she said, "Cash back?"

"Nah, I'm still good, as she slid a form to me, to say, "That is for direct deposit, so if you're out in the field, both of you, your pay will be instant access." We took the forms, back to the comptroller, Miss Tillwater, took them to say, "It will be there just before the first."

"Thanks", I said. Then I said to Brian "Go on the hill and make sure all is going well, I'm going to Anchorage. I went and saw Anna and said goodbye to her, but she said, she was going with me." So we went, I flew out and took some mail and to Anchorage from Whitehorse. We were cleared, and landed, I had a car for me and Anna, and went to the federal building downtown Anchorage. Where the rouse was up, It wasn't a hospital visit, it was an award for my work on the lodges, especially with the Kluane tribe, who were the ones who requested this to happen, as the Vice President Jennifer Jackson of the United States, read off the numerous things I was to have done, and the education, and the forgiving of their debt, over 50 plus things, it ended with the US freedom medal, besides the award, it comes with a monthly cash prize for life, of about 1500 dollars. so said the lady, whom took my bank information, I was well received even Anna was there, afterwards, we had cake, I tried a little piece, the VP Miss Jackson, said, "We would like you to build a similar thing in Fairbanks, a lodge for veterans, on the base." I said "Yes", and knew to get it in soon, as I discovered, anything Yukon wanted, Anchorage was there to give it to us, my new dual citizenship was special, because it allowed me into Alaska, and a special place with the Feds. I went with Anna back to the airport for a physical, the last thing I missed to do, and passed, no problems, and the head was fine. I flew back to Whitehorse, with my award. We got out, I secured it down. Only to hear of a lost miner up in Pelly Crossing, so I called up to Brian, he came down, to tell me it was impressive how well the crew is working. He was going to go through some search and rescue training, but only as a refresher, he once did that in Missouri. So he was my spotter, as he and I were suited up, I was readied the helicopter, and was ready, Brian got in, and I lifted off, and flew along the Yukon river, to the junction at Fort Selkirk, and around to Pelly Crossing, it was bad, it was a strip pit of coal, silver and some gold, the miner was trapped in a crevice that just opened up, he was badly hurt, I came over to the spot, and lowered Brian with a stretcher, he went down, some 100 feet, hooked him up, and then, he snapped on, and I lifted them up, they both cleared the crevice, and then I allowed him back in, and the gurney, it was awkward, knowing we needed another person to help out. I flew to Dawson which was the closet medical center, we landed, as a crash crew was ready, and took him away, Brian went and got another back board as the basket was ready, we were thanked, and I flew off. Back to home as I got word, Dave Scott flew Anna and the diggers home. I landed, to see more snow was down, as it was easier to drag the helicopter under the road roof. But not out of the cold. I put the cover on it and saw the snow accumulation on the two bridges, to realize that would be next, then went in to a nice dinner and went to bed.

September 22 Tuesday 2004

It was day 116, I turned in my physical results when we all three got to Whitehorse. Anna had to go to Pelly Crossing to investigate the crevice, Dave Scott got the job, as I was on the hill, putting together the courthouse, and the fed center. It was mainly for posterity, if it was serious offenses it went to Edmonton, the real center of power, as all we are is provinces, of Canada, that also means the US shares, in need and use. The US provides aid, to those in need. We are officially in winter. It's actually supposed to be fall, but not in minus 20 degree weather and minus 50 with the wind chill factor. All the pilots were out except I, I was in the office, finalizing reports, for the governor, I could be outside, but it's not needed as all the crews are inside, finishing both buildings, I allowed Rob to supervise, while I was doing daring rescues, and making sure we run smoothly, for I was the boss. With that we received a distress call from some hikers on the seaside of Mount Logan, Brian and I were dispatched, we were filled, we were in a heated hanger, and we were ready, as the Coast Guard was also dispatched, out of Anchorage, but was late, I left full bore, to the ocean and cut back for this short jaunt, there they were four guys, hung out to sway in the wind, it was a daring rescue, I was over them, as the line went down, but all were experiencing frost bite and hypothermia, so Brian suited up and was lowered down, he unhooked the first man named Roger, and I winched them both up, Brian tied off, and set the man in, and went for the second, in the line, the bottom man was out, and dangling, just as the Coast Guard arrived, but kept their distance, to watch I fly, the upper currents, to keep it steady, just as I hoisted Brian up, then he went down, for a third, when I received the word, a platform ship was here and to fly them over, and with that as Brian un-hooked the man, I was off, and winched them in, as I went to the ship in minutes, to set down and allowed the men inside, as we got word the last man was consumed and dead. We flew home, I was thinking, it would not have been nice seeing that dead man. The flight back to Whitehorse was disturbing, because one of our men had died as well. We got back, and went in as to a hero's welcome, some said the Coast Guard said it was the highest professional rescue ever witnessed, and the Coast Guard wants me to come to Alaska to train with them."

It would take the governors doing, and he did make it happen. I picked up Anna and Brian and I flew home. The diggers get a special ride, by a rotating pilot crew.

September 23 Wednesday 2004

It is day 117, and we woke up to a blizzard, a massive storm came in here, and just stayed, as I noticed, it wasn't going anywhere, the helicopter was under the roof of the road, as the snow was getting higher, I had all 24 fireplaces roaring and the place was a comfortable 40's, Brian was over to say, "Let's build the cabin."

So with the wood, we had ready, we began to set the foundation, at 20x20, with a two bedrooms in the back, a dining and kitchen off the front, and several doors, and windows, Brian found my stash, he went crazy over the windows, four across the north side, and the rest all around.

You could see in all rooms, that let the light in, I finished the top, as the roof was laid at an angle, this was an all day job. We finished as I put the mortar on, and Brian, Lily Anna and the girls, finished the roof, in slats, and I added a custom door. This was still my house technically, as I use the smoker and the horseshoe.

September 24 Thursday 2004

It was day 118, and the storm broke, Brian and I pulled out the helicopter, I de-iced it, and set it ready for takeoff, Brian was ready as was Anna, I started it up and flew off, and below it was whiteout conditions, all the way, as I took above the highway in places, all the way to Whitehorse, where it was chaos, all the other helicopters were gone, on missions, the governor was in panic mode. He told me, we need a short wave radio, calls for help were all over as the first big storm wiped out power lines and stranded people, he told me, "Go over to the Carmacks, a family is covered, and is using Morse code, for help, Anna wanted to go too, so I said "Sure, let's go, but you're in the back helping Brian, as we were refueled, by Joe Smith the motor pool guy, as this place was buzzing, activity at an all-time high, my crews were at a snail pace, as I flew off over the new courthouse, and up a valley on the other side was Dawson's range. I got to the valley, to see several homes were engulfed in the deep snow, really not prepared for any of this, as the first family was on their roof, waving, I sent Brian down, and they were hoisted up and to safety, I turned to say, "How long have you been up here?"

"Oh two years", said the father.

"How was it a year ago,?"

"It was nice, but not like this", then it hit me, to hear, "We were the ones who almost made the challenge, and was given 40 acres, in the valley, so we built a cabin, and hunt and fish."

"What about a place to do things?"

"Like what?"

248

"Never mind", as Brian was lowered, and another husband and wife team, all from last year's challenge till all eight were picked up, which was my max of ten, and flew them to town of Carmacks. I landed at the hospital, for checkup, one had hypothermia. I was thanked by all and the staff. I noticed on my list was a hospital from here to build, maybe in December, I thought, it was treacherous out here, the conditions were bad, the whole town was engulfed, by snow, except the hospital, it cared for those of the population of over 275. A mechanic, came to us, and set in a short wave high intensity radio, that worked for our system, to say, "This one here is for warm hot weather, that's why you got all this static, as he tuned it in and said, "Your all set", as was that radio, it had more distress calls, in around there, we responded as Anna stayed to help the others. We flew many patterns, to pick up all that was left, some twenty in all, and then we left to go back to home as it was closer than going back to Whitehorse. We had dinner by the two girls, and Lily, then went to sleep.

September 25 Friday 2004

It was day 119, and up for another day of flying, as it was 0700, and another rescue was about a man who fell into the Yukon river, from a raft, who can respond, I spoke up, and we were off, all three of us. I flew the pattern to the location, and doubled back, as he was holding on the raft, but couldn't get up, as I lowered down Brian, he hit the deck, and lassoed the man, and I winched him up out of the water, Anna was there to receive him, he was in shock, as she wrapped him in blankets, as I sent the hook down, and hoisted Brian up and we were going to Dawson, our closest point, as I radioed them, we were coming, and when we arrived, they took the man, and another back board, so Brian got another one, as we got word of a mine cave in at Old Crow, so we loaded, as an emergency nurse wanted to come, so she and her stuff, as we flew fast, from Dawson it was two hours, which was fast, I came in on the approach, to see the platform, and landed, they exited, while I waited, I saw the structure was still intact for literally the time it took to construct it, two foot of snow had fallen, gurneys were ready, as Brian helped those to the helicopter, with that nurse, when ready, I cranked it back up and off we went back to Dawson and to the ER. I flew back to Whitehorse, and realized, this was just the beginning, because the building projects slowed, the rescues soared. On the squawk box, was more people stranded, I also came to find out, that the challenge was fixed, to draw people up there to live, as one of that last group said, "They had all stuck it out, but it was boring so said them and shut it down after 90 days, if after 90 days you make it, the rest is easy. But had heard of that guy building lodges was the clear winner, and thus would get all the land", I kept to myself, thinking of the land, I dug what I had, as it was getting late, as I was diverted to another rescue. It was south of Whitehorse, as I heard all the helicopters were still out. It was non-stop, as we reached the distress signal, it was a family on foot stranded, I set it down as close as I could as Brian winched down, to assess the little children, then one by one was hauled up, Anna held the line, and wrapped each up, as Brian then was lifted up, as they were complaining that the weight of the snow, flatten their home and homestead." We flew them into Whitehorse memorial hospital, as it was 8 pm, and I called us in to the admin building and they said, all is handled, I said we were going home. I flew back, after a stop at the airport for refueling, then it was off to home, I landed at the road, as all seem intact and strong, I also noticed my roof was clean, as all the fireplaces, heat melted the roof, that's it.

We went in as Lily and the girls had dinner ready, it was vegetable soup, and fresh oat meal bread. Afterwards I showered, then Anna. Brian, was with Lily at the south compound, then I went to bed and to sleep.

September 26 Saturday 2004

I awoke, holding onto Anna, as the new squawk box in the house was looking for help as an expedition was lost, south of Dawson, and I now knew it was us, I sprang up, and answered the call, to almost hear, "Finally." I like the building part better, but I was now part of the search and rescue teams, I'm supposed to go to the Coast Guard on Monday with Brian and Anna as we have this new team. We had a hearty breakfast, and we were off, the tricky part to all this by using GPS is the coves, the ranges and the depth, we could be over them, and still not see them, as we came upon them, and no one was in sight. I would think hearing that helicopter would get them up, or it was serious, I sent Brian down, he did a scramble criss crossing positions, come to find out we were a mile off course, all because of such high minerals in these parts, as I kept drifting over, to say to Brian, "Over more", then in the distance was a signal flare, I picked up Brian, and flew to them, they were ready, as they were trapped, on an island, in a lake. One by one to all eight boarded fine, then wanted me to drop them off, on the ridge, I called it in, and they said, "Allow them that", so I did, and they were happy, as I flew off, to another complaint of a home collapse, and rescue in the Carmacks, I made a bee line, to another house on the string of homesteads, a small family of three, each were loaded, and we flew off, to Carmacks hospital. I landed on the top, and they were whisked off. We flew back home, only to be told, that the earlier party had one fall and is badly injured, all wished to be picked up. I plotted the course, and with grease pencil, circled their spot, on a heads up display, I flew to their location, and it was a mess, hikers on all parts of that hill, the top, middle and down below, a woman was mangled. Both Anna and Brian were dropped down to help her first, she had a broken leg, her name was Megan, they immobilized it, and was hoisted in, then worked our way up, taking the rest off the hill, and on to the top, all in, I flew back to Whitehorse, as they were complaining to go to their cars, I slide the center door shut, to knock out their noise, we landed at the airport, they were still bitching, as they got the bill, 20K, and paid it and were waiting a transport back to their cars, as we flew to Whitehorse medical, and dropped off Megan, I was dispatched to take them back, so I flew to them, they all got on, as I flew out to another spot, some place called Canyon

Springs State Park, I reached there and dropped them off, to their cars, engulfed in snow, only to think I'll be back, as I flew up to a hill top and shut it down for lunch, after lunch, I got another call, for a rescue on the coast, near Mount Elias, as I went down, south of where I was at, it was a tricky place, a small plane had crashed, as I was at hovered, the wind currents were something fierce, as the remnants of the plane was in a cove of sorts, it was engine down, as I winched Brian down, as he was getting tossed back and forth, by the winds, off the coast, the ocean looked spectacular as another storm was coming. Down below, some hundred feet down, Brian saw a pilot dead, and a young couple, he harness them both up, and tied them off, as I winched them up, only when told to me by Brian, till finally, Anna had the two secured, and the third, also, below him, as I winched up, all the while I was trying to keep it still, as I was being forced into the mountains, till finally the woman was first in, then the man, and then Brian, and the dead guy, as he was sat up, he looked normal, as the door closed, as I flew off, up and over as it calmed, we landed at Whitehorse memorial, where I shut it down, and all were taken in, when I got another distress signal, from that hiking crew, they were all stuck, and sinking. Both Brian and Anna got back, as I flew off, as I had half tank, but on one gauge was aux, and it said it was full. And flew to their location, and sure enough all four cars, were in the water, they were on their roofs, as I sent Brian down, to harness them up, and then hoist them, individually, till all seven were up, and off we went back to Whitehorse memorial, I then, let them off, some for hypothermia. Then flew to the airport to refuel, and shut it down, we took a break as the old guy Williams, said, "It's been a flurry of rescues, and then a sad news one of our own was down, near a lake, for a boat rescue, I asked, "Anyone pick them up?"

"Yes, there on their way back."

We took off, to the air, and over to the admin offices and put it down, and shut it off, set the lift blade, and put a custom tarp over it to secure it, from the deadly wind, and tied it to the four points, and went in. the admin center was a buzz on

Saturday, usually not a working day, but since the helicopter went down, the entire station here was on high alert. It was Moore and Adams, both good rescue guys, come to find out a bird flew through their rudder, and they crash landed in the lake, both suffer frost bite, and hypothermia. It was a mess, I went upstairs to see it was empty, but well organized. We waited our next call there was none, so we went home. We had dinner, then a shower, and off to bed.

September 27 Sunday 2004

It was day 121, and it was just like a Monday morning, the alarm went off, as it was a call for some help on the Yukon river, by Dawson, several men were in the water, we responded, as so did others, but it was just a matter of time, as three rescuers were coming, and believe it or not, we were there first, it was a large raft, overturned, and more than that people were all over the place, funny I thought they said, just two, it was eighteen, of two rafts, we hoisted, Brian was in the water, he had an all-weather survival suit on, as he helped those in the water, and hoisted others, on the upside down raft, all while traveling down the river, in swift current, then it was our first hoist, then another one, as some wore wet suits, then we had six, as we just kept hoisting, now I was closing in on my, max at ten, and as the last one was in, I radioed down to Brian, "Keep them all together, Anna took the front seat, as I waved her back to say, over the engine, "Keep them calm."

She did so, and said, "We could probably take six more, then I said, "Keep winching", so we took in six more, and that extra weight was pushing our limits, as we had sixteen, and that left two and Brian, as I flew off to Dawson, a good ten mile run, as another helicopter came to help, but had no winch, not able to do anything they just hovered. I made it to Dawson, and landed as workers and crash crews ascended on us, and took them off, as I flew back, as Brian and the others were down river some twenty miles more, I spotted them, and the hoist was ready, and plucked up the two, and Brian, also, the two rafts, were swinging in the air, as they were close, and one of them, deflated, them as they were loaded in. I flew to Dawson, and landed at the hospital. We all went in for some coffee, and rest. For the rest of the day nothing. We were officially off duty, as the next two weeks on to the Coast Guard, in Anchorage. We refilled at the Dawson airport and flew home. Set it down, and the jeep, drug it under the roof, I secured it and tarped it. We went in for dinner, with the two girls, and Lily had vegetable soup for us, it was decided, Lily would go with us to Anchorage.

CH 13

Were at the Coast Guard in Anchorage having fun.

September 28 Monday 2004

I t was early and we were loaded up as we pulled the helicopter out, and uncovered, we were loaded up, the girls, would handle the operations, Nina and Hailey was here, and the other two girls, took a snowmobile to the warehouse. I flew us out, and down to Anchorage, and got clearance to land on the Coast Guard base. We had a reception staff, very nice, and they though Lily was part of the first responders, and she accepted, each went a different way, I was at flight school, Brian was with swimmers, and the girls as first responders, Anna was the crew chief. We were all treated with high esteem, as I went in many classes, some on do's and don'ts, some on conduct and purpose, but what I got out of it, was never leave part of your crew behind, as the instructor was beating it in my head, "That person has a seat on that helio, they risk their lives, for those needed to be rescued. I felt bad for Brian now, as it was his helicopter too, so never leave him behind, and the last thing was never overload the craft, if ten is the max then the crew is counted, and then how many, as we went outside, to see their deluxe helicopter with the state of the art gear, was easily a half of a million dollars as it was a high production rated helicopter, and it was set for ten passengers, in seats, to include a crew of four, two pilots, a crew chief, who does not leave the helio at all costs, and a rescue diver, who rides the cable. This was an eye opener, and how dangerous this was. I flew the Coast Guard's advantage one, a super helicopter, that can carry, ten like mine, but I had an instructor by my side, a Col Tom Davis, he was the stickler for the rules, not saying I break them, I just didn't know them. He liked my steady hand, and how, I held the stick, I was the only one of all he instructed to extend my stick, and add the T-bar. I was steady, and set on positioning. And all this we done was in a flight simulator, I would need to pass this even before I flew a single mission. Up on the flight deck, my helicopter, was wheeled in to a hanger, to be kept safe. At 9 pm we were done with day one. Halfway through the night, an alarm went off, a boat was in trouble, as I was dressed, and was running out to the helicopter, but was told to take the other seat, as Col Tom Davis took the lead, as I got in, and crew was ready as we took off, leaving his second behind, who was slow anyway. The Colonel in the pilot's seat and we were up and we were racing at top speed to the capsized boat, survivors were in the water as we got there. The door opened, and the rescue swimmer was sent down, I watched and I was the spotter, as I called positions, to the Colonel, as the helio moved, to what I said, "Stop, turn five clicks, stop, first pick up", was hoisted up, "Turn five clicks stop, hold", as another was hoisted, "Have the rescue swimmer to go off as one is floating away", as the swimmer responded, I was doing the Colonel's job, as I should have been flying, as he was stuck, so I ran the show, and said, "Hoist now", as I saw them working, extracting them one at a time, till all six were accounted for, and hoisted up, the last was the swimmer, and the other crew member, to the back. They were all in, the door slid shut, as the big vessel, went up and sunk. The Colonel flew the helicopter back, we landed like a plane, and taxied in, as all were alright, all had survival suits, I exited, to hear, "I made a mistake, I should of let you fly her out."

"That's alright, I will next time."

"Sorry there won't be a next time, you're supposed to be training here, so on alarm your off, my second will be next."

September 29 Tuesday 2004

It was day 123, as I woke, it was 0700, and reveille was played, meant all up, each of my crew I hadn't seen them, I was in the officers chow, it was spectacular, on every level, as I wore a uniform, with gold bars on them, which meant Lieutenant to me. I sat alone, until another pilot took a seat, to say, "That was some ballsy shit, you ordered the XO around, it takes years to get in that position."

"It was reflexes, I get a call, and spring up for work, as other pilots joined me, then an announcement came through for me to visit the base commander and so I was off, we had a golf cart to move around with, to a place on the hill I went, to whom he was, we were going to the strategic command center, as I was whisked into his office, for him to say, "Please take a seat", I did just that, as I didn't feel like I was in trouble, for him to say, "I want to first start by commending you on your willingness to be part of a rescue, and I reviewed the tape, and what you did, was all you were supposed to, as the commander, you controlled all that was necessary for a complete and accurate rescue, also spotting a missing man, and directing the swimmer, I have a commendation for you, to a rank of Captain, I checked with your governor, and he accepted, as your commission as such, so your now Captain, says here you were a scout, not just only but one of the best ever, well by this action, it shows you're doing this job well, I'd like to formally offer you a place in the coast guard reserves, says here you're a former Marine, so there is no boot camp required, all I need is for you to sign that form, and take that rank and your with us." In a demanding sort of way, he kept talking about big things, as I was only here to learn, as he finally wrapped it up, to say, "So think on it, good job, do take your promotion", at first I had no idea what that even meant, that was till I went back to class, and was up front, and truly apart of all them, instead of some given title I earned that, it was indeed different. The rest of the day was course work, and then chow and to bed early.

September 30 Wednesday 2004

It was day 124, should I stop writing this journal, as the challenge is over, I don't know it's kind of fun talking about what I do, so here is Wednesday and back to classes, they talked of a PT test we had to run a mile in less than fifteen minutes. The officers, all paced each other, far below that as we all qualified, then on to pushup and sit-ups, all way to easy, for us pilots, it was now to qualify on the simulator, it was a 100 % for I, it was easy, and in the afternoon, it was onto the real attack rescue helicopters, I was a lead pilot, and It was Jack Aimes, from the royal air force from London, I took the reins, taxied the aircraft, and then lifted off, and flew a pattern, as prescribed to me, I had everything on heads up, and part of our mission was a test, to drop a swimmer, retrieve and extract, when it so happened a distress call, for an injured crewman on a fishing vessel, I was closest, so I radioed it back, it was a long pause, to say, "Alright proceed with caution, as I made a bee-line to the ship, it was listing, to the left, as this was a full ship rescue, when I arrived, I radioed back, the conditions, and status, to say, "One half on side, ready to go under, request to extract whole crew, and possible back up, over?"

"Roger, take your limit, Col Davis is enroute."

"Roger, I said, to intercom, "Send the swimmer down", the door slid open, as the winds picked up and so did the rain, it was a full blown storm out there, as I held it steady, to find out it was a crew of eighteen, our capacity was ten at the most, trying to remember, the person count for each helicopter, and thought mine was ten, so I said, "Make sure to send out a rescue raft."

"Aye, Aye Captain said the crew chief, doing as I said, as the first person was brought up, as the raft, was slung out, the line to the rescue swimmer, he set it aside, as it inflated, for the next crewman, as the boat was now sinking, it was another, as "I said, "Faster, Chief, I don't have all day, get ten and pull the swimmer." Production sped up, till all ten was aboard, then the rescue swimmer, placed everyone else in the raft, the boat was on its side as all got in, as the swimmer was hauled up, and in, as I banked off, as the door slid shut. The boat went slowly down, as the raft was free, and in the stormy seas, as I was making a way back to Anchorage, passing the Colonel, and went back to base. I flew the pattern and was cleared to land, and set it down on the runway, and slowed and taxied in, and was sent to a hanger, as the storm was coming in, all the planes and helicopters were in bays, I pulled in and shut it down, crews secured it as was ready to exit, my copilot looked sick, he was pale in the face, as I exited, to hear, "No, the General wants you back out."

"Well I need a second", looking over at Jack Aimes, who bailed out.

"Then it shall be I", he said, he was a Major, Steven Miles, as we were refueled, I offered the pilots seat, and he said, "No", so I took it, the crew chief said, "Were ready, Captain, Major, as the door slid shut, I was led out, and away we went, as I taxied, instead of a direct straight up, all the lines and power lines, I was given the clearance, and I took off like a plane, as the major said, "Why the extension?"

"Oh, for a way to not extend, when I'm in my heads up."

"Clever", he said, as we were going back, to that site, as a cutter was in sight, but the Colonel had enough, and we took over for them, as I said, "Rescue swimmer out, oh sorry, that is your call", "Go ahead, make the call Captain," as the door opened and he was lowered, into the raft, as more were inside, of the eighteen one said, swelled to 24, as we took the last six, and the rescue raft was collected by the cutter, as the Colonel left, then when the rescue swimmer was aboard, and the door shut, I flew off. The mission was complete. It was only day three, and I had passed the course, as I was given a certificate, and was told, you have everything it takes to be a phenomenal pilot, my skills were mad and then told me of the reserves, and said, "It could be, let me think on it?" I said.

As for Brian he was on the slow pace, and so forth for Lily and Anna, so I flew my helicopter home.

October 1 Thursday 2004

It was day 125, and all alone waking up, as I got up did the chores at home, as Nina cooked breakfast, I pulled the helicopter out, uncovered it, and was set. I said my good byes, and flew to Whitehorse, and set it down by the admin building, and went to work, I spent the good part, up on the hill, supervising the construction, of both buildings of logs, it was fun, to see them both go up, but not me physically, doing anything, it was at the end of the day, I went to comptroller Tillwater and she said, "It's in the bank, not to worry, as I went out and got into the helicopter and flew off, to home. I had dinner and rested, then went to bed.

October 2 Friday 2004

It was day 126, I was up and then flew into Whitehorse, only to go visit the governor, whom said, "He was amaze how fast I progressed, but wanted me to stay there in Anchorage, to make sure the team gets home safely. He was telling me to take time off, so I flew home. Parked it, and drug it under the roof, secured it down, and went checking my traps, on my new snowmobile. Most had rabbits in them, as I had a trailer I pulled behind me, to exchange those I had something in them to a new trap, then it was into the wet boots, as I went to the first box, it was empty besides the gold, inside, I took handfuls of mix and filled the bags, it was time consuming, and next was the other box, same results, gold, up the ladder and the rungs, I scraped off the rung to fill the bag, it took all day, to check the traps and collect 30 bags of gold mix. I was in the canyon, when I saw what appeared to be a rock, it was huge, and very shiny, it was too heavy for me to pick up, and so a tomorrow project. I went in, and secured the new animals, and checked on the others, the mink bred successfully, and so did the otter. I had dinner, vegetable soup and fresh made bread, then showered and went to sleep.

October 3 Saturday 2004

It was day 127 and I was at home, with a nice problem, construct a tripod, and lift up that huge shiny rock, that appeared to be broken off from somewhere and was here now, so I did just that had three twenty foot poles, lashed them together, and made a loop for the block and tackle, then took the jeep four wheeling driving, into the back woods, I took a different trail than the snowmobile, to this place, and set up the tripod, then took a harness strap, and went into the calm flowing river and hooked it up, then began to hoist it up, it was about 100 pounds, far less than a pole, as I easily put it in the jeep's back, secured it down and broke down the tripod, that itself weighs hundreds of pounds, and on the back of the jeep, and tied them down, got in backed up and drove down a firm trail, back to the home, using higher ground, all the way back, then at the road, undid the tripod, and off the gold went, to a piece of plywood, on skids, and then to a top and used straps, to secure it together, then I pulled the helicopter over it, and secured it under it by using the skids, and the winch, to hold it, under the craft, I used a cable hook under the helicopter to hold it in place, and then strapped it to the skids, and got in, and fired up the helicopter, and took off, and flied to Whitehorse, admin building, and I was looking for the governor, Jim Hickson, as he was in meetings, then a break, Gladys let me in, for him to say, "I thought, I told you to go back to Anchorage?"

"Well I will, but I discovered something of value, I don't know for tourism?"

"What is it?"

"Ah a huge gold nugget."

"Really how big?"

"About 100 pounds."

"That would be the largest ever found, and you say you have it?"

"Yes."

"Where did you find it?"

"On, Beaver creek at White river junction, I imagine in was unearthed by the last storm."

"What do you want to do with it?"

"Sell it to the government, for display."

"Alright what do you want?"

"I don't know what gold even goes for?"

He looked it up on his phone to say "12 ounces equal a pound, and a ounce goes for 1292 x 12= 15,504 times 100 = 1.5 million dollars, can I see it?" said the governor.

"Sure, it on the pad", as he called in some help from the assayers office, they came, and we all went outside, as I undid it, and winched it up to a trailer, as I set it down, for one to say, "That is the largest nugget vein in history of the world, you just hit the lottery, it has to be over 120 pounds, as they took it away, I would never see it again, as the comptroller issued me a check for five million dollars, I signed it as if I was going to cash it right there, and decided to go outside and over to the credit union, and made one of the largest deposit for just that day, as Jelville Grant wasn't that impressed. The gold went through some processes, as it was from a vein, so said the report, of something even bigger, so I left, and flew home, richer. Set the helicopter down, took some dinner and went to sleep.

October 4 Sunday 2004

It was day 128, I was up early, anxious, and with shovel in hand, and the jeep, I drove back up to that spot, got out, to see the dirt that was near it, and began to dig, and what I discovered was what dreams are made of, I dug out a vein, as it took all day, to visualize the vein, it was inverted, in the ground, and could see where this one was, it was easily 500 pounds or more, and long, as it made up a section, I dug out to the water line, and all around as this day was done. I went back in had dinner then a shower and went to sleep.

October 5 Monday 2004

It was day 129 I was up early, and with a plan, Nina fried up potatoes, and I had four eggs, with bacon, and fresh bread. I went out with jeep, and left, I was on a mission, as I came up on my find, today, I continued to dig out the vein, using a harness, I was able to get one side, as the strap stayed, as I set the tripod, I pulled down on the rope, and nothing it was stuck. So for the rest of that day dug it out. I went back, had dinner with the girls, and a quick shower, and off to bed.

October 6 Tuesday 2004

It was day 130 here, and I was in a routine, it was actually warm today, as most of the snow had settled to form ice, I was off after breakfast to visit the vein, unfortunately two bears, were eating salmon as for our supply we were loaded with smoked salmon, I waited and watched, till finally, they moseyed off. I went back to digging, with the Enfield on my back, it was a slow go, when I thought I could yank it up, it was still stuck, I needed some help, so it was another day of digging, I went back, to the north compound, and loaded a digging bar, and parked the jeep, had dinner, and went in my shop, to work on some more traps, later that night I went to bed.

October 7 Wednesday 2004

It was day 131, it was warm again, to the point of melting, I was on a mission that vein was coming up, as I went out there, the tripod was in place, the line taunt, I placed a digging bar in, and tried to pop it, as I held on to the slack, till it was taunt, then tried to crack it open, as I held it with my arm, leg and hand, till I heard a pop. It was free, as it easily went up, swung around, to the bank, then moved the tripod, by the jeep, and lifted that massive chunk of gold, the jeep went down, I went back and retrieved the digging bar, and looked at the massive hole I created, and below was remnance of the vein. I took my time getting back, to the road, then back by the helicopter, there wasn't much chatter, so I used the tripod, to lift off the vein, and set it down, I found an old blanket, and put it over it, then moved the tripod, and position the jeep, to pull the helicopter out, so it was over the top of it, it was as long as it was thick, kinda like an oversized match stick, I used the winch to hold it up, and then strapping it to the skids, it was ready, but it was nearing dinner, so I put the jeep away, and had dinner, then, took a showered and went to bed.

October 8 Thursday 2004

It was day 132, as I had a great breakfast, and then set up the helicopter, and started it up, and flew out, it seemed to ride easy, all the way to the admin building, I landed, and went in to see the governor, Jim was resting as I barged in, he sat up to say, "What is it son?"

"I have the vein."

"Seriously."

"Yes, come take a look" I said.

He called up the assayers to meet us out there, they had truck and equipment to move it, as the governor was excited, to say, "I want to mount this on the front of the new building, this is the largest second piece, sure to draw tourism, come in let's cut you a check." I followed him in, as I was officially on leave, for him to say, "Now this was a find, I want to go over something with you, as I followed him in, as his office looked like that of the white house oval office, I sat, for him to say, "You impressed the Alaskans especially the Coast Guard, whom would love to have you, what do you say?"

"No, you have me, I'm loyal to you."

"Fine, fine, as he received a call, he said, "Yes, I want that encased naturally in front of the mansion, to read discovered in Beaver creek, October 8th 2004, by Matt Michales, really, I'll tell him. He turned to say, "How about a check for ten million dollars."

"I can deal with that."

"So I guess you'll retire now?"

"No on the contrary, I have lots to still do, money isn't everything, but it helps, I guess the next big thing is a spring wedding."

"Have it at the mansion, you built, I'll arrange the event."

"You better check it over with Anna." I said.

"Oh believe me I will" as I got up and shook his hand, to say, "I just got word, the rest of my team is graduating today and tomorrow" I shook the governors hand, he smiled, as I left he called Miss Tillwater, as I went to see her, entered, as she was finishing printing it up, got up, and set it down, to sign it, for I to say, "Is this the largest amount you had ever printed?"

"Nope, as she went to the wall, and showed me the picture, 280 million."

"I bet they didn't cash it here."

"As a matter of fact they did, it was the mining company we bought some time ago, and to tell you the truth, were about break even, so sign, if you want I could cash it."

"Nah, I'll take it next store."

"So now you plan on retiring?"

"No, whatever gave you that idea, I like it here."

"And we like that you are here" she said with a smile, as I pondered what she just asked, then thought nothing else, as I lefted the admin building and entered the credit union, it was not busy, as Jelville took her time to say, "Ah if it isn't Mister Michales, what do you have today?" I presented the check, for her to stamp it, and endorse it, she had me sign, I put, "For deposit only", she smiled to say, "Now I will hold this for three days."

"No problem."

"I was just kidding, you're getting a great reputation around here, I have a daughter who is single, shall I set you up?"

"No thanks, I'm engaged."

"Oh too bad, I would of made a great mother-in-law."

"I'm sure you will in time."

"Thank you for the compliment."

"You're welcome." I said as I left, and was fifteen million dollars richer, I went out to my helicopter, I got in to see Joe Smith had refilled me, it was topped off, and some maintenance, as he greased the doors, and pedals, I put on my head set, started up the helicopter, and flew off. The one in half hours later, to Anchorage it was fast due to the coastal inlands, straight to from Whitehorse, was cleared to land, and set it down, a crew came out, and secured the helicopter. I had my uniform with me, and when I went into officers' quarters I changed, and came out, as Brian was graduating, himself, to a front of his peers, and given title of diver one. He was swimming qualified, at a rank of sergeant, he was paid for his training, in a form of pay was at the rate of 135 per day, so his check was 1620, he was ecstatic, for the twelve days. I was proud of him, as I shook his hand, for him to say, "I'll take you out", he was all smiles, to say, "Have you seen Lily or Anna?"

"No, I was with the officers."

"And so was them, as their barracks, is in your complex."

"Nope, sorry", I said as it was a distant memory, as I took Brian out to a steak place, on the port, which featured Kansas grown beef and the fresh seafood. I took the seafood platter, with an appetizer of mussels. Brian had oysters on the half shell, with jalapeno's and lime juice. He had a steak, potatoes and cream corn. We both had tall frosted mugs of root beer, brewed next door. It was nice to see my new friend, he looked trim and fit, for he talked of running every day and of protocol's, and what to do and what not to do. We went back to the base, I dropped him off and went back to officers' quarters, and to my assigned room. And went to sleep.

October 9 Friday 2004

It was graduation day, day 133, I woke to reveille 0600, and was up, dressed in uniform, and gathered up all my stuff, I had a printed ticket, to put on my bag, as I set it outside of the door, and placed a card, "To be cleaned, thank you." I set a 20 bill in the tip folder. I left, and fell in line, to chow, it was the top officers first, but we all went in line, as I could have anything to order, or whatever was in front of me, I choose bacon, two eggs sunny side up, and hash browns, and some toast, and half of an avocado. I took two chocolate milks, and swiped my per diem card. I ate by myself, afterwards, deposited my platter, and went to the auditorium. And found my assigned seating and sat, about a half hour later, people filed in, then it started, all the enlisted were given an award, then it was graduation for Anna Long, and Lily White. Anna was given the title of crew chief, and a printed check of 2000, and for Lily helper one, and a check for 1200, they were all smiles as they got off, then the General Edwin Louis said, "Now for our officer, he has surpassed many records, in only three days, he graduates as a promotion to Captain, he is Matt Michales, as I stood and salute him, he hands me another certificate, and a check for 6432. I looked at it, and sat down, as it was over, and Anna embraced me to say, "Boy I missed you, sounds like you had some fun with these guys."

"Yeah it was a blast, they want me to join them."

"Of course they do, what about us?"

"Don't worry, were getting married this spring."

"Really."

"Yes, you have waited too long" she was so happy, to hear, "Hey no fraternization with the Captain", said Brian as we all embraced, they had a cake, and it was fun, a pair of jet fighters landed, and was giving free rides, both Anna and Lily did it, while I stayed grounded, each cashed their check, I held onto mine, afterwards we took an officers rental car to the mall, for Anna and Lily to shop, I rode the amusement rides, and played a round of putt putt golf. Afterwards, I rode back, and into my room then settled my affairs, that meant another visit from Colonel Tom Davis, trying to convince me to join, as he went over the advantages of being in the reserves, and the support and I finally said "Yes" as he wore me down, as all I saw was the 2500 dollars per weekend per month, to be added to my already time, in the Marine Corps, and from a Sergeant to a Captain, and somebody whom is wanted, I signed off on the paperwork, I went through processing, and was given an ID card and a reserves package, then went to uniform, and was fitted right there. In addition a flight suit, a set of wings, and an official letter welcoming me to the search and rescue group. Later, I flew my team off in my new uniform, and back home. That night we had dinner, a shower and before bed, put away the uniform, as she said, "No wear it, it looks nice on you." As Anna was happy I was officially back in the service, but she mention of joining herself, just for the PX privileges.

October 10 Saturday 2004

It was day 134, and we were still off, till Monday, so after breakfast I went into the woods, and drove my jeep, to that spot the honey hole of huge gold, and got out, and with ten buckets, and a shovel and hammer, across the shallow river, to the massive opening, I flatten out as I dug it out, and on the bank. I kept on working, as I was going around the remainder, it was massive, and down about three feet, to uncover a deeper vein, my keeping this a secret, was right, as all anyone ever does is complain about money. And this was a find, it was dirty work, as I kept digging it out, it was about six feet down, but realized it was now free, as I used my digging bar to break up the last, I walked up and out, and went back to the compound to get my tripod, and rope, and went back out, and when I got back, I pulled out this blanket, I wrapped it around it, and strapped it together, it resembled a scepter, in shape, probably 200 pound, as I lifted it with the tripod, and swung it away, and down on the bank, picked up the tripod, and hoisted it up and set it in the jeep standing up, tied it off, and secured the tripod down, I went back for my digging bar, to see it was now a perfect place for a bear or the whole family. I drove off and back to the road, then over to the helicopter, and set out the tripod, off loaded the gold, and placed it underneath the helicopter, and put the jeep away. It was now or never, so I told Anna I was going into Whitehorse, and she said, "Have fun", So I flew off, and it was sort of fun, being by myself, all the way there, I landed at the admin building, and went in to see the governor, who was in between meetings, for him to say, "Ah my son, what do you have?"

"Well the last of the deep vein."

"Seriously?"

"Yep, care to take a look?"

He made a call, and we waited when, we got word of the assayers we went out to my helicopter, as they were already on it, they took it off with a cherry picker, like a car's engines hoist, and over to their truck, and took off. As the governor, had his hand on my back, to say, "That area is gold enriched, from Mount Logan, the Indian's know about it but aren't doing anything with it and that comes to you, you have probably not even scratched the surface, so keep this up, we may be buying up your property, next I wanna give a congratulations to you for joining the Coast Guard reserves."

"You're not mad?"

"Oh heck no, that means we have a partnership with them now, and will help us out in the future, No Matt this was a good thing, and lastly I have a deed here, from Rick Dawson's family, he had requested that this property should go to the person, who will use it accordingly and not just sell it off, as he handed me the deed to all of Dawson's range. This was over 90,000 acres, so it said, for the Governor, to say, "It's actually over, 100,000, acres but officially, set at 90,000, but who's counting the division which is known as Dawson's range on the west side the Carmacks on the other, your girlfriend Anna, has discovered a vein for us, so I guess were even", as we sat in his office when he received the call, to say, "They think it's worth another ten million, but altogether, over 100 million, so say I cut you a check for 50 million and were good?"

I looked at him and was stunned, to say, "Sure."

The Governor got up, to come to my side, to say, "It's just a number, as you don't know what that means do you?"

"No" I said.

"Come with me, let me show you what 50 million dollars looks like", as I got up and followed him, as we took a back entrance, into a waiting area, where, Miss Tillwater was, as she was there to say, "So what would the Governor like today?"

"For you to open the vault to allow Mister Michales the opportunity to see what 50 million dollars looks like."

"It's open", as she set in her hand print, and the door, had a key pad, and next she turned the key, and it opened a massive round door, to see stacks of money, for her to say, "This is 50 million dollars, sent every month from the US in exchange for the gold we send them, go ahead, touch it and see that its real, although it's in stacks, I was in marvel at its size and magnitude, I left feeling good, with a check in hand for 50 million dollars, I went to the credit union, and deposited it, as I got an eye raise over this one, but not a word, as she saw the "for deposit only" she gave me a balance and I left. I flew back to home, shut it down, and secured the helicopter. I went back to woodworking, as Anna was gathering meat, I guess were having another get together, Billy and Laurie showed up, we offered a place, but they said, they were going home. But will be back tomorrow. I went back to working my boxes, as I had gold fever. Brian showed up, he was helping me, as I cleaned up the rest of the gold, and bagged it. Then Brian and I finished the chores, to see the greenhouse was swamped with snow, and it was a real mess, So I and Brian went back on the top roof. Since it had snowed it engulfed anything exposed, so we set the rest of the two logs over the exposed greenhouse were laid, mortared, and shingled, as it was lunch time, we all ate a fine meal, of venison and vegetables, I had tea. After lunch, Brian and I placed six more boxes along the water, and checked the thirteen other large boxes, no animals just plain gold, so I pulled up the box, Brian and I carried it to the jeep, got in, and took it back. The next process was time consuming, to dry out the gold, I scooped it out, and into a bucket, it was flake and little nugget, I had, Brian wash it, with the hose as the water filtered the gold he seemed pretty sincere about helping out. Dinner was upon us, the girls fixed fried potatoes with meat it was always so good, after dinner, we sat for a talk of the future and what our plans were, I said, "Stay here awhile, marry Anna in the spring, and maybe find a challenge on an island, nah just kidding, I love it here, the people are nice and friendly, and our mushroom business is flourishing, just as I had predicted, we have enough to get us by for the winter, which I think is already here, we have a good side job, so let's see after this year is up and we are at Jun 1st again, Brian and Lily spent the night.

October 11 Sunday 2004

It was day 135, we were at home cleaning up the animals, and seeing another successful breeding of the rabbits, the Mink and Otter, Chickens, were harder, as I had to make a brooder(A warm box), for the eggs to hatch, the goats were milked daily, and churned for butter, yogurt and cheese, my favorite, Anna just loved to do this. The TV was put on hold, I mean nightly watching, for now, she still tapes her shows, but might watch about two hours tops, then it's the chores, fireplaces, and bricks to make, as were laying them in the courtyard inside the north and south compounds. I and Brian set up a winch to drag the helicopter into the brick factory, as little by little, bricks were making it out from under the front awning to the bridge. I set up a wheels for the skids, so we could push and pull it out, there was work everywhere, and I might not talk about it, but there is so much to list and so little time. I do think about our monthly feasts, as it was in the middle of our north compound, so today, Billy and Laurie brought up some side of beef she received for a payment, and Anna cut it up, and grill it, as I and Billy, and Brian, was working on my gate, to open on both sides, to spring back, it was clearing easy, and a door, to open for going back and forth, the teepee was set aside and will be used in different places, for the cabin in the south compound well that was just complete and finishing touches applied. It was where they stayed, or on their land. John and Kim arrived, surprised to see the serious spread of foods, birds, and dried salmon, we were all out when someone screamed, as I looked up and saw a bear scale the ten foot fence, to the south compound, I got my Enfield, and just like that it was a plethora of them, climbing the walls, of the north and I went to shooting, I dropped a bear, it fell and was dead, the one over at the south compound, I shot, it fell inside, but it was literally forty of them, no joke. My well placed shots, dropped two more, as the others backed off, to think I need to put up a fence like the reservation, I stood in the road, as bears were everywhere, I fired overhead on the rest and ran them off, all in all six were down, I took the jeep to drag them to the smoke house, all in all it was a process of bear day, knowing I couldn't keep them out or off, we skinned them, salvaged the inners, and I took the six hides, and tanned them, later returned to the party, as it was in full swing, John and Billy were playing pool. I and the other girls had swimsuits on and in the laundry pools, to rest and relax, while listening to Laurie tell us all about Whitehorse, and her practice, everyone was looking for handouts, especially the farm owners, for her to say, "Did you know, every year for the last nine, those who participated in the challenge all get some property and all live up here, tax and property free, one guy told me he got a 536 acre parcel, for free, now is the largest sheep producers in this area, so if you want sheep, let me know?"

"Nah, I'm good with what I have, well to be honest, I had some wolves pups, but at first chance ran off, but maybe Siberian husky's?"

"Yes I'd agree with that, having dogs here is a blessing, like the surprise attack from the bears" said Anna.

"You're in luck the Governor, raises them, well not him specifically, but his tribe, in Old Crow, and are shipped down, but let me talk with him and I can get you 9 solid runners." Said Laurie the center of attention as all she did was brag about the new mall going in, with a planned amusement rides and indoor water works, not to mention 200 shops, as they approved a plan from this company to build them, once the overhead structure is built."

I kept that to myself, as she went on, about the huge hole where once the mall stood, and even getting bigger. A room to house the water was built 20 feet down."

I personally had not seen David's drawings as my concern was the Fed center and the host of them coming, the recent snow didn't stop our momentum, as it was on time and on budget. I let her spout off, about a new metropolis happening in Whitehorse."

It was a close for the feast, Billy and Laurie were leaving, till next month, and left. Then John and Kim left, we finished cleanup.

We all cleaned up the shower room, and then went to bed.

October 12 Monday 2004

It was day 136, and we were back on the clock, as the rescue team, minus Lily, whom was harvesting mushroom, for shipment, I flew, Anna and Brian in, I went and saw Miss Tillwater, whom was in the hallway, for her to say, "You have been busy, many a man spent years trying to get what you got in a week, as she hands me the final report, for me to sign. She leaned in, to say, "This happens about every day, we have gold strikes all over, especially up in Old Crow, but I think yours in Dawson range is leading, good job, as she handed to me, the receipt and off I went to drive up to the court house, and the construction, was near complete, as Rob said, "After this next week, were going to start the mall". So I went down the hill over to the mall, looked like a huge hole rectangular in size take up four blocks wide as long, I could visualize the water park on one end, amusement park on the other, and in the middle shops, three levels, which I needed to build a box for the elevator, going in. It was going to be all log construction, as David Burke showed up to show me the plans, split log construction for the floor, along with side beams to hold it firm. Engineering crews were below, making sure we were ready, to pour, and set in the poles, we were using the three footers in diameter, at forty foot long sections, were on the ready, waiting us, later a crane arrived, parked and left. I went back, dropped off my vehicle, and collected up Brian and Anna, I flew off to home.

October 13 Tuesday 2004

It was day 137, and the three of us flew from home to the admin building, and Anna went with an expedition for the day, as she told me in confidence, that she had discovered a gold vein, but to keep a secret.

I said, "I knew already."

"How did you know already?"

"The Governor told me."

"He did, did he", as she laughed, and so did I.

Brian and I went to the mall, as construction began, forty footers dropped in, to form a south wall, in front of it was boxes for the elevators, the sides were left alone, as the next line was the north wall, the basis for all of our supports, along the north wall to the street. Now it was down the middle, another wall, to form a long box. Now the concrete was poured in, as the log ends were buried, we used fourteen concrete trucks, to bury the basement. We cover the entire thing to cure. And it was the day. I flew us all back. The days were sunny, it was rather nice.

October 14 Wednesday 2004

It was day 138, and the three of us flew back, in went Anna as I and a crew on the ground, waited till I flew up to them in the forests, I set it down on the hill top and landed, Brian and I met with them, as they were ready to clear cut, but leaving selective trees, I marked them while a crew cut them down, till I was done.

The day was nice and buggy up here, and sunny, but many a workers were concerned, with the haze, and that a storm was coming to kick off winter, I said "Whatever, get back to work."

Later in the day, a few rain clouds, and then a dumping, but that was the last of it, as I flew Brian and myself off the mountain, as trucks, trucked the selected cut logs back to town, and to the mall. I landed before them, and in a clear parking lot. Brian got out to cone it off, so others would not park there. Looking down I saw the carpenters, setting logs in place, to section off the bladder for the water portion of the amusement side, as another crew worked to set out and frame the east side, it too had a solid bottom base, as the other custom bladder the size of a whale, was set in, firmed up, it was filled by the fire department, main fire truck and hose company, they came because some guy fell in, and we didn't know it, so when they arrived, we were like, "We didn't know, sorry, so they rescued him and stayed, to fill those bladders, till they were full, and holding the water, next was another floor to show case the ends, and the middle was the mall shops. I was using the same principle as the governor's house and put a hall in the middle, with the wood floor, and side logs, were set as another day ended. I flew home with Anna and Brian.

October 15 Thursday 2004

It was day 139, all was clear as I flew out, it was an overcast day in places, as some were still glistening snow, as I crossed over that and onto Whitehorse, dropped off Anna, and flew to the mall, where it was day four, piling were set in place, and the water park was mapped out, on the west side, to showcase the log run. On the east side was the supposed amusement rides. I had the lower floor of the mall in place, two elevators were installed on each side, the ambience of the wood was fantastic, as a lot of people could not believe how fast it went up, and the structural frame was done. The amusement company was ready to go, as was the water park, some german companies for both. This is where the progress went down to nil, it was a slow go, as we waited, to roof the thing, in the middle I had the top of the forty feet, and began to add a top log to tie it together, as our focus was on the shops, each received 20x20, a back door, that had a walkway to the elevator and a wide sliding front door. The first two levels were under the ground. A floor of wood, then plywood, under lament and carpet or linoleum. We were on time and working hard, plastering the walls, to create a nice space, for the 200 shops. Fifty per level, 25 per side for four floors. My design and build crew was doing a fabulous job, but nothing was happening with the german companies, so I pressed on, to finish the day, as the workers were on three shifts, around the clock. I left, and back to the admin, to see the governor. Whom wasn't too happy, to say, "What is your assessment of the two bids?"

"They're taking their time, I'd like to get the roof on the mall before it snows again."

"Have you heard something?"

"No it was a figure of speech."

"Oh, yes, stay on course." Said Jim, back happy, as I collected up Anna and we took off, I flew back home.

October 16 Friday 2004

It was day 140, and I flew in clear skies, to the admin building in Whitehorse, dropped off Anna, then on to the mall, I landed and construction for the roof was well under way, as crew finished the shops, and all the windows were in. Now it was on to the roofs, for the massive split logs 3 foot wide, was going down on three levels, they started on the ends, to set the first, logs down, with a 5 foot overhang, at 55 feet, and the roof crew was on that to 200 feet wide, 68 logs, nailed down, then mortared, and then shingled. They then made the next transition to the next part, as logs were set, nailed down, another 68, 55 feet long, a portable saw mill, cut all of them, and set in the pairs, to make it even. Hammered down, then mortared, to the line, let set, to the next row or third high, another 68, set and nailed down, then a mortar crew, filled the gaps, then the shingles went on. It was lunch for some, but us running this we watched at the final 68 went to the top pole, it was a little slope, but nailing it down, while standing on scaffolding was nice. I was in the thick of it all, as the mortar crew came up in buckets, and a truck pumper. It was fast work, but quickly firmed up the structure, as lunch came and went, while on the west end, the first of the logs went on. They were nailed down, mortared, then it was the next level, our goal was work till the mall roof was on, as the second row went on, we were forty strong doing this work, mortared, then the next level, as the mall was taking shape, it was nailed down, then mortared, then the last level went on, I came out, and helped as the roof was sealed up, mortared, and then shingled, I set the top cap on, all the way, 200 feet. It was done.

I flew Brian over to admin, and picked up Anna, and went home.

October 17 Saturday 2004

It was day 141, and we both slept in, and the girls made breakfast, it was nice, and relaxing. I had a mission to go on, and that was to check my trap line, Anna came with me, it was fun being with her, as she was easy to get along with, as she said, "When were you gonna tell me?"

"Tell you what?"

"Well apparently the whole admin building knows, you struck it rich."

"Oh about that, well I didn't want to let it out I had found it here, so it was a secret."

"Fifteen million dollars was a secret" she said, helping me in with the boxes, on the trailer, for me to say, "Yes, but it was actually 50 million, as her eyes were wide, for her to hit me in the arm, to say, "Why keep it a secret from me?"

"I was going to tell you, once the checks cleared, but I also knew it wasn't about money for you, I did however, put you down as my beneficiary, if I were to die."

"Hush up, you're not going to get dead anytime soon?"

"Who knows, I could lose power and drop from the sky and it would be over."

"Shut up", she said smiling. As gold was all among us, as, not to mention, these are sure heavy. The boxes were all full of gold. With all nineteen collected, and all the little rabbit trap boxes collected we went back. Off loaded into the north compound's horseshoe and began to sift the gold out on to a makeshift cleaner, to a dryer, and then finally to a sort table, where nuggets were bagged, and the flakes in a bucket. All in all about thirteen 5 pound buckets of flake, to be worth at a million dollars, and another ten pounds @ 15,000 each was worth 150,000 plus, we retired that night feeling good.

CH 14

Snow storm of epic proportions and beyond

October 18 Sunday 2004

It was day 141, and we were back on the trail, after a hearty breakfast, we were at home, we had a little rain, but not much, all the boxes were cleaned, and we set each one up in the river, it took the better of half the day, then the little box traps, as we caught four more rabbits, as they were slowing down and setting in for the winter, as it was mainly muskrat, a quick blow to the head and they were killed, and skinned. They are a nuisance, around here, so it's make sure we kill them, and move on. The trap line was reset, and we went back. It was all a day of rest, no calls especially to our area, and we hit the laundry tubs to swim and frolicked the day away. Just Anna and I, as our two girls, were on their own, doing their crafts, I was able to have Charley buy a rug loom, from Anchorage, which he brought up, and set up for Nina, and several bolts of fiber, as for Hailey, she loved gardening, and maintained both greenhouses, the two girls taught us a valuable lesson, on how to raise and care for children, as we both loved them equally, but Nina, proclaimed I was still her favorite, and Hailey was Anna's, or Lily's it was a tie..

October 19 Monday 2004

It was day 142, and the three of us, flew to the admin building, Joe Smith was there to fill up, and top off my tanks, he showed me the auxiliary switch, because sometimes it's good to use both tanks. Also he said the Coast Guard sent over a new radio, for me to carry around, as he handed to me. I clipped it on my belt, I dropped off Anna and Brian I flew to the mall, and landed. It looked spectacular, as I got out, to see it was our crew, finishing up the middle. We walked the nearly complete mall, it was huge and spectacular. All we had to do now was wait for the amusement and water park builders, they had huge end clearances, so I wasn't worried, as lunch was called we Brian and I went to a local burger place, I had a double, with fries and a chocolate milk shake. Brian had the same except Vanilla. We ate, and he told me how happy he was over our partnership, and he looked forward to the future, I said, "I agree with you, you have been truly a great friend." He smiled.

"Great friend huh" he said.

"Sure, not many people are as strong a worker as you are, plus your loyal, a rare commodity in these times we live in."

"Thanks."

"Oh another thing lets stock up on provisions, while were here in the city, will you do that, for us?"

"How will I pay for it?"

I gave him my credit card, and wrote a note, that authorized Brian to use the card, he took it, to say, "Anything you want in particular?"

"Got artichokes?"

"You know it, but instead of store bought, I'll have some of mine own for you, we have some in the greenhouse."

"So bring them and some butter, maybe some mayo."

"Alright I get the point" said Brian as we finished he walked over to the store, as I went back in the massive building, it was nice to see down the middle, as Rob came up to me and said, "Sir we are finished any idea where you wanna go from here?"

"Yeah the Carmacks, let's build a lodge for each of the past contestants."

"Alright I'll have the crews, go up, as he leaned in to say, "Your one hell of a builder."

"I am ain't I" I said smugly, but he already knew me, so what I said they did, I was the extreme boss. I did my final inspections, as I had a clip board. I wrote down the corrections, as my crew pulled the last of the homemade scaffolding. Brian was back and loaded up the back of the helicopter, and the perishable was in two coolers on ice, so he told me, we got in and flew back to admin building, Joe Smith was out, servicing the other helicopters, he told me a big storm was coming in, as he had my engine panel off, checking fluids, and set in the gas, he clicked over to the auxiliary, and wiped off the seat, and cleaned the windshield. Brian and I went into the admin building, and the first person I saw was the Governor, with the Alaskan Governor, to say, "Hold on, Matt, I want you to meet, Alaskan Governor Jay Zeigler", I shook his hand, for him to say, "You getting quite a reputation, we have several projects we would love for you to take on, their calling you the next best thing for great lodges, will you come this summer to help us out?"

I looked over at Jim, who nodded, and I said, "Yes sir, it would be my pleasure."

"Good, good", as the two went their separate ways, as the Governor, lead me into his office, and offered a seat, to say, "Care for anything to drink?"

"Sure, what do you have?"

"You name it, I'm the Governor."

"Alright sparkling water with pineapple add in."

"That sounds good, as he called someone, then to say, "I want to first commend you on the mall, next all that you're doing with the rescues, were now getting in the treacherous times, where being here isn't a big an issue as being out there, so, think of yourself first, and if you do need to come in, do so, but you're not tied to be here at any time, while were in the heart of winter."

I shook my head in acknowledgement, as a lady came in with a beverage cart, to hand me a big bottle, I undid it and squirted in the additive, as did the governor, to take a swig, to say, "Wow, now that was refreshing" I agreed with him as she left. "Now for the real reason I have you here, the Kluane tribe, has put you as their executor for their holdings, and has transferred 90,000 acres of land in your name, all of Dawson's range on the southwest side, also five head of bison of your choosing, as part of what you did for them, I wasn't aware they were in a medical crisis, and you and Anna came to their rescue, and you're on going teachings and cleanup has given them hope and flourishing, also the hiring of the diggers, you singlehanded changed their whole perspective, thank you, as he slid the document, in front of me, I looked at it to say, "What kind of tax will be on this?"

"None, actually were paying you a per diem, of about 1500 a month, plus the land, is for conservation, and restocking, John Hughes tells me you are breeding Mink, and Otter which was an extinct species in this area, that is conservation, and for each animal you release, I will pay you 10,000, it's in all these documents. I signed the first one, not really knowing why me, but the governor said, "When a native American finds someone they can trust, they allow that person to support them, by being the executor of their trust, you are allowed the privilege of visiting them as you see fit, and report anything they may need, you can work with Old Crow, fish hatchery, about a restock in the spring of white fish, and rainbow trout. You get to authorize a breeding and animal program, not familiar to their way of life, once ocean people, now inland, so your work has been valuable, and now its rewarded."

I signed all the documents, as he had all kinds of smiles, as he shook my hand to say, "Welcome to the family."

I got up with copies of all that I signed, and left out a side door, went up, to my office, and to a desk, high with papers, to see my secretary Karlotta, she gave me lots of papers to sign, looking them over, to see a GPS of the crew moving up to the Carmacks. 49 home sites, will be set as a lodge. It was on the other side of Dawson's range. I signed off on all the forms, and cleared up my desk, as I found an empty briefcase, and stuffed all that in, to say, "See you in a while" to Karlotta.

"I know I heard" she said.

"Heard what?"

"That the Kluane Indians, have given you the largest prime real estate, that many have coveted, to drill for oil, and they found you to handle their affairs, I myself is part Indian, and those that feel that way about you means your special, every day I get people in passing, they gush over you, and seeing that Governor's mansion, there are a lot of people that would do anything for you."

"Thanks that is nice to hear that, as she embraced me, I was crying so was she, as I heard, "Am I interrupting something?", as we both broke the embrace, to see Anna, I wiped away a tear, for her to say, "So when you're ready, come by I have to go see the Governor about something" said Anna.

"Alright", as she was only kidding, as she knows I rarely embrace anyone, I filled out some more papers to file them, as I said, "Karlotta file these with legal, and if you could call me on Fridays to let me know the status of our projects, for I will be out in the fields."

"Will do Mister Michales."

I left, to go down to the comptroller, to see Anneillea Tillwater, she received me to say, "I have made out the following checks, for all of what has happen, besides the wages you earn, and the per diem, you get proceeds, for the land surplus, and division act, so your borders go all the way to Mount Logan, as you share with the Kluane tribe, and as their executor, you are their spokesperson, I gather your saying no to oil drilling?"

"Yes, its farm land, and were growing crop, for the northern district." Said I.

"This includes the town of Beaver creek?" asked Miss Tillwater.

"Yes, what of Jake and Rita Wilson?"

"Would you like them to stay on?"

"Yes, I like them very well, if they want to."

"Alright, I see if their interested."

I signed all the checks, and received them, as she said "Wanna cash them here?"

"Nah, I'll take my chances across the street."

"You know there moving to the mall."

"Then I will just have to visit the mall."

I left, and went out the south door, and into the quiet non activity office, as Jelville Grant said, "So a deposit today?"

"Yes, 12 checks, as I presented them to her, she endorsed all of them, to say, a deposit of 145,654. 92 cents, care for anything back?"

"Nah, I'm fine, as I left, and went to a florist and botany shop, I found a basil plant and bought that, and was given cash for the 100, I had 82.12, and went back over to the admin building, and swiped my pass, and went inside, to see Anna leaving, as she hugged the governor, and was happy, as she came out to see me and I gave her the present, for her to say, "That's nice, are we ready to go?"

"Yes, let's go" I said.

Brian was waiting as we got in, as Brian went out to un latch us, and the helicopter was being pushed by the wind, as I got it going, then lifted off, and away we went to home. I flew in, but decided to park on the road, I used the jeep to pull it under cover, and secure it as the two girls, Nina which has grown incredibly and Hailey also was maturing into a woman, helped off load the supplies, and clean it out, that night we had a meal of spare ribs, off the bear, they were good, twice baked potatoes, and green beans, then the surprise, my artichokes, she had two massive ones for me. I dipped them in butter, and ketchup, it was good, we had a feast, I took a shower, and went to bed. Anna stayed up with Lily, when it began to snow.

October 20 Tuesday 2004

It was a disastrous day, 143, as snow was acculating everywhere, I heard on the radio, the work crews were evacuated, and safe, helicopter travel was at a minimum due to the wet snow, weigh's them down, that's when Anna received a distress signal, from a plane, flying over our position, in ten minutes, the call out was that pilots Corbin and Edwards, were having trouble with their plane, and was losing altitude, from Fairbanks, trying for Whitehorse, but was going down, as Anna came to me, to say, "An aircraft is going down, we must go out and rescue it."

I told her, "It's crazy, we would likely go down ourselves, due to the heavy snow." But I gathered up Brian who was chopping wood, and we went out, to see at least two foot of snow, we dug out, the east side, by the gates, and pulled the helicopter forward, it was freezing conditions, I got in, did a precheck, and it started up, Brian got in, as did Anna and Lily, as I flew it off, the snow was relentless, as it came down it stuck, then melted, as Anna was next to me as my spotter, it was white out conditions, as she said, "Over there is some tracks" she pointed.

I saw and swung down to see a two mile wide debris field, as they thought was a flat surface was actually creeks, and as I set it down, they sprung into action, to get to the passengers, eight others were un-harmed, led by Stephanie, she was helping the others, as the two pilots, and others received whip lash, as I was being weighted down by the snow, as I landed, I was out brushing off the snow. Brian took, whomever he could, as it was a volleyball team, as Anna stayed behind, to help assess the others, it was Megan, the coach, Taima, Marissa, Maurissa, Nicole, Natalie, Lexie, Miranda, Page, and Sydney. All in, and was injured in some form, I flew off, as a warning light instantly came on, too much weight it was struggling, back to our lodge, I landed, and Brian helped them, out as both Nina and Hailey helped them in, and Lily stayed to see that they were taken care of, as we flew off, and landed. As the following was next, Rob, the pilot, Dennis the pilot, Rachel, Morgan, Stacey, Selene, Mia, Tiffany, Selma, and Sabrina. Brian got in up front, as we went home, the helicopter had that same warning, as I had two left on the ground and Anna came with us, we got back, as everyone was helping out, I had to shut it down, to clear off all the snow, it stuck to everything, and then we were ready, Brian and I and went back, for the last two, Stephanie, the strong one and asst coach Kimberly, and took them to the lodge, we could accommodate them, but before this gets any worse, I knew I needed to fly to Whitehorse, and alone, as ten in the back and one upfront. So I said count off, we had 22, eleven each, I took the wounded first. A girl named Page, sat next to me, and as the following got in the back, after a bowl of hot soup. It was Miranda, Lexie, Natalie, Nicole, Maurissa, Marissa Taima, Megan, the coach, whom was really bad off was Kimberly, and Sydney, we took off, in a beeline to Whitehorse, and to the medical center an hour later, the hospital, was waiting, as it was empty, I landed, and crews ascended on them, to take them inside, Page reached over to give me a hug, to say, "Thank you for rescuing my volleyball team, I'd kiss you if you didn't have that helmet on."

"Oh, my girl would mind."

"Not for an appreciation kiss."

Alright so I took off my helmet, she kissed me on the cheek, I'd have to say it was rather very nice. She left, as I lifted off, and went back, got home, it was clearing, as the next group got in, and it was Stephanie up front, and the rest in the back, as it was, Sabrina, Selma, Tiffany, Mia, Selene, Stacey, Morgan, Rachel, and the two pilots, Dennis, and Rob. We took off, and again made a bee line to Whitehorse hospital, at the hospital, I landed, everyone exited, as Stephanie just said, "Good bye", and was gone, as I went to the admin, to refuel, Joe Smith was out in those conditions, as from inside you could see people watching Joe got pelted with snow, refueled me, and clicked it back, to say, "That gives you more range", he took off, as I lifted up and off, and away, back to home, as it was snowing worse, and landed by the lodge, in the road, Brian was out, to help clean off the snow, I went in for a good hot meal. It was accumulating snow, as the jeep pulled the helicopter back under the roof, it was solidly coming down. As it was getting dark, when another distress signal came out, and it was lost, as Anna was trying to get, their directions, as finally someone named Lauren got on there to say, "We have crash landed on some rocks, some are killed, some are injured, and some are just beat up, so I have taken charge, when can you rescue us?"

"We are digging out, and should be there soon" said Anna.

"Hurry, we are all hurt and cold."

Brian and I dug out, was able to pull the helicopter out, I got in and did all my checks, then Brian got in the back, and was ready, as he put on his survival suit. I was ready, so was Brian and we left, they were located, by a locating beacon, on our GPS, they were above Dawson's range, we came upon, a disastrous crash, right straight into, the rocks above the river, which was flowing good, I hovered, as I sent Brian, down, as the door was open, and the snow was blowing in, as Brian got down there, and one at a time, and took, Gianna, next was April, then Julia, Emily, Jocelyn, Bridget, Daphne, Gabrielle, Jamie, and Jackie as Brian was in and we were off, back to the lodge, as the warning light was on again for weight, we off loaded them, and we went back, as the light stayed on, I didn't know what was wrong, the helicopter seemed to be flying fine, all other gauges seemed fine. We got there, and Brian went back at it, this time, all was well, It was, Alex, Danielle, Eva Marie, Felicity, just then the warning lights were going crazy, as the lift was being affected, as so was my steering, and told Brian, get the girls off, was the last thing I remember........

"So I'm going to allow Brian to finish this, "I immediately saw the helicopter was compromised, as it was going up and down, so I ascended with my line, up to the girls, and one by one, they zip lined, off and as I was free. The helicopter, was losing height and I held on for as long as I could, then the engine just seemed to freeze up and went down, into the icy waters, and was gone, underwater, as I fell to my knees, and was crying, as I noticed the line, was still, and got up and tied it off, and took out my phone, to call for help, I said, "May day, May day, Matt Michales is down in the Yukon, please send help. That message was well received, as Anna was frantic. The Governor of the Yukon territories sent everyone, from all over the territory. The Coast Guard, sent a K-C 130, loaded with responders, I knew if he had any chance I would need to save him, and with that I dove in, much to the protest of the women, the icy waters were chilly, I got to the door, it was open, and Matt was out, as I pulled him out, and we floated, to a shore near Stewart, where, I did mouth to mouth, and he came back as I had two choices, pull him from the water, or allow the water to slow down his body, as I had no way of warming, him, and from the sky, was parachutes, in all red survival suits, I looked at my friend who was out and cold, as two men nearly landed on top of us, instantly pushing me away, and stabilized, and moved you to the beach, then blanked you, in a backpack gurney, they spoke among themselves, as one, hitched up you Matt, as the other spun you around, as he inflated an air balloon, as it soared to the sky, the plane came back, and just like that the three of you were gone, up in the sky and away. It was just minutes, when a huge dual helicopter came in, and the rest of the women were picked up, as was the plane and lifted off. Our helicopter, also was rescued, as another of the same kind, from the National Guard, came in, undid the winch line, and sent in divers, while I to was rescued by a little helicopter, and saw our helicopter, being hoisted out, as we all went to Dawson. I had no idea on your (Matt's) status, as I knew, it was out of our hands. I was flown into Anchorage, and debriefed on your status, you're in a coma, but resting, as your strong, a fighter.

October 21 Wednesday 2004

I don't know what I'm doing here, My name is Brian Lewis, so I will put down the rest of the story, it was officially day 144, but since my ride came in, it was Captain Dave Scott, came to us, at Dawson, and we left, for our lodge, that was where I embraced Anna, and Lily, both extremely upset, Lily more so than Anna as she was crying uncontrollably. I tried to calm her but couldn't, as it was Anna. Captain Dave arrived, then flew us to Anchorage, where we had a hero's welcome, Matt was at memorial hospital in the ICU. A call out to his parents, was received and family was flying up today, I volunteered to receive them, as both Lily and Anna were on both sides of your bed, holding your hand. Grief was received by everyone, to include both Governors, who made a visit, both saying, "Whatever it took, would be had". The doctors prognosis was grim at best. I took a courtesy car to the airport, and went in and waited, as your family of four disembarked, I shook your father's hand, it was firm, he was like I a big man, you never told me you had a hot sister, Emily, and your mom, Ruth was nice, and your brother, was a mess, Gary. I drove them to the front, they got out, and I returned the vehicle. I got back, up and it was a cry fest, your sister, your brother, Mom and Dad, Anna, and Lily. This went on for several days, and then you improved a bit. Your family had to leave, then it was Anna's family, and what a clan, 14 came off that plane, and whoa, my vehicle wasn't large enough, so I took her parents and grandparents, whom embraced Anna, and then later the rest showed up, Anna has a huge family, and some tough brothers, but all were here, to help out, they all stay at Charley's and Tiffany's, of the four girls it was Karen taking up your care duties, both her mom and dad, were distraught, but strong, like Anna and all were excited she had the coveted ring, and now talk was how many babies she was to have. The boys went back to the lodge to help out, as they felt it was better to appreciate what you did, and now the wedding, Anna wanted it done in the spring, but the governor wanted to wait till you were up, and celebrate you then, so wake up my friend, God bless.

CH 15

The aftermath.

A lot has changed since, my last entry and this one, some ten years, I didn't feel much like writing, or even a conclusion, who cares about one's life, let alone mine, but after much prodding from my wife, and others, wanted a conclusion to this tale, so I've decided to finish this diary, after the summer of 2004, I awoke one day, to see, Karen Long, Anna's sister, whom was closest to me, then Anna's mother, Aileen, and grandmother Jane, all were extremely happy and I awoke, as if everything was fine. Lots of hugs and kisses, I accepted them, they put their lives on hold for me, imagine that, for eight months. The challenge was officially over that day in October 21st, and all was revealed, but it was my attempted rescue that increased the whole population by tens of thousands plus, as lodges were the new home for a community, in Yukon and Alaska, my helicopter was rebuilt for free from the company who built it, it was or had a defect, to cold temperatures. I still have an office at the admin building, even though its named in my honor, the town of Whitehorse had tripled, and the mall is all the rage, national companies are in there, so it's quite diverse. I especially love the log ride and the roller coaster, the governor shut it down for the day, for all of us to enjoy it. We, Anna and I got married in front of the governor's mansion, on June 21 2004, the entire town was there, to include my new coast Guard buddies, a national wood company, offered us up an all-expense paid trip to anywhere we wanted and took a honeymoon, on our new 90,000 acres, collecting gold nuggets and exploring. Beaver creek was rebuilt, using the lodge theme, and its habitants are, people who work for us, either in the mushroom business, or the gold business. Anna's family is here, as they all moved up to be closer to us, and I guess to support me, I still see Jelville Grant at the credit union, she just told me, I was one of the richest men in the territory, I shrugged it off, as I didn't care, I still do search and rescue with Brian, whom still lives with his wife Lily, and a brood of children. He has six and still counting, we have since enlarged and modernized his south compound. I'm not as lucky, we have two sons, Jeremy and Landon. 8 & 6 respectfully. Every September my Marine friends come to visit, and both Russ and Paul, married both Nina and Hailey, both first child's were named for me Matt and for the first girl Anna, then Brian and Lily respectfully, whom also have families. Now it comes to my complex, to the east going towards Brian's, we clear cut that, all the way to the bridge and made several more lodges, for all our friends and family, well all of her family lives with us to include a structure over the road. As for my daily routine, is but pretty simple, go into my horseshoe, and work on making something, with all my wealth, I bought a lathe and tools, for I love working with wood, then it's on to my trap lines, and find a surprise from time to time, as I catch a trapped animal, if it's not an Otter or a Mink, I let it go, and lots of gold, and now have over fifty boxes, on both rivers. Then in that hole, where I found that vein, was a perfect place for a family of foxes, as I enclosed the front to save them from bears. From time to time, I also train scouts sent to me by the Marine Corps, on my vast property, which I share now with the Kluane tribe, I was awarded with additional 90,000 acres of land to close the gap between the Kluane tribe and ourselves. I still have yet to scout, and it's been ten years, oh how the time flies by. I cut hay, with a combine, and have a huge warehouse on the Kluane tribes shared land. Anna's family have adopted the tribe, cleaned it up, and set in a school, to better educate them. I go to town about every other day, I also go to Anchorage, to spend time with the Coast Guard, as I spend a week at a time a month and this supplements the two weeks in the summer. I know Anna loves the PX and so do the boys, as they stay with me. I hold a title with the Coast Guard of Major or assistant XO, as for what they did for me when I was laid out, all medical expenses were taken care of, and I also got paid, as money is more of a reward then a necessity and go out on special missions from time to time. While I do that, Anna, spends time with Lily, and her family. Anna's brothers, work up here, as each holding different jobs, as weekly, I run an outfitters and tours in and around, we have the largest amount of game possible, especially, the wild turkey breeding program, whereas, we have released, over ten thousand, we all share, with the Kluane tribe, and our Sunday ritual is with them now, at their massive lodge, and for really big celebrations, it's here at My place. I also made a mistake to tell the chief, I lost our helpers, and now we have two new girls, helping us, named Kavi and Ayita. He did mention to me for the rest of my life he would send me as many girls as I needed. Of the other two we had, who worked in the mushroom plant, they also wed, Keith took Marian, and Jason married Aileena both Anna's brothers. They man our convenience store, and hardware store complex, behind is a giant warehouse, where we re-route, from Beaver Creek to Anchorage, to Whitehorse. As for Rita and Jake Wilson, they officially retired and moved to a lodge, on a clear cut hillside overlooking the lodge outside of Beaver creek, for they are Grand Pa and Grand Ma to all the kids. For it's all a family affair. As for Charley and Tiffany, they too wed, and all our differences were settled, they have two children, also 8 & 6, Michael, and Barbara. I think that about wraps it up. I guess I didn't talk about the other contestants, well Billy and Laurie did break up, as he went back to his hometown, as for Laurie, she carried on and stayed and married Mark, Anna's other brother. Next is John and Kim, both stayed, and relocated, just south of my compound to the south, behind the berry patch, whereas I gave them 40 acres, in a secluded valley, next to the moss valley, but on higher ground, I built them a lodge, and a pathway to our house. We see them almost every day, they have two girls, ages 8& 6 names Madison and Gretchen. The cattle herd has blown up to 2000 head plus. Each month we get a beef cow, in exchange for our pigs we raise. We also have goats and husky dogs. This whole thing is in a family trust to be protected forever. Life is grand in the Yukon territory.

The End.

Printed in the United States
By Bookmasters